MONSOON QUEEN

Twenty-year-old Noor has been hiding her magic and biding her time in the spice markets of 1812 Tajoura as she and her neighbours wait for the ravenous British Empire to sail into their homeport, cannons blazing. But when the HMS Victory arrives, so does the chance of a lifetime to join a found family in the Yemeni resistance. Noor finds herself caught up in the fight against the Empire's battle mages and Rami, the dark prince who leads them.

In a case of mistaken identity, Noor heals Rami before a decisive battle. She sees the good in him, and her heart is torn.

Noor's new friend Razan—a brilliant and beautiful inventor for the resistance—has no such qualms. She hates Rami for his role in the raid that killed her parents. Razan has found a way to harness Noor's power to defeat the British, and the two women grow ever closer. On a perilous camel ride to the coffee roasting city of Mocha, Rami strikes, kidnapping Noor and taking her back to his cruel master on the HMS Victory.

In order to survive, Noor will need to call on everything she learned in the spice markets and the Yemeni resistance.

Rebels, mages, lovers. With the final battle looming and the resistance struggling without her, Noor must keep her eye on the prize: saving Yemen from the British Empire. If she can keep Razan in her bed and save Rami from the Empire, she will have the future she's always dreamed of. But first, Noor has to survive the storms to come.

Dream Swimmers

Every night, Noor saves a drowning prince.

In her dreams, she finds him drifting deeper, ever farther from the midnight stars of a half-remembered Gaza. She hauls him to the surface, forces him to breathe, to talk, to tell her where he is.

He doesn't know.

Noor awakens on the Cormorant, a once-and-future pirate ship searching for Rami, the former prince of Yemen whom she aims to rescue from his British captors before it's too late. While Rami fights to survive the secret British prison, Noor will have to use her magic, cunning, and skill to find him. But she won't be alone. Her found family is with her. Lovers, inventors, pirates, rebels, and deserters, they all must come together as they hunt the Arabian Sea for the lost prince.

Dream magic connects Noor and Rami, but in the end, what saves him won't be magic or science or even love, but the stars themselves.

THE WAR BETWEEN CEDAR AND OAK

BOOKS ONE AND TWO

JO CARTHAGE

A NineStar Press Publication
www.ninestarpress.com

The War Between Cedar and Oak Collection

First Edition, August 2025

ISBN: 978-1-64890-894-1

CONTENT WARNING:
This book contains sexually explicit content, which may only be suitable for mature readers. Depictions of torture by severe whipping; bondage; enslavement.

To A., seeing you grow is the greatest joy of my life. To M., you have my whole heart.

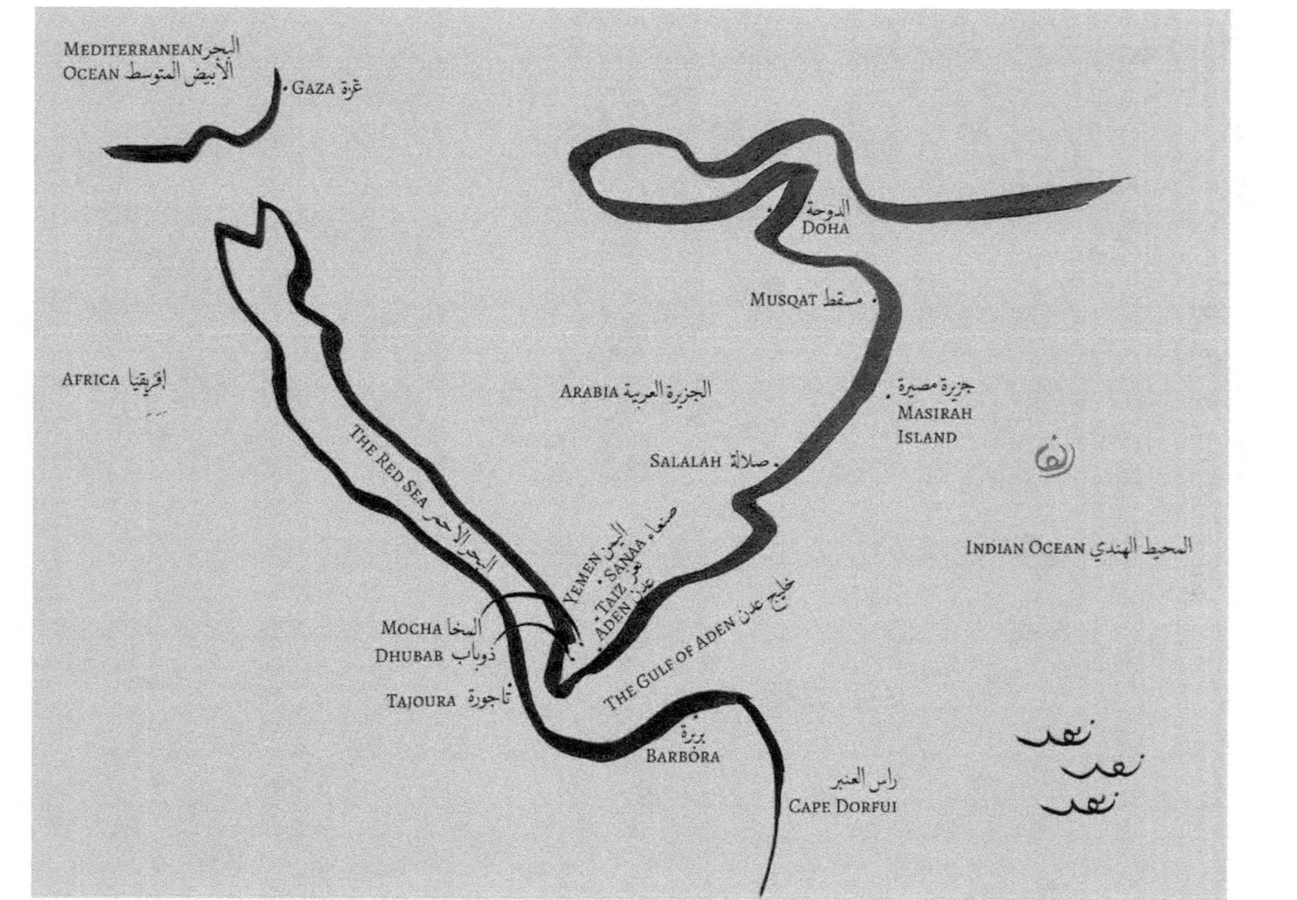

MEDITERRANEAN البحر
OCEAN الأبيض المتوسط
GAZA غزة
DOHA الدوحة
MUSQAT مسقط
AFRICA إفريقيا
ARABIA الجزيرة العربية
جزيرة مصيرة
MASIRAH ISLAND
SALALAH صلالة
THE RED SEA البحر الأحمر
YEMEN اليمن
SANAA صنعاء
TAIZ تعز
ADEN عدن
INDIAN OCEAN المحيط الهندي
MOCHA المخا
DHUBAB ذوباب
THE GULF OF ADEN خليج عدن
TAJOURA تاجورة
BARBORA بربرة
CAPE DORFUI رأس العنبر

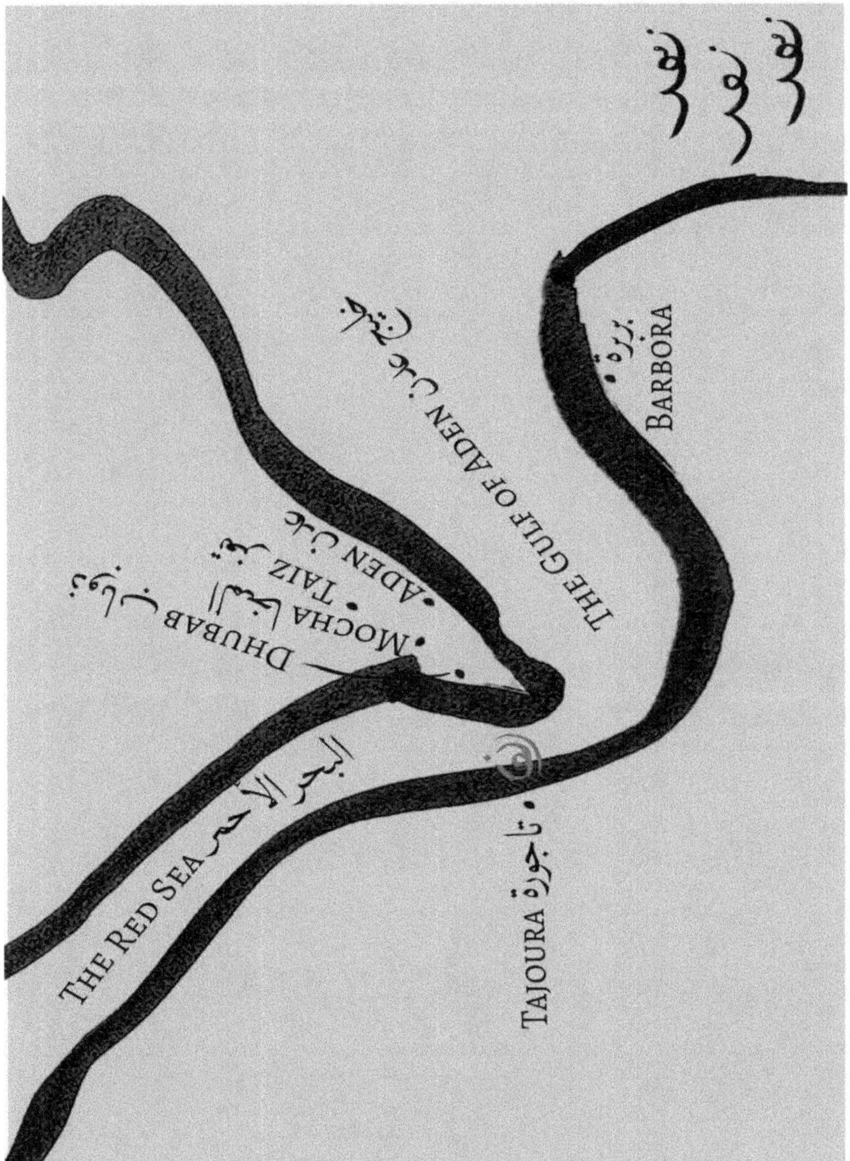

Tajoura, on the Horn of Africa
Three months before winter monsoon season
Just after Ramadan 1227 A.H. / October 1812 A.D.

Chapter One

THE JUTE ROPE flowed through Noor's hands as she climbed down into the shipwreck. The shallow waters of the Gulf of Tajoura filled the creaking hold, but the crew deck was just above the lapping waves. She landed, and her sandals crunched on salt-encrusted cedar. Noor breathed a sigh of relief. *At least this deck isn't entirely rotted.* Though she'd lived all of her twenty-one years within smelling distance of the sea, she could not swim. She hadn't been permitted to learn.

Noor stood in a pillar of noonday sun shining through the hole she'd hacked in the deck above. Everywhere else was darkness. Noor peered into the gloom, checking for any cracks of sunlight on the side of the wreck where she knew her master, Musa, had anchored his *dhow*.

When she was certain he couldn't see, she let a gentle glow rise in her fingertips, lighting the hold. Musa didn't know she could cast light or move objects with her mind. He hadn't been there when she'd found her magic that past summer, her hands on the body of a soft black cat who'd been trampled by a British officer's horse. If he had seen her healing, he'd have had her killed.

Slaves could not be mages in Tajoura.

Before her magic had come, Noor had thought she would be trapped with Musa for the rest of her life; now, she studied with her imam every chance she got, gaining control over her power and searching for a chink in the world she could pry open long enough to escape.

The shipwreck jerked, a low wave slamming into the side.

Noor got back to work. She surveyed the crew deck, checking every corner and cavity until...*there*. A small tumble of rags and arm-length splinters of cedar shielded a glint of silver.

She hitched up her *guntiino*, the long red and yellow striped wrap she wore like an Indian woman's sari, and raised her hand to light her way into the darkness.

Noor pulled Musa's leather purse from under her guntiino and began filling it with silver coins.

"Teach that captain to talk too freely in the hookah shop," she muttered as she swept up the treasure. "Or maybe just to know a thief when he sees one."

Musa had overheard this dhow's former captain in the hookah shop the night before, moaning about his sailors abandoning their backpay as they scrambled to escape the wreck two monsoon seasons ago. This boat was one of many. Ever since the British Empire had set their sights on Aden to the East across the Gulf and rumours of sightings of Lord Admiral Nelson's *Victory* had been reported from the Cape northwards, merchants who'd never plied Tajoura's shallow and reef-filled waters were trying their luck on the last free port on the Horn of Africa.

Many didn't survive the experience.

Musa had sailed her out here on his rickety dhow several times a month for years, ordering her to loot the remains of shattered ships. He claimed any treasure she found or took it out of her hide if she tried to conceal it, to save up enough to buy passage somewhere else, anywhere else. *Musa forgets that the alternative to allowing slaves to buy our freedom is having his throat slit in the night.* Noor dreamed about it, but she didn't kill, wouldn't risk her secret connection to *haya* magic by using it for violence. Her imam had warned her that to do so might sever her connection forever. But even without knowing she had powers,

Musa should have been more cautious. For now, Noor was biding her time, trying to find another way out.

So here Noor was, collecting other people's pay for someone else's profit; it wasn't the first time and it wouldn't be the last. She was relacing the purse when something else glimmered in the heap of mouldering cloth.

Noor's fingers were delicate and careful of scurrying crabs and cedar splinters. *There.* She found what had caught her eye: a Yemeni dagger, a *jambiya*, with a pearl-dotted sheath and a polished moon-coloured lunella shell as a pommel.

It shone in her light.

"What kind of Yemeni man would abandon his family's jambiya?" she muttered.

Beautiful weapons were impossibly expensive for someone like her and far too dangerous to own. She took a breath and stuffed it down the front of her guntiino. The dagger fit snugly between her belt and her belly. The leather purse went between her teeth. She climbed up her rope, arm over arm. Noor extinguished her light as the sun hit her upturned face. She reached the bare bit of stable hull that she'd tied onto and stood up on it, gripping the gunwale as the rising tide shook the wreck.

Noor glanced over the edge to see Musa glaring up at her from the helm of his tiny, shallow-drafted dhow, bobbing only a few arm lengths away from the wreck. His bald head glittered with sweat. His mouth was twisted and red.

"That's it?" he shouted, gesturing at the purse between her lips.

She turned to descend the rope ladder, making a face where he could not see. Her sandaled feet slipped on the slimy, fraying rope, hands cramping tightly above the knots. A wave bucked the ship, and she slammed into the hull, the contents of the purse bruising her lips. The rope *snapped*—

Noor fell, and the warm water was over her head in seconds. She forced herself to hold her breath, struggled to look up, eyes burning with the salt. There it was, Musa's hand lowering to rip the purse from between her teeth.

The current shoved her back against the hull of the wreck, and she lost hold of her climbing rope.

Noor shoved her panic away and pushed away from the wreck, tried to think of how she could use her magic, but her mind thrashed as the water forced itself between her lips. She couldn't *focus*. She crunched against the hull again and turned into it, fingers digging into the rotting wood, forcing herself up one handhold at a time until she got her bruised lips above the water and gasped in sweet, salty air. A wave filled her mouth. She slipped and found a new hold, again and again, each breath a little shallower, until she felt Musa's fingers dig in around her elbow before wrenching her over the side and throwing her to the deck.

As she tried to stand, he hissed, "You ugly idiot, I got my sandals wet because of you," and cuffed her hard to the deck.

The jambiya's sheath jammed into her stomach, and she curled around it protectively.

He hasn't seen the blade yet.

Musa had already turned back to the helm, cursing her loudly as he adjusted the rudder, his fishing spear bloodied across his back. She had a moment to catch her breath.

Unfortunately, what she breathed in was the smell of a freshly killed dugong. The gentle creatures were like horses or the cows the Afar herdsman brought to the annual bazaar that had started just the prior month. With soft grey skin and silly faces, the dugong bore live babies. Her master liked to hunt them while he waited for her to scavenge for him, though Noor knew it was no real hunt. The sweet things would gather around any boat, as curious as kittens. She rolled away from the corpse, trying to keep her disgust off her face.

Then she froze. Strange bells sounded from across the harbour. Turning, Noor cocked her head, trying to find the source.

Silence.

Somali traders' ships didn't use bells. Neither did the double-masted Yemeni dhow that slipped into port under cover of night to avoid British patrols.

Only British imperial warships rang bells when they entered a harbour. She'd heard that from refugees, from women who'd escaped Mocha and Sidon.

No British warship had ever yet entered Tajoura's harbour.

The bells rang again, and Noor's breathing kicked up when she saw their source. At the mouth of the harbour, a ship as massive as the biggest mosque in Gaza, crowded out the sky. Its dozen square sails covered the faces of the clouds, each deck painted black and gold in succession, the colours wavering in the golden morning light.

"I've heard of that ship," Musa growled behind her. "Striped like a bee, stung Napoleon in their last wars. The *Victory*. Their great Admiral Nelson died there." He slapped at the ropes in the rigging, jerking the knots, swinging the sail out and into the wind. "They'll blow us out of the water as soon look at us, with their *alam* mages or cannons or both."

The bells rang louder.

Noor stared at Musa, the jambiya heavy against her stomach. If Musa stayed facing away from her, she could creep up behind him, slide the dagger out, and slit his throat the way he had the dugong's.

There was a reason slaves weren't allowed weapons.

The bells sounded, and she felt the weight of the knife like the promise she'd made to herself years ago: *free yourself so you may remain free.* She kept her eyes on the *Victory* as Musa hurried them back to port.

*

NOOR TROTTED BEHIND Musa's donkey as he rode, her body aching. Thankfully, it was a short walk from the harbour to his stall in the *souq*, the vast market of saffron-and-butter-coloured tents in the heart of the city. They left the dugong carcass with a butcher, who shared Noor's grimace of distaste. The entire way back into town from the harbour, Noor could smell the fear in the streets as old fighters gathered their guns and wide-eyed fathers hurried their children away from the continuing sound of bells.

They reached the tiny stall where Musa repaired and traded the treasures Noor scavenged. It was also where he drank all his profits away. The din of the British bells had Musa reaching for his palm wine the instant he unlocked the doors of the stall.

Within moments, he was out.

Noor closed the doors behind him. Only he had the key to lock them, but everyone on the street knew he was a mean drunk with an uncanny ability to catch thieves in the act. She casually walked around a corner, and then she ran. She sprinted to the highest place in the city—the minaret of her imam's mosque.

She pushed past fruit sellers and chicken pluckers, dodging between spice heaps and hookah shops, ducking through fabric stores and between hagglers. She passed a dozen men and women who would report her passage to Musa, but as long as she was seen going into the mosque, it would be a favourable report.

She made it to the white mosque steps as the bells rang out again.

Noor dashed up and then came to a skidding halt before Imam Tariq. A tall, slender man with greying hair, he unfolded himself from where he'd been sitting at the base of a towering, white pillar, his eyes still fixed on the harbour and lined face worried. He drew a leather thong with a heavy key hanging from it from under his long *khameez* and handed it to Noor.

"I can guess why you're here. Remember—"

She gave him her first smile of the day. "I won't let anyone else up in the minaret; I promise. Musa is down for the afternoon. I want to see what the British are doing."

Imam Tariq nodded. "Are you thinking of fighting them if they attack?"

She frowned. "I'm not sure what little light bursts and dust spinners are going to do against a warship."

"You can do more than conjure dust spinners, Noor. You and I both know that." He gestured to the bruise rising red on her cheek.

Noor touched the mark, drawing a strand of life from the imam and weaving its invisible light into her skin, the sensation like the taps of butterfly wings in the morning light.

Imam Tariq nodded at her good work, then turned to the harbour. "Remember to get back before he wakes."

She ran up the tight circle of well-worn steps, hand on the *jambiya* hidden beneath her clothing to keep it from slipping. Normally, no one but the *muezzin* and the imam was allowed here, but in the past few months, it had become her sanctuary. She reached the top of a minaret and looked out over the only city she had ever called home.

Tajoura sprawled before her, representing thousands of years of trade and growth and tribes coming together, fighting, and making peace. Here, Yemeni traders drank tea with Chinese merchants and Somali craftswomen from the south. To the north was one of the largest slave markets in the region. Her parents had sold her when she was small, her mother layering her hair in thick protective braids before she left. Noor still wore them that way. Since her hair style matched the traders from Mogadishu, Noor figured she was probably from there. To the west lounged the beautiful Lake Ghoubbet with its swift currents and massive, slow-moving sharks.

And there, to the east, the imperial warship hung against the sky like visiting death. It seemed to be anchored in the deepest part of the harbour. Their navigator had probably never been to Tajoura before and hadn't been up for trying to dock. It didn't really matter. Their battle mages and cannons could obliterate the city from the middle of the bay just as well as from the docks.

Noor squinted at boats with bands of yellow, black, and white around their edges being lowered from the sides of the warship, shallow-draft vessels that could be rowed over the reefs. A crowd moved from the souq to the docks. Some were bound to be armed; she hoped they had someone with them who spoke English because none of the British who had wandered through the souq during her time here could speak a passable sentence of Arabic or Afar.

She considered offering the crowd her help to translate, to avert bloodshed. Her skill with languages was one of the few things Musa had given her besides beatings. Noor had a knack for finding books in the tumbled-down wrecks of others' lives and livelihoods—histories and mysteries, poetry and proverbs, stories holy and profane, and sometimes all of those at once. The right book in the right hands could be worth more than her weight in gold, and Musa knew it. He sold her finds to a wide range of traders, some of whom corresponded with him for months before arriving to purchase certain books when she could find them. He preferred his palm wine to writing, so he had made sure she'd learned to read and write Arabic, French, English, and to transcribe Afar and Kiswahili into English and Arabic. She could also speak passable Amharic and Mandarin, practicing those with the Ethiopian caravans and Chinese tea traders. But the thought of being surrounded by the sweating, shoving men on the docks, of seeing armed British men again so soon—

Noor could not touch the memories those feelings brought, the singed aching of her scars.

Instead, she watched.

A man stood in the *Victory*'s shore boat, his jacket a bloody red with bone-white bands crossing his chest. He stepped onto the dock, moving towards the crowd, hands outstretched, holding a box. He came bearing a gift. Something in Noor's shoulders relaxed; perhaps this was just a resupply, not the dawn of war.

A man wearing the clothing of an administrator of the Ottoman Empire, which theoretically ruled here, intercepted the soldier, accepting the gift. There was a conversation between the two men, with a third waved forwards from the crowd. *Ah, they did find a translator.* The crowd softened, edges flowing away. When the men broke apart, the sailor went back to his boat, where he gestured for his comrades to disembark, and the Ottoman administrator waved the remaining people away. Noor watched as the sailors moved through the dispersing crowd towards the souq.

She remembered another group of British men. They had been army men coming down from the Red Sea.

They had moved in a pack too.

Some of these ones seemed to be heading for the fruit stalls, others towards the grain market, still others towards the stockyard. She wondered how many multiples of the base price they would end up paying, or if they would pay at all, waiting until the delicate moment when a trader brought up the price to gesture towards their warship's dozens of cannons. There was no reason but honour that kept them from buying goods in the market today and bombing the city tomorrow.

That thought stuck with her.

Noor saw a group of them heading towards the hookah shops. Knowing she still had time before Musa woke and wanting to see if her haya magic would guide her next steps, she returned to the cool dark of the minaret, passing the muezzin on his way up. Imam Tariq would be busy welcoming people for the *dhuhr* prayer; she would give him the key back later. She would also make up the prayer later.

Sailors in strange ports spoke freely when they thought no one could understand them; their tongues were even looser when surrounded by sweet hookah smoke. Noor needed to know their plans if she was going to use them to get free. If nothing else, this would be a chance to practice her listening English. As she made her way to the hookah shops, the call to prayer, the *athan*, floated out over the city, lilting and strident and beckoning as always.

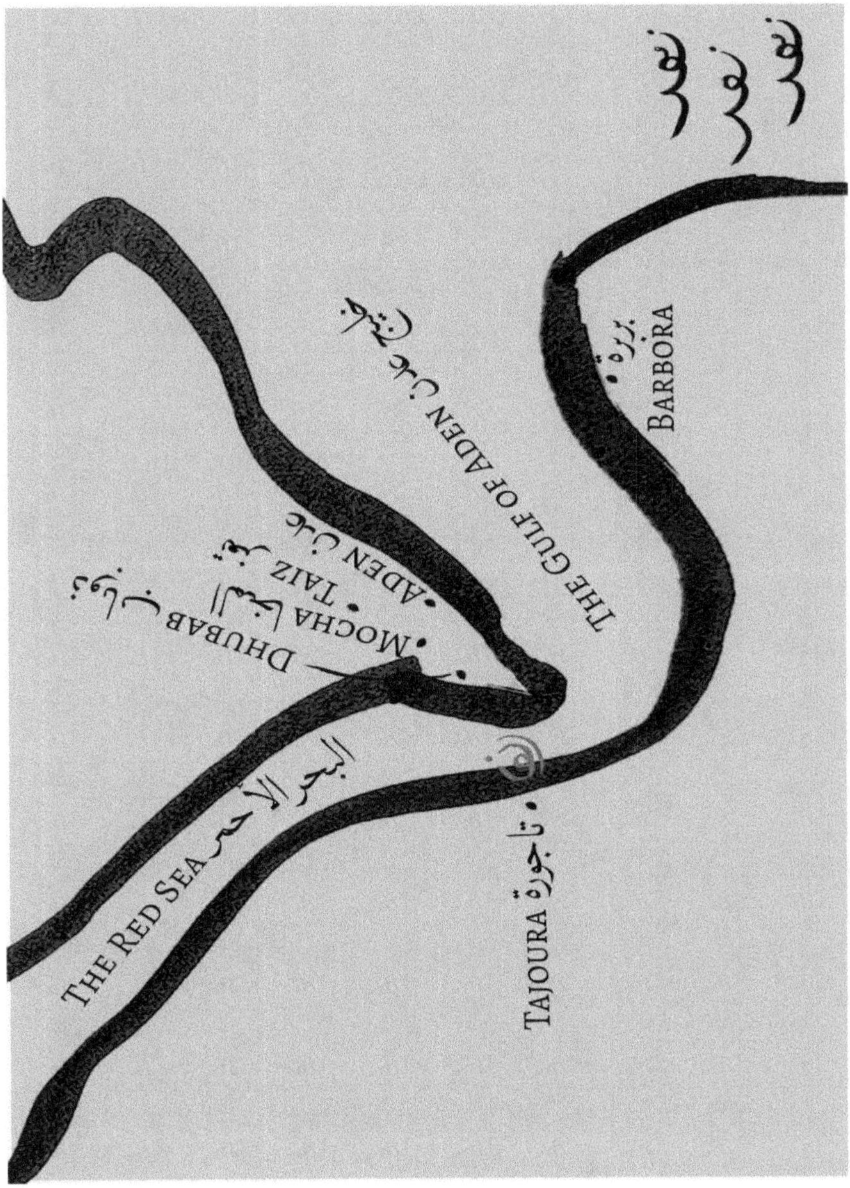

THE GULF OF ADEN
BARBORA
ADEN
TAIZ
MOCHA
DHUBAB
THE RED SEA
TAJOURA
بربرة
خليج عدن
عدن
تعز
المخا
ذباب
البحر الاحمر
تاجورة

Chapter Two

THE BRITISH SAILORS were laughing around a half-dozen shared hookahs, swaying on Mama Halima's red-embroidered floor pillows, knees bent awkwardly. Most wore deep-blue jackets; a few who sat apart wore the red and white. Noor had her back to the wall in a far corner, the jambiya's pearled hilt jamming against her skin until she rearranged it. The sailors' voices were loud and blaring, and she let herself settle into the sounds of the language.

"I could have sworn I saw the *Cormorant* in port—"

"The *what*?"

"I heard he's being lashed right now, the rat bastard, private-like in the sultan's quarters—"

"I can't believe the admiral sent the *Victory* here. After Trafalgar, after Ushant, the ship Lord Admiral Nelson captained and *died on* deserves better than this backwater—"

"Did you hear that yelling from the mosque? I've never heard anything as chilling in my life—"

"Look, it's not Portsmouth, but Aden is the key to the Red Sea, the key to all trade with India, with China, it's the *key*—"

"I can't believe they let that teakettle get shore leave—"

"These Yemeni resistance bastards are really fucking with our supply schedule. I can't believe we had to come here—"

"It's only so he can bargain for us. These bastards will take us for all we're worth—"

"She's a pirate ship. The Yemeni vermin use it to terrorise God-fearing merchants—"

"He probably likes it. You saw how he was in Sidon—"

"I can't believe we're stuck here for two days, just to get the sultan some fresh meat—"

"Is Aden really next? We're going for it?"

"Hush your fool mouth, Tomfellow—"

"I heard the sultan does his own flogging—"

"Can't get a decent drink to save your life around here—"

"This hookah isn't half bad. I can barely see through the smoke—give it here—"

A sailor crashed through the entrance, red-faced and spluttering, "The teakettle bloody scarpered!"

The sailors rose as a mass, shouting and shoving and, Noor noted, uniformly failing to pay for the hookahs they had used. They charged out the door, officers shouting them into search parties. Noor picked two of the younger ones to follow through the heavy afternoon crowd of women carrying woven baskets and men in bright colours.

"With that face of his, he'd just need to put on one of these, what do you call them, caps—"

"Turbans?"

"No, not turbans, Daniels. Kaffiyehs? No. *God's name*, I don't know what these people call them; I can't keep all these new words straight. We need to find him—"

"But that's what I'm trying to say, George. He could have put on one of those hat things, and he would be gone."

"The penalty for desertion is hanging; I don't know how many lashes it is to fail to catch a deserter as ordered. Do you want to find out?"

Noor frowned. Were they talking about an African British sailor? She knew they used impressment—really sanctioned kidnapping—to fill their warships. In the souq, she had seen British sailors who hailed from India, and ships flying under their flag were rumoured to steal entire towns on the other side of the continent. Entire tribes, erased in their slave ships. She'd heard from a condescending book trader that their people were very proud slavery was illegal on English soil.

She noticed they had done next to nothing to prevent their countrymen from profiting from it everywhere else in the world.

Something twisted inside Noor, near where she thought of her haya magic connecting. Like a piece of twine around her heart, it tugged and inched her closer to the unknown. Could it be this man, this escaped sailor? Even if this man might be indistinguishable to British eyes, he could hardly hide his face to anyone actually *from* here. Noor checked the angle of the setting sun; Musa might wake any moment now. As she gathered her strength to return to his stall, someone said in Afar—

"He looked like a Mende man, oh yes, running from the cattle enclosure—"

Noor turned slowly, searching out the voice.

The woman speaking had tight dark braids and wore a loose, comfortable guntiino.

Noor sidled up to her. "My friend, did you see the African sailor?"

The other woman sized her up before a spark of recognition lit in her eyes. Noor knew she had been placed, her position catalogued, her stooped shoulders and humble voice appreciated.

Thus fixed in her mind, the woman replied, "Little one, I did. He was running off from the cattle."

"Thank you," Noor said, hiked up her guntiino, and sprinted towards the smell of manure and the opposite direction of most of the British sailors.

She was cornering around Woubzena Haji's fabric shop when a man ran into her, full force. Noor was a good head shorter than him and was used to using men's size against them. Without thinking, she tucked her shoulder into the impact so it was he who went sprawling into a heap of fabric inside the shop. Woubzena took one look and began smacking him out of her shop with a grass broom, not bothering to regather the fabric he'd spilled as she got him outside and slammed her doors shut.

As the man staggered to his feet, Noor took in his hair—tightly kinked like hers but cut *terribly*. His face was round as if he was from the Atlantic coast, his eyes wide, searching. And he was babbling. Was that English? It sounded strange and slow in his mouth. Then she took in his blue British imperial uniform jacket and knew.

"Are you the 'teapot' who ran away?" she asked in English.

His face collapsed, eyes narrowing as he was startled into saying, "What—why would you use that word? Don't you know what it means?"

Noor shook her head. "I know what a teapot is, idiot, but I don't know why the other sailors call you that."

He leaned closer, eyes searching for a sign of the sailors. "They're saying we're dirty, like a teapot covered in soot. If you don't understand that, I won't be the one to explain it to you. I have to *go—*"

Noor's connection to her magic tugged again, and she grabbed his arm. She had to be sure. "Why did you run?"

He shook his head and dashed into the space between two shops, but then he got stuck, obviously unaware which of these openings were alleys and which dead ends. When he turned around to backtrack, Noor blocked his exit, knowing they were invisible from the street for now.

"Are you with them?" he asked, eyes wide, flicking from side to side.

Noor gestured at herself. "You think the British would trust a woman to spy for them? A slave?"

He shook his head, trying to edge around her, unwilling to shove her the way most would. He said, voice rushed, "They sent me to negotiate for the cows; they thought I could get a better price because—" He waved at his face. "The officer I was with hadn't brought the right currency—paper British pounds mean next to nothing. He told me to wait for his comrade to get back with something real to trade. A Yemeni man who'd been chatting with the cattle market's owner came up to me once he'd gone. He said his name was Usama. He asked how I came to wear the uniform of an empire dedicated to domination and pain. I told him my story; the officer was taking his time. Usama offered to help me get free, said they could use a man like me in their resistance. I didn't believe him. But he said he had a ship, the *Cormorant*, hidden in the harbour. He said he could take me there." His eyes were bright as he spoke about the man who'd promised him freedom.

He rubbed his hands over his face then, and a chill came across his warm features. "I agreed. But then the officer I was supposed to be negotiating for came back. I had to finish the sale. He was talking with the herder, and they pointed, first at me, then at Usama." He shuddered. "The officer drew his pistol. Forced Usama into irons. The officer was screaming about how Usama was a Yemeni resistance leader, and the sultan was going to have his hide for a tablecloth. Other officers came and dragged him back to the ship's brig; I ran. I've been running for what seems like hours."

There was shouting in the distance; it was in English.

Noor made a decision. "I can hide you. I speak English and Arabic and Afar and Mandarin and French—"

"What?" He leaned down to her level, eyes narrow. "Why should I trust you? Do you know what they'll do with me when they catch me? My God, I don't even know what I was *thinking*—"

Noor turned her back on him and flipped the edge of her guntiino over her shoulder, exposing her wing bones. The low afternoon light filtered between the stalls, revealing deep, repeated whip scars.

She looked over her shoulder and saw the realization rise in his eyes. "I know what they will do to you. I have a safe place I can take you." Noor covered herself and turned to face him.

"They'll hunt you too," he cautioned, and Noor grew serious.

She squatted and reached an arm out to snag one of the lengths of spilled fabric from the street. She would find a way to repay Woubzena. Noor held up the white and green striped fabric, measuring the shape of his shoulders. She could fashion a rough guntiino that would pass one moment's inspection but not two. They would have to walk fast.

The man stared at her, uncomprehending. "With Usama in the *Victory*'s brig, I don't know how either of us are going to get to freedom."

The shouts were getting closer. On the other side of the souq, Noor heard the muezzin begin to call out the *asr* prayer.

"One problem at a time. I need out of here, and you know a ship. I'll hide you and figure out a way to get Usama and then get all three of us to this *Cormorant*." Noor would figure out how later. This might be her only chance to find a friendly ship with a captain who owed Musa nothing and had no reason to turn her in. "Now kneel so I can get this fabric around you. That ridiculous jacket will give you away, but we might need it later, so keep it covered. The loose trousers are fine."

He knelt, raising his arms for her to loop the fabric under them. "They could kill us both. I don't even know your name."

She smiled, showing teeth. "I'm Noor."

He held up his hand, and she stared at it, unsure what he was trying to do. He lowered it with a slow smile. "I'm James."

"Nice to meet you, James," she said.

A few moments later, James muttered, "I've never worn a headscarf before," as she wrapped fabric under his eyes like he was about to walk into a sandstorm.

"Keep your hand under your chin to keep it from slipping since you don't know the trick of it, and I don't have a pin to spare. Then, keep your eyes down and follow me."

Noor pushed him out of the dead end and through saffron stalls, urging him deeper into the gap between the two tents and towards the rising call to prayer. They wove into and out of animal pens, using every short cut and duck through she knew. Groups of British sailors shoved past them several times, hollering and shouting, outraging the chickens and frightening the children. Noor kept them to the edges of crowds, and James kept his guntiino over his face. The athan got louder and louder. *Nearly safe.*

They were within sight of the minaret when it all fell apart.

They'd wedged themselves between two stalls, squeezing James's bulk through an opening Noor had slid past without touching the walls a dozen times.

James's half-hung guntiino caught on a splinter, ripping right off his head—

Three British sailors wearing red and white jackets looked up from interrogating a tradeswoman to see James's bare face—

Noor heard Musa's scream of rage—

Musa roared again and charged her where she was hunched over James, his massive fists raised. The sailors drew their sabres, advancing towards James. James turned to her, loss in his eyes.

Noor dropped to her knees, yanking James down with her. She scrambled in the sand, getting whole handfuls of the thick yellow stuff. Closing her eyes, Noor dragged on her magic and it rose, swirling. She let it spill out of her, billowing from her guntiino like a windstorm. The grit flew from her hands straight into the eyes and down the throats of the sailors and Musa. They scrabbled at their sandblasted faces, coughing violently and cursing, swords and fists flailing. Noor reached inside her guntiino to grasp the jambiya's pearled sheath and jammed it into the front of her belt where everyone could see it.

She drew the blade.

She met James's eyes. "I won't let them take us."

He nodded and launched himself at the legs of the sailors, knocking all three down into the massive piles of white rice arrayed in front of the seller's stall, blue-coated bodies disappearing in a puff of chaff. James scrambled to his feet, grabbed a hanging rice bag the size of a toddler and swung it at the head of the sailor who was getting to his knees. Noor sliced a break into the clouds of dust to find Musa nearly on top of her—

"You *whore*! Just you wait until I get you home—" he screamed as he swung at her. Noor's mind flashed to every moment he'd towered over her, fist raised, every name called, every bruise, cut, or whip mark laid. She silenced all her magic and shoved the point of the jambiya deep into his thick gut, standing as she sliced up. He hissed, his eyes bulging, tongue flailing as his fists unclenched.

Noor yanked her jambiya free, hands wet and warm with blood. She stood up tall, staring directly into his eyes. It must have been years since they were of a height, but she had never noticed, stooped as she'd always been. She raised the dripping blade, voice low and calm and only for her own ears.

"I'm not waiting anymore. And you are not my home."

She slit his throat and turned to look for James, not waiting to see Musa's limp body fall but feeling his life leave him through her magic. It felt like a back blow; the last one he would ever land on her.

James had knocked two of the sailors out, but the third was wrapped around him like a wrestler, one arm tight against his neck as James's fingers scratched and scrambled at the thick wool of the sailor's jacket. Noor sprinted forward and then hit the sailor in the side of the head with the pommel of her jambiya, expecting to hear the delicate shell crunch. It didn't, and neither did the sailor's skull, though he slumped off of James, dead to the world. She glanced down at the dagger. The shell had been filled in with some hard substance. She sheathed the blade. A crowd was gathering, the unfriendly sound of it rising.

There was a reason slaves weren't allowed weapons.

"Run!" she yelled at James, and he scrambled up, coughing hard but standing. They raced towards the mosque, the crowd behind them bellowing and screeching.

They stumbled up the stairs to the mosque as the crowd of worshippers flowed out. Imam Tariq stood at the top of the stairs, arms crossed.

"I'm bringing you trouble," Noor gasped in Arabic, voice tight, hands on her knees. "Again."

The Imam said, "This is the second time you've come to my mosque covered in blood. I take it this is not your blood. You are free of Musa?"

She nodded, heart as blank as endpaper and somehow as light as silk, all at the same time.

"You should not have killed him. I told you. Islam forbids killing, and you know this to be true. If you used your magic to do it, you may have lost it all today." He took a deep breath. "But I don't wish to see two more people dead today. We need to get you out of here."

He looked over at James. "Is this the runaway sailor?"

Noor tripped over her words. "He's trying to make it to the *Cormorant*; I think it's a Yemeni resistance ship. A man in the market recruited him, said his name was Usama. The British took his recruiter to their brig. If we can get him back, James says they will help me escape." She shot a look at James, knowing he had no idea what she was saying. "I want to help him."

The Imam quirked a smile, putting his hand on her shoulder. "Let's get you inside." He met James's eyes and spoke slowly, his English curling thickly over his tongue. "You are safe in this place."

Imam Tariq narrowed his eyes at the souq, and Noor imagined he could see through the stalls, see into the hearts of the slaveowners slowly deciding they would need to string her up as an example to others.

The imam then corrected himself with a wry smile. "In reality, you are safe here for perhaps an hour."

He gestured them inside.

James ducked his head and stepped into the soaring mosque. The main hall was empty, and the polished stone floor bounced the golden light of the low afternoon sun across its expanse. Imam Tariq led them down into the storeroom. It was damp and warm and dark, smelling of half-mended prayer rugs and the patina of all of the serving platters used during Ramadan. He dug out a spare guntiino from the donated pile and held it out.

Noor looked down at herself. Musa's blood had dried during their run, crusty and flaking against her skin. She accepted the clean clothing, wrapping it over her guntiino. Imam Tariq tossed James a spare *thobe* in the Yemeni style—an off-white long shirt, unbelted, with buttons down the front.

"Perhaps it will suit your Yemeni friend if you can get him free."

The imam went to an unremarkable section of the stone wall, with a head-height stack of carpets awaiting repair against it. "Help me with this, would you?"

James started to step forward, but Noor was already there and tossed him a rug. They built a rhythm, her passing, him stacking as they cleared the door. When it was nearly bare, Noor squinted and drew on her magic, lighting up her fingers and holding them out. James fumbled the final rug, but Noor ignored that in order to focus on the mystery before her.

"A secret passageway?" she asked.

"It was used before the Adal Kingdom fell to the Ottomans. During the fighting, it allowed messengers from the king to make it to the harbour."

Noor's eyes widened. "It goes all the way to the water?"

"It's pretty muddy in there, and the smoke from a torch might choke anyone else, but with your haya magic—"

Noor smiled, wiggling her fingers. "I'll give us a breeze. We can go the whole way."

She turned to James, but her smile fell when she saw his frightened eyes fixed on her light. She snuffed them out, hiding her hands behind her back as he continued to stare at her from where he sat on a pile of rugs.

The imam murmured in Arabic to Noor, "You didn't tell him you're a mage?"

"No, Imam, I didn't get the chance."

"You have your chance now."

Noor tucked her lips between her teeth and blew out a loud breath. She walked over to James, looking down at his terrible haircut.

"I've always been a scavenger. I didn't ask for this, but it came to me a few months ago. I thought I was going to die. I didn't. I healed. I lived. I learned to heal others. I'm a haya mage, James. I use life magic, fuelled by my own and the lives of those around me. It doesn't shorten anyone's life when I use magic, it simply leaves me or those I use tired." She knelt in front of him, holding up her hand, letting her fingers gently glow in the dim light of the storeroom.

Something clicked in James, and he was back, leaning forward. "You can heal?"

She nodded, cocking her head.

James spoke quickly, his English flying too fast for the imam to follow. "One of the things I have been worrying about is how we'll get Usama out of the brig. We'll be going up the rudder to get on the *Victory* and need to get back down it too."

He paused, hand rubbing the back of his neck. "They'll have whipped Usama badly by now. He's probably too hurt to move on his own, and I didn't know how I could carry him out and not get caught. But if you can heal him enough, he can climb himself, and we'd have a chance."

"Do the British whip all their prisoners?" Noor asked icily.

James's expression was grim. "Corporal punishment is legal, but torture is not. The captain makes an exception for the sultan and his apprentice, the Sword of Sidon—"

"The so-called 'sultan'," Imam Tariq cut in, his Arabic academic and measured but with heat under it. "Do you know what the so-called sultan's real name is? The one his Christian mother gave him? Jack Gibbons. A man named Jack Gibbons came to Yemen and called himself 'sultan'. His name was not read in the mosques; his family is not named in the Yemeni histories. He had no place there. Then, what, fifteen years ago, the empire's pet sultan turned Asma bint Arwa's only child into his hand-picked weapon. He took Rami ibn Arwa wa Nuri on as an apprentice, stole him from the haya magic school in Taiz, and trained him to be an alam mage. Turned him inside out. Turned him into the Sword of Sidon."

James turned to Noor, eyes questioning, not understanding.

She translated, but James was unapologetic.

"I don't know who the Sword of Sidon's mother is, and I am sorry to say it, but I do not care."

The imam moved to interrupt, but James held up his hand.

"I've lived under them, him and his master, for four years. They're *monsters*. They'll tell the captain they're extracting information from Usama, and he'll look the other way, let them gorge themselves on his screams, fuelling their alam magic." James closed his eyes, pressing his fingers over his eyelids. "I've seen it happen. I was ordered to clean the rooms they used. I know every place Usama might be as well as you know that market back there, Noor." He took a breath, refocussing, voice calmer. "I've been finding flaws in their control since I was taken from Freetown. With your magic, we can do this."

"You're from Freetown—?" Just as Noor asked, she was interrupted by tiny bare feet slapping on stone steps, the echoes moving towards them. The imam's little boy appeared, looking frantically back and forth in the darkness. He saw the imam, but his eyes were still too sun-dazzled to discern Noor and James where they sat, unmoving.

"There's a crowd coming, Baba. They want Noor-Noor."

The imam put his hand on the back of the little boy's head and pulled him in tight.

"Tell them I will speak to them on the steps. That I have her captive here and will bring her out, but only after *maghrib* prayers."

The little boy turned around, eyes finally adjusting enough to see Noor. He ran to her for a quick hug, nodded to his father, and then sprinted back up the stairs.

The imam sighed hard, then said in Arabic, "Let's get you going. Stay in the tunnels until after full dark, until you hear the athan for *isha* prayer. I'll hide the door once you're through. There are many branches in the tunnel, but stay to the right and you'll come out nearest where the British shore boat is anchored. Their ship's boats will be guarded, but I trust you'll find a way to lure them off." He quirked a smile at Noor. "Perhaps a dust spinner?"

Noor smiled. Then she remembered. "When things calm down, can you tell Woubzena that the guntiino I stole for James is hanging outside Hamadou's shop? It may be torn. I'll pay her back when I can. Though she may get more for such an infamous garment."

The imam nodded. "Time to go. Remember everything I taught you. Free yourself so you may remain free."

She raised her chin. "I will."

They headed into the safety of darkness.

*

JAMES AND NOOR picked their way through the damp, deep underground passageway, peering through the thick gloom until they found the hidden exit, right where the imam had promised it would be. The rightmost tunnel emptied into the dhow repair yard, deserted after dark. As they waited for the isha prayer, James told her how he'd come to be on board the *Victory*.

"I was born in 1783, at the end of the Revolutionary War. My mother was a slave in South Carolina. The man who called himself our master supported the revolutionaries. We were able to stay together for a time—before an overseer killed my mother and I was sold. I was forced to work in the new master's shrimping business, working every day with his sons out on the shoals. I escaped when I was seventeen. I had heard there was a boat of British abolitionists in Charleston. I ran and hid with the others who escaped with me. They dropped me off in Freetown, in Sierra Leone, to join a colony of freed people there. The people in Freetown were from hundreds of tribes, speaking just as many languages and worshipping just as many gods, but it was some kind of home." He had a smile on his face when he spoke of Sierra Leone, like the one he'd worn when he'd spoken of Usama. But then his tone hardened.

"It was only a few years later when the British declared Freetown a Crown Colony. That was in '08, and with that, the Navy began 'impressing' able-bodied, English-speaking sailors. Even those of us with American colonial accents. I managed to avoid them for a few months. The *HMS Victory* came into port on her way to the Cape of Good Hope, desperate for more sailors. There had been a sickness. They grabbed me right off the street, held me in the brig until we'd left port, and ordered me below the waterline, shovelling shit and cleaning up after sailors. They called me a 'landsman' the first year, though I'd been sailing since I was a child. That was, when they weren't calling me 'teapot'. I didn't set foot on dry land until today." He stretched his strong legs out on the floor of the tunnel, rolling his ankles.

"Why'd they let you out today?" Noor asked.

James ran a hand through his hair. If they got out of this, Noor was going to have to find a gentle way to offer to fix the mess the British barber had made of his hair, at least get him a proper comb.

"I guess they figured I was broken in," he said. "As if there was anything they could do to make me stop wanting to escape. People always underestimate how much freedom means to those without it."

"Today is the first day I remember being free." Her voice was quiet in the enclosing dark. "I wasn't born a slave. I was sold. By my parents."

James was silent, the tunnel melding the sound of their breathing with that of the waves.

After a moment, James turned to her. "I'm not sure when that prayer, the 'iza'—"

"Isha," Noor corrected.

"That one," James said with an uneven smile. He leaned closer; she leaned back. He gave her an odd look but gave her space. "I don't know very much about Islam. I've met imams before, in Freetown, since most of the locals mix Islam with some traditional beliefs. But he—"

"Imam Tariq," Noor supplied.

James nodded. "He seemed kind."

She stared back down the dark tunnel to the only place she'd felt safe her entire life. "When I stumbled into his mosque those months ago, blood soaking through my guntiino, Imam Tariq didn't have any place to hide me but the minaret. That was before he cleared the storeroom. I went to the mosque because I half remembered a half-heard sermon he'd given cautioning against the abuses of British soldiers against local women. When my magic came in, the taste of it rich under my tongue, he was the only one I knew of who had seen my kind of magic before and not only the alam magic, which is the pain magic wielded by the battle mages of the European Empires."

Noor was deep in the story; she'd never had anyone but the imam want to listen to her before, and the moon was slow to rise tonight.

"The first day I came to him for help, I only hoped he wouldn't turn me away while I healed, knowing his protection was the kind that even Musa's rages couldn't break. He found me blankets and a clean guntiino, gave me tea and bread and quiet. I slept on the little balcony at the top of the minaret for those first few days.

"I took months to heal properly. I did little jobs around the mosque, too scared to go out into the market. Until, one day, I wasn't. I went out to buy bread, and it was as if something was tugging me out, a string around my heart. It led me to just the right place, a shop I'd never shopped at before. While I was visiting with the shop owner, a British soldier came roaring through the market on his horse. A little stray cat got in his way, and he—"

She choked, thinking of that small, broken body. "But I decided—or it was decided for me, was how it felt at the time—this would not be so. This would not happen. They would not hurt one more thing. So, I scooped her up and healed her." Noor shrugged a shoulder. "I brought her back to the mosque where she lived until the imam's son took her home.

"At that point, I knew, and the imam knew, I had haya magic. At the start, I had little control over my magic. Once I was ready, the first thing he told me was that mages—a title we give freely here to anyone with a connection to magic—are extremely rare. Most tribes only see one every few generations. That means that for many years, we'd had no single reputation as a group. Some mages became healers, some warriors, some hateful and some loved. It was like the skill with a blade or a gift for oratory. It could be used for evil or for good.

"But Imam Tariq told me that neutral reputation was before the British war mages had gone against the Mughals in India, had used their alam magic to raze cities and destroy fleets. They called them the Anglo-Mysorean Wars, but it had been a massacre. Now, all mages are suspected of being in league with the imperialists. Yet another reason to keep my magic a secret."

James nodded, shifting uncomfortably.

She kept going. "After I healed and every week since, I helped Imam Tariq clean the mosque after the big end-of-week service. As we swept and scrubbed and polished, he told me what he'd learned from reading about every mention of magic in the small library he kept. He told me about the lives of mages past, how they used their power, how it worked."

She took a breath. "Again and again, he told me the story of a great Yemeni *emira*, a haya mage who used her magic during a war, killing with it. And with every death, her connection to the haya magic frayed until, one day, it snapped, and she and her people were left magic-less for a generation. Imam Tariq gathered more stories, told me them over and over as he found them. He taught me everything I know of magic. I suspected he used his small savings to buy more books and scrolls on magic to help, but when I asked, he always simply smiled and changed the subject."

A fond smile hovered on her face.

It faded as she said, "Most evenings, he reminded me that my magic was a gift, as much a part of me as my brown eyes, and I had a duty to Allah to use it well. Imam Tariq would talk about the pillars of faith as guides for people in all different kinds of lives, mages not excluded. He reminded me of *salat*, prayers, not only the daily requirements, which I was the only one keeping in Musa's household, but of praying to quiet the storms inside. He taught me ways of calming, controlling, centring, and focusing. He gave me exercises that had worked for other women he had counselled, who had survived some of what I had survived. Imam Tariq reminded me of *sadaqa*, the importance of giving to others."

She shook her head. "It wasn't all lectures and cleaning. We tested the boundaries of my magic whenever we could."

"What boundaries did you find?"

Noor held up her palms. "I can call light. I can move objects that come in waves, mostly water and sand. I made a dust spinner dance in the market, and this little girl ran through it; I'd never seen such joy. You saw today how I can use that, when I have to, to hurt. I healed a paper cut on the imam's finger. I healed the cat. Its fur was soft and black, and it screeched, raking my thighs to ribbons once it could race away up the minaret steps on newly healed legs. That healing nearly knocked me out. I slept all afternoon, through maghrib prayers until after dark. Thankfully, Musa always slept through them too."

She looked James in his thoughtful, considering eyes. "Imam Tariq gave me what sanctuary he could, when he could. Risking himself, risking his family, to get me free; that is part of who he is. He's a good man."

James nodded. "I could see that."

They both paused, letting the quiet of the moonlight shudder around them to the steady beat of the rising tide. Then James traced his fingers in the mud, drawing an outline of the *Victory*.

"Here is what I'm thinking for a plan," James said finally. "We'll go up the rudder. No one will see us as the guards avoid patrolling around the sultan's quarters because no one can take the screaming. There'll only be one guard at the brig since everyone else on the roster has shore leave. I'll distract him; they won't have heard about my desertion, so I'll stay in my uniform."

James began shucking the thobe Imam Tariq had given him, revealing the blue wool uniform underneath. "Usama will be the only Yemeni in the *Victory*'s brig. You get in, get Usama, get back to me quick. You can heal him enough so he can walk; we can get back to the ship's boat, get to shore; and Usama can take us to the *Cormorant*."

Noor took out her jambiya and tested the edge on a reed growing from the corridor floor. A light touch sliced it in half, and she watched it drift to the muddy ground to land in a puddle of moonlight. She met James's eyes and saw hope there. Noor found herself unwilling to dim it.

"Sounds like a plan."

The isha prayer began to roll out across the city as they set out for the docks to borrow a British boat.

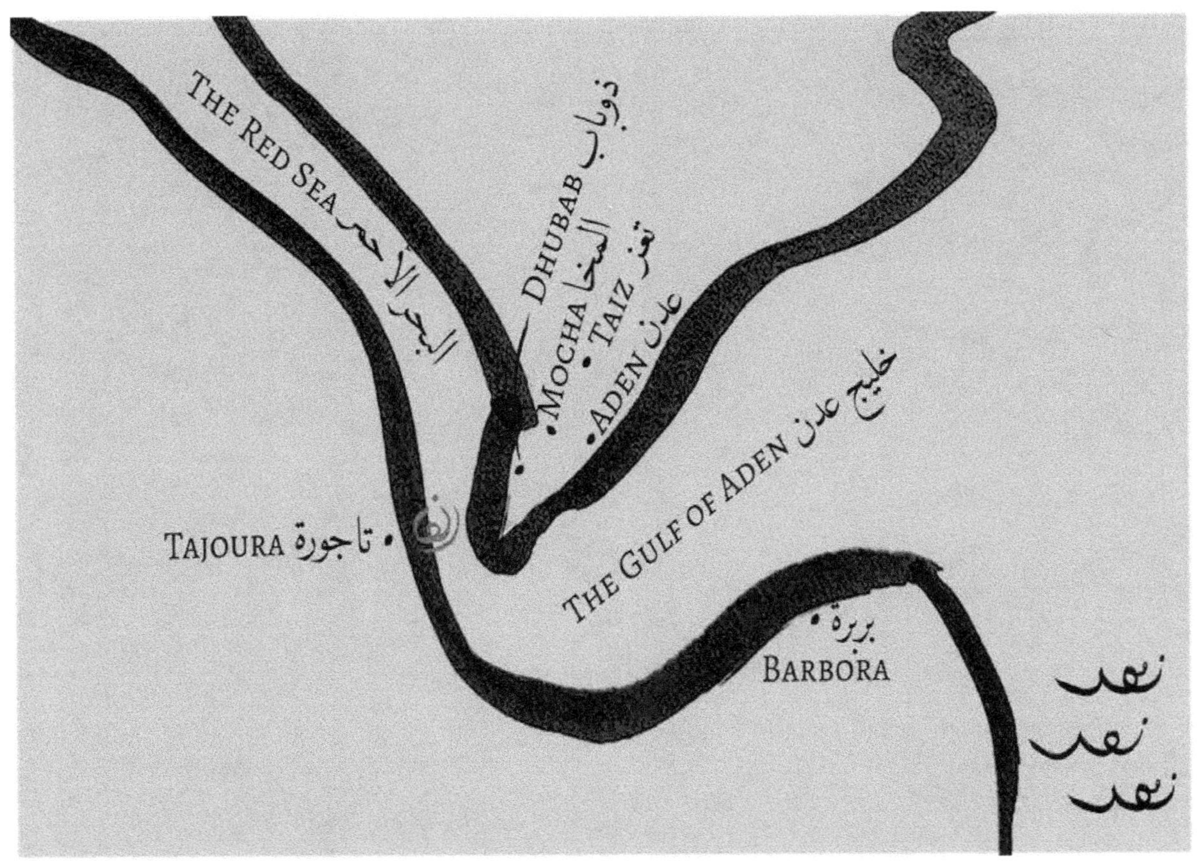

THE RED SEA
البحر الأحمر
DHUBAB
ذباب
MOCHA
المخا
TAIZ
تعز
ADEN
عدن
THE GULF OF ADEN
خليج عدن
TAJOURA
تاجورة
BARBORA
بربرة

Chapter Three

NOOR SUMMONED HER light to her fingertips, holding them in front of her as she edged down the whitewashed hallway of the *HMS Victory*. The steady tip and pitch of the warship at anchor was subtle compared with the rowboat they'd come in on.

A smell, raw and red, flowed from the end of the corridor.

The brig.

Noor slipped forward, her leather sandals light on the deck.

Heavy boots beat around the corner where James was, so she hid her light in her palm, breath tight in her chest, and held still. Then came James's voice.

"Lieutenant, could I get your help for a moment?"

The guard growled, "What do you think you're doing up here, teapot?"

Right on time.

Noor hurried forward, just out of his eyesight. Six doors stood at the end of the corridor, three on either side of a small open area, right as James had sketched out for her on the quick walk to the docks. Each white door had a barred window and a deadbolt thrown across it. She reminded herself: *one young Yemeni man, badly hurt.*

No one was visible outside the cells, the only sound that of the low conversation between James and the man who was supposed to be guarding the brig. No shouting.

Yet.

Noor approached the first cell and peeked through the high barred window. The pale features of a sleeping man shone back at her on a low bunk. He murmured something, rolling towards the light. She ducked and tucked her fingers in tight, listening for any more movement. Sweat walked like an insect down her spine. The ship's huge square sails cracked overhead, but the first cell stayed quiet.

Noor crept to the next window. The room held an empty bed with bedding carefully folded on the cream-coloured mattress, ready for the next insubordinate sailor or member of the Yemeni resistance.

A nightwatchman's boots beat on the deck above, steady and slow; that deck's guard on his rounds. They were three decks deep into the *HMS Victory* and surrounded by the nearly five hundred men James had said served on board. It was a miracle they'd come this far without being spotted.

Noor moved to the last door on this side, and her sandal slipped before she caught herself against the doorframe. She glanced down, holding her fingers out wide, shining her light on—blood, a spreading pool of it. It dripped from a thing hanging beside the door, black like a branch. She leaned closer to it, chest tight with memory—a cat-o'-nine-tails, knotted, and winking with blood. She looked through the barred window, knowing what she would see.

A broad-shouldered, dark-skinned back, scored and striped with cuts and gouges from the cruel knots of the whip. The marks started at the nape of his neck and scratched down to the belt of his soft-looking black pants. What skin that remained untouched dripped with sweat, probably from a rising fever from the cuts. The man on the bunk breathed in shallow pants, his forearm covering his face, blocking out his view of the cell. His long feet were naked and hanging off the end of the bed.

James didn't say Usama was this big.

Noor slid the bolt and stepped inside, keeping her light low, and tugged the door against the frame. It swung back open on the next rock of the ship, and she caught it with her pinky; no lock on the inside. She clenched her jaw and slipped a foot out of her sandal, the rough-cut whitewashed oak boards threatening splinters as she eased onto them. Noor wedged the shoe between the lintel and the door, then tugged it to make sure it would not swing.

It held.

She turned around and studied the man on the bunk, seemingly dead to the world. Kneeling to shake his shoulder, Noor hesitated, hand hovering above his skin. She didn't want to touch him, didn't want the feeling of a strange man's sweat on her palm. She examined at his injuries, gathering her strength.

Deep bruising spread over his shoulders as though he'd been kicked repeatedly before the whipping. She knew those kinds of injuries. She shivered hard, once. Moving away from that memory, Noor forced herself to lay her palm on his shoulder. As soon as her skin touched his, something tugged low in her stomach, warmth spreading, her magic rising to meet another's.

Is Usama a mage too? James has to learn to be more specific in his briefings.

He didn't wake, but he rolled a little. Blood matted his dark hair along the side of his angular face.

Healing first, then.

Noor drew on the long thread connecting her to her magic, letting it build in her stomach, hot and soothing and *hers*. She felt hers slip beneath his skin into the deepest hurts first and then the bruising inside his skull and a broken ankle. *The British work quickly.* She slid the edges of his whip cuts back together, healing the torn muscles, easing the bruises across his spine. He would still be in pain, but he'd be able to climb down the rudder with her and James. Masses of scars crossed his back. *Not his first whipping, then.* She had many of the same scars. She'd learned she couldn't heal the old ones, just live with them.

When she'd finished, she opened her eyes to him watching her, his expression strangely soft. A constellation of moles ranged across his face, and she caught herself trying to discern a pattern in them. His eyes were dark, drowning deep as he stared up at her.

"Thank you," he murmured in Arabic, hand drifting up to her cheek.

"We have to go!" she hissed, jerking back as his eyes widened. "I healed you so you could walk. Can you walk?" He swung himself up to standing—and then fell back against the bed with a *thump*. She froze, worried the other prisoners on the block might wake.

She heard movement.

"Here," she said, and before he could do more than give her a dubious scowl, she'd bent her knees, got her arm under his, and had hefted him back onto his feet, a good half of his weight across her shoulders.

He gazed down at her, seeming slow to catch up.

James didn't say Usama was stupid; maybe I didn't heal his head right.

He murmured, "Is this a dream? Does he know?"

She frowned, answering as she maneuvered them towards the door. "He sent me. My name is Noor."

The man jerked, breathing harshly, then sagged even further. She pinched his ribs, and he startled, glaring at her.

"Noor? Where did you come from?"

"Let's *go*," she said.

He bent his head and started shuffling stiffly with her. She eased the door open and moved them into the corridor, bare foot landing squarely in the puddle of blood. She grimaced but kept moving.

In the cell across the way, a shape stepped up to the bars. Noor shoved them both around the corner, getting them into the still empty corridor.

The man's breathing was steadier now he was up and moving. She very much hoped he wouldn't pull his fainting act again until they were off the rudder and into the rowboat they'd hidden in the ship-shadowed water there.

Noor rounded the last corner before the ladderlike stairs that zigzagged through the ship and let the starlight in even on the third deck down. James slid out of a shadow, eyes wide. The guard must have gone on whatever snipe hunt James had concocted for him.

Noor jerked her head towards the man hanging off her shoulders, but instead of helping carry the load, horror flared across James's face. Noor slowed. She glanced over at the man as he stared up at James from under his long hair.

"Get away from her!" James hissed barely above a whisper. Noor's eyes widened. She'd only known James for a few hours, but that tone was recognizable anywhere—hatred.

"What's going on?" she whispered.

"That's not Usama," James replied, face twisting. "That's the Sword of Sidon."

Noor wasn't sure she'd heard right, but then James's fist was smashing against the man's jaw. He flew back, and an echo of it hit Noor, her body bending with it, his head slamming against the wall making her skull ache. It was over in a second, his body collapsing to the ground, shaking the oak deck. Noor dropped beside him, fingers going to his forehead, drawing on her magic—he was unconscious, not dead.

She glared up at James, heart racing, skin clammy. "Why did—"

James was already hustling back towards the brig, leaving the man crumpled against the wall. Noor stood slowly, one eye on the man she'd healed. Noor could hear his blood in her ears, but over it, from the end of the corridor, a bright tenor whispered:

"*Habibi!*"

It came from inside a cell.

"What are you doing here, habibi? And why did I just see a young woman carry the Sword of Sidon out of here like a sack of fish?"

"We're here to rescue you," James hissed as he unlatched the door. "That is Noor back there. She's helping us in exchange for a ride out of Tajoura."

Noor watched the other man swagger out of his cell, snagging a bag of his personal effects hanging beside the door without stopping. As he walked through the gloom towards her, she saw he was about a decade older than she was and wore his long, black hair in a neat braid down his back. He pulled out a leather thong strung through a key and settled it around his neck. Then he slid a jambiya out of the sack. When he tucked it in his belt, his entire body seemed to steady, with his shoulders square and his smile that much brighter. James looped behind him, urging him forward.

Usama wouldn't be hurried. He met Noor's eyes and pressed his hand to his collarbone where it showed through a rip in his white thobe. "Nice to meet you, Noor. Thank you for your help."

His smile was infectious, but Noor kept glancing at the man they'd left crumpled at her feet. Usama's eyes widened when he followed her gaze. He leaned into James, speaking soft English, perhaps thinking Noor could not understand.

"Ah, habibi, not to be ungrateful, but I fear it may be important. Why precisely did our new friend free Rami ibn Arwa wa Nuri only to leave him on the floor of his master's ship?"

James glanced at her apologetically before saying. "She mixed you two up. I told her to rescue a Yemeni man in a cell while I distracted the guards, and I had no idea the sultan was going to send him here tonight."

Usama shook his head. "The guards were so busy whipping him on his master's orders, they never got around to me. Is he still breathing?" He shook his head at himself, braid winding against his back. "No, wait. You know what? I don't care. Let's go."

And he started up the stairs—only to halt before the sight of a half-dozen muskets pointed at his chest.

The snipe hunt must have ended early.

James's eyes darted side to side, searching for an escape. But Noor had seen the faces of the men behind the muskets. She knew men like them, knew what they looked like sweating and heaving, and her voice came out as cold as a winter storm as she raised her hands.

"Stand back."

Usama took one look at her face and, with the rising heat of haya magic in the air, tackled James to the side.

Noor pulled her arms to her chest, sensing the life of every man on this ship, all of the fish and sharks and tiny creatures below and around it, and the birds in the night sky. She held it all in her mind's eye and slipped a small piece of it away from all of them, throwing all of that power, all of that energy into the ocean behind the men and pulling up a giant, spinning column of water. It was thick with sand and silt and the nails and screws of the shipwrecks she'd spent her life scavenging. She whipped it across the top deck, down the stairs to where they stood. She wrapped the coil of roiling bay around the sailor's chests and *yanked*. They flew back up to the deck, screaming in terror as their bodies tumbled like toys.

"*Run!*" she shouted at James and Usama, voice harsh and strange. They stared at her, mouths hanging open before Usama scrambled up the stairs, dragging James along with him. Noor turned to Rami, struggling to sit up, his eyes wide, still, and dark. On his face was an unlooked-for recognition.

"You're a haya mage," he said loudly in the sudden quiet.

She held her breath for a moment, the change in James and Usama's footfalls telling her they had made it clear to the top deck. Then, she nodded before sprinting up the stairs, half expecting him to follow her, to yank her back with his own power.

He didn't.

Why not?

Noor caught up with James and Usama only to find them surrounded by sailors wearing the red uniforms. She flung her arms up, throwing sprays of sandy saltwater into their eyes, before grabbing the other two men as the sailors howled in pain.

They sprinted toward the rudder, James leading, Usama's hand in his. Noor bred chaos on the deck with handspun waves, shoving the crowds of men trying to force their way up from the underdecks back beneath the oak. James made it over the side and helped Usama get his hold on the ladder to the rudder. Noor couldn't climb and keep aiming the water.

She called in Arabic, "I'll be right behind you. Keep going!"

She sensed something, some kind of alam magic boiling up from the sultan's quarters in the aft of the ship under her feet, coming for her like a tide, rising deck after deck after deck. Different from the Sword of Sidon's magic, it was cold like grave dirt, shredding like a whip.

They needed to get out before whoever was wielding that magic arrived. Noor closed her eyes and slipped a bit more life off the top of some of the sailors. She gathered it between her hands, kneading and kneading and kneading it. Though she knew the price of all this magic came for her from a long way off, she was flying high now. She stood and nearly grinned at the shock on the British men's faces as she, a Somali woman, wrapped in her red and yellow guntiino, jambiya at her waist, stared them and their muskets down.

"Look at me!" she cried in English, and when she could see the whites of their eyes, she threw her hands wide, casting a blazing light across the entire *Victory*, the power of it knocking the sailors nearest her off their aim, musket bolts skipping harmlessly out into the harbour.

A deep voice screamed in English, "Don't *look* at her, you reprobates! You three, get the lamps lit! Else you won't be able to see them in the water!"

Noor saw three huge lanterns swinging from the mast. She called up a swirling waterspout and flung it at the lanterns, knocking all three into the harbour. She slid over the gunwale and climbed as fast as she could down the rudder, not thinking about the frosting deep water below. The alam magic seemed to have been extinguished by her display, like sand on a cooking fire.

"They won't be able to aim for anything after that, lady mage. Very good thinking," Usama said as soon as she dropped onto the boat. His grin was huge as he and James began rowing them away from the *Victory* as quickly as they could.

A bolt hissed into the water beside them, and Usama turned wide eyes to her.

She narrowed her eyes. "It looks like they're willing to try."

Noor turned and pulled up more of her magic, exhaustion dragging at her bones, but she forced another burst of light, sending it flaring across the harbour into the searching eyes of the sailors.

"We can compliment each other on our beauty and smarts later," James huffed. "Where's your *Cormorant*?"

Usama turned so James's back pressed into his front and lay his arm over his shoulder to point to where a double-masted Yemeni dhow was coming out from behind an anchored bark, on their starboard side.

"Right there."

The cedar-hulled ship could easily fit three dozen sailors or enough goods to feed a family for years. It tacked over to them, putting its bulk between them and the *Victory* as more musket bolts flew, the sound of them growing dull as the ship's body protected the three of them.

"The only woman I will ever love," Usama said, patting the hull as it slid easily around them. On the deck, a woman wearing a black headscarf threw down a ladder for them and waved with a welcoming smirk over the gunwale.

As he climbed, Usama called up, "The emira will get a kick out of this mission report. I got the information we needed, and I brought back an imperial deserter and a haya mage. It's going to be a glorious dawn."

"Let's get out of here in one piece before you crow too loudly, my friend," the woman said as she hauled him over the rail.

Once he was over the side, Noor grabbed the bottom rung and worked her way up, James ready to follow. Right as she reached the top, a hard, warm hand gripped hers, pulling her over. It was the other woman, her eyes bright and smiling and hands now on Noor's elbows to keep her steady in the pitching ship. Vibrant red embroidery covered her *abaya* as if she were Palestinian, or at least the dress was. It was beautiful. Noor's breath caught, and she gently eased herself away, making room for James to climb up behind her. A tall Chinese man working the sails assessed them with a glance before returning to his work.

The ship was old but well cared for. Wide, steep stairs descended in the middle to the hold below, which was divided into two sections with a curtain. The top deck had two cabins, for the captain and a guest, if Noor had to guess, and there were probably dozens of smuggler's hidey-holes across the ship.

They swept into the dark of the night, leaving the chaos of the *Victory* in their wake.

*

ONCE THEY WERE safely in the Gulf, Usama told her they would head directly to the Yemeni emira's secret base north of Aden. From there, Noor could go on her own way or stay with them in the fight.

"Your choice, *habibati*."

Once they were in the Gulf, the man who'd thrown down the ladder introduced himself as Mianning, originally from Shanghai. He'd been in the Gulf for forty years. His Arabic was rough, and Noor got the sense he was never a big talker, but the smile she got when she answered him in Mandarin was genuine.

The woman in black introduced herself as Razan bint Adla, a shipwright and tinkerer with the resistance. She was about Noor's age, shorter than Noor, with intelligent eyes, strong hands with quick fingers, and a Palestinian or Syrian accent. Her abaya reminded Noor of the ones she'd seen women wearing in Gaza during a caravan Musa had brought her on. Razan led her down into the hold to a collection of hammocks.

"The others will sleep in the cabins above deck, and we'll have the hold to ourselves, sort of like a women's quarters." Razan's tone was competent, and something eased in Noor's chest now she knew she had another woman to rely on.

Noor could barely keep her eyes open. A full day of magic, carrying the Sword of Sidon over her shoulders, the race off the *Victory*—it all fell on her like a dead dugong.

"Is it safe if I—" She gestured to the hammocks.

Razan's eyes were serious and her tone remained steady. "I will stay with you. These are good men. You are safe here."

Noor gave her a weak smile before climbing into the highest hammock. It would be better to fight back from up high if someone came for her in the night. She held her jambiya tight and was nearly out when she felt someone approach. Her opened her eyes to Razan holding a thickly woven blanket.

"It'll be cold out in the Gulf this close to monsoon season," Razan whispered.

Noor took the blanket, trying to think of the last time she'd slept with one. The weight was unfamiliar but deeply comforting. Razan's watchful warm brown eyes were the last thing Noor saw before sleep took her under.

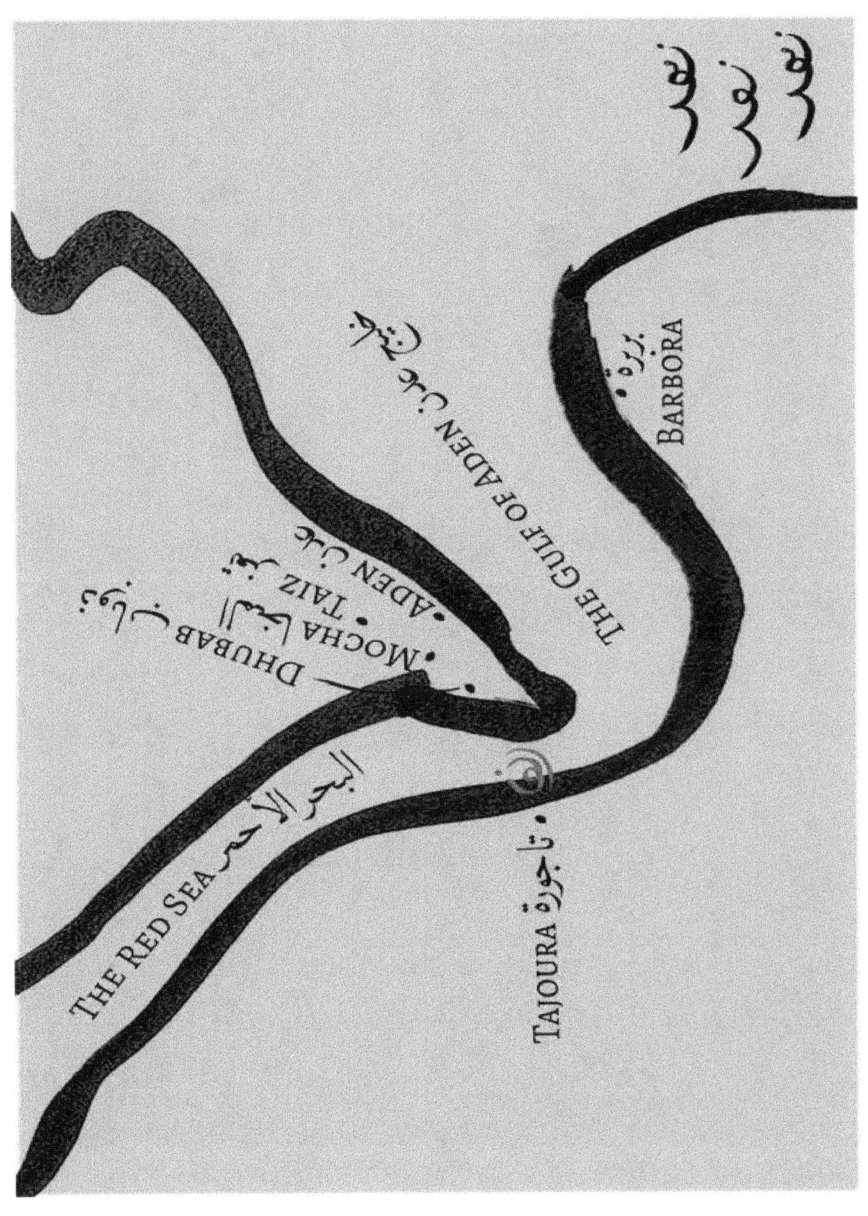

BARBORA
THE GULF OF ADEN
ADEN
TAIZ
MOCHA
DHUBAB
THE RED SEA
TAJOURA

Chapter Four

NOOR WOKE MIDMORNING. Razan slept in the hammock below, her brown face relaxed, lips slightly open. Noor watched her chest rise and fall, how her tall body swayed with the waves, curled carefully on her side facing the entrance. *It's been a long time since I've had a friend.*

Noor climbed out of the hammock, trying not to disturb Razan. She paused at a little snort and a shift in Razan's hammock, but she didn't wake as Noor pushed past the curtain marking off their space and out to the lower deck. Even here, it smelled of open water, sweet and salty and bright with none of the rotting seaweed mustiness of the harbour.

She found a washroom, really, a closet against the hull that drained directly into the sea, equipped with a small barrel of fresh water. With the door shut, she took a deep breath, all of yesterday's mad rush flowing over her, threatening to drown her again. She was on this ship until they made port, and then she would need to have a plan.

I can do this.

Noor climbed the stairs to the deck to find Usama navigating and James keeping him company. Razan had made it up and was tinkering with something on a table that folded out from the hull. Mianning was probably resting in his cabin. Noor took a moment to gaze at the impossible and infinite horizon. Sea blue and sky blue nearly melded into each other, so it was as if they were standing in the centre of a globe; it pulled something deep in her chest, that impossible horizon. That sense of falling and flying had always been her favourite part of the few times she'd been out on the Gulf. Usama smiled when he saw her, keeping his eye on the waves ahead.

"We'll first spy land by midnight—we're taking the long route to avoid patrols. We should make it to the base by first light."

Noor glanced around, searching for some kind of food.

Usama smiled. "There's some good *kidem* bread in the basket over there, along with a nice bunch of fresh fruit. Eat as much as you like; it'll spoil otherwise. For longer journeys, we'll be eating off the land. Or the sea, as the case may be. But Razan made a run to the market while I was gathering information about the *Victory*, so we're comfortably supplied for now."

Noor nearly skipped over to the open-air kitchen. She sat with her back against the hull and began to eat. Razan locked her bench and wandered over, her hips swaying easily with the rocking of the ship. She plucked. a yellow fruit Noor had seen but never tried from the bag and munched on it, skin and all. She folded herself onto the deck opposite Noor, skirts flowing around her knees, and smiled.

"We didn't get a chance to do much more than exchange names last night. Since we have a few hours, and a break from chores until Mianning gets up, I figured I would see if you had any questions."

Noor chewed slowly, thinking. "Are you in the resistance, too, or is it only Usama?"

"It's all of us here, though Mianning only dives in a few months at a time when the emira catches him in port without a clear excuse as to why he can't help." Razan grinned. "Mianning's mostly a smuggler and occasional pirate. He used to run with the emira's husband before he was killed by the British, *Allah yarhamhu*. When was it—?"

Razan called over to Usama, "When did Yusef ibn Nuri die?"

"*Allah yarhamhu*, two years ago this spring, trying to defend Mocha from the *Victory*," he called back from the wheel. James looked at him and then at Noor to translate, which she did.

"He was a good man," Razan said sadly. "A scoundrel, a pirate, and a card cheat. But a good man."

Noor said, "It sounds like you miss him."

Razan bit her lip. "We all do."

Noor studied the sea, chewing on the bread, sun warmed, buttery, and delicious. Razan snagged a piece and bit into it.

"I saw Usama wears a key. Is it to his home in Aden?"

Razan shook her head. "No, it was to his mother's home in Mocha. Destroyed when the British took the port. He worries it when he's troubled."

Noor turned to the other woman. "How did you come to join the resistance?"

"I'm from Sidon." Razan replied as if that was enough, her voice as distant as the clouds. "After the Sword of Sidon razed the city—my parents were dead, my sister was dead. I've always been good with tools. My father built houses; my mother was a weaver. I figured if I could join a group, build for them, maybe I could fight back. The emira took me in, after Sidon."

Noor said. "I met him."

"Who?"

"The Sword of Sidon. On the *Victory*."

"Did you kill him?"

"No. Why?"

"How did you meet him?"

Noor's cheeks flushed hot. "I thought he was Usama. James said to bring out the only Yemeni man in the brig, so I brought out the first Yemeni man I saw in the brig."

Razan's lips quirked as though she was suppressing a smile. Then her face grew serious. "But now, you know what he looks like."

"Yes."

"Then, next time you see him, kill him. Kill him with your magic."

"I can't use my magic to kill," Noor replied, frowning.

"Why not? He does. He does it all the time. He feeds from pain—"

"That's why."

"What?" Razan said sharply.

"The way my imam taught me, there's two kinds of magic. There's alam magic, where mages hurt themselves or other people and use that pain to fuel their magic. Then there's haya magic, which comes from the little edges of life. It's the same energy you use to get up in the morning, to walk. The same energy you can restore with food, so when I take some, it leaves people a little tired, a little hungry. Killing with it—it would be like trying to grow a plant by tearing out its roots. It makes no sense."

Razan's eyes were calculating. "Have you tried eating raw sugar?"

"What?" Noor asked.

Razan reached into her abaya's pocket, jingling what sounded like rocks, pegs, nails, and a pair of small tin cups. She pulled out a hunk of something wrapped in wax paper.

"Here, it's my last one. It makes me feel like I have more energy. Maybe this will help feed your magic."

"No, I can't take your last piece." Noor raised her palms to ward off the sweet.

"You saved Usama. Knowing them, they're never going to thank you." At Noor's widened eyes, Razan hastened to add, "It's not that they're bad men, them and Mianning. It's simply that they've been in this fight their whole lives. Daring rescues, dagger fights, escaping the empire—it's all a normal day for them. It was a little shocking for me when I joined. I figure it doesn't have to be shocking for you."

Noor accepted the gift and unwrapped the paper, revealing a hunk of brown crystallised sugar, such as the Indian traders in the market sold for far more than she'd ever been able to pay. She scraped off a piece with her fingernail and popped it in her mouth. Closing her eyes, she let the taste fill her mouth.

"Oh, that's so—"

"'Sweet'?" Razan asked, grinning.

"So sweet!"

"Take a bite of it. It's different when you fill your whole mouth."

Noor laughed and settled back a little against the hull, holding the sweet in a careful hand.

"What else should I know? Are they—?" She nodded to James and Usama, sitting with legs and shoulders pressed together. She could have sworn James was nearing a giggle; he was so happy. Usama's face was less mobile, but a light shone in his eyes that Noor had seen in her friends who had married for love. She smiled, glad to see someone happy.

She finished her thought. "Are they safe?"

"I don't know James. But Usama usually has a good sense for men. As for Usama and Mianning, yes, they are. They don't care who beds whom as long as everyone is happy about it." At Noor's startled expression, she paused. "I am very direct. Many people don't like that about me, but it's also a part of me I'm willing to change. So, I'm going to say some things that sound very direct, and I hope you will forgive me."

Noor folded her candy up in the wax paper and met Razan's dark eyes.

"Rape is very common in many places," Razan continued. "Rape in marriage, rape of children, of little girls. Sometimes tolerated, sometimes banned, sometimes put into rituals, sometimes tribes chop the cocks off men who try. But the tribes that make up the resistance are led by a woman—Arwa. She sets the rules. She doesn't tolerate any kind of rape; she doesn't tolerate forced or arranged marriage. She believes all people should be free. Free from force, free to love who and how they want and need to."

Noor frowned. "I've never heard of a tribe running itself like that."

"It seemed as if in the city where you lived, the men had a lot of control?"

Noor rolled her eyes and nodded, mouth twisting.

Razan continued, her eyes filled with laughter. "Did you ever know men to concede power, to share stories about places where people like them had less power?"

Razan leaned in when Noor shook her head. "I think you may find, in the way that I have found, that there are many more ways of being a woman in the world than the ways you and most others were raised to believe."

Noor's heart kicked up, jolting against her chest, her mouth watering. *It must be from that sugar.* She let go of the breath she'd been holding, and then Razan gave her a crooked smile and leaned back.

Grinning suddenly, Razan jumped subjects. "Do you want to see a trick I made?"

"Uh, sure."

Razan held up a finger. "Wait."

She shoved her hands into her pockets and pulled out a long piece of copper wire and two metal cups like the ones sailors used. The bottom of each cup had a hole with the wire tied through it, connecting both of them. Noor narrowed her eyes; it was a waste to destroy cups.

Razan handed her one and kept the other for herself. "You speak into it, and when you want to hear me, you put it up against your ear."

"But I can hear you just fine."

"Wait. You'll see."

Razan took her cup and walked slowly, stretching her wire all the way across the deck, maybe fifty paces. Usama grinned, then turned back to the sea, clearly having seen this before.

Razan put the cup to her mouth, and Noor dutifully put hers to her ear.

"Can you hear me?" Razan said into the cup.

The words warbled like birdsong but were still recognizable. Noor widened her eyes, and she glanced down at the cup, mind racing. She put hers to her mouth, and Razan cupped hers around her ear.

Noor said, "How does this work?"

"You see how the wire moves when I speak?"

Noor squinted at the wire. But they were on a ship; everything was moving. She shook her head, a blush rising.

Razan gestured for her to raise the cup to her ear again.

"I'll keep talking, but put your hand on the wire while I do so."

Noor did, and it was like a trapped bee buzzed against her palm. When she gripped the wire tightly, there was silence even as she could see Razan's mouth moving. Then Noor took her hand off the wire.

"—sound stops when you touch the wire." Razan grinned as she walked back to Noor, coiling the wire as she went. Noor reluctantly let go of the can when Razan tugged it from her hands.

"My mother showed this to me," Razan said conspiratorially. "She discovered it when she was weaving a metal screen. I think our words move on the wire itself. It doesn't work with the cups alone or the wire alone. She thought the cup focuses the sound and sends it on the wire."

Noor cocked her head. "You know, when I think about my haya magic, sometimes I think about it as tugging on a thread, pulling the life of those around me closer to me. I don't know if you saw, but I can make things move with my magic?"

Noor continued after Razan's nod. "Usually, only things that come in waves. I don't really know why. My magic came to me when I was on the sand; sand dunes are like still waves. It's mostly water and sand that I seem able to move."

Razan's eyes twinkled. "Do you think you could make the wire move? A little bit, but very fast?"

"I could try."

"Let's see!" Razan uncoiled the wire from around her cup.

Once she was in position, Noor tried. At first, the wire made a low, pounding sound, like the biggest of drums at the beach bazaar. She concentrated, thinking about moving it back and forth, faster and faster, until it was a high-pitched screaming whine—

Usama marched over, clapping his hands around the wire. "Habibati," he said, his usually cheerful face as close to stern as Noor had seen him get. "Perhaps it is worth it reminding you both that we are—" He held up a finger. "—on a pirate ship—" He pointed to Mianning and held up another finger. "—transporting resistance leaders—" Pointing to himself and Razan, he held up another finger. "—wanted deserters from the Royal Navy—" He now pointed to James and then to Noor. "—escaped slaves—" A fifth circled his head. "—in the middle of imperial patrolled waters. And so, perhaps, we should not be making loud noises at this time."

Razan coiled up the wire, shame-faced.

Noor shared her blush.

"Sorry, Usama." Razan shoved the cups into her abaya's pockets, a few small shells falling out. She picked them up and fiddled with them as she and Noor sat together, backs against the curving hull.

Noor adjusted her jambiya so the lunella shell pommel didn't jab into her stomach.

"May I?" Razan asked, reaching for the weapon.

Noor slid the Damascus blade out of her belt and handed it to Razan, hilt first.

Razan examined the pommel, not the waves on the blade, her long, slim fingers careful on the delicate-looking shell. "When I was a little girl, we would go down to the beaches of Sidon and collect shells. When we found big ones such as this beauty, we'd put them to our ears. My father would tell me we could hear what the animal inside it heard, the sound of the deepest oceans, the heartbeat of *other* oceans, oceans I'd never seen, never even heard named."

Noor's gut tightened, the nudge of haya magic. It rose in her like a tide. "Do you have a bigger shell?"

Razan turned to her, noting the change in her tone. "Yes," she said slowly.

Noor's words were distant now. "Do you have two?"

Razan went to her workstation and rifled around in the bag that hung from one end of it.

"Here." she said, handing Noor the shells. "But what—"

Noor interrupted, voice still distant as the tide tugged inside her. "I must do some magic before the feeling passes, but I will explain after."

The lunella shells were shaped like the turbans of Sikh men, only small, the size of a young girl's fist. Noor closed her eyes and brought the two shells together in her hands, openings aligned gently. She pulled at her haya magic, pulled and pulled, took a little bit from Usama and James, a bit more from Razan, from the fish below her, the whales and sharks, the birds flying high above the sea. She left Mianning alone, not wanting to compromise their navigator. She pulled until the light between her hands glowed against the backs of her eyelids.

Until Razan whispered, "Whoa."

Noor pulled a little bit more, and then she pushed the energy into the shells and whispered to them, "You are connected." It took the same inner muscles as twisting stiff metal into the links of a salvaged chain, locking them into place so they made something contiguous that had previously never been whole.

Noor let the magic ease back and opened her eyes. She tilted her head all the way back.

Razan, James, and Usama stood over her, staring down with wide eyes. Razan spoke first.

"Did you use some of my life?"

Noor's eyes felt heavy as fishing weights as she nodded. She'd used much more of her own.

Razan's face was tight. "How about you ask me next time?"

Noor's cheeks heated, but the shame was as distant as of the cresting wave dizzy giddiness that came from such a big piece of magic. She was *tired*.

She handed Razan one of the shells, aware of Usama and James's eyes following. "Try it."

Razan looked down at the shell, face querulous but game. She moved to the far end of the dhow and held the shell up to her ear.

Noor held her shell to her mouth. "Can you hear me?"

And Razan's eyes got huge. "No," she gasped, and Noor frowned as Razan stumbled over herself. "Yes, I mean, yes, I can hear you!"

Razan put the shell back to her mouth. "How far do you think this goes?"

"We'd have to test it, but I don't think distance will affect it. It's—" Noor sagged against the hull, even as she tried to stay upright with two men standing over her, even as her eyes crept closed. She mumbled, "It's more about sameness."

Razan spoke again, beyond excitement with joy. "Noor, do you know what you've done?"

Noor shook her head, or rather, rolled it against the hull.

"Noor, you could have changed the course of the fight."

Noor spoke through a yawn, stumbling over the words. "I told James I'd be useful."

Razan returned and knelt in front of Noor, hands gentle on hers. She said, low and warm, "You look terrible, Noor. Let's get you in your hammock."

"Mmmm," Noor managed.

Razan stood and stooped to gently take Noor's weight, letting her lean hard on her strong, slim shoulders. She elbowed Usama and James out of their path and headed for the stairs.

Shuffling, Noor followed her lead, yawning again. "I never slept in a hammock before last night."

Razan frowned a little. "I thought a lot of folks used hammocks in Tajoura?"

Noor dropped her gaze, working her jaw.

Razan leaned in. "Where did you sleep?"

"Outside. Unless I brought enough treasure back. Then inside."

"On a pallet, a mat?"

Noor couldn't keep her eyes open. "In the sand, on the street."

Razan's answer was as cold as starlight. "If we go back to Tajoura, I am going to kill your master."

Noor crooked a smile and stumbled after her into the hold. "I took care of it before I left." She hurried to clarify, thinking of Imam Tariq's story of the emira who lost her powers. "Not using magic," she said as she patted her jambiya. "Using this."

"Good woman."

Razan drew her towards their sleeping area. At the curtain, she narrowed her eyes at Noor's upper hammock and seemed to make a decision. She pulled Noor's blanket into her lower hammock and poured the other woman on top of it, tucking it carefully around her waist and ankles.

The blanket smelled of Razan, honey and cedar, metal and shell. Noor snuggled into it and could almost feel the heat of Razan's body in the weave of the hammock.

Razan stepped away, and a little time passed, Noor drowsing, enjoying the sway of the hammock and the comforting scents around her.

She was nearly asleep when Usama spoke up from outside the hold. "Will these work for anybody?"

Noor called out, slurring her words, "We'll have to test it. But I think it will only work on the ones whose life I used."

A footfall sounded on the stairs, and Razan seemed closer. "Did you use all of ours?"

Noor shook her head, lowering her face to the hammock, blocking out the sunlight through the hatch. She spoke to the canvas. "No, not Mianning's. I didn't want to make him sleepy."

She could hear the smile in Razan's tone. "You're a smart woman, Noor."

Noor nodded, turning further from the light, the canvas mussing her hair. She was too tired to do anything about it.

She dreamed of the *Victory*, of long corridors, of bright sails.

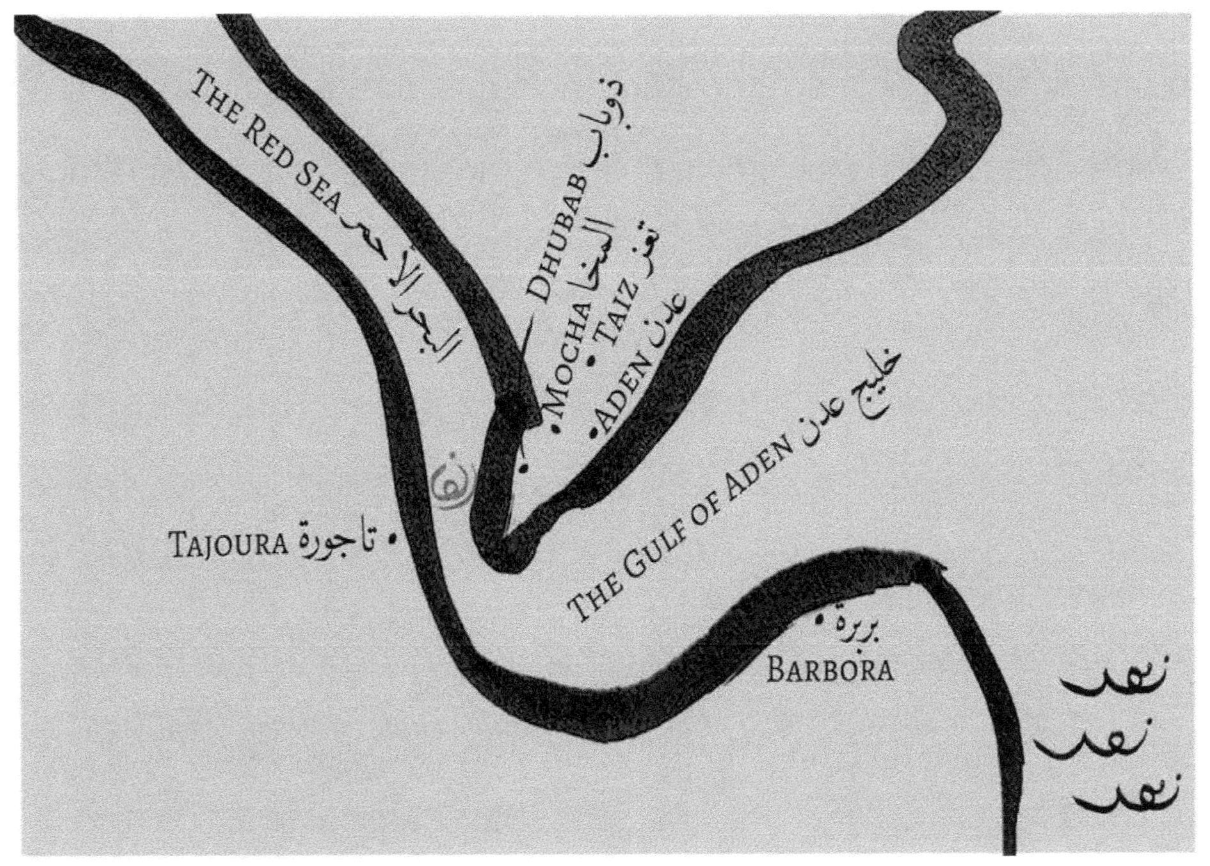
THE RED SEA البحر الاحمر
DHUBAB ذباب
MOCHA المخا
TAIZ تعز
ADEN عدن
THE GULF OF ADEN خليج عدن
TAJOURA تاجورة
BARBORA بربرة

Chapter Five

WHEN NOOR WOKE up a few hours later, it was midafternoon. She climbed the ladder to see James and Razan still experimenting with the shells, mostly using gestures and some of their limited shared French as they hollered across the length of the dhow. Usama was still at the helm, and Mianning was off sleeping in the captain's cabin. When Razan saw Noor was awake, she bounded over with a flask of cool water and a fresh mango.

"We've been working for hours and hours, and we think we figured out how it works."

Noor smiled and held up her hand. "Can I eat first?"

Razan, chastened, said, "Sure." She stood in front of Noor, rocking from foot to foot, out of tune with the dhow's rhythm as Noor ate.

As soon as Noor had bitten the last orange flesh from around the large seed at the heart of the mango, Razan said, "So, I have a couple of questions."

The rest of the day's light was spent testing different types and sizes of shells. It ended up that the lunella shells they'd started with were a fine size and shape, but a variety could work. Adding additional shells didn't take nearly as much energy as establishing the connection in the first place. Noor had a clear picture in her mind each time they added a new shell to the system. She imagined she was weaving another strand into a vast and growing fishing net, with a shell at the intersection of each and every thread. Noor was right that only those who had life drawn from them to enchant any particular set of shells could use them.

She could use all of them.

Razan asked a lot of questions about how far Noor needed to be from someone to include them in her magic, whether she needed to be able to see them. Noor couldn't see the sharks, whales, birds, and bugs she'd used on their first shell, but she could sense them through her magic and so draw power from them. She couldn't pull life much farther away than she could see over open water, but if James went to hide in one of the many smuggler's niches in the *Cormorant*, Noor could still draw from him.

Razan made him test this. Repeatedly.

Usama pulled up some fishing lines as the sun set bloody against the horizon. He cooked his catch in a small oven on the deck and asked for Noor's help turning them. They worked in silence for long moments, and then he spoke.

"James told me a little bit about your history." He glanced towards her back, then met her eyes, his gaze sincere and clear. "I don't want you to feel—trapped. Here. With us. You can leave. I mean, not right now..." He gazed out over the open Gulf of Aden all around them. "But once we get to port... Look, I don't have a lot of money, but you saved my life, saved James's life. I have enough. I can set you up with what you need to go wherever you want— Home?"

"I don't have a home. My parents sold me when I was a child. Maybe, someday, I'll want to go back to where I think they were from, to try and find them, to give them a piece of my mind. But I need to have peace of mind before I do it so I don't bring them back the same pain they gave me."

Usama's eyes widened a little. "That's very...kind of you."

She quirked a smile. "I've had a lot of time alone to think about it."

He rubbed his stubble, studying her, eyes sharp and kind all at once. In a flash, she saw how he could convince someone to desert the British Empire in the time it took most people to drink a cup of tea.

"Well, if you're searching for a home, we're fresh out of haya mages—by 'fresh' I mean before the Rami started calling himself the Sword of Sidon and turned turncoat, he'd been the only one we had—and if you want a home in the Yemeni resistance, you've got it."

Noor traced the cedar beams and planks of the dhow with her eyes. It was old but well-maintained. *Clearly loved.* Usama seemed to have plans, networks, ideas.

No one seemed to be starving.

Everyone seemed to care for one another.

He leaned in. "I won't keep selling when it looks like you might be buying, particularly since you can't walk away right now, but we're at what the emira would call a fulcrum point."

She frowned, not knowing the word.

Usama pulled out his jambiya and balanced the flat of the blade, near the hilt, on a fingertip. "The place where my finger touches the blade is a fulcrum. I move it a little bit one way—" He walked his fingers up the blade, and it tipped, flipping. He caught it smoothly by the hilt, then rebalanced it on his fingertip again. "I go another way—" And it fell, stabbing into the cedar deck. At Mianning's glare, Usama knelt, pulled the blade out, and rubbed over the mark with the edge of his thobe, his key slipping out from under it at the motion.

"So, there is a kind of balance right now?" Noor asked.

"No, more like a *waiting.* I couldn't hold the jambiya on my finger for long, with the waves rocking the boat around us. There are waves moving across the world right now, rocking everything—Napoleon, Al-Wahhab's people, and the so-called sultan are the three biggest waves in this part of the world. Nothing holds at a fulcrum point for long. Today, this week, this month, this year, we're inside of a long breath. We've got six months, maybe a year, before the British are done with whatever they're doing in the Americas with their most recent war there with the United States and before they decide to refocus on their moneymaker—

getting trade to and from India and the east. That's all, of course, assuming Napoleon doesn't try to break across the Channel again. But no matter which other wars they're fighting, to fund them properly, they need Aden. Sure, they could pay us to run our port, they could pay our tariffs and dues, the taxes that would let us build more schools, keep the water clean, care for the aquifers and cistern systems and keep streets safe. But they're not going to want to. They want to be able to charge everyone *else* those dues, those tariffs, to use the money for *their* warships and iron rockets. They want total control."

He frowned. "I don't know if you know a lot of Yemenis, but regardless of tribe, we don't particularly like being under anyone's thumb. We're going to fight." He set his jaw. "Just like people fought in Sierra Leone and Hong Kong and everywhere else they've beaten people, taken over. Their *colonies*."

Noor broke in. "But they lost in the former American colonies the last time, just as France lost in Haiti. They've been outside of European control ever since James was small."

"Yes. But our war isn't theirs."

"What do you mean?"

He paused, running his hand down the bow of the ship, the long grain of the cedarwood guiding his fingertips.

"Have you ever seen the cedars of Lebanon?"

"No. The farthest north I've ever been was Gaza," Noor said, cocking her head at the swerve in subject.

"You should go. Razan will take you one of these days. She has people there." He closed his eyes, tilting his head back. "The cedars are as tall as mountains, and the smell—if you think it smells good cut and dried and shaped into a dhow, you should smell them *alive*."

"I'd love to someday."

"James told me the *Victory* was built of two thousand English oaks. Two thousand. And when I've met American ships, they're made of the same—oak and some pine. But their ships look like British ships. They're made by the same shipbuilders, sometimes bought from the same shipyards. No matter their leaders' wars, their ships look the same."

"I don't think I've ever seen an American ship."

"I spent some time on the Barbary Coast, getting to know the Arab fleet there, trying to drum up support for our cause." Usama gave a big sigh. "Maybe someday. Not now. But I saw my fair share of American ships." He opened his eyes, meeting hers. "Do you think the people who lived in the Americas a hundred, a thousand years ago, do you think their ships looked like that? Massive white sails and spiderwebs of rigging and canons for days?"

"I don't know if I've ever thought of it."

"I've seen drawings—Razan collects them, designs of other nations' ships, boats, anything that floats—including those made by the people who lived there before Amerigo Vespucci named their home in 'the New World.' They made their ships for their great and small waters, their tidelands and wild and cared-for places. They are *different* from what came across from Europe. Brilliantly, perfectly, beautifully different. Unique to their time and place and people."

He looked down at his hands, slowly tracing the lines of the cedar in front of him. "That is what we are fighting for in this war between cedar and oak. Not the sameness of colonialism and European expansion, but the right, the *freedom*, to continue on our own paths, to make new ideas as we see them, to build new worlds of our own in our own times and places."

Noor thought about that. "Where do people like James and I fit in? And Mianning and Razan? We're no more Yemeni than the so-called sultan is."

"To me, to most people whose opinions I care for, getting to choose who our people are is part of that freedom too. It's not about purity of the blood or being an unchanging nation; it is about having the dignity of choice. It's about not having colonies, armies, faiths, and leaders forced on us but allowing us to become who we are meant to be."

"So, when you say 'our war isn't theirs...'"

"I mean we're trying to do something that has never been done in this part of the world—to force the British Empire to treat people who were here first, people outside of Europe, as equals. Treat our home not as a place to be colonised, not as a source of slaves, but as a force to be reckoned with.

"That's the fulcrum." Usama tucked the jambiya back into his belt. Then he held up one finger. "Will we be colonised, enslaved, turned into yet another of their conquests? Dhows sunk and great masted ships raised up in their place, shadowing our coastlines with their acres of sails? Will Aden become New London or New Portsmouth? Will we be ruled by people who do not speak our language, whose grandmothers and grandfathers are not buried in our soil, who known nothing—care nothing—of our own unique ways, our hopes, our dreams?" He held up another finger. "Or will we survive, fight back, remain our own people, unbowed, unbroken?" Usama dropped his hand and rubbed his neck before continuing.

"I'm usually the one who gives the rousing speeches before battles, so that's why that sounds like a speech. But it's also true. And after what I saw on the *Victory*, you could be the whole difference, Noor. With you, we could stop the *Victory* from taking Aden, which is what my sources in Tajoura told me is their next port of call after a weapons resupply at Mocha. With you, we could sink them in the harbour of Aden. Our dhows, our smaller boats, they can get around the sunken *Victory* and keep trade flowing. But that hulking mass in the mouth of the harbour would protect us from their warships."

He considered her. "Of course, scavengers will take her apart, use that pale oak wood for crossbeams in their houses, use those sails for their dhows. In six months, a year, the *Victory* will disappear into Aden like it never was. But those six months will give us the time to prepare, to get ready."

"What about the Sword of Sidon and the so-called sultan?"

Usama sighed, hand going through his hair. "You know I used to babysit him?"

Noor gave him an incredulous look.

"I don't know if anyone told you. He's our emira's son. There's some whole long story about how the so-called sultan whispered to him in the night through his magic, twisting his mind, kidnapping him in the dark.

But I really don't care. He chose to kill more of his own people, people who weren't hurting him, than most British do in a lifetime. He left his people to die, and there's no coming back from that. But to sink the *Victory*, to win this fight, we'd have to find a way to deal with him and his master. I just have no idea how to do it."

Noor held up a hand, pausing him before his next speech. "I want to help. I want to give Aden the chance that so many other people haven't had against this empire, against the men who run it. They think they can take what they want. They'll keep taking until someone stops them. We need to stop them."

Usama clapped her shoulder, grinning; when she flinched, he yanked his hand back. "Sorry, sorry. It's been a long time since I could see a path to, if you'll excuse the expression, victory."

She groaned.

His face grew serious. "But Noor, I don't want you to be deceived. This is going to be a tough fight. We have books, scrolls, memories about haya mages, but we have no one who can teach you. Our last school ended in flames. You'll be figuring it out on your own."

He paused and seemed to make himself say it. "You might die. But I can promise that we'll all be dying together if that happens. We don't leave our own behind."

James sauntered up, smiling, and put his arm around Usama's shoulders. "What are you all talking about so seriously over here? The fish aren't going to cook themselves."

Usama smiled, switching to careful English. "Then I had better light a fire. I'm starving."

Usama sauntered over to where Mianning was pulling out the fruits they'd bought in the market and where his lines were tied over the side. He checked the lines for another course for dinner before ducking below to gather some well-dried driftwood for the small brick oven.

James lowered his head, speaking softly. "Is everything all right?"

Noor leaned against the gunwale. "I agreed to join the resistance. I think it's my best chance of staying free. And I want to protect others from going through what we went through at British hands."

James's eyes were approving. Then he shuffled his feet, clearly working his way up to asking a question. She let him get to it in his own time, watching Razan and Usama bicker over how to cut fruit.

James said it all in a rush. "Will you teach me Arabic?"

Startled, Noor replied, "I would think Usama would be happy to."

"He will, and he is, but I don't want to spend all our time together teaching and learning. And I kind of want it to be—" He searched for the phrase.

Noor offered, "A gift?"

"I want to surprise him, to show him I want to be a part of this, of all this."

"I would be happy to. I'd recommend you also listen to Razan because she speaks the Lebanese dialect, and Usama speaks the Yemeni dialect, and I speak a version of all of them. So, listen to how they pronounce different words."

James grinned.

"Here's your first word. 'Noor.'"

"'Noor,'" he dutifully repeated, face confused. "Isn't that just your name?"

"In Arabic-speaking cultures, names also often mean something. They might refer to a historical figure or an ancestor—or an idea. 'Noor' means 'light.'"

"'Noor means light'," he repeated.

"Good," she said as she moved past him. "Now, let's eat."

They started on the fruit, and in minutes, Usama was cooking the fish, muttering to it conspiratorially through the small oven's door. When he served it to them, the meat was pale and sweet, the skin crispy. Noor couldn't remember feeling so comfortably full.

After they all cleared up and Mianning took the helm, and Razan and Noor headed down to their hammocks. It was early for bed, so they sat together against the fine-smelling cedar wall of the ship, shoulders pressed tight together in a long line. The sun had long-since set, and the stars were out in force. With the waves hushed in the low wind, they could have been in Lake Ghoubbet or the middle of another ocean entirely for all Noor knew.

"You know what I wish," Razan said wistfully, "and I'm not trying to be ungrateful because these shells are incredible, world-changing even. But I wish there were some equivalent of this except with things we can see with our eyes."

"What for?"

Razan tipped her head back against the slow curving hull. "Well, like sharing the maps our spies have seen in London rather than having to wait months and knowing we're only seeing a copy of the battle plans. It would be faster than the British with their semaphore flags and their mail ships."

"You have spies in London?"

"The British don't make a lot of friends with how they are out in the world, and sometimes, we have ways of making our own friends." Razan paused. "Is it—would it be possible to share what we can see?"

Noor's contemplative silence drew Razan's eyes to her.

"I haven't known you very long," Razan said, "but I'm starting to think of this as your 'engineer face,'"

"I don't think I qualify as an engineer."

Razan shrugged. "What are qualifications? What school would let us in, precisely? We make our own qualifications. I'm an engineer; you're an engineer." She held out her hand, fingers straight, pointing towards Noor.

Noor thought for a moment, frowning. In the souq, she'd tried to never show ignorance because revealing it meant someone would take advantage. But in the day that she'd known these people, that didn't seem to be how they moved through the world. "I don't know what that gesture means."

Razan's eyes lit up. "Oh! Here it is." She grabbed Noor's wrist, slapped their hands together, and bounced them up and down. "It's a form of greeting. I learned it when I was studying with my French tutor in Beirut. It's *very* European."

Noor shook her head. "You say that like it's a good thing."

Razan looked down before meeting Noor's eyes. "Yeah, I guess I did."

Then, she returned to task. "Anyway, engineer, what are you thinking?"

Noor held out her hands, filling them and the space between them with a lambent glow. She thought of the green and red skin of the mango Razan had given her. Dutifully, the ball of light changed colour. Not only colour but shape, becoming a fuzzy idea of a mango.

Razan's eyes widened, so the whites shone all the way around. She whispered, "Can you do that anywhere other than between your hands?"

Noor considered, then turned her palms to face the hull. The ball of light drifted over to the side, flattening against it.

Razan approached the shape, holding out a hand to touch it before freezing and glancing back at Noor.

"I don't think it will hurt you," Noor said.

Razan reached out farther. "It's just—it's just wood. It's just light on wood. It would be hard to see during the daytime unless we were in a dark place or at night." The possibilities raced across her face. "I know this stuff makes you tired, but please, please, please, can we keep working on this? You have my permission to draw life from me anytime we're working on it."

Noor laughed. "And you've got me until I'm too tired to keep my eyes open."

"Great. Now, can you make anything or only mangoes?"

Noor closed her eyes and brought up the first image that came to her—Musa's screaming face. Razan gasped, scrambling away. Noor clapped her hands together, killing the image.

Razan clapped her hand over her mouth. "Sorry. I didn't—"

"No, I'm sorry. I—"

Razan huddled beside her, back against the hull. "Was that the master you killed?"

Noor nodded.

"All right, try to think of something else."

With thoughts of Imam Tariq's little boy, Noor filled the light with his image until she held a doll-sized version of his body between her hands. She sent him running and playing through the hold. Then Noor showed Razan the cat she'd healed from the market and a happy, living dugong swimming and twining around her hammock, followed by her pups. She brought up Imam Tariq and Woubzena Haji's faces. As they lay on their backs, hair and headscarves intertwining, Noor showed Razan the shapes of clouds, scrolling across the sky.

Razan sighed. "This is incredible. Can you make images that someone else sees? Like you did with the shell, how it conveys others' voices? So you don't have to control it?"

Noor chewed her cheek, thinking aloud. "The shells worked because we already knew we could hear things through them."

"That was just a story my father told me."

"But stories have power."

Razan held her gaze. "They do."

"But—we can tell a new story," Noor said slowly. "About—" She scanned the hull, searching for a feasible option. "—about two women who could see through each other's eyes using a—" She grabbed it. "—a mango seed!"

Razan burst out laughing.

Noor held the edge of her guntiino over her eyes. "Through veils?"

Razan laughed again, pulling the cloth away from Noor's smiling face. "No, we want a thing men and women can use."

"I made James wear a guntiino with a headscarf to get through the souq."

Razan grinned. "As is right and appropriate."

Noor turned, scanning the hold for anything they could attach a vision to. Her jambiya jabbed her stomach. She pulled it out, the rolling Damascus layers of it dancing like waves and undertow currents, tugging that thread inside her. Noor polished it against her guntiino and then held the flat of it across her eyes, carefully keeping its edge away from the bridge of her nose. She drew life, carefully this time and only from herself and Razan, from the birds in the air, the fish in the sea, all the insects, and the great whales she could sense in the distance. Noor put that between her fingers and pushed it into the waves of the Damascus, making them spring up and over her hands, a wavering light, dark, and in many, many colours.

She would sleep so very well tonight.

Noor held up the polished blade, and reflected in it were her own eyes. And then, in the flat of it, she saw a clear blue sky with soft white clouds scampering across it.

Razan's face showed amazement, but there was a bit of disappointment in her voice. "It's good when it's flat, but I wish I could see the shape of them again; they were so beautiful."

Noor closed her eyes, sinking back into herself and *tweaked*. It took the same effort hitching her guntiino or adjusting her hair—a small movement that realigned everything around it. When she opened her eyes, a covey of small clouds hovered above the knife's blade, bumping into one another.

"Now you try," Noor said, handing the blade over. Razan stared at the jambiya, concentrating. A woman materialised, sitting on the flat of the blade, her eyes like Razan's. The figure stood, tugged her abaya straight, and then she laughed silently, joyfully, arms going around her stomach with glee.

A tear slipped down Razan's cheek. Noor didn't know what to do—should she hold her? Look away? Touch her arm? She'd comforted hurt animals in the market, but a cat always let you know precisely what kind of touch it wanted. Noor settled for carefully laying her palm at the base of Razan's neck. The other woman collapsed forward, her tears against Noor's throat.

Razan's whole body shook wordlessly. The woman on the jambiya faded, laughing and waving. Noor patted a gentle pattern along the safe middle of Razan's spine, counting her breaths and wishing she knew if she was helping.

Finally, Razan muttered, "My mother. She—she died in Sidon. When the empire attacked. I miss her so much, but I didn't have a painting of her, nothing like that. We don't have images of living things—"

Noor shivered hard, her stomach knotting. Was this a depiction of a living thing? She knew many Shi'a people didn't mind. Zaidi believers in Yemen had some beautiful images of men and women and animals, and she'd seen Persian carvings and bowls and rugs and hangings in the market that showed living things. Making images of living things wasn't a major prohibition where she lived, but she'd heard of groups, followers of Al-Wahhab, coming down from the holy cities, men who enforced these kinds of rules much more strictly.

Razan seemed to follow her thinking. "To me, this can't be worshiped as an idol since it is so fleeting. It shouldn't be *haram*." She paused, thinking a moment. "Can you make the blade show us impossible things? A blue mango?"

Noor focused on the blade, trying to imagine a blue mango. She could see it in her mind's eye, but it didn't—what kind of blue? Would it be lighter and darker the way a mango skin was, or would it look entirely different? A regular mango appeared, its image flickering like a candle.

"Fascinating. You know, I think that might mean we cannot use these to lie." Her eyes shone. "The first-ever form of communication that is entirely truthful. Can you imagine, Noor, if we showed this to the British subjects, the people whose boys are being press-ganged into service of the empire, who spend their lives working to fuel a war effort, and they don't even know what it looks like?"

Noor smiled a little at Razan's enthusiasm, but she doubted they would care. She'd met a lot of British men who'd seen for themselves the brutality of what 'empire' meant; it didn't seem to have changed anything about how they acted in the world.

But she couldn't bear to unmake her friend's hope.

Razan studied the blade. "So, the people whose lives fuelled the creation of this blade's images can use it to show any memory, accurate and true to that memory. They can show it flat or whole, larger or smaller. They can control what is shown but not modify how it looks." She squinted up the stairs as if she could see through the deck to where Mianning managed the helm.

"Can anyone see this?"

Noor frowned, shrugging. "I don't know. I would think so? I would guess that anyone can overhear something on the lunella shells if a person is speaking loudly enough."

"Let's go test," Razan said.

They staggered up the ladder and over to Mianning, Noor's legs half asleep, Razan clutching the blade. He narrowed his eyes at them, one hand on the wheel.

"Noor, think of that little boy you showed me before," Razan said.

She did, the imam's son climbing up and out of the dagger and striding across it, the little cat tagging along behind him.

Mianning's eyes narrowed as he asked Noor in Mandarin, "Did you do this, little one?"

She was unsure if it was said with pride or fear.

He leaned down, squinting at the little figure. "I cared for a boy that age once, a long time ago."

Noor recognised pain in his words; she would know it in any language.

Mianning stood up straight and said to Razan in careful Arabic, "I can see it. Can you show anything?"

Noor nodded, answering in Arabic, "Anything that is true."

The corner of his mouth quirked a little. "The emira is going to love it."

Suspicions confirmed, the two women stumbled towards the ladder leading to the hold, giddy and exhausted. Before descending, Noor checked around the deck.

"Where are Usama and James? We should show them too."

Razan cleared her throat, tugging Noor towards the ladder. "Well, uh, there's a guest cabin."

"I saw. And a captain's cabin."

Razan scanned the deck, eyes moving as though she were reading a script, then tugged Noor down the ladder to the hold. "I think James and Usama are...getting to know each other." Her tone was careful.

Noor pondered how to navigate the suddenly tense waters. She spoke slowly. "They seem to like each other very much."

Razan's eyes were full of a world of thoughts, but she waited for her to continue.

Noor tried again. "I knew two men who also liked each other very much. It didn't concern me or those who cared for them."

Razan's shoulders moved away from her ears, but she still said cautiously, "I've known people for whom it was a concern."

Noor grimaced. "Me too."

Razan collapsed back against the hull. "I won't pretend; I think it's cute."

Noor burst out giggling. "You think it's *what*?"

"Cute, adorable, nice! This world is too hard not to spend time with people you like."

"Agreed. And the emira?"

Razan smiled, but her eyes remained serious. "She believes people should be free."

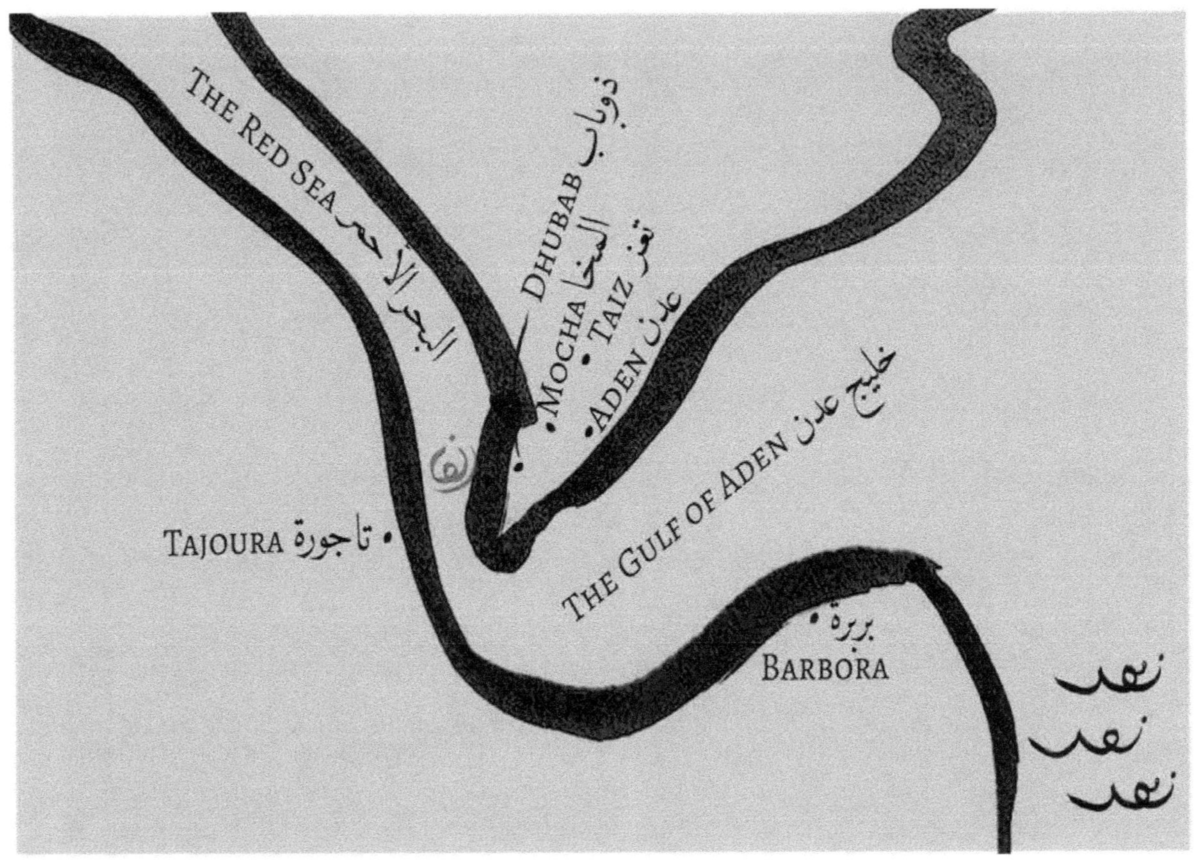
THE RED SEA
البحر الأحمر
DHUBAB ذباب
MOCHA المخا
TAIZ تعز
ADEN عدن
THE GULF OF ADEN خليج عدن
TAJOURA تاجورة
BARBORA بربرة

Chapter Six

A WINTER MONSOON wind had picked up overnight, slowing their progress. It held its rains back, barely. Unlike its summer sister, the winter monsoon season was shorter, wet in some places and fiercely dry in others. And like its summer sister, once it started, it made the Gulf nearly impassable for all but the most daring sailors.

They spied their destination mid-morning, the emira's compound, just north of Dhubab on the Red Sea. The gulf here was shallow and clear, and Noor peered over the gunwale at fish she'd never seen in Tajoura—from the tiny silver runners to a massive, big-headed thing that tried to intimidate the *Cormorant* hull into moving out of its path.

The family compound had four long, high white walls surrounding a collection of homes and a single tall gate with red flags on either side of it in the middle of the longest wall. From the mast, Noor saw a half-dozen little girls running outside the walls, colourful clothes streaming behind them, screaming in their games. She smiled; *children are the same everywhere.*

As they neared the makeshift dock, Usama came to lean against the gunwale with her. "The emira is going to be thrilled to see you," he said.

"Since Rami left, we haven't had even the hope of a mage."

Usama turned to her. "The *Victory* could be in Aden within days, so the emira will be in the midst of battle planning. We need to think of a way to quickly convey the value you bring to the effort, to get all of the *sheikhs* and *sheikhas* on her council on board."

"What do you have in mind?"

*

USAMA HAD A flair for the dramatic.

Noor loved it.

Usama and Mianning went ahead, up the sloping sandy beach towards the compound. Usama carried Noor's jambiya and one of the lunella shells. Noor waited until he'd passed the guards who had come outside the wall to observe their docking. Then, she, James, and Razan climbed down the ladder to the sand below. Noor moved to stand a few hundred paces from the compound, slightly in front of Razan to her right and James to her left.

As Usama had promised, Yemeni men and women began to wander out the open gate, children milling and scampering around them, continuing their game of tag. Noor held up her lunella shell and spoke into it, hoping Usama was where he'd said he would be.

"Are you ready?"

"Habibati, I have never been more ready for anything in my entire life."

A commotion started up outside the compound as the watchers gleaned her voice was coming from the shell.

"Good."

She raised her hands, tugging on that place inside where she kept her connection to haya magic. She called up a dozen dust spinners twice her height and walked forward, her friends following with the whirling winds flanking them. Noor crossed her arms as the first tremor of exhaustion worked its way down her arms. She kept going. The spinners raced faster than any horse could run, whirling to double, triple, quadruple the height of the white walls before falling harmlessly into piles of dust at the feet of the gathered families.

Noor raised her shaking hands again, her feet keeping a steady beat on the hard packed earth as she summoned a wall of dust in front of the three of them, totally blocking them from the compound crowd's sight. Without breaking her stride, Noor took three deep breaths and then allowed the sand to dissipate.

She was close enough to the crowd that she thought she could pick out the emira, an older woman in a brightly coloured abaya, her grey hair showing under a headscarf. A number of older women stood in the crowd, but it was this woman's eyes that caught and held Noor. They were the same drowning dark as the Sword of Sidon's eyes.

From within the low waves of the Red Sea behind her, Noor called up a curling rope of water, a sister of the one she'd used to drive off the British sailors on the *Victory* but thinner and carefully free of fish. She drifted it across the sand in front of the crowd, spelling out the word 'Yemen' in looping, curling Arabic script, stream steady even as her feet slowed. She wouldn't have been able to write as elegantly in English, which broke space between most letters, but in a scripting language with fewer of those breaks, it was simple work.

She was close enough that a few steps would bring her within touching distance of the frozen crowd. Usama bridged the distance, stepping forward, and handed back her jambiya. She accepted it and knelt, holding it high above her head as James and Razan knelt behind her. Noor didn't miss how many of the sheikhs and sheikhas had their hands on their own family daggers as they eyed her. She tried to control her breathing, to keep from gasping from the effort of the magic.

Noor's words rang out clear and strong. "What would the emira like to see?"

The emira's tone was low and hard, but Noor heard a smile in it. "Show me the *Victory* as you last saw her."

Noor closed her eyes, picturing the black-and-gold striped ship, its dozens of sails, its rigging, its fallen whale-oil lamps, still flickering in their glass cages. She opened her eyes, and the ship floated in miniature above her jambiya.

"Can you make it life-sized?" the emira asked.

"Yes. Do you want the view from the top deck?"

"Can you show me any part of the ship?"

Noor glanced at James. "I can show you only what I have seen, but if you give me a moment, I can allow James to control this blade. After four years on the vessel, he should be able to show you anywhere you want."

James and the emira nodded. Noor bowed her head, focussing on that tug of her haya magic as it grew and grew between her hands, weaving James in between her and Razan's connection to the blade. The light glowed pink through her eyelids, and she heard people shuffling away from her. But when Noor opened her eyes, the emira hadn't moved, still watching with such fierce wonder. Noor couldn't stop her lips from quirking into a smile. She turned to James.

He took the blade, saying, "Emira, where would you like to see?"

"Where do they keep the powder for their cannons?"

James blanched; if he hadn't understood before how his knowledge of the ship would be used, he knew now. He visibly steeled himself and answered, "The hold, Emira."

And there, all around them and as large as life, was the hold of the *Victory*. They stood on oak planks, far below the waterline, the ribs of the ship arcing up and fading into the high blue sky above them like thick smoke. Thousands and thousands of barrels, ballast that kept the ship upright, were stacked around them.

James pointed to a section of casks set aside from the rest. "Those are the powder kegs."

The emira walked closer. She reached her hand out for the keg. It passed right through. She turned to one of the sheikhas who hung back. "As I said, Tawakkol, if we target the powder, we can blow a hole right through the hull and sink the *Victory* in the mouth of Aden harbour."

The other woman stared with wide eyes as she nodded distractedly. When the image shuddered, the emira turned sharp eyes to Noor. Noor bit her lip, and the image clarified again. Sweat dripped down her back.

"Does showing us this image cost you?"

Noor closed her eyes. "Some, Emira, at this size. But it is a cost I can bear."

The emira waved her hand through the casks once again. "You may drop this vision."

Noor did, her eyes falling closed before she forced them open again.

The emira raised her hands slowly and placed them lightly on Noor's shoulders to lift her from kneeling. As she met Noor's eyes, she quietly said, "You may have saved us all."

Noor dropped her gaze, jaw working.

Usama stepped forward. "Emira Arwa bint Asma, may I introduce Noor of Tajoura and James of Sierra Leone and South Carolina, lately of the *Victory*."

Noor hastened to cut in, "The lunella shells and the images from the jambiya—I never could have done those without Razan."

And the emira laughed, a bright cackle. "Oh, Noor, we all know Razan is brilliant. She designed my own ship; I would trust that task to no one less."

Noor flushed a little but flicked her eyes to Razan, who grinned wide and proud. The emira turned and waved them into the compound, walking with a slight limp.

Usama stepped up close to her and said in a low murmur. "Noor can also heal."

The emira paused, the flowing crowd pausing with her, and turned to Noor. "How do you heal?"

"I am a haya mage, so I draw a small piece of...let's call it 'the life' of the person I am healing, or of myself if they have little to spare. And then I can heal."

"Can you heal sicknesses or just injuries?"

"Emira, I do not know. I have only known my connection to magic for a few months."

The emira's eyes widened. "Only a few months?"

Noor ducked her head, and the emira stepped forward.

"I have a sickness; my people know of it. It saps my strength day by day. Can you heal it?"

Noor stepped forward, reaching for the emira's hands. "I will do my best."

The emira laid her hard, calloused hands in Noor's equally rough palms. Noor closed her eyes, the morning sun beating down on the back of her neck, a dozen eyes on her face.

She found it almost immediately. The sickness started on the skin of her leg and seeped into the blood and bones. Noor took a breath, drawing from herself, trying to unpick the sickness from the emira's tough old body. She got a piece loose, only to find it tightening its hold elsewhere; she tried to shrink it, only to see it trying to move deeper. She pulled back.

"I am so sorry, but I can't. Maybe if I had more experience—"

But the emira was smiling, her eyes a bit sad, but a real smile nonetheless.

"Death comes for us all, Noor. My healers tell me I have a year or more—more time than the British will give us. Perhaps we can try later. But no matter what, you have brought my people life. It would be too much to ask for you to bring me the same. Noor of Tajoura, I am glad you are here."

Noor's eyes prickled at the failure. But the emira turned to the crowd, raising Noor's hands.

"Join me in welcoming our new haya mage—Noor!"

Cheers and trills rang out as hands came to embrace her. Three hugs in and with Razan at her back, Noor began to relax into the wide welcome, her body tingling, mind sparking and alive and ready to fight.

She thought she would explode from the joy of it.

*

NOOR SPENT THE rest of the afternoon enchanting lunella shells and jambiya blades in a side room off the red-pillow-strewn *majilis* while the emira finalised the new battle plan with her council inside. Sometime during the afternoon, a group of little girls cadged two of the lunella shells from one of the more indulgent fathers. They raced around, inventing increasingly complex games with them. As the council was packing up and collecting their newly enchanted family weapons to bring home to demonstrate the emira's power, the emira herself came over to sit beside Noor, a rolled-up map in her hands.

Noor turned to her slowly; she could barely keep her eyes open after using her magic for so many hours.

The emira murmured, "We have a great library in my family home in Aden. Centuries of scrolls and books on magic, both haya and the other kinds." She closed her eyes. "Usama probably told you, but we have had mages in my family. Not me, of course, but my mother. And my son."

Noor wanted to ask about the Sword of Sidon. But the emira kept going.

"Before you arrived, we spent days arguing; nearly half of my council insisted we simply give in, try to negotiate a peace that allowed the British everything they wanted in exchange for not destroying Aden with the *Victory*'s one hundred and four cannons. But with these incredible tools and the promise of your magic, the majority finally swung around. They're willing to fight for Aden."

Noor's cheeks warmed. "That's wonderful."

The emira nodded, her eyes troubled. "It is, but they needed to have decided this weeks ago for it to mean anything. It will take at least a week to gather our forces. Usama told you the plan?"

"He did."

The emira rolled out the map, showing the breadth of the Red Sea and the Gulf where Africa and Arabia met. "We can have a half-hundred ships in Aden's harbour in a week. That includes travel time back up the coast or into the mountains for each of the dozen sheikhas and sheikhs, time for them to demonstrate our newfound power with your gifts, time to lockdown their compounds, divvy up who will manage the babies and elders and farming and animals while their usual tenders and keepers are gone, time to travel to Aden, and a night to gather and finalise the plans." The emira patted her jambiya at her waist. "These will help since they'll allow us to agree on tactics and strategies while they travel. But it is barely enough time.

"Barely enough time and also three days more than we *have*. Even with the *Victory* delayed by hunting for James and repairing what you did to her—good job by the way—Usama predicts the British will be in Aden in four days."

The emira traced the map with her fingers. "They will go to Mocha to meet a shipment of weapons sent across Sinai and down the Red Sea." She pointed to a city on the western coast, north of Tajoura. The name of the city reminded Noor of something, but her mind was so tired she couldn't place it.

The emira traced again, looping south and into the port of Aden. "Then, the *Victory* will sail to Aden, and they will either level her with their cannons, see her surrender—or sink."

The emira leaned closer to Noor, brown eyes serious. "We have asked so much of you and you have given us a fighting chance where we had none before. I cannot ever thank you enough for that, Noor. But if we don't stall the *Victory*, if we don't delay her at Mocha, we cannot win at Aden. We won't have the time we need."

Noor tried to pull her exhausted thoughts together. "You have allies in Mocha who can sabotage the *Victory*?"

"One of the sheikhas on my council has family in Mocha and says they will help. I sent her to them hours ago on my fastest Arabian stallion, and she should be there before midnight."

James approached, and at the emira's gesture, sat beside them. He passed Noor a fresh cup of tea, which she took gratefully, its heat between her palms more solid than any magic.

"None for me?" The emira said in careful English. But when James started to stutter and offer to get one, she patted the ground, smiling. Then in Arabic, looking to Noor to translate, she continued.

"I'm teasing. So, James is our expert on the *Victory*. Knowing what he does about your powers, Noor, what could you do to the *Victory* that would stall her for at least three days but not much longer than a week?" At Noor's questioning glance, she explained, "I don't think the sheikhas and sheiks can keep their people from returning home for that long if there's no fight coming."

Noor translated.

James thought about it, chewing on a bit of *qat*; Usama must have given it to him.

"The only time I saw the *Victory* stalled in port was for repairs or when the sultan wanted something. It would have to be a part they could repair with local materials, so not destroying the cannons or anchor or ripping a hole in the side. They're meeting a supply ship?"

Noor translated for the emira.

"They are—I see where you're going. If we could have delayed the supply of weapons, that would have been ideal." The emira shook her head. "But they're already in Mocha."

He met Noor's eyes. "I think anything you can do to damage but not destroy some part of the ship would be best. Breaking all the glass in the captain's cabin, swamping the supply of fresh water with sea water, ripping the sails, that kind of thing."

"It sounds like you need me to go to Mocha."

"Yes. But we've asked so much of you—"

Noor made to stand, then wobbled and sat back down quickly, her legs shaking. "I'll go. But I don't know the way."

"I can—" James started, but the emira held up her hand, a twinkle in her eye.

She called for Razan.

The young woman came running, abaya fluttering around her strong legs.

She met Noor's eyes with a grin and flopped down on the ground beside them.

"Razan, you know the way to Mocha?"

"It's just up the coast, Emira."

"I know that, Razan. I was asking—never mind. You will take Noor there, to Sheikha abu Bakkr's family inside the walled city. They live beside the Bundar family. You'll need to be there before dawn, before the gates to the walled city open. The sheikha will meet you outside of the gates." The emira looked over at Noor, who couldn't help listing to the side like a drifting ship.

Razan smiled fondly and spoke over Noor's head. "I'll pack a bag for her. We're taking a camel?"

The emira nodded. "We need the horses for the messengers to the sheikhs and sheikhas who did not send representatives. You have until after dinner, that's the soonest we can have a mount ready." The emira rose slowly, grimacing. Noor wanted to ask about her son, to tell her what she'd seen on the *Victory*, but didn't know where to begin. She watched the older woman walk stiffly out of the room.

James leaned in close to Noor and murmured, "She's sending you and Razan someplace without me?"

"Yes, I think she needs your knowledge of the *Victory* here; you'll probably go in the caravan to Aden with her and Usama and the rest of the household."

He continued tightly, "I didn't want to bring it up while she was here, but, Noor, there's something you need to know about the Sword of Sidon. He's going to be on the *Victory*. He never leaves. You'll have to be prepared to kill him."

"Why?"

He began to speak, paused, then asked, "Can you let me use your—what do you call it—knife?"

Noor pulled her jambiya out. "It's a jambiya. Jam-BEE-yah." He repeated the word, held the knife out, and concentrated. Out of the blade rose flames, entire buildings and blocks of housing burning. There was no sound of voices, for which she was deeply grateful as she saw a body jump from the top of a building at the tip of the blade and plummet down, down into the floor.

"What—"

"Just watch."

The vision turned from burning homes to the deck of a ship—the *Victory*. The view shook as it moved forward as if James had been running in his memory, running towards—

Noor's mind struggled to make sense of what she saw. First, bare backs. Then, a line of six men, kneeling on all fours, heads bent. Above them stood a figure in a long, dark blue jacket. In one hand, he held a cat-o'-nine-tails, its ends wickedly knotted. He struck across two of their shoulders at once, throwing his weight into the motion, and the men below him jerked. He raised his other hand, and the flames jumped from the buildings to the harbour-bound ships.

Their sails turned into beacons of deathly light.

In the flaring brightness, Noor saw who the man holding the whip was.

The Sword of Sidon.

Blood covered his hands, his eyes wild and a sickly green in the dark light of the burning city.

James let the image fade, and Noor took her jambiya back, hands trembling. She saw no evidence of the man she'd healed on the *Victory* in that man's face.

"I understand it is war, and we can't stay safe now if we want to be safe later. But, Noor, be careful. And—" He paused as Razan came back into the room. Noor was glad she'd missed James's vision, if only for her own peace of mind. "Take care of Razan too. I know she's been in this longer than we have—"

"James," Noor said, "the babies you were playing tag with have been in this longer than we have."

He nodded, sharing a smile. "I know, I know. But she's—she's special. You're special too. You need to protect each other."

She reached out and patted his shoulder. "I'll do my best."

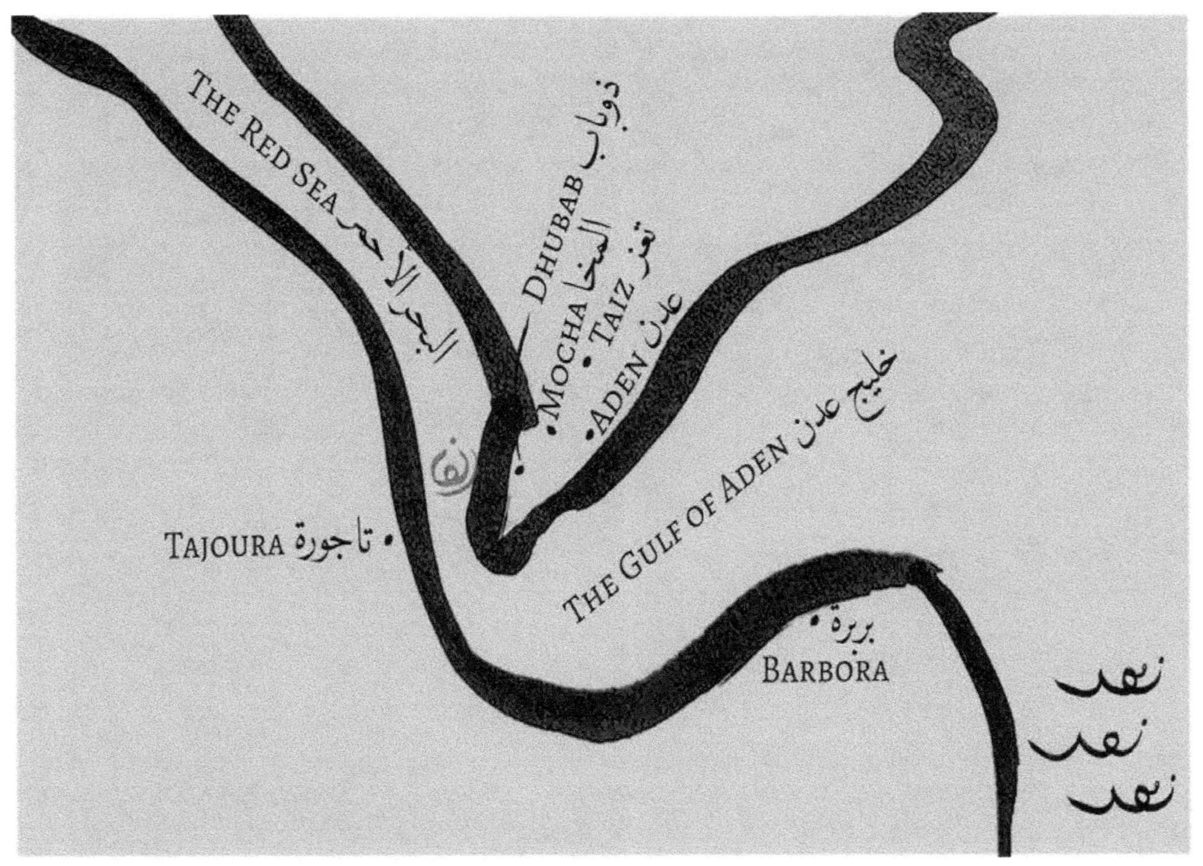
THE RED SEA البحر الأحمر
DHUBAB ذوباب
MOCHA المخا
TAIZ تعز
ADEN عدن
THE GULF OF ADEN خليج عدن
TAJOURA تاجورة
BARBORA بربرة

Chapter Seven

THEY HAD A little bit of time, just bare hours, before she and Razan needed to leave.

They spent it together.

Razan had quarters deep in the warren of buildings that made up the much-built-upon complex of houses and granaries and wells and stables and storage areas of the emira's compound. Her room was tidy with a wide window shaded by delicate latticework and looking onto a neat courtyard below. The burble of a fountain filled the late afternoon air, water trickling over stones to keep the inner garden cool. Various pieces of wood stacked the walls of her room, models of ships Razan had built or wanted to build someday, as well as scrolls and books of designs from past shipwrights. Swooping, swirling lines of calligraphy that reminded Noor of the prows of ships decorated every spare bit of wall.

A heap of blankets for the cool desert nights covered a pallet bed.

"You should rest," Razan said, still halfway in the doorway.

"I don't know if I can rest." Noor half laughed.

The late afternoon sun filled the room with honeyed light, dripping down the heap of blankets, trickling over Razan's bare toes where they scrunched in the pile of rugs.

She stepped closer to Noor, her black abaya swaying around her ankles.

"Everything is going to change tomorrow," she said. "It's already started to change."

Noor's heart was at the base of her throat, flickering fast and faster.

"I hope not everything," Noor said, slipping her fingertips around Razan's elbow, savouring the strength of that arm under the fabric. "There are wonderful things I have now I would never want to give up."

"Hmm," Razan murmured, covering Noor's hand with her own. She intertwined their fingers, calluses rough but the touch so, so soft. "It feels…"

"'It feels'?" Noor managed.

"Like we've known each other, known this was coming. Prepared for it, even."

"It's all new to me," Noor whispered, daring to drag her thumb over the back of Razan's hand, the strong tendons there like ridges of a mountain range.

"But good?" Razan checked, stepping a bit closer, her warm breath on Noor's face.

Noor nodded. "Good, yes."

Razan quirked an eyebrow, easing her weight back. "If we could do anything right now, what would you want to do?"

Noor glanced down at Razan's toes curling in the thick pile of the rug. *Maybe she's nervous too.*

She eased her hand out of Razan's, but before the other woman could tense at the possible rejection, Noor settled it firmly on the curve of her hip. "I'd like to touch you. Have you touch me."

"I'd like that too. But I want you to tell me what you like. I want—I want to know that everything I'm doing is what you want."

Something opened, bloomed in Noor at that simple, powerful request. It meant so much that she didn't have to request this, that it was offered, freely given.

"I want you to touch my cheek," she whispered.

Razan raised her hand, barely grazing her knuckles down Noor's cheek. Noor catted into the movement, body lighting from it.

"Again, please."

Razan repeated the gesture with her palm, hot and healing and close. "For now," she said breathily, "can you do to me what you ask for? I'm not sure I can take asking too."

Noor nodded, carefully stroking her fingertips down Razan's cheek, enjoying the smooth lushness of it against her skin, the gentle give and the firm bones beneath.

When she finished, Noor said, "Can you hold me close to you, tight?"

Razan nodded, gathering her up, arms slipping behind Noor's back and crossing, gripping her until every breath was given, a gift. A shared gift. Noor returned the strength of her hug, letting the power of her muscles draw a small sigh from Razan.

Noor buried her face in Razan's neck, the hot smell of her becoming her whole world for a moment. She let her lips brush Razan's ear. "Kiss my neck."

"Yes." Razan gave Noor an open-mouthed press of her lips, holding for a long second, and then a quick swipe of her tongue.

Noor bent to do the same, brushing aside Razan's headscarf to find the soft skin. She tasted of sea salt and sweat and fire smoke; she tasted like freedom. "And again?"

Razan switched sides and slid her teeth up the big tendon in Noor's neck, making her whole body shiver. Unsure how to do that trick safely, Noor kissed the strong round of her shoulder through the fabric of Razan's abaya.

Razan gasped. "I want to touch your hair; can I?"

"Please," Noor said, and Razan stroked her hand over her tightly kinked curls.

"It's so soft," Razan said. "It's almost alive."

Noor snickered. "It's just hair."

Razan shook her head, pulling back to meet Noor's eyes. "It's your crown. I love it."

Noor smiled, leaning in. "Kiss me?"

Razan nodded and pressed her lips to Noor's. The bright magic of it, sparking and sparkling between them, made Noor's toes curl and stomach clench, and she never wanted it to end. Razan moved her lips against Noor's, the sweet slide of them enough to pull a deep sigh from Noor. She collapsed forward, arms winding around Razan's waist, Razan's hands tight on her shoulders, their bodies barely brushing, sliding and slipping, learning the shape of each other.

Noor, gasping, pulled back. "Lie with me?"

Razan nodded and began to unwind her headscarf. In a moment, she was done, the black fabric in a heap on the floor. She eased onto a pile of blankets, arms raised up to Noor and beckoning.

Noor knelt and crawled into Razan's lap as the other woman lay back, so they were lying side by side. Razan slipped a curl behind Noor's ear, eyes fond and so, so close.

"What now?" Razan asked.

Noor frowned. "What feels good to you?"

Razan slid a thigh over her hip, tucking her other knee between Noor's knees. "If we start like this and then—" She arched forward, bringing her thigh into sudden, brilliant contact with Noor's body.

"Yes, yes," Noor gasped, "more of that."

"Your wish is my command," Razan said, rearranging their arms so she was better braced. Noor's hand found hers, and she held on for dear life.

It was like dancing, if dancing had lit up her body and soul with each flex of the beat. Razan set an easy place, sliding and grinding against her, taking her own pleasure against Noor's thigh. A peak seemed to come much too soon, but also as though it was a million years in coming.

"My chest," Noor gasped, "touch my chest."

Razan shoved her hand beneath Noor's guntiino, skin touching hot skin before finding her breast. She cupped it in her palm and swiped a firm finger once, twice, a third time across her nipple.

"You, can I, you—" Noor tried, but Razan shook her head, laughing easily.

"Not to my tastes. But you, hot and comfortable and making those beautiful sounds in my arms—it's more than enough, habibati."

"Happy to be of service," Noor managed, and Razan tweaked her nipple in response.

Somehow, the lightness of it, the teasing in the midst of something that could be so serious and sacred but was just real and safe and *fun*, was enough to send Noor flying over the edge, with a grunt and a cry. She shook in Razan's arms, Razan's stifled moans telling Noor she was soaring with her.

Noor lost time, curling into Razan's body, cheek on her soft breast as she followed the rise and fall of her slowing gasps. They lay together, the smell of their bodies in the blankets, legs intertwined, relaxed and easy from their release and the sense of safety they found in each other's arms.

*

THEY WOKE FOR dinner, giggling as they straightened each other's clothes. As soon as their bellies were full, the emira's aide hustled them to a tall, grumpy camel she claimed was named "Daphne," and they lunged up and headed north. As the sun set over the Red Sea, Noor found herself on the way to Mocha, Razan holding her upright as they swayed across the sand. Razan had shoved an oversized red pillow in front of Noor and hooked her chin over her shoulder to murmur in her ear.

"You sleep, Noor. I've got you."

The stars wheeled above them, true and bright, but Noor could not keep her eyes open long enough to enjoy the new constellations she could see from this coast.

"I can take first watch—" Noor offered, hoping the responsibility of it would keep her awake.

Razan tightened her grip and chuckled against her shoulder. She began to hum, something quiet and lilting.

Noor's eyelids began to droop as she sagged against Razan's strong arms.

Noor drew herself together for a moment and then hitched her leg in front of her, shin against the rising saddle, and let Razan slowly lower her onto the pillow. Razan's hands on her back soothed and kept her steady, and she breathed to the breaking waves to her left. She fell asleep to Razan's humming, the heat of her body behind her, and the quiet comfort of the open sky.

*

NOOR AWOKE TO predawn darkness, oddly refreshed for having slept on camelback, the crash of the surf beating the same rhythm beside her. The most amazing smell filled the salt air.

"What *is* that," she asked.

Razan searched around and then took a breath. "Ah, did no one tell you about Mocha? We're nearly there."

"I remember something about it—is it where the emira's husband died?"

There was a pause. "Yes, that too."

Noor didn't want to stick her thumb in what seemed like a still-un-healed wound, but if she was going to go face-to-face with his son, she wanted to know as much as she could.

"How did he die?"

Razan took a moment, leaning over to flick the reins against the camel's neck to warn him away from a thatchy bit of scrub he was eying beside the path. Noor took in the land before them, wide open to the base of the far-off mountains on their right, the brush flowing to a nar-row strip of sand and then straight to the sea on their left. Dark green scrub no taller than Noor's knee, dappled the flat land between them and the mountains. Though the sky behind the mountains had bright-ened, the sun was still low enough that she, Razan, and the entire coast-line, as far as she could see, remained within the mountains' shadow.

Razan finally spoke. "The British control Mocha today. Two years ago, they demanded the key to the city gates and a tariff be paid in return for their unwanted patrols." She sniffed derisively. "The sheikhs and sheikhas and Jewish leaders in the city didn't want to pay it. The emira sent her husband, Yusef, to negotiate for them. I think she wanted him to try to bring the Sword of Sidon home, but Mianning said they never saw his face. They went onto the *Victory*, met with the so-called sultan, told him their terms, and were rejected. They returned to the dock, and both sides prepared for battle. Yusef insisted on captaining a borrowed ship, leaving Mianning the *Cormorant*. I think Yusef was hoping that the Sword of Sidon wouldn't attack his own father or his adoptive uncle, and that would allow them to get further inside the *Victory*'s guard."

She took a breath. "It didn't go that way. The *Victory*'s cannons started firing into the ships at harbour at dawn, and Yusef's ship was the first to sink. A dozen ships sank that day before the sheikhs and sheikhas surrendered and opened the city gates to the British. Mocha has been under their control ever since."

"So, the Sword killed his father?"

"Yes—" Razan started, and then Noor could feel Razan shaking her head behind her. "—and no. Mianning said he didn't, or he tried not to. Mianning said that, right as the first cannon was firing, a massive wall of water rose between the Mocha fleet and the *Victory*, like the wall of sand you made back at the compound. The ships arranged themselves behind the lead boats while they had cover, but then something changed, the wall fell, and every level of cannons began to fire all at once, wrecking the ships. Dozens died. Mianning says that was the Sword of Sidon trying to save his father's life." She huffed. "I don't buy it. Why didn't he jump ship and leave? If he didn't love the empire, why would he stay?"

Noor let that hang in the air. She went back to the original question. "Why did they want Mocha so badly?"

Razan's raised arm swept out towards the city whose walls made a dark line on the horizon. "Coffee."

"Coffee?" The smell was luscious, and Noor tried to imagine drinking it. She might have smelled it somewhere in the market—coffee was common enough with the number of Ethiopian traders—but this was different, sweeter. She squinted toward the horizon. The gates were easier to see now, the wall around the city low and dark in the shadow-cast light.

"They roast it here so the buyers can't plant the beans, but it also makes it taste like chocolate from South America. It's the favourite of a lot of Europeans, and they can only get it here."

"And the British wanted the export tariffs for themselves?"

"They did."

Noor squinted again at some kind of commotion at the gates. She wondered if it had to do with the sheikha they were supposed to be meeting.

She peered closer, and then a brush of magic moved across her, its scent familiar.

She reared back, shouting. "We have to turn back—"

A musket exploded at the gate, its round burying in the scrub brush beside them, the branches snapping like bones in the quiet predawn air—

The camel startled and bolted away from the muskets—

Then it seized, grinding all four feet into the sand, grunting in terror as a towering column of fire blocked its retreat—

The column reached up above their heads. The heat blasted across their faces as if the door of a baking oven had opened in front of them, a story high and rising. The camel turned tail and bolted back towards the city, the pillar chasing them. Razan hauled on the reins, and Noor made ready to jump off, but in the time it took them to try to wrangle the poor panicked beast back to a walk, they were nearly at the gate.

A dozen British sailors stood arrayed between them and any safety the city might have offered. Some were mounted on hired horses, some afoot. Standing in front of them: the Sword of Sidon, eyes like green fire.

Razan swore, yanking the reins again. Finally getting the camel to slow, she tried to turn the animal around. But the burning column was still behind them, creeping closer, urging the terrified beast forward one shuddering step at a time. They were near enough to hear the city waking, the roosters and donkeys competing for most obnoxious now that the camel's hooves had stopped beating thunder beneath the two women.

The Sword stood, staring vacantly past them.

No one spoke for a long minute. Over the city walls rose tall buildings of dark grey mudbrick with arching white windows, families coming awake within them. A bird flew over the city, searching for prey. Under all of it, Noor thought she could hear the Sword of Sidon muttering to himself as the men behind him shifted uneasily.

Before the Sword could move, Noor whispered to Razan, "Do they know who you are?"

She shook her head.

"Then stay back. I'll try to keep them from taking you too."

"I'm not going to *abandon* you—" Razan started, fumbling for her lunella shell. "The emira will know what to do—"

"We can't reveal the shells. What if they make their own? We'd squander the advantage they give us."

"I'm not leaving you," Razan repeated through gritted teeth, her arm tightening protectively round Noor's waist. But she kept her lunella shell hidden in her sleeve. "Look, fine, pretend I'm a guide. I'll act terrified, and once we stop, I'll hide behind the camel, pretend I'm praying. I'll keep the shell in my hands and whisper. Noor, *please*, let me try."

Razan didn't wait for her to reply. She hurled herself to the ground out of reach of the pillar of fire, turned her back on it, knelt, and began to pray.

Noor dismounted more slowly, never taking her eyes off the Sword. His eyes, green like from James's memory, held a wildness—a barely contained violence—that hadn't been there the night she'd healed him. She held her hands up as if he were a hurt animal and approached slowly, trying to make distance between him and Razan.

He called out in English, "You're coming with us."

Noor kept her hands raised and stopped in her tracks.

"Why?" she returned in the same language.

"My master commands it." He stood slightly hunched in his heavy wool as though protecting an injury. But she'd healed all of the cuts he'd had two days ago; this one must be fresh.

Noor wondered in a flash what his punishment had been for letting her go.

"What does your master want with me?"

He smirked, but it seemed uneven—as if he wasn't pulling his own strings.

"You are to serve him as I do."

Noor shook her head twice, hard, but instead of the defiance she expected from her response, she uttered a question in Arabic. "Is he a kind master?"

The Sword checked behind him, the men growing uneasy at their lack of understanding. "What?" he hissed, also in Arabic.

Noor lowered her voice, speaking quickly, still in Arabic. "Did he hurt you again?"

The Sword clenched his jaw. "I'm an alam mage. I gain power from pain."

Noor narrowed her eyes. "You're not looking particularly powerful right now."

He slammed his hand into his chest, then flung it out. Another whirlwind of fire joined the one behind them, right beside where Razan knelt with the camel, hands folded in front of her mouth, whispering into the hidden shell. The columns smashed together and doubled in breadth and height. The camel moaned and sidled, but Razan hauled it down beside her, forcing the beast to sit. Noor saw her friend's eyes flash white, but she kept going.

Noor turned slowly back to the Sword. "You have to hurt yourself to do that?"

She closed her eyes, drawing a sliver of life from each of the men in his guard, leaving him untouched. She called a small stream of water up from the tip of a wave breaking on the beach beside them. It ran through the sand, sinking in and then coming up again, running uphill and twining between the rocks edging the road. Then, she pulled it in a great glittering arch over her head, the spray from it glittering a thousand colours as the dawn broke over the mountaintops. She dipped the tip of it down to the top of the fire spout. At first, the water vaporised, hissing and filling the air with the smell of burning salt.

She pulled up more water, the tug deeper in her belly as she drew on her reserves. The water began to quench the tower of fire. She could sense the Sword of Sidon pushing back, slamming his fist into his chest to fuel it.

But she had more life to draw from than he could create pain.

The fire fizzled out.

Noor turned back to the group of men, and the Sword's eyes were hungry. When she let the water cease, the Sword turned to the men, speaking in English.

"You see now why we delayed a day to acquire her?" The men had moved their muskets to their shoulders, aiming directly at her.

In the morning quiet, she heard Razan arguing through the shell.

"There has to be another way, *please*—"

Noor glanced back as Razan shoved the shell angrily back inside her abaya, her face defiant.

Razan stood and moved forward, keeping Noor between her and the armed men. She folded herself against Noor's back, sure and tight, and whispered into Noor's shoulder, lips sweet against her body despite everything, "The emira said she tried to raise her allies in Mocha. They're not responding and are either dead or betrayers. She said we're on our own."

Noor's mind was spinning, head feeling a little light.

Razan whispered again, hand going to Noor's wrist. "Can't you just—call up the water again, knock them all into the sea, and run?"

Noor turned to embrace her, making it appear to be a goodbye, whispering into her scarf. Razan smelled like fresh baked bread from the market. "Run where? Into Mocha with no allies? We still need to stall the *Victory*, and maybe—" She closed her eyes, thinking quickly. "Look, it doesn't sound like they want to kill me. I can—" Her breath tightened in her chest, but she forced herself to speak, trying to forgive herself for how her voice shook. "I *will* find a way to stall them. I can't risk my magic by killing with it, but I can defend myself for the three days we need. You get help; get a dhow so that when I call you on the lunella shell, you can come and get me when the *Victory* gets to Aden, before she sinks."

Noor smiled, knowing Razan was too close to see it. "I still can't swim."

Razan's breathing was harsh, a sob coming up from her chest. "This is *wrong* Noor. You just got free."

Noor scanned the assembled men, and her insides ran cold. She gripped Razan's wrist, fingers tight on the delicate brown skin, and a bracelet moved, cool and patterned beneath her touch. Noor forced herself to whisper, "Three days. Then you'll get me out. The resistance needs your mind. I'll see you in Aden."

She turned quickly and strode towards the pack of men before Razan could stop her. She called out in English, watching as all of the musket muzzles followed her and not her friend. "I will come with you without a fight as long as you let my guide go. She's a shepherd's daughter and has no part in this. Otherwise, we will try my water against your fire again and see if it goes better for you than last time."

Some of the men leered and stepped towards her, but the Sword held up his hand and they grudgingly halted.

"You have made a wise choice."

Razan, already on the camel, had turned the muttering animal around. Noor forced herself to look away before she could change her mind. The Sword gestured her to come closer.

She went.

*

THE TRIP THROUGH the city was quick and uncomfortable with her hands tied behind her back. No one would meet her eyes once they saw her bonds. She shook her head in disgust.

Noor had decided a long time ago that if she saw someone being collared or punished, she would meet their eyes. It had hurt to do, particularly during the public whippings the Ottoman officials occasionally preferred, but she'd made a commitment to herself. If another person could go through that kind of pain, then she could see them do it and acknowledge them as a person, be with them in some small way while it happened.

It seemed no one on the morning streets of Mocha held the same belief.

The Sword guided her onto a boat waiting between two European trade barks in the harbour. The *Victory* sat at anchor farther out. Noor spotted a half-dozen European merchant's ships with big sails, the same dimensions as the *Victory*'s.

She hid a smirk.

She bided her time until they were midway between the docks and the *Victory*, where the water was deep enough to swim and not get slammed into the rocks. The Sword stood beside her, focussed on the *Victory*. His eyes had returned to a dark brown, and he wore his own face again.

Noor braced her feet on the deck and peered up at him. "Can you swim?" she asked in Arabic.

"What?"

"I'll take that as a yes."

She threw herself upwards, shoulder hitting him in the stomach, knocking him ass over teakettle into the harbour, and barely catching herself before she went in after him. Still hanging on to the side of the boat, Noor closed her eyes, slicing energy from each of the men around her. Throwing it all up, she yanked into reality a screaming, shearing wind that barrelled into the *Victory*'s sails, tearing them in great slashing gashes.

She was jerked back, a fist connecting with the slide of her face, knocking her to the deck. The next blow split her lip as she tried to get her legs in front of her, to kick her attacker away—one of the men in the red jackets—

"Stop!"

It came from over her head, a furious but sodden growl. She squinted up at the Sword of Sidon pulling his sopping-wet self out of the harbour. His long blue wool coat poured water onto her face as he clambered to get between her and the soldiers.

She coughed, making a face at the unrisen bruises moving uncomfortably under her skin.

"Not much fun, is it?" he hissed in Arabic before turning to the soldiers. "The sultan commanded she remain unharmed. Which one of you hit her?"

None of them raised their hands, instead, frowning resentfully at one another and not speaking.

The Sword wrung water out of his long hair, back into the harbour. "Fine, then, all of you will go onto the whipping roster."

"No, sir," one of them started—a blond man, his face already reddening from the morning sun. "It was me, sir. Look what she did to the sails, sir."

The Sword glared at him and then turned his face up. His mouth dropped open, and he stared down at her, now more considering than ever, before he schooled his expression.

Now he knows what my powers can do in war.

The Sword swept his sodden blue coat behind him and sat between her and the men in the boat, giving them his back. She was strangely grateful that he didn't try to help her up; maybe he understood why she didn't want anyone hauling her back to sitting. She inched herself up, tonguing at the split in her lip. It would heal; she wouldn't use the energy to do it now.

The Sword turned and reached towards her face, then, at her glare, stilled his hand before dropping it.

"My master will heal you," he said.

She spat blood overboard.

Those were the last words spoken until they reached the ship.

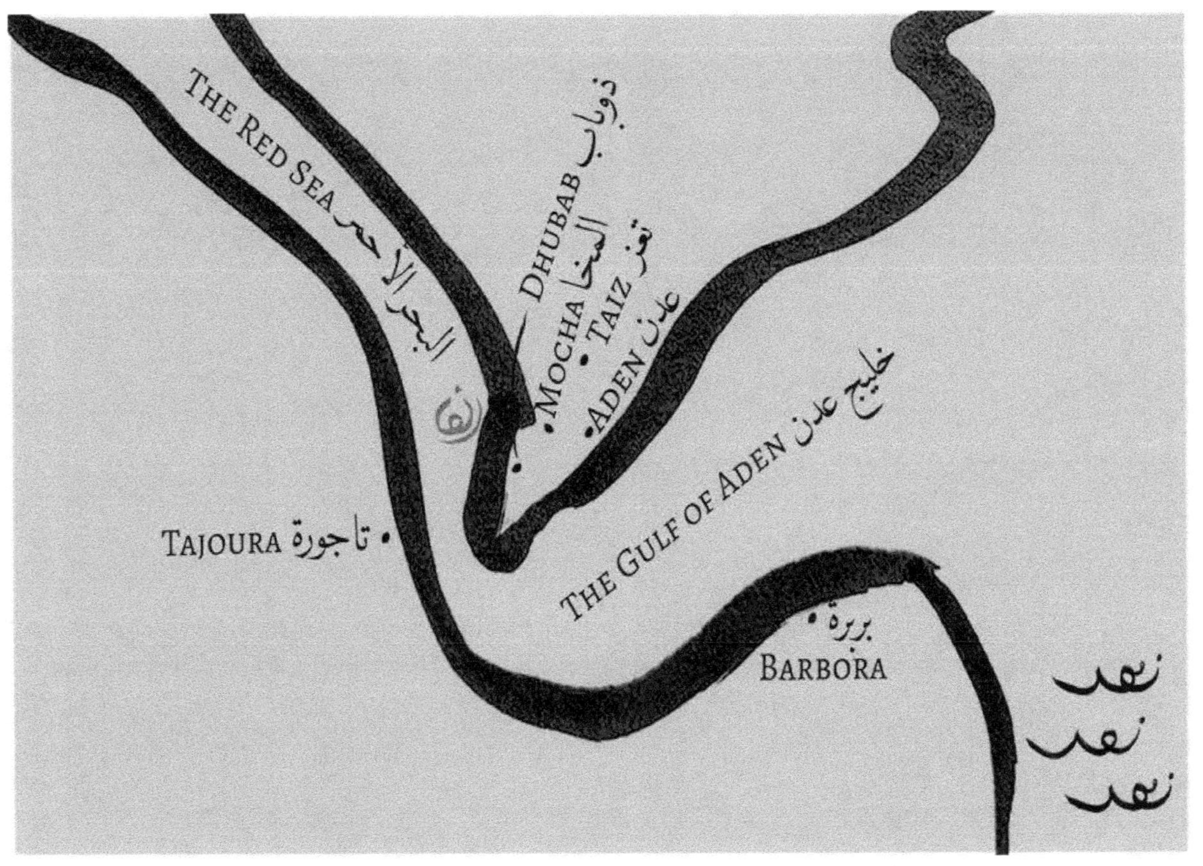

THE RED SEA   البحر الأحمر
DHUBAB   ذباب
MOCHA   المخا
TAIZ   تعز
ADEN   عدن
THE GULF OF ADEN   خليج عدن
TAJOURA   تاجورة
BARBORA   بربرة

Chapter Eight

THE SWORD TOOK her directly to his master in the stern of the ship. Now he wasn't hanging off her shoulders, she saw he was so tall he had to stoop under the exposed beams to walk through the ship. He could only stand fully between them. The British Navy was built for smaller men.

Noor had no such problem; she was exactly the right size for this mission, awful though it was. She tried to distract herself from the leers of the crew by wondering what it would be like to always live half crouched.

It wasn't distraction enough.

The Sword knocked on a glass-windowed double door with shabby white lace curtains closed up tight.

A cracked, grating voice called out, "Enter."

One glance at the so-called sultan was enough to make Noor's blood run cold, so she focused on the room itself. A rich blue Persian carpet covered the floor, and large square-paned windows framing Mocha's soaring white minaret made up the back wall and half of each of the side walls. There were two doors on either side of the windows, which she remembered James had told her were to the open-air toilets. The room also held a dark wood desk, a sleeping cot, and a rack of cat-o'-nine-tails of differing lengths and thickness, carefully arranged. One was missing, leaving a yawning blank on the white wall.

That drew her back to the figure seated on a spindly legged chair in the middle of the room. A whip hung from his arm, the knotted ends slithering across the carpet with every rock of the ship.

"You're late," the body gurgled.

The thing on the chair looked worse than any three corpses Noor had found in shipwrecks. His face, swollen and sunken in turns, had great creeping brown cancers bulged out across it, glazing over one sea-weed-green eye and moving towards the next. His hands were clawed and shaking as he grasped the handle of his weapon. A weeping open wound gaped across the back of one hand, the flesh the colour of sea-weed.

The hand held a flail.

"Fifteen should do it."

The Sword nodded and began to strip out of his still-wet jacket. Noor lurched away from him, stumbling back until her shoulders slammed against the wall. Her movement drew the Sword's eye. He jerked his head as if to tell her she had the wrong idea. Then he went back to unbuttoning his undershirt. He stepped towards his master, then turned to face her and knelt.

"No," she whispered when her mind caught up with what she was about to witness. A dozen blows was considered extreme. Fifteen could be enough to kill a man.

The sultan raised his shaking hand over the Sword's back and snapped the leather so that, even with his weak grip, the knots cut into the skin. The Sword's eyes met hers as the whip again fell across his shoulders, and he flinched forward onto his hands. The sultan's other hand hovered over him as if warming himself at a fire—the next blow was stronger. Noor held the Sword's eyes as he was struck, again and again. At the ninth blow, he dropped his head, his breathing pained as each intake of air stretched the torn skin across his back. As she glanced up at the sultan, it felt like the ship was tilting under her feet.

The sultan's face evened out, the rot sinking into it before disappearing under pale, smooth skin. He sat up straighter, swinging his arm with a viscous twist to that forced the air from the Sword's chest.

The Sword held up a warning hand, gazing at Noor from under his long hair, and she found she'd pushed away from the wall, moved towards him.

"We are alam mages," the sultan said in a deep baritone, nearly healed of its cracks. "Isn't that right, apprentice?"

The Sword nodded, jolting in the middle of the gesture as the whip cracked across his back.

The sultan continued, his words melodious now, the kind a young man might follow in the night if it promised the right kind of power and freedom. "When you heard that we fed our magic on pain, what precisely did you think that meant, if not this?"

Noor stayed silent, horror vibrating through her body.

"Only two left," he crooned.

She didn't know why he needed them—he looked healthy now, far better than the Sword did. His arm arced forward, once, twice, and the Sword took a moment to breathe, twitching with the pain of the motion. Then he turned on his knees, head going to the floor, a crawling bow. The sultan put a booted foot on his shoulder, pressing him lower into the floor. He kept it there, and Noor watched as the cuts in the Sword's skin stopped bleeding and began to ease closed. His breathing was harsh, but he didn't move away from the man who had hurt and was now healing him. When the sultan removed his boot, the skin was still pink and tender, the healing not entirely done, but the Sword could stand. He moved stiffly as he began to rebutton his shirt.

"Take her to the cells. I will see her in the morning. Stand guard over her so she remains whole."

The Sword opened the door, and she glared at him.

"I know the way."

He gestured silently for her to move, and she strode in front of him, through the crowd of idling sailors, straight to the brig.

The guard, chatting with one of the men in the cells, stiffened when he saw the Sword, staring straight ahead at the opposite wall. The Sword found an empty cell and gestured for her to move inside. Once in, he undid her manacles and stepped back, blocking the door.

In Arabic, he said softly, "Do you still have that jambiya?"

"Yes," she replied in the same language.

"Good," he said and shut the door.

She examined the room. It was clean. *One thing you could say about the British navy—they certainly liked their whitewash.* A chamber pot with a heavy cover squatted in a corner, and she noted a satchel with water and a box with hard tack. They must have brought in the water from the port because she'd understood from James they hadn't yet learned the trick of keeping water fresh at sea. *Maybe that's why their sailors drink so much alcohol.*

The door shuddered, and she peered through the window, seeing nothing. Then she glanced straight down into the mussed hair of the Sword of Sidon. He sat tailor style, straight backed, not resting against the door.

Noor slammed her shoulder into the door to see if there was any give in the lock. It bowed a bit, smacking him in the back. The Sword craned his neck upwards to glare at her, his face pale with pain, and she ducked under the window. She had guessed right. The so-called sultan hadn't healed him entirely. She wondered if he could heal himself or if that was a skill his master kept a secret.

Noor sat with her shoulders braced against the door. She'd never been in a formal prison before—choosing not to think of that month in the compound—but people she'd known who'd been to prison had told her the boredom was the worst part. She wondered if she would be able to hear the calls to prayer from Mocha, or if the ship and the distance over the water would keep her ignorant of them.

She tapped absently on the door behind her: *one, two,* pause, *three; one, two,* pause, *three.* It sounded like '*alive and here, alive and here, alive and here*'.

Through the door, she felt: *one, two,* pause, *three; one, two,* pause, *three.* Noor jerked away from the door. Again, she heard it: *one, two,* pause, *three*; *one, two,* pause, *three.*

She didn't respond.

Noor thought back to the past two days, calculating how many prayers she'd missed. She started making them up. She knew it didn't really work that way, that the whole point was taking time five times a day, but she needed something to occupy her. With five hundred men surrounding her, she wasn't going to be sleeping.

*

THE WATCH PASSED while she reviewed everything she knew about alam mages. It wasn't much, and it wasn't good. Imam Tariq had focused on teaching her about her style of magic; they'd both hoped she would never encounter the other kind. The next guard bantered quietly with the men in the cells but didn't approach hers. She wondered if the Sword was glaring him down or if his mere presence was enough to protect her. Every time she peeked, he was there, sitting, back held carefully away from her door. At the next shift change, the bell sounded, and she stood watching. The guard left.

She hissed down at the Sword in Arabic, "Stand up and give me your hand. I can finish the healing before the next one comes."

He stood, keeping his hands at his sides. "Why?"

"How are you supposed to protect me if you can't move properly?"

He narrowed his eyes, somehow knowing that wasn't her true reason. But he held his hand out, wincing at the movement. Noor grabbed a hold of his fingers, her grip none too soft. He had sabre callouses across the side of his pointer finger. She closed her eyes and slipped a bit of life from each of the men around them and poured it into him—into torn muscles, bruises on top of those, a cracked rib—that's what he must have been breathing around back at the city gates. When she finished, his dark eyes were wide.

"You have no shields," he whispered.

"What?"

"You have no—" He stopped himself, hand pulling away from hers to cover his eyes. "When you were healing me, I could see how you were doing it, who you were drawing life from, what you were *thinking*. When you touch another mage, you can hear their unguarded thoughts— Do you know *nothing*? If you do magic with a mage enough, you don't have to touch. Here—" He held out his hand again. "Try to get inside, to see what I'm feeling."

"Inside what?"

"Close your eyes and try to see what I'm feeling."

"I know what you're feeling from your face."

"Try again."

"You're not my teacher."

He made a frustrated noise, and she grabbed his fingers and slipped inside. She saw frustration and pain and a roiling, rage-fuelled madness that made her heart stutter, and she yanked herself back.

"See?" he said smugly. "That's with my shields down. Try again."

She rolled her eyes, but curiosity tickled at her, like when Imam Tariq brought her a new book. She touched her fingertips to the back of his hand and found nothing but a smooth, cold wall.

"How?" she asked.

"Think about someplace where you were entirely alone, and no one could get at you. My safe place has many rooms, so even if someone gets into one, doesn't mean they've broken into others. There are some so secret, I have trouble getting in myself."

Noor closed her eyes, and for a moment, she was at the top of the minaret, a thick wooden door and a hundred spiralling steps between her and the rest of the world, able to see everything, entirely unseen. His magic reached out, tapped on her door, but the lock was sound, and the door barely shook when he knocked on it. She pulled her hand away, more slowly this time.

"Why don't you just try not to invade my mind, so I don't need walls? Non-mages can't do this."

He clenched his jaw. "It's not likely that I'll have a choice."

"That's ridiculous. You always have a choice."

He turned his head to the side. "The guard is coming."

She ducked down to sitting, and he returned to his position on the floor.

*

THE SULTAN DIDN'T call for her until midafternoon the next day. She didn't know if he'd been busy or if it was a tactic designed to throw her off-balance or both. She'd used the time to retell herself the favourite stories she'd heard in the markets, stories in Somali and Afar, in Arabic, and translated from Greek. There hadn't been a gap between guards, and she and the Sword didn't speak again. His meals had been delivered to him, and he'd only left for a few moments every few hours, at random times, always warning her beforehand.

It was right after the afternoon shift change when she heard him say from her door. "He's ready."

She stood, making sure her jambiya was secured inside her guntiino. She wanted to ask what to expect, but she bit her tongue. The Sword might choose to be friendly when she was in a cell, but she had no idea how far that went.

He marched her back through the columns of sleeping and card-playing sailors. She sensed their eyes like drawn daggers.

They came to the door, and the Sword of Sidon knocked.

"Come in."

She entered the room; the sultan appeared older, his skin greyish, but nothing as he'd been when she'd first seen him.

His spoke, low and soft. "So, Noor, how was your night in the cells?"

She said nothing.

"As I'm sure you've gathered, mages together are much stronger than mages alone. No one in the resistance that you've so eagerly thrown your lot in with or in that hole where you came from will ever understand you the way we do." The sultan held up one hand, now wrinkled but clean of the cancer she could sense eating him from the inside.

She wondered how long it would be until the Sword's next whipping.

The sultan spoke again. "Show me what you can do."

"I'm not auditioning for your circus troupe."

He hissed. "You will show respect."

Her knees hit the floor. She hadn't meant to kneel; the Sword hadn't laid a hand on her. It was as if something had come inside her body and ordered her muscles to move.

Is this how he controls the Sword?

She ducked her head, displaying submission while fighting to control her real panic. She had to keep him talking; talking, she could survive.

"My apprentice tells me you can call light, manipulate dust and water and air, turning them into weapons. Is that the extent of your haya magic?"

"Yes," she said.

Why hasn't the Sword told him I can heal?

"Those are common abilities, though most are like a candle. If reports are correct, you are more like wildfire. I could help you tame it. I could make you rich."

"I don't need to be rich."

"You could be powerful if you served the empire."

"I didn't know that the British Navy accepted women."

He scoffed. It was as though he was working from a script he'd used for years and never thought of changing. "We would make an exception for a power such as yours."

"Where would I sleep?"

He frowned at her question. "You would have chambers on the *Victory*."

"No, I wouldn't. One woman and five hundred men. You think I would sleep here and remain—what did you say last night—'whole'?"

"You are insubordinate," he snarled.

"I am not your subordinate."

He turned to the Sword of Sidon. "You said something similar to me once."

"Yes, master."

"She will learn, won't she?"

"Yes, master."

"Take her back to her cell and remove the food. Let's see how long she lasts."

The Sword drew his breath as if he was going to speak, but then his body stiffened. He moved jerkily towards Noor, but before he could touch her, she rose under her own power once again. The Sword opened the door for her, taking care not to touch her. With him at her back, Noor walked down the corridor filled with leering eyes and back into the cell.

Once the cell door was locked, Noor leaned against it, breathing a sigh of relief. "That wasn't so bad."

The Sword stood stiffly, and he was sweating, even though it wasn't any hotter here than in the so-called sultan's chambers.

"What's wrong—"

He turned to her, and it was the so-called sultan's cruel smile on his face, eyes flashing bottle green. "You've been making *friends*."

It wasn't the Sword's voice and wasn't the sultan's, but more like hearing the sultan speak through the Sword's mouth. *The sultan is inside his shields, wielding him like a sabre.*

Noor drew her blade. A thick door stood between them, but that meant next to nothing since *he could open it*. The Sword stepped closer to the door, and she put the wall at her back so she could brace against it, so she could kick, bite, *fight—*

And he relaxed, breathing a deep sigh. He ran a shaking hand through his hair.

"We shouldn't speak again," the Sword said.

Then he sank to the floor and sat tailor style with his hands in his lap, back braced against the door this time.

Noor didn't put her jambiya away until long into the next shift. That guard was the loud, chatty one. When an argument between him and another inmate grew heated, she held the lunella shell on her pommel to her mouth and whispered, "Razan. Razan, can you hear me?"

As soft as a breeze from the shell came, "Yes, oh, Noor, it is good to hear you."

Razan's voice was like a cool river on a hot summer's day, an anchor, a connection to life outside of this madness.

"You too," Noor said. "I tore the sails. They'll be in port for three, four days." She paused as the fight got louder. A key issue seemed to involve gin's superiority to beer.

Noor leaned close, covering her mouth so as little of the sound travelled as possible. "I only have moments— Do you have a ship? Can you meet me on the port side tomorrow in Mocha at the *fajr* call to prayer, just before dawn?"

"Oh, Noor—" There was a commotion on Razan's end, and Noor muffled the shell with her hand. When it ceased, her friend's next words here soft, pained. "I'm with Mianning on the *Cormorant* on the way to Aden; we can't get to you. We need to meet you in Aden."

"I thought I could last here, but I can't. The Sword of Sidon is—"

Razan spoke quickly, "Noor, the *Victory* must have sent for reinforcements after Tajoura. British barks are swarming the Red Sea. We'd be sunk before we could get in sight of you. You need to stand fast, Noor. Stay strong, habibati. You know the plan in Aden. We'll get you then. I promise."

Pressure built behind Noor's eyes, but she held her breath until it passed. She wouldn't cry where anyone else could hear. She thought of dry deserts and the quiet in the minaret and whispered coldly, "I will see you in Aden."

"Noor, please—" came Razan's soft response, but Noor cut it off. The argument outside was easing down.

The Sword shifted against the door, and she tried to slip inside his mind, to see if he had heard. But his walls were as tall and smooth as ever.

Noor might have drifted for a bit, what with the exhaustion of the ride and the fight and the two days in captivity. She still tracked the shifts, ears straining for the call to prayer, but the sound never made it through the whitewashed walls. She noted the sailors moving around her as they got to work on finishing repairs, ate, argued, and laughed. At some point in the late evening, the ship heaved, the direction of the rocking changing. They must be underway to Aden. The men must have worked double time to repair or replace the sails, but she'd given the resistance the time they'd asked for.

She hoped it was enough.

The Sword of Sidon kept watch at her door all night long.

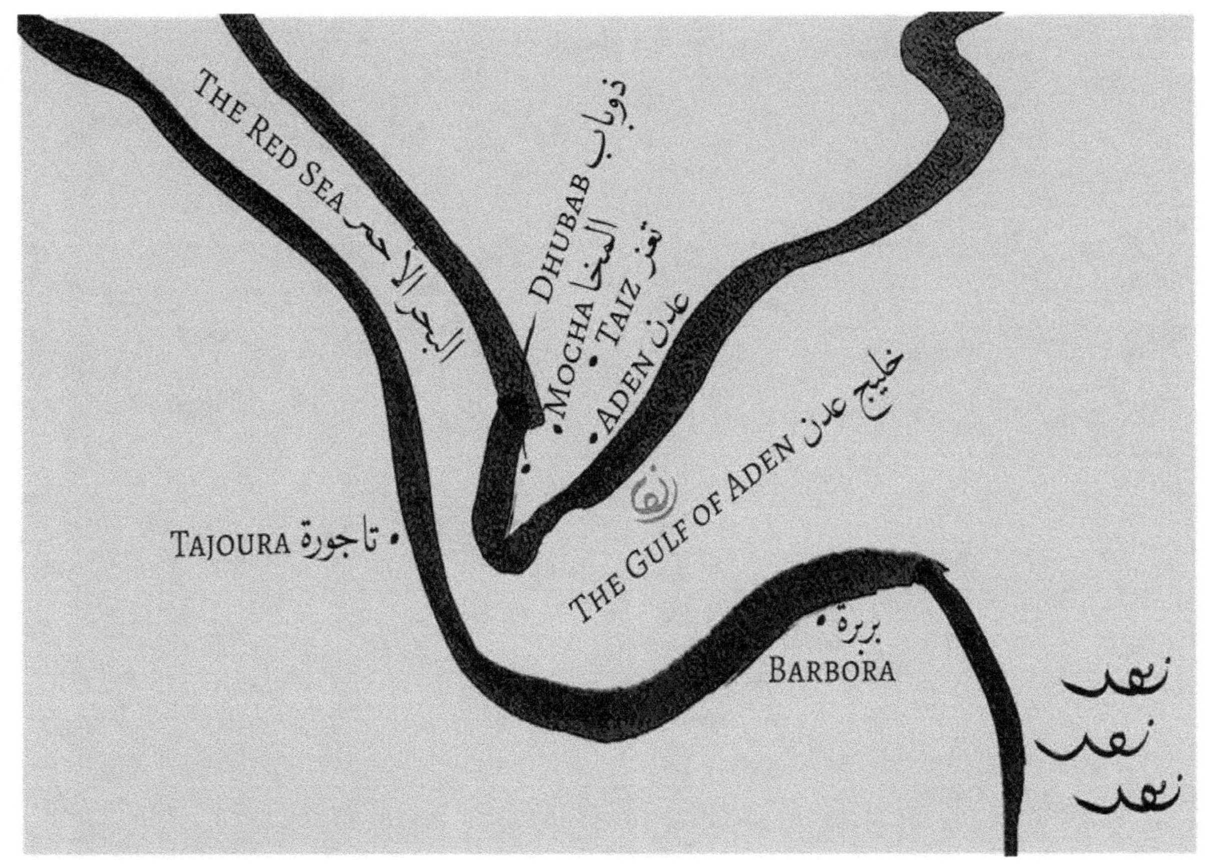
THE RED SEA البحر الأحمر
DHUBAB ذوباب
MOCHA المخا
TAIZ تعز
ADEN عدن
THE GULF OF ADEN خليج عدن
TAJOURA تاجورة
BARBORA بربرة

Chapter Nine

RIGHT BEFORE DAWN, Noor heard the echo of fajr prayer across the water. *The ship must have moved closer to one of the mosques on the coast in the night.*

There was a knock. Noor bolted to her feet and peered through the barred window in the door, into the Sword's eyes. It seemed it was only him in there this time, his eyes a rich brown, but she had no way of knowing.

"He's ready for you," he said quietly.

She stood, stretched out her shoulders, then nodded. He opened the door and motioned for her to turn. He shackled her hands behind her back and led her out into a ship wrapped in controlled chaos, to men readying the cannons, carrying cask after cask of gunpowder up from the hold. The two of them moved through the crowds, the Sword making a path through the rush.

"You should just give in," he murmured in English. And it didn't sound like a threat, more like when Imam Tariq had given her advice about managing Musa's moods. It wasn't hopeful, and it wouldn't fix tomorrow's problems; it was meant to help her survive today.

But she shook her head and said in Arabic, "I won't have another master."

He looked at her oddly, replying in Arabic, "In Tajoura, I thought you were—"

Then he clenched his jaw, glancing to where a sailor was eying him closely. He switched to English, speaking quickly. "He's going to take Aden. You know it. I know it. Everyone on this ship and everyone in your pitiful resistance knows it. But after that, he'll need to break up the sultanate, with Aden as a Crown Colony and the rest of Yemen as a protectorate." His eyes were bright, feverish. "He'll need another sultan; the governor will appoint whomever my master recommends. I'm going to be the next sultan of Yemen."

She shook her head, saying softly in Arabic, "The governor's never going to choose you."

He flinched away from her as though he'd been struck.

She stared up at him, trying to drive the point past his shields. "They'll never choose a Yemeni man. Can you think of anytime a person from a European colonised place was appointed to rule it? Anytime in British history? I've never heard of one."

He frowned. "It's a new century. We've lost in the Americas, we're fighting Napoleon on the continent, and we'll be refocussing on where we're strongest. I could be the *first*."

"But you won't."

His face froze, eyes glazing. "He's calling for you."

She locked her shields in place, gritting her teeth with the effort as the sultan's magic came for her. They entered the room to find it lit by whale oil lamps, air greasy, and the window barely cracked to let in the predawn sea breezes.

The so-called sultan was aged again, cancer spots upon his skin. But his eyes were sharp, green as a corpse; she thought that was probably their natural shade.

"Hungry yet?" he asked with a self-satisfied smile.

Noor paused. She guessed she was. Going without meals for a day and a half must have seemed like a deprivation to someone who'd had his multiple daily meals delivered on a naval schedule. She was more aware of her shoulders aching from the heavy shackles, not her hunger. She wondered if she should fake it, but she'd already waited too long to respond. His eyes flared with rage, and he raised his hand.

Reconsidering, he pointed a twitching finger out the window. "Have you ever seen Aden?"

Noor shook her head.

"You may be one of the last to see it as it is. The captain anticipates having to level the city, so fill your memory now."

The *Victory* swept around an outcropping, and the dawn flooded across Noor's vision. She gazed out over the waves as the Sword of Sidon moved up beside her.

The buildings in Aden were the tallest she'd ever seen. Some had to be ten floors high, made of brick the colour of fresh bread, with white ornate frames around windows and ample balconies. Nothing in Gaza was this tall, nothing in Tajoura this tightly packed. Great black mountains with jagged peaks encircled the city. She'd heard traders describe it as a city of pearls held in a dark palm. The less poetic spoke of how it was nestled in the crater of a quiet volcano.

A fierce grin rose to her face when she saw in the harbour what the sultan couldn't with his back turned: over a hundred dhows with the *Asma's Dhow* and the *Cormorant* heading two waiting columns.

Shouting resounded on the deck above them, and Noor wanted to look back at the so-called sultan's reaction, but she couldn't tear her eyes away from the fleet, every one of them flying the emira's red flags.

"Master—" The Sword of Sidon interrupted her reverie, pointing over her shoulder to the ships.

At the sultan's grunt of surprise, the stench of grave dirt rose around them, stifling and hot— "Your mother will rue the day she stood against me."

A cruel power threw Noor's body backwards. She hit the floor hard with her shoulders, bound hands bruising beneath her hips, barely keeping her head from slamming into the oak, muscles near-tearing with the force of his magical shove. The sultan's hand raised, gnarled fingers curling.

A cruel smile moved across his ruined face. "I will destroy her myself," he said in a rasping hiss. "And I will do it using the power of her slave mage."

She took in his torn, terrible face, so lost to humanity, his green eyes so cruel, and the quiet peace she'd always known at the top of the minaret rose up through her.

She met his sickly green eyes and shoved herself to standing. Her muscles screamed against the sultan's magic dragging her down, but she held on to that calm and ripped past his hold as if tearing through rotted fabric.

The Sword of Sidon stared at her, mouth agape, his mother's ships at his back.

Noor gazed down at the sultan, hearing only the quiet of the morning, watching his hands claw, gripping the air, trying to force her back to her knees. He shoved his hand towards her and her knees buckled—then straightened. A wall of magic burst between them—Rami. She felt the weakness in it, the pain driving it too thin to hold, but she only needed a few more breaths.

As she gazed down at the so-called sultan, she said, quiet yet piercing, "You don't know my name."

His face twisted up at her, rage and disgust making him more horrible than any cancer as he screamed his defiance, redoubling his efforts, yanking power from the Sword and taking him to his knees. But he held his shield around Noor, bolstering her power with his wavering magic.

"My name is Noor," she said as she pulled her magic from the deepest reservoir she had, her own pain receding before it, the one built over cold nights sleeping on the street, shaking days working at sea and unable to swim, that gruesome month in the compound, and every moment she'd spent in the lonesome quiet of the minaret.

A light blazed from her hands, hot in a way it had never been before. Her shackles melted from around her wrists, lighting the carpet behind her on fire but leaving her untouched.

She held out her palms as they burned as bright as fresh hope. She drew from her memories of pain and of peace, yanking on that thread until it reached its very end. She stretched out and grasped the sultan's frail hands.

"Noor means light."

Her light jerked and lit, transforming into a torrent of flame flowing from her palms, engulfing the so-called sultan and burning the screams from his throat.

The fire felt cool to her hands as it burst through the shattered windows behind him, erupting into the air behind the ship.

The flame caught, lighting the rudder and climbing up the ship as men screamed.

The howling of the figure in front of her took a long time to stop, long after his magic drifted away. But finally, there was only the stomach-churning smell of cooking meat and the horrible pop and crunch of crackling flesh.

The screaming on the decks above only got louder. Noor called a twist of water from the harbour and drenched the state room with it, killing the remaining fire but leaving the rudder alight.

"Get the bloody fire hoses and pumps, you pox-ridden bastards!" came the battle shout from above deck, accompanied by the whistle and pop of gunfire from the armada in the harbour.

The commander roared, "Get at least one bloody cannon pointed at the goddamned pirate ship!"

Noor peered out the broken window at the *Cormorant* far ahead of the rest of the waiting fleet, tacking so hard to gain speed that the sail grazed the tips of the waves. She heard a footstep behind her.

She turned as the Sword of Sidon strode towards her with his fist raised. But his eyes didn't track her, instead remaining fixed and unwavering as he buried his fist in the charcoal chest of the so-called sultan with a torn shout. He punched again and again, long hair covering his face, embers coating his skin, screaming, voice cracking, and face stretched to madness.

When the body was a pile of cinders and smoking ash, the Sword stopped, breathing heavily, burn blisters criss-crossing his knuckles.

Noor stepped towards him, and he didn't react.

"He's gone," she said in Arabic.

"How did you do it?" he asked in English raggedly, still staring at the heap. "You're a haya mage; you can't kill."

She studied the heap where the man had been, responding in Arabic. "I have no idea. But he cannot hurt anyone anymore."

The Sword squared his shoulders, standing between the beams so he could reach his full height, still not looking at her as the fire raged above them. He was steady when he said in English, "Now I'm the sultan."

She froze. "What?"

Why won't he speak Arabic? He's acting like he doesn't understand me.

She stepped towards him, switching to English, "Why would you want that?"

He didn't respond.

She stepped towards him, holding out her hand. "I'm getting out of here before the ship burns around us. Come with me."

"No."

"Rami," she said, and he shook his head, like he was trying to shake a fly off, hair across his eyes.

"You'll have to go through me." Rami's words shook, ash and blood mixing on his knuckles.

"What?"

He shouted, high and reedy, "Guards! The prisoner mage killed the sultan and is attempting to escape! To me! To me!"

The door burst open as if they'd been waiting for his command, and a dozen men in their red jackets with white bands crossing at the breast stumbled into the room. They held their muskets, faces sweating, red, vicious. They filled the room, surrounding her—

Noor stumbled back, memory driving hard through her like a blow from Musa's fist. Rami's mind caught on the edge of her panic, reaching for hers, and she threw up her shields, forcing herself high, high up in the minaret tower and then slammed the door.

Her mind still high in the minaret, Noor threw her fear and her magic out across the sailors and *yanked*, pulling more life from each of the men outside than she ever had before, draining them down to the dregs.

The sailors dropped. They fell in circles, red on the deck, and then blue. The whole deck was out, and Rami was back on his knees.

The power she'd seized was immense, building faster and faster, and she didn't know where to put it. Her skin glowed golden with it as it sought any pathway out. Noor turned to Rami behind her. He reached for her and grabbed her bare wrist. She shuddered, looking into his eyes and found them a rotting green.

It wasn't him in there.

It was the sultan's strength crushing her wrist, dragging her to him. But she had the jambiya in her other hand, and she slashed across his face, the two men's cries mixing as the blade dragged from his lip up to his hairline.

She didn't know if she'd taken his eye, but the pain must have been blinding. He staggered back, his grip loosening on her wrist as he forced the remains of the sultan out.

In the moment his shields were down, Noor yanked again, sending him into the safety of sleep, his body in a heap at her feet.

The power inside her billowed and grew, Rami's life energy more powerful than any she had ever touched before. Chaos swarmed above her with the thunder of a hundred hard-heeled boots and the roar of a single cannon. Her friends must still be evading destruction out in Aden's harbour.

Noor picked her way across the men to the hole where the windows had been, stepping on any solid foothold be it sea-soaked oak or red-shirted chest. She looked out over the water and called up a much sturdier waterspout, this one full of rocks and sandy grit, and set it to drilling through the oak exactly at the waterline. The spout punched a hole through in seconds, the ship lurching with the damage. She hoped it would give the crew the maximum amount of time to evacuate. The ship tilted, and the sleeping men slid around her as she held on to the top of the window frame, bracing her body. She glanced back. Rami was wedged against the wall, safe for now.

She stepped up to former windows, and there it was—the *Cormorant*, swooping through the water, well within cannon range, but no one was firing. She heard the cannons rolling across the deck with the listing ship.

Noor called the waterspout up to her, spinning and spraying her with a mix of sand and seaweed. She ordered the spout to pull away the great yellow and black painted timbers of the hull, widening the hole she'd drilled, and build a spiral staircase with it, held up by the spout and leading across the harbour right to the *Cormorant*.

Behind her came thick-soled boots pounding on the ladder stairs and then armed men gaping at the sleeping marines, the blasted-out windows, and the still-smouldering chair. Most of all, they stared at her, glowing wildfire bright in the middle of it all.

"Stand back—" she said in English, but they raised their weapons. "Stop!"

They fired, bolts throwing up sprays of splinters that cut into her legs, pain slashing at her connection to her magic. She reached out her hand for Rami, ordering a sliver of the waterspout to snake up and over to seize his wrist. One of the sailors dove for him, caught his hand, and dragged his body away, his friends helping. Noor tightened her grip and felt his muscles begin to stretch, to give.

She shouted, "Stop, *now!*"

But the man kept dragging him away.

She screamed in frustration and let go of his wrist, unwilling to break his bones as another man aimed a musket squarely at her chest.

Another musket bolt slammed into the wood at her feet, and she jumped out onto what had been open air a moment before. The steps shook under her weight, but held. She ran down the spiral of them, thin sandals slapping on the black and golden wood. When she reached the bottom at the water level, gasping, hands on her knees, she let the spout lower, sliding the planks across the water in front of her. The water around her splashed up in tiny fountains, and Noor glared into a row of muzzles, firing down at her from the top deck. But the angle was strange, so she began to run, ordering the planks where her feet would land as she sent up a sister spout to knock the men at the gunwale back.

On her next step, Noor slipped on a split plank, and her leg punched down through the water, a loose nail gouging into her calf. She caught herself on the board beneath her, holding her balance as the pain sang through her, breaking the trance she'd found herself in since the so-called sultan had forced her to her knees. She drew her leg back up, careful to avoid the nail, and pushed a bit of her swirling energy into healing the wound. She looked up at the *Cormorant* swinging towards her, Razan waving her arms.

"Come *on* Noor!" her friend shouted.

She pushed herself up, staggered, and strode the rest of the way. Her power was flagging, and the terror of the fall gripped her, but then Razan threw down the ladder. Noor wrapped her hands around the smooth, dry cedar, and the tightness in her back eased.

She began the climb back up. When she reached the top, Razan's face was as admiring as Usama's was dumbstruck.

"That was some kind of show you put on there, Noor." Usama said with a grin.

Noor threw her arms around Razan, breathing in deeply, getting her sopping wet and not caring even the tiniest bit. She smelled like their last night together, and her strong arms held all of Noor's weight and fear and hope for one impossible, perfect moment. Then Noor pulled back.

"Wait, wait please," she said. "I have to get them off the ship."

"Get *who* off the ship?" asked Razan, but Noor held up her palm.

Noor raised her hands, pulling the waterspout back up as her friend hovered behind her. About half of the ship's boats were in the water, with the other half blocked by her flames. She doused the flames enough to allow a path to the boats. Then Noor slipped her waterspout into the hole she'd made in the stern. She pulled out man after man after man and lowered them into the boats. Her vision was blacking out, and she couldn't see who each of the men she saved were, but she hoped Rami was one of them.

The sailors stopped firing on her waterspout after she pulled the first dozen rescued men out, and the men in the boats began to help around the twentieth. Her strength started dragging, lagging in a way she'd never felt before, but Noor kept going until she knew all of the men she'd stolen life from were in the boats.

In the time it had taken her to save them, the emira's fleet had surrounded the sinking *Victory*, and one of the quicker officer's had run up a white shirt on an oar: the flag of surrender.

When she felt the last man's back touch the bottom of the boat, she let her legs collapse.

"It's done," she gasped.

Usama knelt before her. "Noor, Noor, I hate to do this, but the emira needs to know— Are the sultan and the Sword of Sidon alive?"

"I killed the so-called sultan," she said, her voice a bare scrape. "The Sword...I don't know."

"Why did you let him live?" Betrayal infected Razan's tone as she knelt beside her.

Noor shook her head, feeling as if she were floating in counterbalance to the rocking waves. She tried to think of how to explain but couldn't think of anything her friends would listen to.

Noor was suddenly so tired.

She settled for saying, "I injured him," and that seemed to settle them.

Noor thought of his face, split open and bleeding, a scar that would mark him for the rest of his life. She considered her friends' satisfaction at knowing he was injured. Something inside her tore, and she found herself crying. Noor couldn't remember the last time she'd cried outside of someone actively hurting her, but this was as if something was bleeding inside her. All of those men, leering at her, sleeping in the ship. The sultan now no more than embers in a sinking wreck.

All of it.

Razan's face eased, her expression of betrayal shifting to concern. She reached out her arms and tucked Noor in under her shoulder, and Noor's body relaxed before her mind did. "I'm sorry, Noor. I know you tried."

She tried to explain through her sobs that she *hadn't* tried, that she'd *had* the chance, a hundred chances. Noor could have knocked him out the way she had the sailors at any time, could have done the same—maybe?—to the sultan. She could have *ended it*.

Instead, she'd healed the Sword, let him teach her, protect her.

But none of her words came through, only her sobs.

After long moments, face hidden in Razan's shoulder, her scent surrounding her, Noor fell into the same dark where she'd sent Rami ibn Arwa wa Nuri.

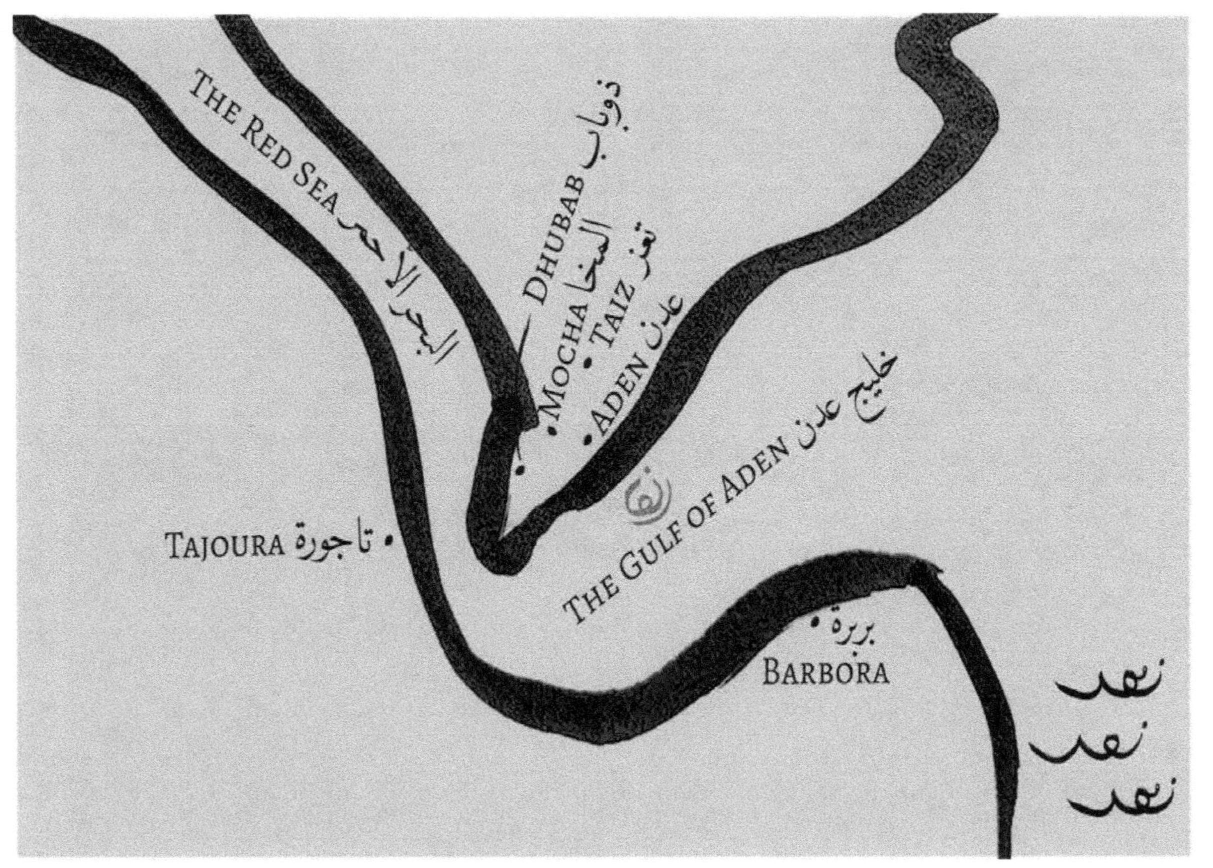
THE RED SEA البحر الأحمر
DHUBAB ذوباب
MOCHA المخا
TAIZ تعز
ADEN عدن
THE GULF OF ADEN خليج عدن
TAJOURA تاجورة
BARBORA بربرة

Chapter Ten

SOMETIME LATER, NOOR awoke. She eased her eyes open to a familiar cedar ceiling. Razan stood beside her hammock, a flask of cool water in her hands.

"Thank you," Noor said and took a long and slow drink.

"The emira and her council are impatient to speak with you, to thank you, but I told them to leave you alone until you'd eaten."

"You're a good friend, Razan. Thank you."

Her friend shared a quiet smile and held out a strong hand to help her out of the hammock.

Above in the kitchen area, as Noor ate dried fish, Razan told her about how she had raced the camel along the road away from Mocha until she found a caravan heading south later in the afternoon—a Jewish family travelling to Aden for a wedding. She'd recognised their names as being relatives of a family who had worked closely with the emira, so she'd asked for their protection as they journeyed. They gave it with grace, and Razan had stayed with them.

Noor didn't remember much about that afternoon—the party at the emira's compound in the heart of Aden, the crowds of well-wishers, soaked sailors, and allies. All she remembered was how the emira's arms had closed tight around her and the smile on James's face as he clapped her on the shoulder. Before the sun had set but long before the festivities were over, Razan helped Noor find a quiet place to sit at the edge of the central courtyard where the roast and the women's dancing were. She stood guard, keeping Noor's well-wishers from overwhelming her.

Noor went to bed in a room shared with Razan long before the rest of the resistance thought of sleep. Her friend wrapped strong arms around her, holding Noor tight until she could sleep.

*

NOOR SLEPT THROUGH the night and through the following day, only waking when Razan insisted she eat. She accepted leftovers from the party gratefully and then burrowed back under a thick blanket and fell into sleep again, knowing Razan was keeping watch.

*

NOOR OPENED HER eyes and found herself drowning in night-dark waters. She moved her arms and discovered she could swim. Breaching the surface, she imagined she could tread water; she'd always been able to in her dreams. Noor looked around; she wasn't in the Tajoura harbour or the Red Sea but in the silica-filled waters off a lagoon on the coast of Gaza. She'd been here once, years ago, on a caravan with Musa.

A dark form appeared in the water, and she froze, trying to calculate if it was heading towards her or would let her pass unharmed. But the shape drifted downwards into the blackest deep—and it was human.

She dove and saw—his face with her gash across it. His chest was bare, legs still clad in the impractical imperial wool pants.

Noor looped her arm around his still-warm body and dragged him through the lagoon and into the cave she knew was there beneath the ancient city. Big for a cave, the space was thirty paces across, its mouth full of gentle waves when the tide was high, the sand a dark slate grey, and the ceiling high enough for even Rami to stand. When Noor had last been here, it had housed a dozen families from her trading caravan. But now it was bare, empty except for the two of them. When Rami's eyes flew open, he threw himself away from her, coughing the remaining water from his lungs and trying to get his hands in front of him, eyes frantic, wild for a weapon.

"What are you doing here?" he gasped in Arabic. His eyes were his own again.

"Where is 'here' for you?" she asked in the same language, hands up, palms out.

He spluttered and looked around, raking his hand through his hair. "I don't know where I am."

"Well, this is a cave in Gaza."

"You can't be here with me," he said, seemingly not hearing her. "It must be a trick, something they—"

And he disappeared.

Noor searched the area. She'd never had a dream where someone had popped in and out of it before. She turned to the water, dove in.

She enjoyed imagining she could grace the dark and rushing waters with the stars high above her and never fear drowning in the undertow.

*

THE NEXT MORNING the emira decided Noor had had enough time to recover and brought her before her allies. The council sat in a circle on thickly embroidered red pillows, hot tea in front of each of them.

Noor twisted her guntiino between her hands.

The emira prompted her. "The Sword of Sidon ambushed you at the gates of Mocha."

Noor told the tale. When she came to the moment when Rami had knelt before the so-called sultan, shirt off, preparing to be whipped, one of the sheikhas interrupted her.

He muttered, "He probably liked it."

Another murmured, "He deserved worse."

Their hard eyes were why she glossed over healing him, how he'd helped her with her shields, and how he'd fought with her at the end.

She was rewarded for her reticence. The harshest questions thrown at her were about why she had tried to save the men on the *Victory*. The sheikhs and sheikhas of the tribes supporting the emira were furious that Noor had allowed most of their crew to escape to a small, fleeing support ship.

Noor finally set her hands flat on her knees. "I am a haya mage. I have been taught that if I kill with my magic, I will lose it. That is what my teacher, Imam Tariq of Tajoura, told me happened to Emira Asma." She glanced at Emira Arwa, wondering how she would react to Noor mentioning her mother.

The emira's eyes were narrowed, but she waved her on.

Noor continued. "I killed the sultan, knowing I might lose my connection to magic and be stranded on the *Victory*. I did it anyway because I freely serve this cause. But many of those men were, like James, conscripted. They were no more willing workers than I was when I was a slave in Tajoura. I would no more burn my fellow slaves to death for doing what they needed to survive their masters than I would willingly go back into bondage."

The sheikhs and sheikhas made disgusted faces as though she were some kind of child who did not understand the ways of war. She didn't know how to explain it to people who had known nothing but freedom, so she kept the rest of her answers short.

The emira dismissed her soon after.

Noor found Usama hanging around in the corridor outside. She leaned back against the brown brick wall, covering her face with her hands.

"That good, huh, habibti?" he asked.

She raked her fingers through her hair, straightening it. "I didn't sleep well is all."

"Sounds like you need a distraction. "Do you know how to ride?"

Noor shook her head. "I rode a donkey sometimes, and as of three days ago, I've ridden a camel. But mostly I was made to walk."

He smiled, eyes softening. "Well, the emira's horses have been cooped up in preparation for the battle, but a little bird told me that you and James would be quite welcome to help exercise them if you'd like to get outside the walls of the compound."

Noor spent the day walking around in the little circle in the paddock on the outskirts of the city, the most beautiful animal she'd ever seen between her legs. She found a power in riding, a danger. These horses could kill if they had a mind for it. But mostly, they wanted grass. They were sleek and tall, their hair the slickest thing Noor had touched outside of water.

Later, she and James and Razan had dinner together since Usama had been pulled into late-night strategy meetings.

She and Razan shared a bed again, falling into a deep, easy sleep.

*

NOOR OPENED HER eyes again under the water of Gaza. This time, she looked around and found a dark shape hanging in the water, his hair a nest of medusan curls. She dove, her dream strength pulling her forward. She grasped him by his white shirt and pulled him to the surface. He struggled in her arms, but Noor dragged him to shore, letting him go once they made the beach. He stumbled to the wall of the cave, putting it at his back.

Before he could disappear again, she said. "Where did you go when you left last night?"

He gritted his teeth. "You can't possibly care."

She frowned. "I tried to get you off the *Victory*. I wouldn't have left you with them if I had any other choice. They wouldn't let you go."

"They still have me," he whispered.

"What does that mean?"

He rolled up his sleeve, uncovering a line of welts across the skin, not something you got from falling in the rigging or during weapons practice.

The lines were parallel, systematic.

"What are they doing to you? Are you with another alam mage?"

He rolled his sleeve back down and growled, "I can take care of myself."

She awoke at the sound of someone in the corridor returning from the strategy session. It took a long time to get back to sleep as she rubbed and rubbed her right arm, searching for marks that weren't there.

*

USAMA'S SPIES HAD taken one of her lunella shells as far as Jerusalem but no farther yet. It would be a month or more of hard travel before they had them in London.

"But once they're there," Usama had said, rubbing his hands together gleefully, "we'll have a real, solid idea of their plans. We'll know when we can rest and when we have to prepare. The first instantaneous information we or anyone else has ever had—all thanks to you, Noor. We're learning incredible things already. Such as the British calling their ships back to India. With only a few months before the winter monsoon season, they're going to wait until it's over to 'reconsider their strategy in Aden.'" He said this, grinning as though it was a resounding victory, though it meant the war had simply moved to some other place, a long sail to the east.

"I also heard a little tidbit as it was being passed back to the lord admiral in Portsmouth." James glanced at Razan before Noor as if he wasn't sure how she'd feel about it. "The Sword of Sidon has been imprisoned. The story going around the navy is that he went mad—madder—and killed their chosen sultan. He's being held until the lord admiral can decide whether to try him for treason or just kill him outright."

*

NOOR SLEPT SOUNDLY that night and didn't remember dreaming of anything.

The following day was more meetings about magic, with an afternoon spent under the brilliant sun with the horses.

*

THE NEXT NIGHT, he was deeper down. Her lungs began to ache as she dragged him to the surface. It took longer to wake him once they were on the shore, long enough she was trying to remember what she had learned on the docks about how to save a drowned man.

But then he woke, confused, his hands came up in front of him, trying to fend her off. Red welts surrounded his wrists.

Rope burns.

A brisk wind blew into the cave, and they both shivered. Noor imagined a campfire between them and a fresh guntiino around her. Rami stayed in his sopping clothing, hunched over, haggard, and glowering at the fire.

"You need to get out of there," she said.

"I can't."

She realised he was speaking Arabic, had only spoken Arabic in this time and place.

"Why not?"

"There's something blocking me— They've severed me from my magic. I don't know how, but I can't get out. It's some kind of prison, and half of the guards were volunteers from the *Victory*, men the sultan and I whipped."

She went quiet at this and then: "So, when you vanished—"

"They had come for me."

She tried to imagine these nights continuing, spending her days enjoying her freedom or securing it for others and her nights doing this. She thought of what the others had said at the council meeting, what Usama had said before they landed at the emira's compound about why so many of the families hated Rami.

She studied him for a moment, and the question burst from her lips. "Why does the council hate you so much?"

He stared at her, confused.

"The sheikhs and the sheikhas who your mother rallies in the resistance. I know it's something to do with Taiz—with dead children, but I don't know what you *did*."

He moved to the mouth of the cave, his back to her, the stars bright and endless in front of him. His tone was flat and lifeless. "I killed their children."

Noor shivered, and it wasn't because of the cold. "No one's story is that simple."

He shook his head. "Fine, since we're trapped here. Fine." He clenched his fists at his side. "I don't remember it. It was—my master he—"

Rami took a breath. "I was at the school in Taiz, studying. Then, I was on the *Victory*. And then, someplace else where I knew no one, and no one knew me." He shrugged a shoulder. "I was young; maybe I did it. Maybe I burned it down."

He spoke as if it were only him and the night as it lay over the waves as if he hadn't spoken to another person in days. He held his hand up as though cupping the cheek of the wind, high above his head.

"At that age, I was still using haya magic." He spoke in a jumble as though trying to get his words out before they caught up with him. "Hadn't found my alam magic. When I think about that night, I think about— I could see the stars, could see them twist. Until then, I'd always looked for the light in the stars; never the void between. But in that moment when it happened and every night since then, when I could see the stars, it's been flipped for me. I can only see the blackness, can barely see the stars. I didn't choose it, but I can't bear to say it is wrong either, even now— There's so much more pain in the world than light. Darkness is what keeps the stars apart. It's a kind of alam magic."

Noor sucked in a breath, pushing her shoulders back against the cold stone. Rami's voice seemed far away, heavy with painful knowledge.

"When I needed pain, it was there for me, Noor. My whole life, pain had seeped in, whispered to me. That's how the sultan found me.

"Those are bullshit excuses. What he said happened was this— My hands, my power brought down the school on the children sleeping there. Most were crushed instantly beneath it, others—" Rami flinched at the next thought, and Noor could feel it then, some long pent-up dam of emotion breaking. What it had held back for so long rushed down like a river, and she knew there was nothing he or she or anyone in this universe could do to stop it. He was in the middle of the story, in the thickest pain of it.

"I dug through the rubble with my hands, trying to get to the scratching noises, to the light of their life forces. Over and over again, I heard them, felt them grow cold and flicker out.

"It wasn't until I got to the lowest level where the littlest ones slept that I finally understood why they were still dying. When the rubble had stopped moving moments after I'd—I'd ripped down the wall between the massive cistern and the basement of the school, I saw the basement where the littlest children slept because it was coolest in the summer. They'd drowned. Been drowning even while I dug through the rubble with my hands because after I'd caused all of that destruction—with my hands because when I tried after, I couldn't lift a single pebble with magic."

He stared down at his broad palms, the jagged working calluses the only dark marks on his skin; Noor doubted it was his hand that he was seeing as he said, "I got some out—" He breathed. "—and a few got themselves out. The ones who were strongest or perhaps the most afraid, the lightest sleepers. The hardest fighters. The ones I brought to the sultan." He made a choking sound, and Noor wanted to reach for him, to bring him back to this time on the sand.

She didn't.

He still stared at his hands, turning them over and over as if asking them where they'd come from, as if wondering what in him had made them into what they were.

He kept going, the anguish still thick in his voice. "We couldn't get help; I'd smashed the only bridge to the rest of Taiz when I let the alam magic out, and the people were always suspicious of us mages up on a hill. And what would we tell people—that I'd killed the teacher, but it was an accident? Was it? Who would believe me?"

He shook his head, trying to convince himself, even now. Noor wasn't so sure Emira Arwa's son couldn't have found a way back home in those bloodied hours, told people some of what the so-called sultan had done, what the teacher had done, and told himself it was worth the attempt.

She thought, in that moment, that if he'd had the enchanted jambiya blades, he should have shown them his memory of his teacher attacking him, and the others would have had to believe him. Noor nearly broke in, to tell him about them—but she stopped herself. As trapped and hurt as he might be right now, she had no assurance he wouldn't someday find himself in a position to trade her information for his safety.

She kept silent.

"It seemed so clear," he said. "It was so clear in here—" He tapped the side of his head. "—that there was no way for me to go back home. I could hear the words so clearly in my head— 'There is no more home.' So, when the sultan's sailors showed up the next night with a rope bridge, we didn't question it. Four more children had died, Noor, between when I—I pulled Taiz down and when the British came for us. They burned it behind us when we left. 'No more home.'

"The others said it was my fault what had happened. All of them. The sultan took them, slipped his magic inside their heads, convinced them to serve him. He sent them for training throughout the empire. Kept us all apart. So, we were always the only ones in ships full of British men."

Rami's back was a long, harsh line in front of the pale moonlight as he turned to look at her over his shoulder. "I learned to use alam magic like breathing, alone in a deserted place. I was hungry, thirsty, terrified of the long-toothed animals that roamed there. After a week, I lost the ability to heal. Another week, I couldn't use it to hide. One by one, all of the things I loved and been good with at Taiz, I lost. All I had was alam magic. By the time they came for me, I'd lost everything else about that life. So when the sultan named me the Sword of Sidon—" He shrugged, voice bleak. "—what did giving up one more thing matter?"

He straightened his shoulders, turning fully to her, his mask firmly back on, his face arrogant as any prince's. "What they're doing to me here is nothing. This is nothing. They're nothing. I'll survive them."

"And then what—what will you do then?" Noor asked, her voice cracking.

But he was gone.

*

SHE AWOKE AND turned to Razan. Her friend sat on their bed in the early morning light, legs folded on her mat as she tinkered with a device like a miniature dhow. Her hair was down around her shoulders.

"I've been dreaming of Gaza," Noor said.

Razan glanced over to her, a question in her eyes.

Noor took a deep breath. "I've been dreaming of Gaza and Rami ibn Arwa wa Nuri."

Her friend's face clouded over, lush eyebrows lowering in a deep frown.

"Why would you dream of Gaza?" Razan asked, ignoring the other part.

"I've been there once, five years ago, part of a caravan selling trinkets to the pilgrims heading to Al-Quds, to Jerusalem. My former master took me along to do the actual work. It was right when the Egyptian ruler, the Ottoman's pasha, invaded the Peninsula and took the holy cities back from Sheikh Al-Wahhab's people.

"The chaos meant a lot of folks went to the Al-Aqsa Mosque rather than Makkah or Medina. Musa—he joined a caravan of traders heading north to take advantage of the crowds. We all stayed in this cave, thirty of us, forty if you counted the children who were, like me, brought to do the actual work. Musa was selling what he called 'holy oil', claimed it was blessed by a saint. *Which* saint varied by the customer. I'd scavenged these deep-blue cut-glass bottles from a Portuguese merchant ship that had run aground in the harbour, hauled boxes and boxes of the pretty things out and back to him. That bastard put lamp oil in them and tripled the price." Noor's cheeks flushed hot as she remembered cheating the pilgrims, having had no choice.

"He was always doing stuff like that, trying to make a cheap profit from someone else's faith and sweat. One night, I told an old Orthodox woman in the Gazan souq not to buy one of the bottles, that it was a cheat. Musa must have heard, but he didn't say anything. He waited until I'd gone to sleep in the cave, and then he attacked me, dragged me to the water, tried to drown me in the lagoon." As her voice filled with heat, Noor was surprised that she could feel angry with him now. At the time, all she'd felt was shame at disappointing him. He'd been so far inside her head back then.

"He knew I couldn't swim, so he tossed me in deeper than I could stand. One of the women dove in, pulled me up, pumped my chest, got me breathing again. She let me sleep with her children that night, but they were gone the next. The beating I caught after that—" She took a breath. "—well, I don't remember most of the rest of the trip.

"When he threw me in, I opened my eyes under the water, and the salt stung, and the rocks were these strange shapes. There were bones of a great whale on the bottom of the cove, and it was—so quiet. No master screaming, no whipped donkeys, no moaning camels, no sellers hawking. Nobody touching me. And then I looked up, and that woman was coming for me, diving down for me, and I thought so clearly in that moment that I deserved to be saved, that I wasn't nothing like he always said. That voice I heard, telling me to wait, not to breathe the water, to wait—I started thinking of it as my survivor's voice."

Noor brought herself back. "So maybe that's why these strange dreams start there. It was when I first decided I would survive him, them, all of it. That I would free myself so I would remain free."

"And the Sword of Sidon?" Razan asked, voice tense. "Why do you think he's there?"

Noor shook her head, covering her eyes with her palm. "I don't know. When I was on the *Victory*, I tried to get him to leave, to desert the way James had." She quickly tried to justify it so Razan would understand. "I thought it might weaken them."

Razan seemed unconvinced but let her keep speaking.

"There isn't another alam mage in the Gulf, right? They're all in Europe fighting Napoleon or in the Americas right now?"

"Usama would know better, but I haven't heard of one."

Noor ran with the thought. "So if Usama said the British are deciding what to do with the Sword and decide to use him again, he could wreak incredible havoc across the Gulf?"

"Yes."

"So what if we took him from them?"

Razan, who had been nodding along, froze, lips curling in distaste. "Why would we want him? Why would you want to get him? Why would you tell *me* about him, ask *me* when he— No, don't answer. Don't. This is the emira's call. You'll need to ask her."

Razan stood and began to get dressed, refusing to meet Noor's eyes, her face pained. Noor was frozen as she watched her close the door between them. Then she dressed as well, feeling a gap in her stomach.

Noor was in meetings again the whole morning, this time, discussing how she healed with a group of healers. There'd been a plague in Persia that had killed millions of people when the emira was a young woman. The threat of it haunted leaders across the region, and they wanted help thinking through how they might use her magic if that form of death came to Aden. The emira sat in on the discussion, listening and considering. When they broke for a midday meal, Noor touched the emira's arm.

"Can I speak with you alone for a moment?"

"Of course." She waved the others on without them.

"It's about your son."

The emira moved to close the door, locking it before turning back to Noor.

"That's a touchy subject around here," she said. "He doesn't have many supporters."

"I've noticed. I'm not sure Razan will speak with me again after I told her what I wanted to ask you."

The emira's eyebrows rose, and she sat down, pouring herself some more tea.

She handed Noor a cup. "This should tide us over, but knowing how they all eat, it may end up being our only meal until dinner."

Noor smiled. "Usama told me the Sword of Sidon is in prison. And—" She rested her eyes on the beautifully embroidered sitting pillows piled to the side of the room, thinking about how she would say this. "I think I'm connected with him. Since the *Victory*. I think he needs our help. What I told Razan is that if we stole him away from the British, they couldn't use him against us. And maybe there's some way he could be of help. The sultan had a terrible sickness, a terrible cancer. Rami used his magic to cure him, at least for a few days at a time. He might be able to heal you."

The emira regarded Noor intently, sipping her tea. "You've told me his method of healing. I may be furious with my son, but I don't want any part of that." She paused. "You seem to have a sympathy for him the others don't, even others who lived with him for years as James did."

Noor dropped her eyes, speaking to her cup of tea. "James saw him hurt others, saw the brutality. I saw him getting hurt. It's a different kind of introduction. And—" She closed her eyes, trying to keep her breathing steady. "—in my experience of the world, there is no way to travel in time, to fix how we were treated, to protect our younger selves. But my imam, the one who trained me in magic for a few months before I met James, he always told me it was my job to free others, once I was free. That's the only kind of time travel I know of, to save others where we ourselves were not saved."

"Even if you're only saving him for a trial among his own people? Even knowing we may put him to death for his crimes?

Noor nodded. "I believe in justice, but I can't see how he can get it under the British. He might see it here, with his own people. Razan deserves to see justice for what happened to her family, whether he is guilty of the razing of Sidon or was controlled by the so-called sultan at the time. Razan deserves to know the truth, to know who to blame. And I think he had less control than the resistance believes. He may be less guilty than others may think."

The emira's dark eyes lit up. "Like I said, you seem to have a sympathy, perhaps an empathy for him." She set her tea down. "I wish that I could share it. I love him, of course, but he has hurt so many of my people." Her tone had taken on a formality that stung. "Perhaps I could have done more for him when he was at the school in Taiz, when he was first taken. But like you said. There is no going into the past to correct our mistakes, and any leader collects them like scars."

Noor needed to push, even as she felt the chance slipping away. "Can you ask the council if we can go and get him?"

The emira stood up. "You make a good case about his usefulness, and about justice. I'll try at the meeting tonight. Now, let's get lunch."

*

NOOR WENT TO bed early, before the council meeting, too anxious to eat. She opened her eyes under the water, the swirling shapes of the rocks beneath her feet strange and beautiful. There he was, hanging in front of her, hands limp at his sides. Noor dragged him to the shore, and he opened his eyes, rubbing the salt water out of them as he stood. He stared down at her, stars at his back, and he had just opened his mouth to speak when Noor jerked awake.

It was Razan, her face triumphant.

"The council came to a decision nearly immediately. The emira's asking for you."

Noor hurried up, trying to shake the memory of the cave. Razan led her to the council meeting room, which was lit with candles that filled it with a liquid light. As the rest of the council filed out, some glared at Noor openly as they passed her; others stared at her from under their eyebrows and scarves.

Not a friendly face in the bunch.

The emira was still in the room. When she saw Noor, she waved her in.

"Noor, it's not good news."

Noor's heart pounded in her ears, and she raised her voice to speak over it. "We're just *abandoning* him?"

The emira stood stiffly, mouth quirking. "You have picked up on so many things here so quickly. It is easy to forget you aren't familiar with how our government works. It's called half a loaf."

At Noor's confused expression, the emira reached over, grabbed a loaf of bread from a platter, and broke it in half.

"You want the whole loaf," she said, then pointed to herself. "I want the whole loaf. But if we both get half—" She handed the half loaf to Noor. "—no one starves. No one is full, but no one starves. Also, don't forget the most important achievement of your young life—you are your own master now. No matter what the council says or doesn't say, you can do what you think is right. You have your own voice, your own power. The first way women give up our power is by assuming we have none."

The emira tossed her half loaf back onto the platter and dusted the crumbs from her hands onto the carpet. "So, here's what the council said. They won't spend any of their time, talent, or treasure on a rescue mission for the Sword of Sidon—" Noor started to interrupt, but the emira held up a long finger.

"But before we met, I had confirmed that Usama and Mianning would volunteer to go with you. I managed to convince the council that James and Razan should be able to go as well. James had to promise he would continue to advise us on imperial plans using your lunella shells and the jambiya. Razan—" She took a deep breath and hissed it out between her teeth. "Razan is willing to go, but it may hurt her to try."

Noor wondered if Razan had requested to be left out of the search or if the emira was familiar with her pain. Her heart twisted at the thought.

"When can we get underway?" Noor asked.

The emira's eyes were serious: "Tomorrow at the earliest. Usama's spies and my ambassadors will try to figure out which of the naval prisons he's being kept in, try to broker a peaceful transfer back to his people. You, of course, will only have until the winter monsoons start or an admiral calls for Rami's execution."

"Thank you." Noor said, voice tight.

The emira nodded and waved her out of the room.

Noor passed Razan on the way back to their room and didn't know what to say. Her friend's angry smile was hard on her heart.

Noor kept going, intent on finding James to make sure he was all right with the plan. When she did find him, he let her know he was glad the emira had asked him and even more glad to be off. He didn't yet speak enough Arabic to be able to casually chat with the busy, intense resistance leaders and their followers who moved around the emira, which must have been lonesome.

Noor suspected he would also be happy to have Usama to himself again.

*

NOOR TRIED TO sleep, but she couldn't get her mind to rest. Finally, she got up to find Mianning. He and Usama sat together in one of the small gardens, enjoying the shade of the jasmine vines and the quiet flow of a small fountain while nibbling on some kidem and cheese. They welcomed her in, and after a few minutes, James joined them, bringing a carafe of fresh water. Razan followed with her maps, her model, and a stiffness to her posture that would not go away. She sat beside Usama, across from Noor, and wouldn't meet her eyes. They began to plan their course.

Through the night, people from the compound came and went, stopping to sit with Usama, and perhaps get an eyeful of Noor and James, before wandering off to their own work and pleasures.

At first light, they went to the souq, the maze of market stalls so like and unlike those Noor had known as well as her own body back in Tajoura. Noor spent the day collecting maps and charts from the palace library. She said goodbye to the horses with James.

And so, with everything they would need for a two-month journey, Noor set off with Mianning, James, Usama, and Razan for the first harbour prison at Socotra, a strange and isolated island in the middle of the Gulf, full of dragon's blood trees and centuries of secrets.

DREAM

SWIMMERS

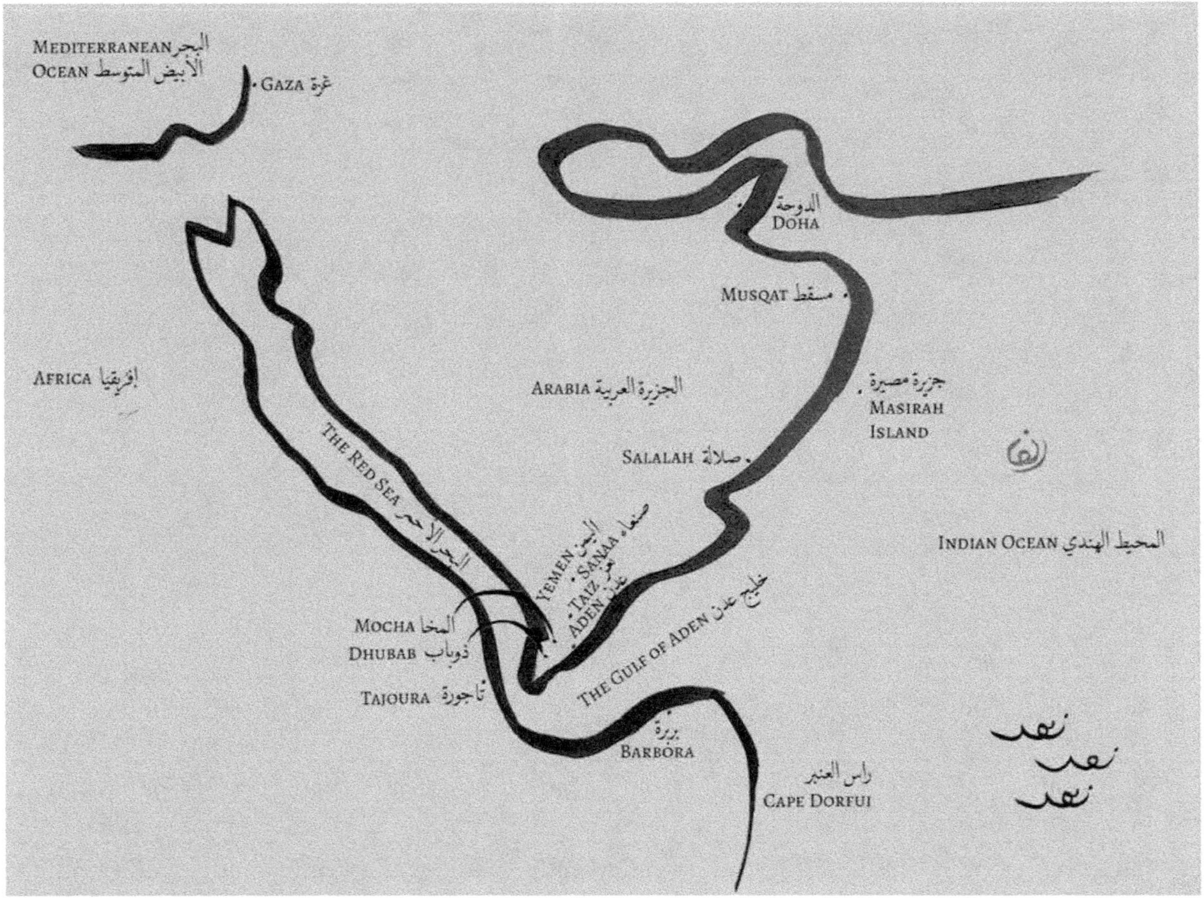

MEDITERRANEAN OCEAN   البحر الأبيض المتوسط
GAZA   غزة
AFRICA   إفريقيا
THE RED SEA   البحر الأحمر
DOHA   الدوحة
MUSQAT   مسقط
ARABIA   الجزيرة العربية
MASIRAH ISLAND   جزيرة مصيرة
SALALAH   صلالة
INDIAN OCEAN   المحيط الهندي
YEMEN   اليمن
SANAA   صنعاء
TAIZ   تعز
ADEN   عدن
THE GULF OF ADEN   خليج عدن
MOCHA   المخا
DHUBAB   ذوباب
TAJOURA   تاجورة
BARBORA   بربرة
CAPE DORFUI   رأس العنبر

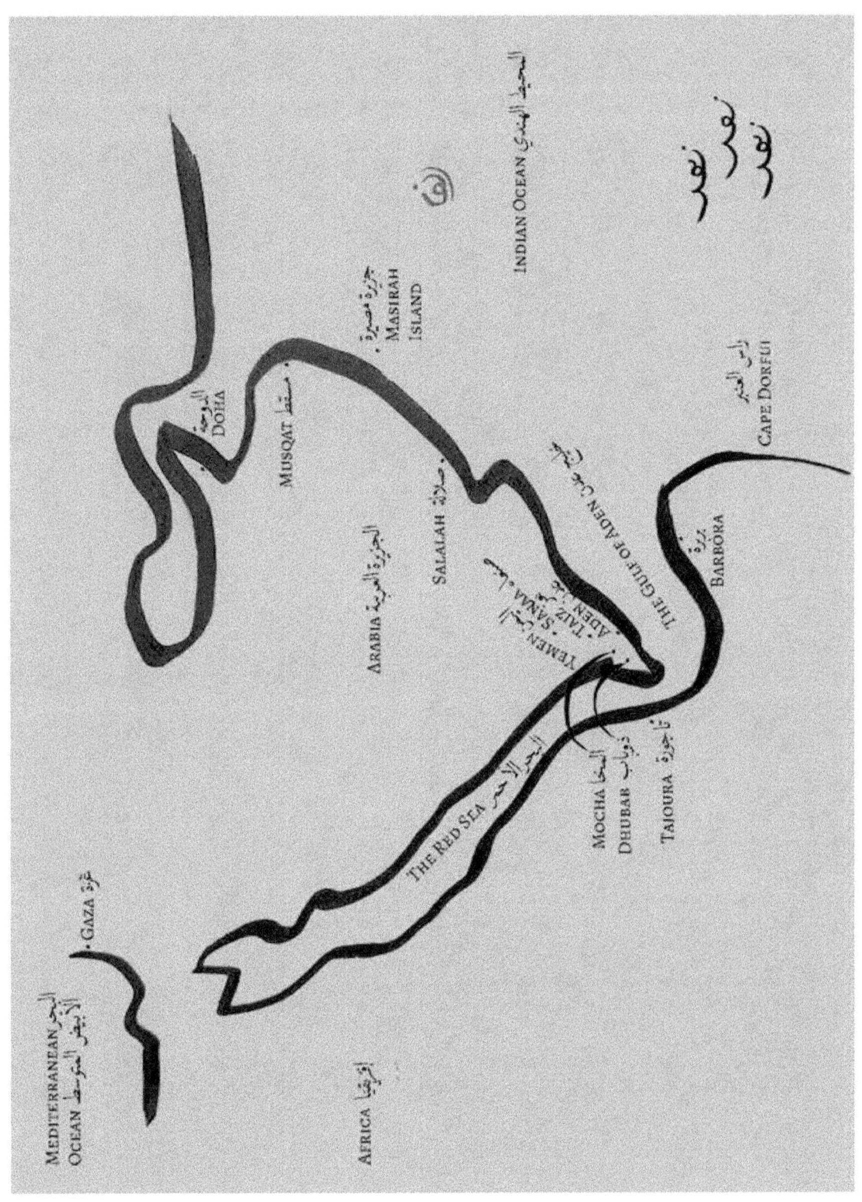

The Arabian Sea
A month before winter monsoon season, Yemen
1227 A.H. / December 1812 A.D.

Chapter One

NOOR FELL ASLEEP in her hammock onboard the *Cormorant* and opened her eyes beneath the cold waters off the coast of Gaza, two thousand imperial miles northwest. The full moon revealed the strange shapes the tides had wrought on the rocks deep in the water beneath her. She searched the sea floor for Rami, born the son of Yemen's rightful ruler, lately a traitor and *alam* mage for the British invaders. Their shared dreams haunted her sleep as Rami rotted in a British prison, and Noor planned to free him and bring him to face his people's justice.

She found his body near the lagoon floor and struck out, able to swim in her dreams. Noor couldn't in the waking world, a still bleeding lacuna from her earlier life when she'd been enslaved by a cruel master in the spice markets of Tadjoura. He'd kept that knowledge and much more from her until she'd killed him with a scavenged dagger and fought her way to freedom. Rami had sunk deeper and deeper in each dream, but Noor didn't let the burning in her lungs pull her back up. She wrapped her arm around his still-warm body and pulled him to the surface. Once there, Noor dragged him through the shallow waves and into the cave she'd once sheltered in with other families beneath the ancient city.

"Breathe, damn you." Noor pumped his chest, willing him to live.

Rami gasped and shot up. He struggled away from her, dark eyes wild. The scar she'd given him on the *HMS Victory* stood out, stark on his dark skin.

"Have it your way," Noor said and moved to the other side of the cave. In the waking world, she'd spent one week here a half-decade ago, camping out as her then-master Musa sold fake holy water to pilgrims.

But in dreams, all things were possible, so Noor concentrated on a patch of brilliantly white sand, and a moment later, a clutter of kindling lay stacked there as if it had always been. It took no *haya* magic, no life power, to conjure here in a dream. She would have never been able to turn nothing into something like this on the *Cormorant*. In dreams though...

"The fire will be ready whenever you are," Noor called out. She folded her legs and gazed out at the moonlit Mediterranean Sea.

Rami approached. He stood so close the water ran out of his long hair and dripped down the back of her *guntiino*—the red-and-gold wrap dress she wore—trickling down her spine. Rami knelt beside her, careful not to touch, and frowned at the wood she'd conjured.

"Let me," he said, and the wood burst into flame, nearly consuming it all in a single fireball.

She laughed at the extravagance, at his powers' excess.

He stiffened and glared.

She couldn't help that she found him absurd sometimes now, this terror of a man who had haunted her friends' nightmares. If he was going to pout, she would just go swimming with the hammerhead sharks and pilot whales off the coast for a few hours before waking up and trying again tomorrow night.

It wasn't as though he could sulk in the waking world.

And it wasn't likely his British jailers allowed it.

He moved to the other side of the fire and grumbled, "What's so funny?"

She bit her lip.

His voice was hoarse and raw. She hated this change in him, the damage done to his deep, soft voice. She'd only heard it a few times during their brief time together aboard the *HMS Victory*. The *Victory* had once been Lord Admiral Nelson's flagship, and Noor had sunk it with her own extravagant display of magic, turning the ship into a burning heap of broken oak planks and sails of flame. It had been enough of a mess to block British warships from taking Aden. And they'd bought Yemen's resistance precious months to prepare to defend themselves again.

Noor had wrecked the ship and freed Rami from a cruel master who'd taught him only pain and the style of magic that came from it, but she'd been unable to take him with her. So here they were, mysteriously connecting through her dreams as he grew thinner and more ragged under his jailer's persistent hatred. The British had once seen the mage as their best weapon and now viewed him as a traitor to their empire. Rami's body showed the wear of their unkind hands, as did his voice's increasing hoarseness. She figured it was from the screaming, his dream mind not remembering how a voice should sound free from hurt.

Noor hated the guards at whatever prison he was in. It didn't matter that he had wielded his master's whip against them when they'd served together on the *Victory*. No one deserved to suffer like this, night after night after night.

He eased a little closer to the fire, drawn to the heat or the company or something else entirely.

"What's so funny?" He repeated.

She had to answer that terrible grate of a voice coming out of his irritated, strange-soft face. "You are."

He huffed and folded his legs, then held two large, sword-calloused hands out to the smaller, swiftly burning fire. She glanced at his arms, but the intricate cuts that had covered them like a trader's route tattoos when she'd seen him in a dream the night before weren't there now. Whether he'd healed himself or his mind wasn't including them, she didn't know. Noor was grateful for the expanse of clean, dark skin, flecked only with moles.

"I think you need to let me go," Rami said, and every bit of the fire's warmth left Noor's body.

She'd thought they wouldn't talk about this, not give voice to it.

"Hmm?" she said, hoping he would drop it.

He leaned around the fire, voice darker and steadier. "Your magic—it's warping. You can't have missed it. You can't be both a haya and an alam mage, not in this world, not in this time. I think—" He choked this time, weakening for the barest of breaths, and it squeezed her heart as if he'd slipped his fingers beneath her skin. "I think you need to let me go. I'll never be free. I'm getting weaker. There's no way you can get to me in time. After Taiz, after Sidon, after everything I've done, there is no one left in the resistance who would want you to."

Noor stood. "Just you try me," she said and strode to the edge of the lagoon. She dove in and let the dark sea close her ears.

But speaking wasn't the only way they could connect in dreams. His words followed her in her mind as, in the darkening deep, she took solace from a world gone mad.

That's what I was afraid you'd say.

*

NOOR WOKE WITH a start, swaying gently in her hammock in the hold of the *Cormorant*. Razan snored gently in the hammock below hers. Noor took a long moment to soak in her lover's sleep-softened features, her tall brow now smooth without the wrinkles of rightful hurt and anger that too often marred her face.

Noor flopped onto her back and took heaving breaths as she combed through her dream for any details that might help her and her crew find Rami more quickly. She scanned the long, arching lines of the cedar planks which made up the hull of the *Cormorant*. Warm, red-gold wood filled the air with sweet spice, nothing like the whitewashed hell of the *HMS Victory* where she'd first met Rami in a prison cell.

Razan stirred, her long black lashes fluttering, and Noor peeked over the edge of her hammock. She watched for wakefulness, unsure she was up for her lover's disappointment so early in the day. Razan settled, and Noor felt her chest loosen. She crept out of her hammock and climbed to the top deck, where she grabbed some dried dates before joining James at the wheel.

"We have to go faster," Noor told James in English as he piloted the *Cormorant* across the vast, dark, dancing waves of the Arabian Sea. "Socotra was a waste of time. It's been three weeks of sneaking lunella shells to Usama's contacts so they can tell us as soon as they know something. Have we narrowed down the list of prisons?"

Her friend shook his head. He'd gotten a proper haircut in Aden by someone familiar with the tightly kinked hair they both shared. Nothing like that hack job the British barber had left him with from his long, unwanted years of indentured servitude on the *Victory* before he'd escaped and freed Noor in the process. James may have known some of the sailors who now guarded Rami, but perhaps not. The *Victory* had a crew of over 800 when Noor sank it, but James had been one of the few men stolen from Freetown. She'd gathered there had been little love lost between them and less socialization.

James's expression was serious when he spoke, his deep voice slow and precise as he repeated their mission's hard facts. "The British navy isn't telling Usama's spies where they're keeping him because the lord admiral hasn't decided if he wants the Sword of Sidon dead or alive." James referred to Rami by his *nom de guerre*, and his hatred for the man showed through in his words.

"I hate this," Noor said, the tiring night catching its claws in her back, pulling her spirit lower, and making her ache.

James laid his hand softly on her shoulder, held her there in the warmth and sunlight among those who loved her.

"Usama's people are doing their best, but there are so many places they could have stashed him. Any harbour prison, any governor's mansion, any embassy."

"Did Razan have any ideas of better ways we could use the lunella shells to coordinate search efforts?"

James flinched. That told Noor all she needed to know. Razan wanted Rami dead by any means necessary. She had accompanied them on the *Cormorant* to retrieve him only once she'd been assured he would be tried for his actions on behalf of the British Empire. Razan was from Sidon, and she blamed Rami's magic for the *Victory* shelling her city and killing her parents. Before Rami had shared Noor's dreams, she and Razan had shared a bed. They still did, but Razan's righteous fury at Rami and confusion that Noor did not see the world as she did had come between them.

"She would tell us if she had," Noor reassured them both, thinking of her friend sleeping in the hammock below. "If only to be done with this mission sooner."

"Give her some time," James said and gave Noor's shoulder a squeeze.

"It's not that I don't understand. I'm bringing him back to face justice, not saying he shouldn't be held accountable."

"I know, Noor." James repeated, "She needs time."

Noor nodded, and he gave her sad smile.

He jerked his head towards the waxed maps she'd borrowed from the *emira*'s library in Aden. "Want to take a turn piloting? I could use the rest."

"Of course," Noor said.

James bumped her shoulder before heading towards the captain's cabin he shared with Usama.

Noor spent the rest of the morning at the wheel, watching the horizon for imperial patrol ships and trying to stay awake. Razan eventually came up to keep her company and record the daily updates from Usama's spies. Usama's contacts were using Noor's lunella shells as if they'd been born to it. She had enchanted dozens of them after being inspired by Razan's brilliant engineering mind. The shells allowed anyone holding them to speak across any distance and share perfectly accurate visual memories as well. After checking in with her contacts in the lunella shell network, Razan had heard nothing to change their current course, so she plotted and replotted their route. The ease and routine of it soothed Noor more than any number of kind words.

Maybe we'll get through this in one piece.

As Noor eyed a cloud bank to the east, Usama sauntered over.

"You're looking tired, *habibati*. Sleeping all right?"

She'd told him before they'd left for Aden that she was dreaming of the Sword of Sidon. Her friends worried when they saw her tumble from her hammock to clean her shaking hands in the sea. They watched silently when they caught her shivering in the tropical air because the winter wind had blown frigid into the cave, and Rami hadn't been able to speak from remembered pain.

"Sleeping is easy, resting is harder. But I've got it under control," she said, casting a smile his way.

Usama tipped his head back to grin up at the sun and soak in its rays. Then he took a long draught of his cup of coffee, made from some of the last free beans from Mocha, as he waited her out for more. Finally, he prompted her.

"You can control your dreams?" he asked.

"Can't everyone?"

"A lot of people probably wish they could, but no, most of us just get to sail into whatever nightmare we've been handed."

"I've never done it any other way. It's—" She reached for a metaphor. "Before James helped me escape Tadjoura, sometimes I would see the theatre troupes in the *souq*. Some characters would sit back, watching, and the whole play would go on without them. Then, they'd step in and start changing things. Once, a troupe from India, in the souq to sell Mysorean rockets, did a play about a woman named Draupadi and her five husbands." The rockets had been for defence, in theory; some of the boys had snagged them and set them off during Eid, nearly blowing themselves up and making the souq stink for weeks.

"Five?" he asked, voice going high.

She nodded with a grin.

"The scheduling must have been intense," he murmured mildly, and Noor chuckled.

Then she grew more serious. "In my dreams, it's as if when I step onto the stage, I can either follow the script or change it. I usually know the plot. I can step away from something if it's too frightening." *Or too disturbing.* "And I can move the plot another way, though it makes the dreams less vivid, paler."

"That's lucky. Do you know that they're *your* dreams though? Since you're sharing dreams, perhaps it's been the Sword of Sidon's dream you've been controlling—easing, perhaps. Maybe he can't control his dreams, even though you can when you're in them. Maybe you could teach him, give him something to hold on to while he waits for us to figure out what British cubbyhole he's been socked away in."

Usama spoke quietly under the waves' tapping against the hull. "But I'm still most worried about you, habibati. If you can find a way to get more rest, I'll be happy for you. I don't really care if it helps him. I'm just worried for you."

"I'll try." Noor checked the sun. She had a half day until she'd sleep again.

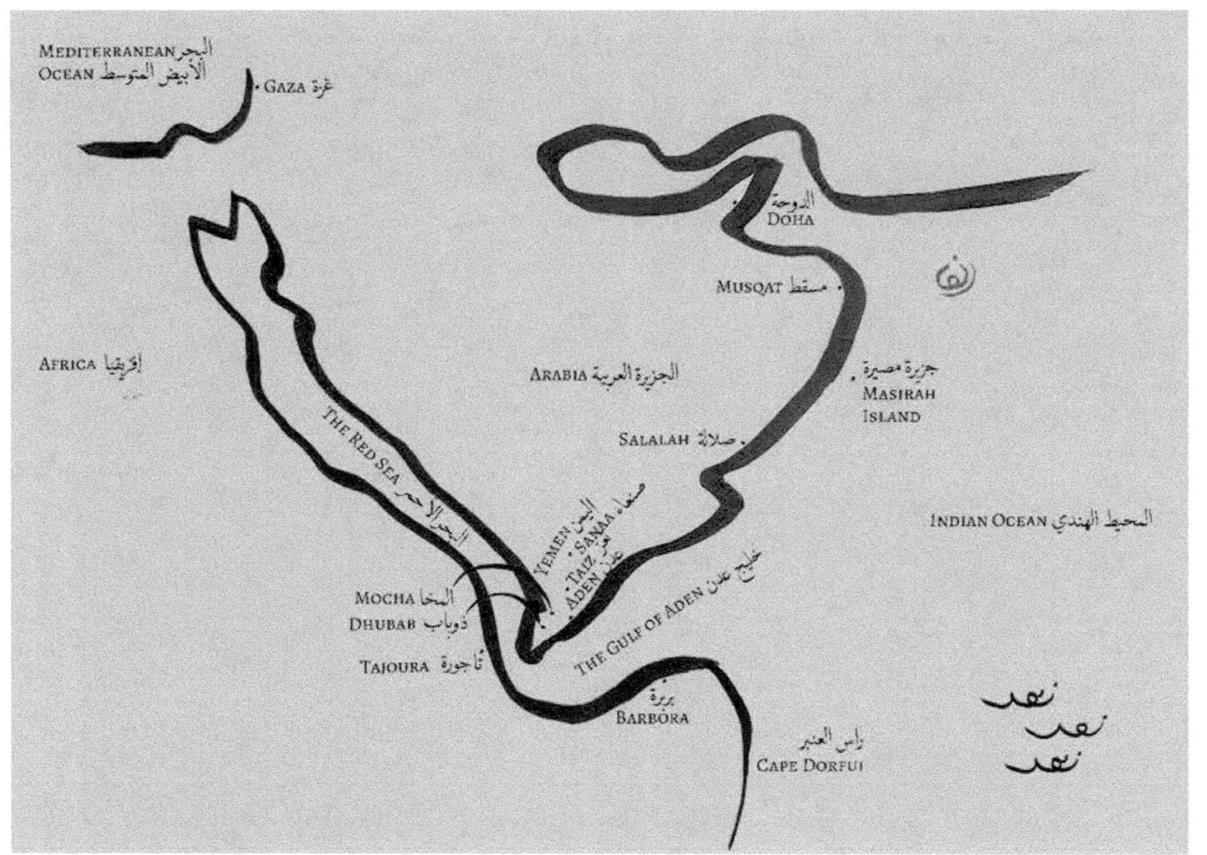
MEDITERRANEAN OCEAN البحر الأبيض المتوسط
GAZA غزة
AFRICA إفريقيا
الدوحة DOHA
MUSQAT مسقط
ARABIA الجزيرة العربية
جزيرة مصيرة MASIRAH ISLAND
SALALAH صلالة
INDIAN OCEAN المحيط الهندي
THE RED SEA البحر الأحمر
YEMEN اليمن
SANAA صنعاء
TAIZ تعز
ADEN عدن
خليج عدن THE GULF OF ADEN
MOCHA المخا
DHUBAB ذباب
TAJOURA تاجورة
بربرة BARBORA
رأس العنبر CAPE DORFUI

Chapter Two

NOOR MET RAMI in a dream again three days later. For three nights, she'd opened her eyes under the blue-grey waters off of Gaza and found herself alone. She'd searched and searched, once swimming far enough out to sea the currents took her, and no matter how hard she fought, she could not get back to land. She'd had to force herself awake before she drowned. Each night, when Noor had come back to the dream, she'd headed straight for shore. She tracked the sweep of the moon as she gathered firewood, prayed, and swam into other dreams, all the while stretching her growing magical senses out, searching for him.

On the third night, she awoke underwater and saw him right in front of her. His hair was a mess, his eyes wide and unseeing. He appeared wilder with her scar pale across his face. She wrapped her arms around his waist and dragged him to the surface, even as he struggled, trying to return to the dark, the quiet, the drowning deep that sometimes seemed to call him.

"Get off of me!" he sputtered.

She released him.

Rami immediately sank, the weight of his British Navy–issued winter coat tangling around his arms and feet. She gave him a moment to soften up and then dove down again. Hauling him up so his face was above the water, she then manoeuvred him, towing them both to the cove.

After he caught his breath, Rami started fighting again, struggling to get free, sinking when he succeeded. Her breath caught in her lungs as she dove again to yank him up.

"Stop," she snapped. "Just stop."

He didn't—because, of course, he didn't. Rami was here and not here. He didn't stop thrashing until she got him up onto the pale sand of the cave. She laid him on his back, and he writhed for a moment before settling down, anguish on his face, his eyes shut tight again.

Rami's hurts wrenched at her chest, and she said for the first time what she'd thought had been obvious. "This is a dream. You can control it."

When he squeezed his eyes tighter, she leaned forward and shook his blue wool collar hard enough to get his attention.

"You're dreaming. You can wake up if you don't want to be here."

He ignored her, his black hair covering his face and longer, more tangled than she remembered from their fight on the *Victory*. She thought he might be trying to get himself so mussed up, so tangled, that even when he had to open his eyes, he would only be able to see darkness.

Noor raised her hands slowly to his face, wanting to catch the thick strands and push them back behind his ears.

She stopped herself.

She didn't think it was pity that moved her, nor kindness, but something else. Like when she'd held an injured, hissing black cat in the souq and then healed it. Noor didn't require the things she cared for to appreciate her—*you'd die waiting for a cat to say thank you*—but she enjoyed the feeling of fixing a problem, even a small one. *It's a dream. What could it hurt?*

She smoothed his dark hair back so he could see.

He arched towards her touch, eyes shut, hunching his shoulder closer to her, trying to catch her hand with his cheek. He didn't raise his hands, did not try to touch her, but tracked her movement, following—what, the warmth of her? Or the tenderness of touch?

She got her fingers caught in a tangle and gentled her grip, but not before he winced and tried to lean away from her into the cold, wet sand at his back. It had no give to it, no more than her hands did. She changed the pressure and eased her fingers between the strands of hair, bringing them into some semblance of order as his breathing evened out, slowed. The texture of it fascinated her, thick and curling, nothing like her tightly kinked, sun-thinned hair. His was dark and rich, like Mocha coffee, like the scrap of velvet Mianning insisted was from his lady love. *Like the softest fur on the sweetest animal, but the kind of sweetness that hid a lion-toothed smile.*

Noor was so focused on his hair, on thoughts of whether his body in the waking world was in danger or had some semblance of peace, that it took a moment for her to realise he'd opened his eyes. Not entirely—just enough so he could see her through lashes so thick she didn't know if he could make her out. She kept her fingertips gentle against his scalp, and in a fluid movement, he turned to give her his back, his cheek on the soft cloth of her knees with his hair spread out across her palms. She wanted to push him, to turn him over, to tell him, *no, no, you don't know if you can trust me—I don't know if I can trust me with you.*

But here he was, trusting her.

She would have to do her best.

They had been dancing around this for the past three weeks. Getting more comfortable touching and being touched, a necessity when every dream started with her deadlifting him from the ocean.

Noor let her fingers trail from the back of his head to the sopping navy blue of his jacket, and he shivered.

"Are you cold?" she asked.

He shook again, not responding.

"Rami, you don't have to be cold. Imagine yourself in dry clothes. This is a dream."

He tensed, clenching his jaw so tight it made a muscle pop in his cheek. Rami held his back and stomach muscles stiff, perhaps trying to control his shaking. He covered his face with his arm, the wet cloth mussing the hair she'd just straightened.

"You can change it," Noor said with a thread of desperation. "You're in a dream, you don't—" She sighed; she was going about this in the wrong way. Noor raised her hand, closed her eyes, and then, a new and larger fire glowed, warm and crispy in front of them.

"Look, Rami, can you see the fire? Did you see any wood there before? How do we always have wood here in this deserted cave?"

He moved his arm away from his face and peered at the crackling fire through the mess he'd made of his hair.

"Someone must have left it." His voice was so much worse than usual, a ragged scrape.

"We're in a dream, Rami, one you can change if you want to."

He shook his head, and she sighed. She didn't want to force this, but she wanted him to have some place where he had some kind of choices, some kind of freedom.

Noor leaned over him a little, hands outstretched towards the fire, her clothes already drying. She'd imagined herself into an already-dry guntiino after they'd hit shore every night and cursed herself for taking this long to wonder why he always stayed in whatever clothes he started in. She had assumed it was contrariness, a personality trait she would now try to leverage.

"If I'm right, and it's a dream, what do you have to lose by proving me wrong?" she asked. "If it's a dream—"

"If this is a dream, then it means I have to wake up," he hissed.

She ran a hand over his back, trying to calm him. At his flinch, she yanked her hand away and paused, a sickness flooding her that the wetness on her hand was not just water, and the darkness of the jacket was not the navy fabric alone. It was stained through and through with blood.

"If this is a dream," Rami continued doggedly, "then I have to remember what happened before I sleep—and I don't want to. I want to be *here*. I want to be *here*." His voice strengthened as he spoke until, with a pained sound, he sat up between her and the fire and turned to face it, the broad expanse of his back within reach.

Noor reached out, gently, slowly. He held as still as the statues of Christian martyrs she'd seen at their churches in Gaza as she unhitched the jacket from his shoulders, and he let her draw it down off of his arms. She gathered it up and tossed it deeper into the cave. Then she searched under his collar for a hook or clasp for his undershirt. It was black, different from any shirt she'd seen him in on the *Victory*. A dress uniform? She fumbled for a moment.

"Here." Rami slipped his fingers under his hair at the nape of his neck, pinched them, and flicked his wrist. The cloth sagged, pulled to the next button that had been cleverly hidden inside the fabric. Noor undid it and then the next and the next, focused on stopping the rough fabric from scraping on the mess of his back.

Starlight shone through the cave entrance, its cool light brightened by the honey light of the fire. It illuminated the harsh red lines and curves scratched across the constellation of moles that freckled his dark skin and marked out the words: "Arab Lord."

Those two words, written over and over and over again across his back, dipped down below the waistband of his pants. Large and small, in different handwriting and blade widths, some had been written in ink, iron nibs scratching his skin, and others seemingly cut with a blade, perhaps a razor. Some still bled sluggishly. He turned away to hide the words, then fumbled to close the buttons as he scrambled to the other side of the blaze.

Noor held her palms up, streaked with his blood, "Rami, Rami, I won't pry. I won't touch you if—"

His eyes widened, his body began to shake again, and then he did something she couldn't have expected—he chuckled.

It was dark and harsh, but it was real.

"There's nothing I want less in the world than that. Yours has been the only kind touch I've felt—well, since Taiz."

She remained as neutral as she could, didn't let him see the agony that blossomed beneath her ribs at the thought of burning schools, fallen stone on small bodies, what followed that night, and his lonely adulthood under the so-called sultan's control. But something in her face made him move farther away from her all the same.

"I don't say this for *pity*, I *don't want pity*," he said, voice petulant and rushed.

She lowered one of her internal magical barriers, just a bit, to give him a sliver of the first memory she recalled, of him teaching her how to build those shields, their hands touching through the bars of her cell on the *Victory*.

The thing was, Noor had no idea what would happen in the breath right after she'd freed him from the British prison, had no idea what would happen the moment she got the manacles off his wrists. Would they be able to keep him long enough to bring him to the resistance for trial? Would he break free, go back to the British to exact revenge on Yemen's replacement sultan for deposing him? Fall into her arms? Go to war against the resistance? Become a fisherman? Go stark, raving mad, only lucid in his dreams? She kept those fears off her face and out of her heart, let him see only that she looked forward to better times.

But Rami stayed away, back bleeding, cloth gaping since he couldn't manage to button his jacket himself. She lowered her barriers further, needing him to understand what brought her here over and over again, to this minute, this moment, this place, this thought. She hoped he might be convinced he could heal himself or let her heal him, at least here in the dream, if he understood why she was here.

She decided to show Rami a vision of what she would do when she found him in the waking world, spooling the thought out as he stopped moving away from her—and more importantly, the warm light of the fire.

Noor hastily arranged her imaginings of how she would free him into rooms lining a corridor of the emira's compound. She placed thick wooden doors between him and everything she didn't want him to see in her mind. Then, she pulled him in. Noor only meant to show Rami one or two visions of the future. But as he stood beside her in the grey brick corridor, tall and healthy in a pure white *thobe*, she realised too late that none of the doors had locks, all of them swinging open in a warm breeze. Noor couldn't control what she revealed in this dream, nor keep the worst of her visions locked away. She wished with a finger-twisting, fervent hope that he would forgive her for what he was about to see.

*

IN HER FIRST vision, Noor found Rami on the ground of a barren, soulless cave, carved out of a cold, harsh grey rock, part of some abandoned mine. She lowered herself into the oubliette on a rope. Musket fire shattered stone above her head, but she just tucked her chin to her chest and levered open the bars of his cell. Rami sat in the tiny space, legs folded, hands on knees, straining to pray through the pain—because now, the Rami in the cell also had the words "Arab Lord" carved into him in unsealing blood.

Noor forced the bars and reached out her hand. He didn't acknowledge her. A magical wall blocked him from his magic, keeping him from knowing he was bare inches from freedom. Perhaps he couldn't even see the dank walls, dripping stones, the water of a thousand, thousand years working its way to the bottom of this chilly mine, leaving his hair mildewy.

Noor focused her haya magic, shoving at the wall with a growing wind, driving all her rage and her light, her pure *will* to save him. One slice, one crack appeared. Noor pushed, and there it was—a blast of air. Rami's eyes snapped to hers, and he stumbled to his feet. She tossed him a *jambiya*, and he grinned, twirling it between the manacles on his hands, prying them apart. Noor lowered the rope, and he began climbing, motivated by hope despite his damaged body. She followed, watching his magic catch and deflect the musket fire as she finished the ascent behind him.

Then that vision faded, the door closing as a second door opened.

This time, Noor found Rami in one of a long line of strange, clear glass cells, grouped in cubes of nine under a wicked yellow light. They were the kind she'd heard a drunk-and-terrified British deserter describe back in Tadjoura. He said they were one of the so-called sultan's concoctions. She'd hoped he was mad because she could not imagine this place being real. This vision of Rami's box barely gave him enough room to stretch his arms out, much less stand up.

This Rami was shaking, shivering in a temperature that would be comfortable for the wintery British but not for a man who'd grown up beneath the Yemeni sun.

Noor cut through the hard glass with her magic, and when he saw her ducked his head.

"Have you come to kill me?" he asked.

She remained quiet, whispering into his mind lest the guards hear her. *No, I'm here to save you.*

Rami hunched further. *You can't. No one can.*

Noor froze, waiting to see if a trap lay hidden in his horrible room. She found none, at least none she could see. She knelt, letting her knees hit the glass with a *crack*. Looking down, she saw a hundred, a thousand other prisoners, straight below in cube upon cube, and on either side of her, constant and following her forever, completely without mercy.

Noor held her hand out to Rami, but he didn't react. She waited, kneeling in front of him. A voice whispered from the lunella shell, connecting her with her crew—the signal that she had only a few breaths to get Rami out before the guards reached her. Noor gave up waiting, yanking his arm over her shoulder and heaved him up, his body limp against hers.

Rami could only shuffle, feet dragging, eyes dull, no light coming into them when he saw the *Cormorant*. His body remained chilled no matter how many blankets she piled on him.

After weeks, Noor realised what no one would tell her: he wouldn't come out of this. She was in charge of a vegetable, an untrained nurse for a formerly untamed man. Her temperament was totally unsuited for his care, but he had no one else to step up for him. No one cared enough to try.

Noor recognised the plot of the third vision as it unwound. She strained to scramble back, to force herself away. She couldn't stop it. The ball had left the musket and she knew Rami watched it unfold with her.

Noor found Rami in a prison with no cells, only rolling grass beside an ornamental lake near Karachi, surrounded by high white walls. He smiled and laughed with other high-born criminals around a delicacy-laden table. The lord admiral was there, as was the new so-called sultan. Rami seemed safe and sane, and he—he laughed at her when she ran towards him, bloodied from fighting her way past the guards. He appeared well-rested, and his expression was hard. He guffawed when she told him about the dreams. Rami stage-whispered to his companions that her dreams were his idea of jokes, his tricks, something he came up with to pass the time, to lure her to capture. He lazily called the guards. They dragged her into a much worse version of that prison, the British, holding her responsible for resistance crimes she did not commit. This Rami laughed as they hurt her, just laughed and laughed and laughed.

Noor finally wrenched them out of that vision, only to fall into one she wasn't sure how she knew about, a room she hadn't allowed herself to set foot in for fear of what it might contain.

In this vision, Noor found Rami bleeding on the floor of a prison cell. He looked as he did now, damaged but not beaten. She stretched her hand through the bars of his cell, and he rushed to her. He threaded his arms between them to wrap around her waist. Noor pressed closer and gripped the nape of his neck, their foreheads held apart only by iron. He pulled away, but she caught his hand, turned it over, and pressed her cold lips to the smooth, undamaged skin of his inner wrist.

"I thought I would never find you," she whispered, surrounded by the smell of him, fantasy pleasant in this dreaming moment. She felt safe in these dreams and basked for a stolen moment in his touch, the reality of him, his smile, his welcoming her help, her *self*. There was a hole in her dream self's belly, aching and raw, that she never knew was there until she had Rami with her again and found it filled. But it lasted only as long as they were touching, only as long as she could count on his hand in hers. Noor squeezed his wrist tight and pressed her lips to it again.

"I knew you would come for me," Rami said, and then he stood back as she drew her jambiya out. She pried open the lock and pulled him out, and he fell into her, arms encircling her, his body warm and whole. Not unharmed—not even in her fantasy did she have that hope—but *whole*. He wasn't in pieces; he wasn't vague and gone. He was hers, and she was his.

The vision let them both go, and they faded back to their surroundings in the cave.

*

FIRST, SOUNDS RETURNED: the break of the water on the stony shore, the pop and crackles of the fire, Rami's controlled breathing.

Then, smells: blood mixed with the salt from the ocean and a whiff of woodsmoke.

Noor sucked a breath between her teeth and kept her eyes closed, the flames dancing red-orange on her eyelids.

She waited for the sound of him moving away. Perhaps his rage at her presumption or offence at her visions of his weakness will have taught him to control his dreams where her words could not. She listened as he stood, stepped around the fire, came nearer to her, until Noor needed to know what he was doing and opened her eyes.

He met her gaze, dark eyes bright in the firelight as he lowered himself to sit beside her. She could have taken a deep breath and pressed their knees together.

She didn't.

Noor was too sure she'd made a fool of herself with this opening up. Even without that, she needed him to have the space to choose if she was something he wanted. And he needed to do it in a time and place when she wasn't undoing him piece by piece. Some part of her knew that, even as she dreamed, her sleeping body lay beside Razan's. Razan, whose heart she did not wish to injure and whose views about Rami she knew all too well. Noor wasn't sure how she could reconcile her dreaming and waking worlds or the fantasies that flew between them. She had no idea how to braid together her fields of feelings and seas of emotions with the scars and histories of these two people whose lives and bodies and souls intersected with hers. But she knew there must be a way; she could feel it in her very bones.

Rami held his hands out to the flames, light flickering through them as he warmed his palms.

"I could see the truth of some of your visions," he said. "The circumstances I am in are most like the first one, but—" His eyes remained fixed on the light. "—if I had to choose a way to see you again in the waking world, I would choose the last one."

Noor leaned back on her hands, letting the firelight sweep across her knees and thighs, letting the barest press of her arm against his send a vision she could not explain.

She made herself tell the truth. "Me as well."

His bare back still bled.

She paused for a moment and then asked, "Would you mind if I healed you?"

He froze, hands covering his face before making an aborted gesture, perhaps to redo the buttons, perhaps something else. She didn't know.

Finally, he sagged. "If you would. Even if it only holds through the end of this dream, I would welcome a few pain-free breaths."

She examined his back. The only way she knew how to heal was skin-to-skin contact, and she would need to rest her whole palm somewhere. The hard curve of his waist was the only area free of marks.

"If something stings, worse than a healing should, tell me immediately. Don't wait." She paused, considering where it might be safe to touch him and held a hand out to his other side.

"Squeeze my hand if you need me to stop." Noor meant it to be practical, aware of her own inability to verbalise when she was in a world of hurt. But the moment his palm touched hers, she was thrown back into that last vision, the feeling of her lips on his skin. She shunted that away and focused on the harm that had been done.

"All right, I'm going to start," she said, and he laced his fingers through hers just as her palm touched his bare skin, and she pulled on that long thread that connected her to haya magic.

"It's not even accurate," she grumbled to herself. The thought nagged at her, kept her afloat, stopped her from sinking into her magic.

"Hmm?" Rami queried, slow breaths marking the rise and fall of his bowed spine, hand tight on hers.

"'Arab Lord,'" Noor said. "You're not a 'lord'. We don't have 'lords'. We have emirs and sheikhs and sometimes sultans. That British bastard who called himself your master, the so-called sultan, at least he got the title right. They don't know what they're talking about."

Rami chuckled and then hissed as the motion disturbed the cuts on his back. "The British aren't really ones for the fine details about the peoples they—" He sucked a breath in as she began healing him in earnest.

The wave of feeling swept her under. The closeness, the warmth, the heat of the fire on the back of her knuckles, the slow swell of his back as he breathed in through his nose, out through his mouth—it was like the gentlest turn on a ship she'd ever experienced, thrumming in waves through her and through him.

Noor spread out his injuries, mapped them, and started at the most aching and debilitating parts. She poured a golden energy into his muscles, torn from writhing, then flowed healing over them, knitted them back together until they were strong and loose, tension fading. Noor found the markers, the little hints from when she'd healed Rami on the *Victory*. A small part of her hated his jailers for undoing all her hard work healing him in the first place. Noor moved to his blood vessels, buttoning their skins closed again like one of Rami's heavy jackets.

She'd stood outside the butcher's stall in the market in Tadjoura for many long afternoons, waiting for him to cut down Musa's order. She'd watched him wield his knife, and in quiet moments, asked to learn, to see how skin and muscle, veins and blood, bone and sinew fit together. It had thrown her, the day it had finally pulled together in her mind like a language. Bodies had their own grammar, their own syntax and needs. Cobbled together with their histories written in their very internal structures, they told their stories just by what they were. When her magic had come to her, saved her, it had seemed as simple as breathing to learn how to use it to stich others back together in the same way she'd been pulled together in the Imam's house. Human or dugong, it didn't really matter: if a living thing could bleed, she could heal it.

Then, Noor began on the lower levels of skin. Rami had started playing his fingers over the back of her hand, gentle brushes across the tendons and veins, a rhythm setting the tempo for the flow of haya magic and warm healing into his body.

After the last of the skin, Noor focused on the many—too many—surface cuts. Wetness covered her cheeks at the thought of how long he must have been face down as this was done to him. She could tell from how his muscles had torn and from his strains and bruises that he'd been tied down. Her mind shied away from that image, the horrible, helpless hurt, as he slipped his thumb between their palms and swept it across her lifeline, exploring back and forth. Rami brought her back, reconnected her to the magic, to her intention, as she finished moulding his body back together again.

Noor took a last pass through, easing bruises and resettling bones from past beatings. She knew none of this would help in the real world. Rami would awaken in hours to these bleeding cuts, strained muscles, and bruised bones. But perhaps he would rest better and heal more while doing so if he was without pain. Noor didn't know if that was how it worked, but she couldn't bear to watch him bleed and not try to help.

When Noor came back to herself, she had rested the side of her tear-wet face on the warm, healed skin of his broad shoulder, both arms around his waist as he played his fingers over her hands, her wrist, tracing the thin lines of her bones.

Before she let go, she let herself feel this thread-hung moment. A different kind of magic lay in holding someone's hand, which had nothing to do with magic and everything to do with the power of insistent bodies. Hands were the most solid thing about a person. They got you your food, and they helped you fight. They showed you your first ideas of the world as a baby, touching everything. Hands could become fists to protect you, could touch softly enough to turn the page of a book or slap hard enough to end a marriage. And sometimes, only with people one trusted, when one really *needed* it, two hands together could open up a perfect, doubled, un-doubleable thing. One's reality could touch theirs and fill up the entire world with the exact sensation they were feeling. Holding hands with someone one cared for was one of the most intimate things Noor could think of.

She let go.

Her arms ached with exhaustion from the work of healing, but Noor redid all but the top button of his jacket, giving him cover and some of his armour back. Then she pulled away, worried she'd pushed a boundary too far. But he turned, knelt to face her, and grabbed her arms, holding on tight. When she kept pulling away, he let her go.

"Thank you, Noor," he said, voice warm and soft.

She glanced towards the fire. They had another few hours before he woke.

"Lie down with me?" Rami said, and immediately, Noor's blood didn't know whether to race for her face or someplace else entirely.

Rami coughed and clarified. "Rest with me. Healing, even in a dream, can take it out of a person. There's a warm fire and no danger here tonight; you can rest."

With her eyelids already heavy with sleep, she lay on her side. Rami settled on his back beside her, and his pinkie brushed hers, calluses catching and skin so warm.

Rami rolled his head to the side, looked at her for a long moment, and played his fingers closer to hers.

Then, Noor locked her critical thoughts in a corner cabinet of her mind and, in one movement, slung her leg over his, pillowed her head on his mostly dry chest, and listened to that big, bruised, heartbeat. She listened and counted the beats—*alive and here, alive and here*, it said—until she drifted off, knowing that for this minute, he was safe and sound enough for her to rest.

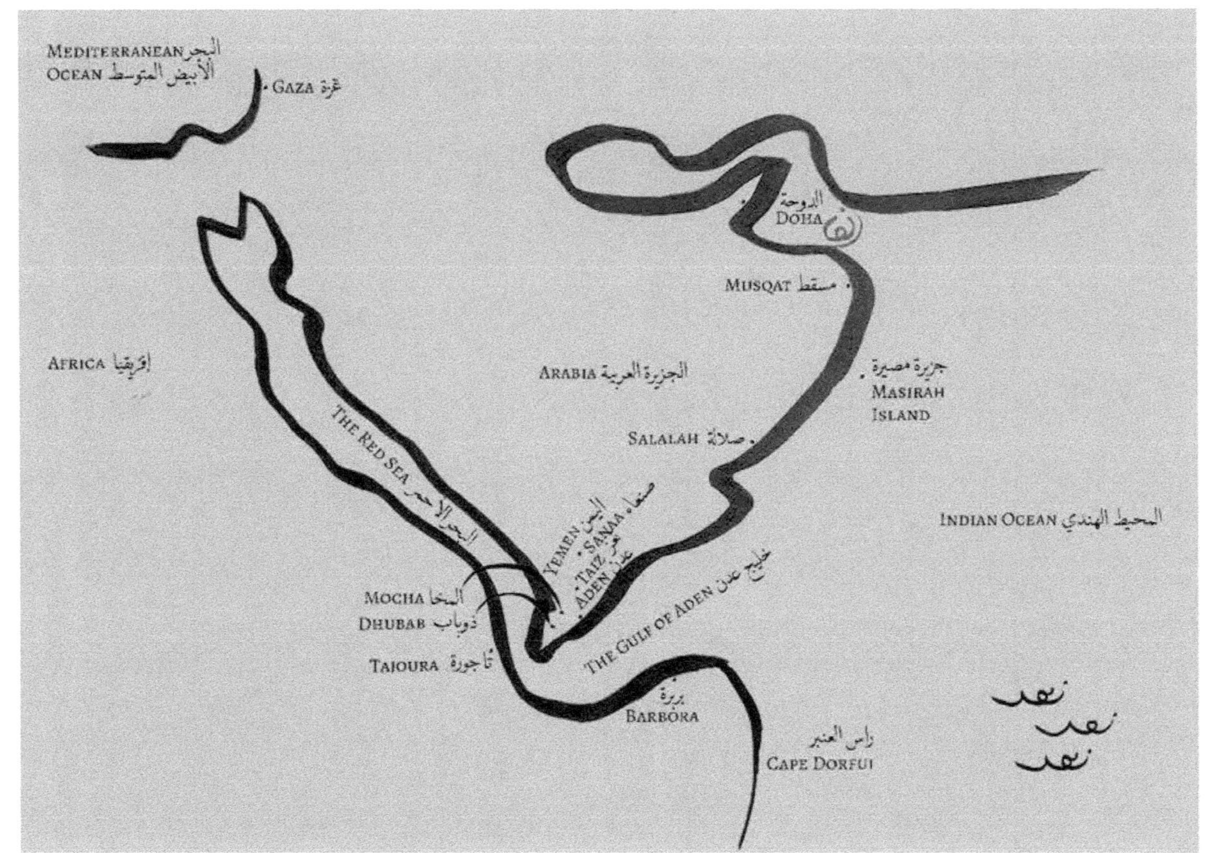

MEDITERRANEAN OCEAN البحر الأبيض المتوسط
GAZA غزة
AFRICA إفريقيا
الدوحة DOHA
MUSQAT مسقط
ARABIA الجزيرة العربية
جزيرة مصيرة MASIRAH ISLAND
SALALAH صلالة
INDIAN OCEAN المحيط الهندي
THE RED SEA البحر الأحمر
YEMEN اليمن
صنعاء SANAA
TAIZ تعز
ADEN عدن
THE GULF OF ADEN خليج عدن
MOCHA المخا
DHUBAB ذوباب
TAJOURA تاجورة
بربرة BARBORA
رأس العنبر CAPE DORFUI

Chapter Three

NOOR STRETCHED AND sat upright, feeling warmer than she had any right to and entirely at a loss for how to explain what had happened in that dream. Razan slept easily on the hammock below hers. *Maybe a day piloting them to Doha to meet with Usama's spy will give me enough time to figure out what* that *was all about.*

Noor climbed to the top deck and grabbed some dried mangoes for breakfast, then joined Usama at the wheel. He gave her a brilliant smile. She remembered it was the first time in a few days his and James's rest shifts would overlap.

"Go on. I'm sure James is waiting," she said with a smile.

Usama started for the captain's quarters, then paused. "How'd it go, habibati?"

She shrugged. "Looks like you were right. He didn't know he could change his dreams. The thing that's blocking his access to magic may be keeping him from controlling them too." Noor had decided after that first morning, after what had happened with the council and Razan, that she would keep the details of what was happening to Rami to herself. Not even the emira would know. It also felt like something Rami wouldn't want shared if he had a choice.

Usama looked like he wanted to continue, fiddling with the key around his neck before smirking.

"Rami's always been stubborn, even when I used to babysit him—"

At Noor's delight, he flapped his hands to shoo her away.

"That's a story for a morning when I haven't been piloting this junk overnight without a break. Catch me when I'm rested, and maybe I'll share."

"I'll do that," Noor replied as he left.

She shared part of the shift with Mianning, who nodded at her on his way out of the hold, on his way to mending ropes. She checked their location. Usama had taken them through the Strait of Hormuz overnight, and they were only a half day away from Doha. As Noor studied the maps, Razan staggered up on deck, bleary-eyed. She never really was a morning person, Noor thought fondly.

"We're docking at the island in the middle of the bay, right?" Noor called over to her once Razan had a chance to have some food and get a bit more prepared for the world.

"More of a sandbar. But if the last monsoon season didn't obliterate it, that's where we'll meet our guide." Razan pulled out the chart she'd made for their approach.

"Sounds good." Noor said and drifted into silence, aware of Razan's gaze, heavy on the side of her face. But when she looked, Razan turned to stare fixedly down at the map.

Noor checked the horizon and found it as vast and empty as before. She scraped a fingernail against carvings in the thick cedar of the wheel as she let the swells and rhythms of the sea ease the tension in her body.

She thought back on the night before. *Why had she let Rami see those visions inside her? What did it mean that he wanted them, wanted that with her? Had he'd felt it before he was imprisoned? Was this some kind of captive's disease, him latching on to the only kind thing in his world? And what did that make her if she took advantage?*

Noor wanted to ask someone for help, for advice. But she didn't think Razan was up for it. Razan had never objected to any of the things

Usama, James, and the council had said about the Sword of Sidon. And her agony over losing her family was justifiably raw.

Noor had another thought, one Razan could probably help her with. "What do you think Emira Arwa will do with him when we get her son back?"

"I don't know—I thought she was going to figure that out once we return with him?"

A wave of exhaustion suddenly hit Noor, and she gripped the wheel.

"That had been my plan, back at the palace," she said slowly. "Everything seemed possible and simple there."

Razan's eyes found hers, full of worry and anger and curiosity. Noor tried to focus on that curiosity and a blazing need to know the world that had drawn her to Razan in the first place.

"But that was nearly a month ago," Noor continued. "A month of handing out shells to all of Usama's spies and waiting and waiting, and the Gulf is so *big*."

Now that she had started talking, she couldn't seem to stop. "I know the British haven't tried to take Aden again and probably can't until after the winter monsoon season has passed. We have no idea what their plan is, how long they will keep him. They could kill him today, and we'd never know. I'd never— Will I keep seeing Gaza in my dreams, seeing that lagoon, forever and ever, always empty, always me alone?"

Her breath hitched. "And if we get him, and if the resistance passes judgement on him, what would that look like? What would that take?"

"I don't know," Razan repeated, rising. She reached a tentative hand for Noor's shoulder, and when Noor sagged into her, gathered her up in her arms.

"Noor, do you need to talk about it?" Razan murmured. And then she squared her shoulders. "I-I can listen if you need me to."

Noor closed her eyes. "I keep thinking of the Ottoman executions I saw in Tadjoura," she whispered. "Hangings, mostly. A drowning, back when I was little. They sewed her up in a bag. It was *horrible*. No drawing and quartering, nothing like what the British do to their own people. But death is death. And the thought of that happening to Rami—" She choked, then continued.

"The so-called sultan whipped him bloody right in front of me on the *Victory*. I got through it at the time, had been through it before, because beatings, whippings, you can survive those. But death, there is no coming back from that, no redemption, no resolution, just a spirit leaving and meat left behind."

"I always wondered how the so-called sultan kept control over such a big man, why Rami never left."

"It isn't always possible to leave even the worst of situations." Noor held her voice steady, but only by the skin of her teeth.

"Noor, I didn't mean—" Razan held her tighter, and Noor slowly relaxed into her body again. But the thought kept coming back to her. It burst out of her.

"Am I freeing him only to have him executed?"

Noor couldn't solve her mixed-up feelings about last night's dream, but this she could do something about. "Will you call the emira with me to ask?"

Razan leaned back, meeting her eyes. "If that's what you need right now, then yes."

Noor found her lunella shell and reached out to the emira's aide, who she'd been told to contact with updates. A wave jostled the boat, and Razan took the shell, letting Noor get both hands on the wheel. Her grip on the steady cedar was like being held in another way.

The emira's assistant answered, and after a few breaths, the emira's voice came through the shell.

"Noor, this is unexpected. Have you found him?" Her voice was low, but Noor thought she could detect a hint of worry, a bit of anticipation.

"No," she answered. "I'm sorry. But what I called about was—"

"And Razan"—Emira Arwa raised her voice over the *muezzin's* athan, the call to prayer echoing in the background—"Mianning, James, and Usama, how are they doing?"

"I am well, Emira," Razan said. "We are getting closer to the next imperial prison in Doha. What Noor called about was—"

"We're doing well here as well," the emira said. "After prayers, I will be opening up the court for this month's criminal cases—"

"That's exactly what I'm calling about," Noor said, wincing as she interrupted her. "What's going to happen to Rami after we get him back?"

Noor waited through a pause.

After hearing nothing but the waves, Razan said, "Did we lose you?"

"No, Razan, you still have me here. I can tell you what I know. The few imperialists we have captured have been tried by a jury of the people in the resistance and sentenced by them. Some have been given prison sentences, some work details, some exile. And some...some have been executed. Those who burned villages and boats, who took children. It's rare, but it is a possibility. And we've never tried someone as high-ranking or who has done as much harm as my son."

More quiet followed, filled by the lapping of the waves, while Noor tried to think.

"Was that all?" The emira asked.

"I think we should tell the resistance what's happening to him." Noor replied, running on instinct, her mouth going faster than her mind.

She could hear the emira starting to interrupt and reached for Razan's hand, squeezing it, begging for her support, and Razan gripped back.

"Look," Noor said, bullying through, "I'm going to get him back. And he deserves to be tried for what he did"—she met Razan's eyes—"even if that ends in prison or execution. The people he whipped to feed his magic and killed by serving the British Empire on the *Victory* deserve justice." The first glimmer of understanding Noor had seen in weeks showed on Razan's face.

Noor spoke to the cedar at her feet, choosing her words carefully.

"Justice is what I want. I think you do too. But if the punishment is pain for pain, I don't think that will help anyone heal their war wounds. Or maybe it will; I can't speak for them. But knowing how Rami's already being punished, badly, in ways that the resistance would never require? Maybe that will help his jury sentence him fairly. I don't think they can if they're only working from memories of Sidon and the *Victory*.

"But if the resistance finds out he's alive, *and* we've been trying to save him with the council's grudging blessing, *and* he was broken but *now* he's all right? How can they make a fair judgement without knowing the whole story? If we let people know *now* that we're going to get him, that he's imprisoned, and we give them news about what's being done to him, maybe they can make the right call."

Noor tried to get her exhausted thoughts in order. "I don't want him to be hurt more than he has already been. Exile is one thing, but torture—"

"My son is being tortured?" Emira Arwa said, her voice harsh.

Noor had a lot of reasons to keep those details to herself, and all of them withered under the emira's brutal tone.

"Yes. I'm sorry for not telling you before, Emira. His living conditions have never been good, but when we communicated last night—" Noor didn't know what to share, what not to.

A cold silence followed, and then, "What are they doing?"

Noor swallowed and forced herself to speak. "They've been cutting him, carving things into his back."

Razan froze beside her.

"Carving what?" the emira said.

Noor wished she'd never called. "I-I don't know if—"

"Noor, if we're going to run an internal sympathy campaign for my son, argue he's suffered enough for his crimes, then I need to know everything that is going on. I don't know why you've kept this from me, kept it from everyone, but that needs to stop now."

Her iron-cast voice softened. "I don't know who made you feel we weren't on the same side here, but I want Rami back—in one piece and repentant—and I'm willing to do the work to make that happen. The British Navy may run horrible prisons, but they aren't *all* butchers. So, if I have the details of Rami's treatment, I can use some of my diplomatic contacts to get more information. Maybe even some help if they decide to sue for peace. But I need you to tell me what's happening."

Noor closed her eyes, saw the blood, black stains spreading over his navy jacket, under her nail beds. "'Arab Lord.' They're carving 'Arab

Lord' over and over into his back. Writing it, too, with iron nibs on their pens so it tears his skin up."

Noor sped up, trying to get it all out before the emira interrupted her. "It's getting worse; they're not giving him as much time to heal. I think some nights, when I don't see him, it's because they haven't allowed him to sleep at all. If they stop him sleeping entirely, I won't be able to help him, won't be able to see him—" She caught her tongue between her teeth, breathing harshly as Razan wrapped her arms around her. Noor gripped Razan's forearm with her free hand, holding on to her like a lifeline.

"I just want to get him out of there," she said, low and firm.

"We will, Noor. Your idea of biasing a potential jury pool is a good one, but we may be able to do more than that. His treatment at the prison guards' hands is either a fulfilment of their orders from the imperial navy, which will make excellent propaganda to pull their support from wavering tribes, or it's a violation of those orders, in which case we may be able to get some clandestine help from the empire in his retrieval." There was a pause, and her voice modulated from emira to mother.

"And Noor, I'm going to ask you to do something difficult. I need you to give my assistant regular reports on his condition. She'll share them with the entire lunella shell network, using my shell. You should tell him you're doing this and why. It sounds like you're helping him, or he wouldn't keep inviting you into his dreams. I don't want to harm that relationship. But I'm going to start a daily update on his status for my commanders to build support for him here and to keep our contacts fully informed. And I hope it will help you too. I know it can feel as if you're helping by keeping such things to yourself, as though you're protecting the people around you, but this much weight is too much for any one person to carry. That's why he's reaching out to you. And that's why you need to *tell your crew*. Not just Razan—James and Usama and Mianning too. Mianning, especially, as he's loved him since he was a little boy. He'll fight like hell to save him. They need to understand what you're going through."

Noor felt wrung out, her bones wobbly with exhaustion, as she said, "I'll try."

"Good girl," Emira Arwa said and then called out to her assistant, who had probably listened to the whole conversation. "Expect to get regular reports on my son's status and distribute them as widely as possible. Razan, are you there?"

"I am, Emira."

"The other survivors of Sidon will be furious. I am not asking you to speak on his behalf—"

"I can't—"

"I know. But I want you to be prepared for what happens next. I can make it clear I ordered you, that this mission was not your choice—"

Razan paused, and then, "No need for that. I chose to come here. Like Noor said, I want justice. Most of us do, under all the fear and fury. I hope my being here helps them see that justice will be done."

"I hope so too," the emira said. "I'll handle Sheikh Koroma. This will light his beard on fire like nothing else."

She took a deep breath, and Noor could imagine her dark eyes clouding.

"Noor, I know Rami will hate it, the talk about him, about what's happening to him. He was always watched as a child, everyone praising him for his power, wanting him to reflect back on them, orbiting him like little moons. Others were afraid of him. He was so filled with magic he shook the palace with his tantrums, scared the other children, terrified the horses. For most mages, their connection to the haya magic comes as soon as they have reached adulthood, the magic seeking a stable vessel before then. Sometimes, it comes later or earlier, in a time of great joy or pain or a return to health, but that is rare. Those whose first touch of magic comes from hurting are often drawn to the alam, and those who dip into its currents in a moment of joy are drawn to the haya. Rami's birth had been hard. He was born breech. We thought for long hours he would die. But the pain of it, mine and his, awakened his powers far too early for him or me to control. The camels wouldn't even let me ride them when I carried him in my arms."

The emira sounded as if she was talking to herself, but this was the first time Noor had heard any stories about Rami's childhood. She soaked them up as the desert sand drinks the first spring rain, and all the while, Razan watched her thoughtfully.

"I didn't think it was because he was made for alam magic," the emira continued, "no matter what his teacher who escaped Taiz told me later. And I didn't know until much later—I *didn't know* that his teacher had become Wahhabi, had met with al-Wahhab or the fanatics he inspired to fight against the Ottoman Empire. I didn't *know* that he had returned to believing people who were drawn to alam magic should be eradicated, not just taught control and kept an eye on as we'd always done." Regret poured through her voice like a great beast in deep water.

"I love him, Noor, as any mother would, but if you get him back, he will face justice. A resistance trial for his crimes against his people. He will face us, not the brutality of the British Empire, but his own people and their fair and full judgement of him. It's what he deserves."

After a pause, the emira added, "And Noor?"

Noor hunched forward to listen closely.

"Do not ever keep something like this about my son from me again, or you will see a side of me you will not like. Are we clear?"

Noor gulped. "Of course."

The channel went dead, and she sucked in a huge breath, Razan's arms around her moving with the motion.

"That went well," Noor said before burying her face in Razan's shoulder.

*

NOOR SENT THE first dispatch to the emira as they were pulling into Doha's bay: *"Rami ibn Arwa wa Nuri is being tortured by the British while in prison. The crew of the* Cormorant *and I are retrieving him for trial by his own people. More tonight."*

Doha was a study in yellows, desert on desert on desert with a massive, repurposed Portuguese fort crouching on the edge of the curving bay. They anchored the *Cormorant* beside the largest sandbar in the harbour on which stood a broad branching sidra tree. The faint call of the *dhuhr* prayer and interweaving cries of many muezzin echoed across the turquoise water. Noor leaned her elbows on the cedar gunwale next to James, her jambiya concealed inside her guntiino, and watched as Usama's spy edge his tiny *dhow* towards them through the shallow, warm waters of the Gulf. James would accompany her into Doha since his English was fluent and Usama's best suited for survival purposes only.

He called himself Ian Tone. A conscripted Irishman, his shock of black hair lay greasily across his forehead, and his pale skin was patchy with sun overexposure. He worked at the prison as a cleaner. Usama had told them that Ian had been disillusioned with his home country's inclusion in the so-called United Kingdom. Ian had told Usama he hoped for help getting new work outside the prison in exchange for his intelligence.

Once Tone had pulled up next to the sandbar, Noor and James climbed down the *Cormorant*'s ladder and boarded his boat. Ian reviewed the day's plan as he piloted the dhow through green-tinted waves.

"We'll pretend you are executors of a Keralan merchant's estate. You've been charged with investing his riches to sustain his grandchildren for their lifetimes. You are looking for a place for his former servants to work to earn good wages for themselves and profits for his house. That will also protect the *Cormorant*, since I believe she still flies the Keralan flag,"

It was one flag among dozens from other states Noor 'flew', but she didn't feel the need to share that. Ian spoke up again as he negotiated his way into the shallows near the base of the Portuguese fort.

"I got the update on the enchanted shell Usama's man gave me last week," he said, his whinging tone implying the gift had been an imposition. "Just before I picked you up, I heard tell there are accusations that the British are torturing the Sword of Sidon. That bastard deserves it, but I've never seen our people do something like that. And if we did, that means I have to get out of here sooner than I'd planned—" He shook his head before turning to them. "Am I leaving with you? Usama said I had to wait, that I knew things about the British no one else could find out. But look, if the officers are abusing people, I want out."

"No." *Better to be honest than get his hopes up.* "We're only going farther into British territory," Noor said. "Nowhere that will be safe for you to go if you defect. But we'll tell the emira what a help you've been. And Usama is right. We have so few true contacts in this part of the British Empire that you may be our only hope of getting the Sword of Sidon back and harnessing his power for the resistance."

"Good luck with that, ma'am. A bastard like him is better off overboard than taking up space on a dhow."

Noor kept her face blank as James glanced at her, but then they were docking and hopping onto the gently shifting dunes. Noor adjusted the scarf she'd tossed over her shoulders but kept it off her hair. She hadn't covered in Tadjoura, hadn't covered in Aden, and she wasn't going to do it here to fit in with whatever stories the soldiers might have come up with about Muslim women.

The Portuguese fort was set back from the water. As they walked across open sand, Noor let her magical senses drift wide. James asked just the right questions, getting morsel after titbit after nibble of information from Ian about how mages were handled in the prisons.

"How do you keep them from just, leaving?" James asked with a mildly curious tone. "If they are powerful enough to wreck empire flagships, surely some bars and muskets would be no issue for them."

"That would be our best-kept secret," Ian said slyly. "You'll see."

They approached the gate to the fort, and the sweating British guards there waved them through.

"Usama asked me to find out something specific last time he and I spoke on his contraption, and I just did this morning," Ian whispered, his breath stinking. "The location of the other two prisons where they keep mages."

He paused for effect, and at Noor's flat stare, continued, "It's Muscat and Salalah. But you won't be able to get in. There's no one like me there, and they're on serious lockdown. All the guards are tested for magical interference, and the names of the prisoners is a closely held secret. I only found out who was holding mages with a little"—he rubbed his fingers together—"*baksheesh.*"

Noor kept her face neutral, even at his poor pronunciation of an Egyptian-Arabic word for bribery that had no real currency in this part of the world.

"Those are the only two places where you're holding mages?" James asked. "What happened to the rest of them?"

Ian shrugged a shoulder. "Don't know, don't care. Probably drowned them all in the sea like bad kittens." Ian's face twisted when he spoke of mages, his sunburned skin nearly cracking with the force of his disgust. Noor had known many men like him, men who hated magic.

When they reached the warden's office, Noor had expected to have to give their entire cover story again, but the warden didn't seem to care. Perhaps it was normal for people to come in and gawk at the prisoners in his care.

Inside the high stone walls of the fort, Noor kept her eyes wide open, counted corners, and studied joints to see where she and James might need to blow a hole through for escape. She carefully avoided the eyes of the prisoners who hung on their bars and watched her walk freely. She refocused when Ian started telling James about a British religious festival, one Noor had seen celebrated in Gaza's oldest churches.

"Christmas is the only night of the year all of our prisoners can request to go outside. We let them see the glory of the stars the same way the Three Wise Men did. Only those prisoners who know the tradition know to ask. But any who ask can go outside for a Christmas Eve service in the harbour as a demonstration of our Regent's charity and goodwill to all his subjects."

"When is the British Christmas again?" Noor asked. She knew it was a different date from Coptic Christmas and Ethiopian Christmas and different still from the Eastern Orthodox Christmas she'd seen celebrated at St. Porphyrius's Church in Gaza. *Christians and their schisms.*

"I forget how ignorant blasphemers can be—it's in a week," Ian replied. "Our preparations are nearly ready." He babbled on again about specially imported food called 'mince-fruit pies' and some kind of colourful decorations made of plants. A few moments later, James got him back onto the topic of mages.

"We only have one mage held here in Doha," Ian said. "Captain Sean O'Reilly. He was a fluke. The only one in his family to feel the call to evil. It's only one in ten thousand children who are cursed with magic, is what I've heard."

Ian paused, considering. "O'Reilly's an old man now, but he enjoys visitors. He's been here for years," he added, his tone a mix of condescension and fondness.

James glanced at Noor, who turned to Ian.

"What was he convicted of?" she asked.

"Oh," Ian said. "I don't ask that question. But I heard he deserted the British Army at Mysore, hired himself and his crew out on a slave ship, but was caught in Africa somewhere. Or maybe he was on the wrong side of something when he was a young man, got caught up with the wrong influences." He shook his head. "It happened wars and wars ago."

They turned a corner to a long hallway with iron-barred cells lining it on either side. That was all Noor caught because she thought they'd come under attack. She couldn't hear, couldn't see, couldn't *feel*. Only James's hand on her elbow kept her steady and moving forward.

Breathe.

Breathe.

Breathe.

The world was colourless, muted, vacant. Magic-less. Noor wanted to run outside into the harsh desert sun and escape the sensory amputation that was the world without magic. She had lived with magic's presence, its hum, glow, and embrace these past few months. At this point, it was as much a part of her than any given limb, and now it was *gone.*

She tried to look normal as she struggled to adjust but mustn't have done a very good job of it because James pulled her into a squat with him, turning them both towards cell bars to hide her blanched face.

"Noor, are you good?" he whispered in halting Arabic as Ian

quieted, observing them.

She caught a bit of movement through the bars, inches from her face, and she gasped.

There, the cell was not full of men, but—something else entirely.

Long, forked tongues flicked the air. Curved and shining claws tipped massive paws. Long mouths held just as many teeth as a crocodile's. Thick tails swished.

A little colour bled back into the world as Noor realised their skin was purple. Riotous, violent purple.

"What the—"

"They sure are something, aren't they," Ian said, standing over James and Noor's stooped bodies. "They're our secret weapon. No mage can work witchcraft within sight or smell of a urodela."

"How?" James breathed.

"Something in their blood, I'm told. The effect is limited to a few long strides, but the more urodelas, the wider the barrier."

Noor, still trying to breathe, gaped at the giant, woman-sized lizards. Two of them shared what looked like two cells with the central wall removed so they could waddle easily between them. One creature was as long as Noor was tall, its scales a pulsing violet. It had a thick, mauve-coloured underbelly and fine, almost frilly scales leading to a ridge on its back. Plants growing in sturdy, handmade wooden boxes filled each cell. The scent of wet earth, the dry smell of all reptiles, and something sweet, almost floral flowed around Noor.

The creature had wide, intelligent brown eyes and a forked tongue about a dozen imperial inches long, which it flicked through the bars to taste her scent. Noor froze, wondering if it would give her away as an undercover mage. But it simply bobbed its head before slipping into a small pool of clean water. Knowing the creature wasn't maliciously blocking her magic, that it couldn't help its abilities any more than she could hers, gave Noor the strength to stand and continue walking.

James dove into chatting with Ian. "Those beauties, how much did you say they went for again? Are they native here or imported?"

Noor examined the area as the two men chatted at the end of a corridor with only six cells on either side. All appeared empty and had been turned into nurseries for the urodelas. Cute critters gambolled around their parents, waddling through overflowing food bowls and clean water bowls. The littlest ones, cute with pudgy purple bodies as long as Noor's foot, had yellow spots rimmed with orange. They watched her sleepily with soft eyes. Fine, strong cloth across the bottom of the cages kept the urodelas from slipping through the bars. Noor could almost forgive them for making her feel like she was missing a lung and an eye.

She reached the end of the cellblock, where a man stood at the bars of his cubicle.

O'Reilly.

Sean O'Reilly observed her through deep-set dark eyes in a heavily wrinkled face. He stooped, though as Noor adjusted to the dim light of his table lamp, she realised it probably wasn't from abuse, but rather a life of reading. Bookshelves, well-built and filled to the edges, covered every wall of his large cell.

Riches beyond measure.

Noor spotted a half-dozen languages on their spines and topics ranging from history to law. O'Reilly reached through the bars to take her hand. It was warm and dry in hers, and kindness radiated from him.

"The other cells are usually full of my papers as well," he said in English, his voice a warm growl. "But it's nesting season, so I had the guards box them up to make way for the babies." He reached into his pocket, pulled out a sweet, and tossed it to one of the littlest urodelas. Its scales flashed bright pink, and its little legs wriggled as it licked the sugary thing up. "I didn't want them to be separated from their families too soon."

Noor's eyes filled with tears; the urodelas's field must be affecting her emotions as well. O'Reilly gave her time to compose herself, occupying himself with his shelves.

"What have you learned here?" she asked, also in English, taking in his books and papers.

He studied her and seemed to make a decision.

"I have learned that what I was taught by the people who sent me here," he said, this time his voice strong, "was only the taste of a raindrop in the tsunami of knowledge that living things have acquired." He spoke as if he'd had elocution training and had worked these thoughts in his mind thousands of times before speaking them aloud. "I have learned there are so many ways of being, and there are as many ways of being broken as there are of building yourself back up again."

He grinned brightly, his white teeth crooked, and she couldn't help but smile back. "Also, I have learned that it is possible to set others free without being free yourself."

"O'Reilly is quite the jailhouse lawyer," Ian said, a fond smile transforming his face, making Noor reconsider her evaluation of him. "He argued in front of the Governor of Bengal, John Shore. It must have been, what, fifteen years ago?"

O'Reilly nodded.

Ian continued, "He made his case that, since the English bastards had defeated the rebellion in Ireland, Irishmen should have the same chance to become officers as everyone else, or at least be released from conscription. There are a lot of Irishmen back home with their families because of his work, including my uncle."

O'Reilly smiled politely and turned to Noor. He looked her over for long moments. Then he turned to slide a long, clean finger over the leatherbound books stacked under his quilted wooden bed. He pulled out a slim black one and flipped it open to a full colour illustration of— some kind of bowl? Noor leaned closer, James at her elbow.

"Have you ever seen one of these?" O'Reilly asked.

"No."

He tilted the page towards her. "This shows a way to repair broken things. A master potter might spend a week or a month making a single vase. Then, one step after taking her work from the kiln, she trips on the cat and drops it, breaking it in two. She could throw the vase away, and many would. Such is a potter's life, this kind of pain. But this happened in a land where the ceramicists have decided that rather than throwing away shards, they repair them. Not with glue and not to hide the broken places, but to highlight them with gold."

As he opened the book to a sketch, she saw what he meant: the grey illustration of a hand-thrown bowl in the picture had cracks filled with gold leaf.

"It's not just that," O'Reilly said quickly, his voice so low, Noor thought perhaps only she and James could hear it. "The repair is *always* done with gold, but sometimes the bowl is dark and sometimes light. What reconnects it is always heated and hardened metal. The power, that *magic* that binds the broken pieces together, can sometimes look light against the dark, or dark against the light. It's about contrast." He said this last part slowly. "It's about the balance, not only between, but *within*."

O'Reilly turned to dig up a waxed waterproof messenger bag from under his bed, placed the volume in it, and pressed it into Noor's hands.

"Keep this—and write me sometime. I get new folios every few months when the ships come through from India or on their way to Iraq. But news from the world outside, the kind that is not yet written about, well, that is something I would treasure."

Noor nodded and slung the bag, the book inside, over her shoulder. She adjusted it as James asked Ian about the best way to get in contact with O'Reilly.

Leaving O'Reilly's cellblock revived Noor's connection to her magic—sweet pain, sweet connection. Leaving the thick prison walls behind provided nearly the same level of comfort.

On the long walk back to the dhow, James kept Ian distracted. Noor wondered what was happening to Rami now as the call to *maghrib* prayer echoed across the city.

After Ian had sailed them back to the *Cormorant*, Noor walked back to her area in the hold and carefully, deliberately hung the messenger bag with its book on the curving cedar wall. She slammed her hands on either side of the bag once, twice, three times, until she misjudged the distance and slashed her hand on a splinter. *We have got to find him before they kill him.*

She returned to the deck at dinner time to eat some fish Mianning had caught. Her friends watched her carefully as she approached. Noor didn't normally spend long hours in the hold alone. James cleared his throat, glanced to Usama, and then to Razan. Razan scooted to the side, making room for Noor to sit beside her, then pressed her shoulder in tightly against her. Razan frowned at the scrape on her palm. She reached for it and moved it towards the firelight.

"Uh, Noor," James said, his voice soft. "What did you do to your hand?"

She ducked her head. "It's—it's frustrating not finding him, not getting anywhere, wasting time. And those *prisons*, that *man*. He's helpless there, has spent so many years there, and no one's coming to visit him; no one's searching for him. *No one else cares*, and—"

Mianning put his hand on her shoulder, and she tensed. He lifted it off but kept his eyes carefully on hers as James broke into the heavy silence.

"Noor, we all saw the message this morning. I didn't want to bring it up on our way to the prison because we needed to focus, to be able to get out of there quickly if it went badly. But you didn't tell us. Not about the torture. Something's changed in how you're communicating with him. It's been different, more intense, the past day or so. You're changing Noor. You're getting closer to him, taking stuff about him personally, and—"

When Razan made a small, wounded sound, Usama broke in, translating between English and Arabic.

"It's weird, is what it is," Usama said. "It's like you have—"

"Sympathy for the devil," James cut in. "When we started, you said it was to get him away from the British so they couldn't use him against us again. I thought that was what we signed up for."

"But now you're talking about saving *him*. About what *he's* going through. The emira said updates on him will be going out to all the commanders with the morning briefing. And my thing is—what happens if we don't get him? How did this mission get so personal?"

"We know you're stepping into his dreams," James said, more calmly. "But we don't know what happens between you two when you're asleep. I'm not trying to judge, but we're here for you, above him, above everything but the cause. So, what has he been doing to you, these past few days?"

Noor hadn't thought, hadn't realised. Her friends thought Rami was hurting her. She shook her head, looking at them as they sat around the work table.

"One of the first nights when I saw him in the dream," she said softly, "there were these patterns, hashes and slashes on his skin. Then there were deep rope burns. They weren't anything he could have done to himself. I kept thinking about it. But who would believe me? I tried to tell Razan but—"

Noor swallowed, unwilling to criticise her friend no matter how much her prior coldness had stung. "I saw him with my own eyes, saw his abuse on the *Victory*. But after everything he'd done— You've heard everyone we've spoken to. Allah, you've said it yourselves. Some pain may be the least that he deserves. But I don't think he deserves to die, not without a chance to defend himself."

She closed her eyes, memory after memory flashing of his cut and bruised skin, his smiling face at the last meeting, his hope. "He's a fighter as much as any of us are, and he deserves the chance to fight back. *They tie him down.* They took his connection to magic, probably using uro-delas like we saw today, James. There's no justice in what's being done to him. Just pain. And he hurt others for his power. He deserves a trial, to be found guilty or innocent of whatever the final charges are. But there's nothing coming of his hurting right now. It's retribution, not justice.

"You asked what I do in his dreams. Every night, I save him from drowning. I find him, nearly dead, under the water in a cave in Gaza. I take him to shore. Sometimes, he's too damaged to talk. Sometimes, whatever they do to him doesn't wreck him as much, doesn't cut as deep. He's never once asked me for help. I don't think he believes he deserves to be saved.

"This is what I was asking you about yesterday, Usama. Every night, I have a choice to let him die. The rules of the dream feel clear. If I see him drowning and don't save him, he will die in the waking world. Then this whole thing would be over. That would free him, permit him to fade away into the magic, to haunt me or not, whatever it is he ended up doing, this broken, fragile, fucked-up man. But I don't sense in him the will to die. I sense the will to live. And I don't think he deserves what's happening to him. Torture isn't justice."

Usama took a deep breath. "Like James said, I'm here for you first. I don't believe in torture, even for torturers. I'm not saying any of us love the Sword of Sidon, but I'm absolutely not in love with the idea of Emira Arwa and Yusef's son suffocating on water or being tortured to death alone while you have to watch it happen." At this, James nodded confirmation. "But you need to tell us if things start to change or get worse. You need to let us know."

There was a long pause, and then Razan's voice came through, quiet and precise. "I—it feels odd to ask, Noor, when there's so much else going on, so tell me to drop it if you need to. But why Gaza?"

Noor set her jaw. "I don't know. The thing, whatever is connecting us, keeps bringing us back there. I was there a long time ago. I told you it was the place where I first decided to fight back?"

"Maybe it's as simple as that," Razan said, turning Noor's hand over in hers, her gaze down. "The story you need to believe in order to save him is the story the dreams are bringing you to, reminding you of."

"Could be," Noor said.

After a long moment, James shrugged. "You know more about how magic works than any of us, and it sounds like this is confusing you too."

"I've never had a teacher. I'm just doing the best I can. And sometimes it feels like it can never be enough." *I can never be enough.*

Razan laid her hands on the table. "I think Noor deserves our support and probably needs her rest."

"I'm sorry to overwhelm you like that, Noor," James said contritely. "You know we're here for you."

Her eyes prickled. "I can stay up for a while." She glanced over at Razan, trying to keep the pleading off her face.

Razan met her eyes. "I'd like to clean that hand up—if you don't mind the help?"

"I can use all the help I can get," Noor said, a little desperation seeping into her voice.

"Then you'll have mine." Razan stood and left for the hold, and Noor watched her go down the stairs, her heart lifting for the first time in weeks.

Later, Razan's voice drifted up from her hammock.

"Noor?"

"Yes?"

A long silence followed, then, "Would—would you like to share my hammock tonight? I can't say I'd be up for more than sleeping, but when you were gone today in Doha, I—I was worried for you. I think my body would appreciate knowing your body is safe, warm, and close."

Noor was already tumbling out of her hammock and crawling into Razan's as she chuckled at her eagerness.

Noor tucked herself in against Razan's side, legs a tangle and Razan's hair in her face. She'd never felt better, safer, than in her arms.

Razan breathed slowly and comfortably under Noor's cheek, and Noor thought she could fall asleep just like this, no need for more talking.

Then, Razan's hand brushed down the back of her head, traced down her nape, held her tight.

"Noor, I need to say something."

Noor tensed. "I'm listening."

"They're just dreams," Razan started. "No, I know, they're magical and intense and consuming, but I wake up at night and see you here, your body here, and I want you to know that I'm here for you. I'll keep you safe, while you're doing what you need to in those dreams. I trust you, Noor, to do what you have to. I'm not—" She paused, seeming to chew through the word.

Noor called on her magic, using her fingertips to gently light her lover's face.

Razan chose every word with care. "I'm not possessive. I've loved women who loved other people and me at the same time, and we found ways to make it work. I don't need to be everything to you or you to be everything to me. However it is, whatever it feels like, just know I'll be here when you wake up. And when we get him out of that prison, we can talk, just you and I, if these dreams need to change anything in the waking world. Is that all right with you?" A flash of worry or something like insecurity crossed her face.

Overwhelming gratitude rushed through Noor, and she wrapped herself even tighter around her lover.

"Yes, Razan. More than all right. Thank you. I cannot tell you how much that means to me." She swallowed. "It's strange, but I can feel there is a plot line in the story, in the dreams themselves, and when I move away from it, the world seems distant, greyer. I—I want to see where it goes. How the story in the dreams moves, how it ends."

"Then follow it to the end. But know when the dream ends, I'll be here in the daylight, waiting for you." Razan took a breath. "Have you ever lived in a family compound?"

"Not that I can remember."

"Where there were families; where more than two people were married?"

"Like Draupadi?" Noor asked.

"Who?"

"She's one of the central characters in the Hindu plays I saw in the souq. The players were selling Mysorean rockets, doing plays on the side while waiting for buyers. Draupadi had five husbands."

"I guess no one ever had to argue about who would do the clearing up with so many hands in the house," Razan said with a grin.

"Or they argued all the time," Noor replied. "I met a Keralan merchant once whose wife had several husbands. They all worked together. He sailed the ship, another sold the goods, another was sick, and they all cared for him. The children were all theirs. I think they called it *sambandham*? Or maybe something else?"

"My brother has two wives," Razan said. "He's still in Sidon. They follow *sharia*, so he treats them each equally. They don't really like each other, Maha and Adla, but they have different homes in the compound, and their children get along, so it works for them."

"My *imam*'s wife always said it was impossible to treat two people the same, so having multiple people in a marriage wasn't something she ever recommended." Noor smiled to herself, remembering. "She also argued that she didn't understand why she needed to cover her hair because the Quran just says to cover your head, and her hair was covering her head."

"She sounds like she would set a lot of people's hair on fire in some places."

"Probably," Noor said. "But the same goes for us. So, I figure we're in good company."

"Fair. There are a lot of ways to live. That's really all I was trying to say—there are a lot of ways to live."

Noor buried her face in Razan's neck as she gave a big yawn. "Thank you for talking it through with me."

"Of course."

Feeling brave, Noor pressed a kiss to Razan's cheek. She gasped as Razan turned her head, caught her lips, and kissed her once, firmly, before nuzzling her face into Noor's hair.

"I'll be here when you wake. Go to sleep, Noor."

And Noor did.

*

AS SOON AS Noor closed her eyes, Rami was there before her, fighting something in the water, something she couldn't see. Nothing was around him, nothing choking him, nothing hitting him, but he struggled, face wild. She dove towards him, shoving a message at him: *You're in a dream, remember, Rami? This is a dream.*

Noor floated in front of him, just out of his grasp. And for the barest of breaths, he stilled, his dark eyes set on her, face frozen, and then it crumbled. She closed the distance and slung an arm around his belly, getting her grip before swimming up with enough force that her shoulder shoved him in the armpit. He startled, and she felt him begin to kick, begin to help.

When they broke the surface under the unending arc of crystalline stars, Rami gasped in huge breaths, his eyes wide and searching. When Noor tried to let him swim on his own, he surged closer to her and refused to break contact. So they swam together towards the cave's shore, his shoulder close to hers, his hand on her arm as they clambered up the well-worn rocks, not letting her out of his touch.

This time, he set the fire, burning the wood she'd collected in past dreams. Rami took off his jacket, lay it where it could drip drain in the moonlight, and sat close beside her, shoulder tight against hers. He scanned the entire cave as if it was new before turning to the fire.

"I rested better last night," he said, his voice hoarse. "Thank you."

"Me too, though today was long."

He quirked an eyebrow at her, and she relayed her conversation with the resistance, that she would be telling them what was happening to him. She didn't say who she'd spoken with, not sure of his relationship with his mother. Noor watched his face freeze as his breathing kicked up. Then, he seemed to take control of himself, his eyes too casually drifting back to the fire, arms around his knees.

"We think you're in Muscat or Salalah," Noor said. "Any idea which it might be?"

He hung his head, frustrated. "This is all so ghastly."

A peal of pure surprise burst out of her at his formal, aristocratic words. Rami startled at it, but before she could smother another laugh, he grinned, bumped her shoulder with his, and chuckled.

"Fine, that's an understatement," he said. "But I don't want my life, what's happening to me, to be some kind of bargaining chip between resistance commanders." He lowered his head. "But I need out, and it sounds like this is the way. A compromise."

She slowly moved a hand towards his knee and patted him gingerly. He leaned into her, and when he spoke next, his voice was a near whisper.

"I rested better, but there isn't any amount of rest that will allow me to survive many more days like yesterday. If they keep me from sleeping, it will start to affect me more, not only because I won't have time to heal, but because it will take me away from, this time, this place. From you." He looked around, everywhere but her. "I've been getting my hope here."

Rami turned towards her, eyes meeting hers, and reached out, slid his fingers to the nape of her neck, not tugging, not pulling, just resting there. Noor's skin was alight, warmth spreading up her entire body, emanating from that point, the two square inches where his fingertips tied their bodies together.

She pressed his fingers tighter against her skin. Slowly, barely moving, he relaxed towards her, his forehead coming to rest against her shoulder. One knee fell to the side, and the other nudged against her leg until she let her legs relax, laying one over his as their breaths came in tandem.

Her arm had tired from holding both of them up, so she squeezed his fingers, intertwined with hers. "Resting in the dream helped me yesterday," she said. "Maybe it will help you tomorrow if you'd like to."

He froze, his leg touching hers, and then he slid away, and she was— cold. Not the cold of clammy clothes but of a lost connection. He returned with his damp cloak, which he wadded up into a pillow that he tucked under his cheek as he lay down, the crackling warmth of the fire beside him. Then he sat up, adjusted the cloak until there was room on it for both of their heads before lying down again.

She snorted at his fussing and lay down, also on her back, her head on the far edge of the cloak. Slower than breathing, light on the ground, Rami turned his head to take a measure of something—in her or in him, she didn't know. He then curled onto his side, faced away from her, and held very still. With his massive back to her, all Noor could think was that it was probably nowhere near healed in the waking world. She put a gentle hand on his hip, and he startled badly.

She rushed to say, "I'm sorry. I didn't mean to— You can just rest—"

"No, now I know it's coming, it's all right," he said, his voice a little higher but reassuring.

He held himself stiffly as she nudged herself forward until the length of her body was a hair's breadth from him. This close, he smelled of seaweed and sweat and something else, something sharp and rich she remembered from when they'd first met. Noor laid her hand on his side again. This time, he sighed, set his head more firmly into the makeshift pillow, and eased his ribs into her palm with a tentative breath. She slid her hand across his stomach, curved it over his hip, and the sensation filled her, the contact, his body so close to hers. Her back was to the entrance; if anything came through, came for them, she could defend them. It made something primal roll and preen in her belly, this possessiveness, this feeling of protection.

After a while, he took a deep, sleepy breath, and his entire back brushed up against her front. It was her turn to freeze, to press her tongue to the roof of her mouth, to try to will away the heat in her belly trickling down between her legs, trying to keep her molten rushing pulse cool. She matched his next breath and followed it as it forced her into deep, meditative breathing since his lungs were so much bigger than hers and his exhausted exhalations slower. To steady herself, in her mind Noor listed the harbour prisons they'd been to as well as the ones they hadn't. She thought about Muscat and Salalah and tried to focus on them rather than his body relaxing under her arm, muscle-by-muscle group gentling.

His entire body tensed one final time before he fell into a restful sleep. With him out, Noor let herself settle a little, moulded herself to him, pressed the tops of her thighs to the backs of his, her chest closer to the skin she'd run her fingertips over as she healed it yesterday. She buried her face in the dampness of his hair to keep from thinking about that. She closed her eyes, and the fire warmed her arm across his stomach, and his body warmed her everywhere else.

When Noor was absolutely sure he was asleep and had been for a while, she whispered, too low to be heard over the crackling of the fire, "I swear to Allah, I will set you free. And we'll both see who you are in the daylight."

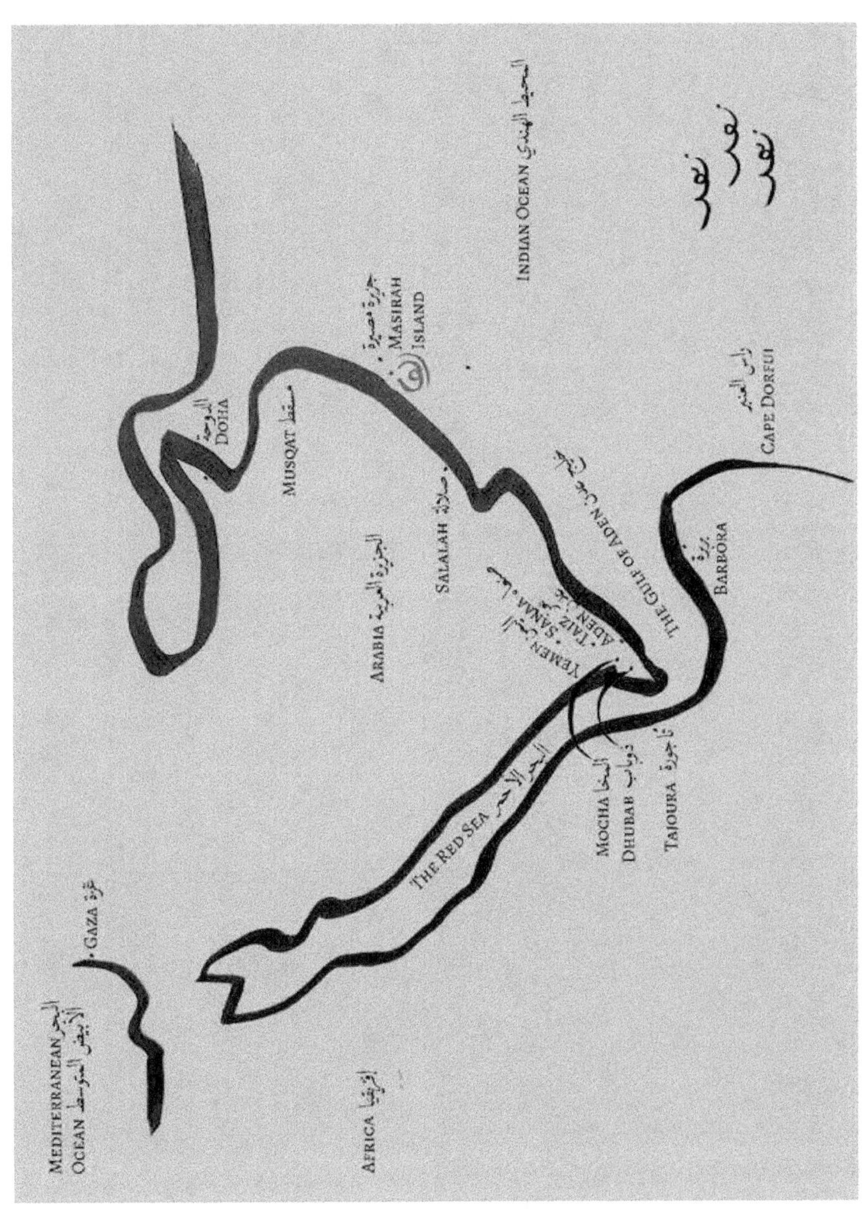
MEDITERRANEAN OCEAN
GAZA
AFRICA
THE RED SEA
MOCHA
DHUBAB
TAIOURA
SANA'A
TAIZ
ADEN
YEMEN
THE GULF OF ADEN
BARBORA
CAPE DORFUI
INDIAN OCEAN
SALALAH
ARABIA
MUSQAT
DOHA
MASIRAH ISLAND

Chapter Four

EARLY WINTER MONSOON rains swept across the Arabian Sea. Massive waves forced the *Cormorant* to shore near Masirah Island as they waited for winds to shuttle the thunderheads towards the east. Mianning set out lines in the warm rains to catch fish disturbed by the waves while the rest of them sheltered in the captain's cabin or the hold. Noor read the book O'Reilly had given her by the light of her magic until night truly fell, and then she went to sleep.

*

THAT NIGHT, NOOR found Rami closer to the bones of the pilot whale than she ever had before, drifting deeper, eyes shut. She grabbed his wrist, her lungs already aching, and pulled his slack, unmoving body. She wanted to shake him, force him back into consciousness, shout at him to fight, to swim with her, to do something other than being a limp sack of rocks for her to carry.

Instead, she dragged him up the shore, then pumped the water from his lungs while trying not to add to the watercolour of bruises across his bare chest. Noor kept at it until he coughed, not waking but certainly breathing. Tonight, he wore only his pants, his feet brown and long on moonlit sand. She got the fire going, envisioned a thick blanket under them and a thicker one around him, and folded her legs to pray.

When Rami stirred again, the moon had made a quarter of its habitual journey across the entrance of the cave. He fought the blanket over him, crawled, and stumbled to the far side of the cave, only to sit with the stone at his back, huddled with his knees against his chest.

Noor stared, unmoving.

When Rami had turned his back to scramble away from her, she'd seen deep bruises shaped like handprints over the dark skin of his hips, his lower back, and on his spine. His eyes were bright, alert, but when she stepped towards him, he startled so hard that his head hit the rough stone wall. Noor put the fire between them. He stayed where he was.

"Do you ever feel that dimness of the soul?" he said finally, his words a mix of harsh whispers and sudden bursts of noise. She cringed at what could make him sound like that.

"I get downhearted sometimes, if that's what you mean," she said, keeping her tone calm.

"Not that. I'm talking about grey times." He shook his head, his face spasming at the small movement. "Not grey fading into darkness, but inner darkness, the shading of the world that lets us see death without looking away, lets us feel pain without wincing, lets us see the world as it is. Or as the worst parts of it are."

Noor thought of the long, moonless nights in Tadjoura, of feeling she knew the truth of the world and that truth was a terrible one: that all people were made up of darkness, and the few, rare, fleeting kindnesses of the world might as well be accidents for how uncommon and how ineffectual they were.

"Are you asking if I ever feel melancholy?"

He grimaced, either at her use of romantic language or some slicing, inner injuries she couldn't see.

"I do," she said, continuing the thought. "I have. I am, right now, actually."

He seemed to withdraw further. Maybe he thought it was catching; maybe he thought there was something about his presence throwing her off her centre; maybe he was injured. She continued the conversation he'd started, trying to draw him out.

"My melancholy is something that comes from inside sometimes, at least, that's how I think about it," she said, and his eyes were on hers, dark and in pain that she wanted to *fix. Cracks in people can't be glued together. They need to be rebound with something else, something of both fire and water.*

Noor kept going. "When I'm filled with melancholy, my world is darkly lit. I find myself expecting all evil. I don't let myself dwell on good things, can't bring myself to be happy for even a few moments at a time." She thought her tone might be too clinical, too vague. She stared into the fire.

"I know, in my mind, those grey days will pass, that everything in this world passes. I don't let myself make big changes until I'm out of the gloom and have time and space to re-heal."

She paused, trying to remember how she thought about it, then sent her words out like darts in the dark cave. "I think of it as holding space for myself, as I would for someone else. If a friend is sick, or wounded, or captive"—she glanced again towards his huddled form pressed tight against the unyielding solidity of the wall—"or if they're dying or missing, I try not to get angry at them for not being what I want or need in that moment. Because nearly everyone will come back if you give them enough space."

"That makes sense," he said, his voice raw, harsh. "But what if I really hate waiting?"

"That hate is part of melancholy. It shows you're still fighting, that you still believe you deserve better than you're getting. That you can still *want.*"

"What happens when I can't get what I want, when what I want is taken from me, when other things are taken from me?" Rami's voice was now so thin and scared Noor didn't know what to do. Her pulse thudded in her stomach and bile rose in her throat.

"What I learned in the desert is all sadnesses pass, all melancholies fail, nothing keeps us away from our futures forever. Until we find a way to survive, we have to endure and take what we need with both hands."

He came to his knees, his face a mask of pain. The firelight showed what she hadn't seen before. Bright red bruises circled his neck—fingertips pressed into his throat from the front and reaching around from behind.

"I want—" He gripped his hands in his lap, eyes downcast. His voice was full of shame when he said, "I want not to hurt."

She slid to her knees. "I will never touch you unless you ask me to, but I can heal you like last time."

He shook his head. She eased back again.

"What they did this time, it's not the same kind of hurt," he whispered, something in his voice so wrong, like a conviction that he was alone in this pain.

Noor knew what she would need to do next, the rules of the dream shifting. "Did you hear the one about the man who fell into a pit?"

Rami shook his head, his eyes wide, confused at her change in tone. He crawled a little closer to the fire, every movement causing agony.

"The man who fell into a pit cried out, 'Help, help!' And an imam came by, wrote a prayer down on a piece of paper, and walked away. The man who fell into a pit called out, 'Help, help!' again. And a sheikh came by, wrote down some sage wisdom on a scrap of parchment, and walked away. He called out, 'Help, help!" again. And his best friend came by."

She began unwrapping her guntiino from her arm.

"His friend jumps down in the hole, and the stuck man says, 'Why'd you do that? Now we're both stuck down here!' And his friend says, 'No, we're not because I've been down here before, and I know the way out.'"

Noor turned her wrist over in the cool night air and angled it towards the fire, showing a thin, long scar. "I ate some bad meat, made me see things, made me try to slice my bones out with a stone. I passed out before going too far."

The flickering firelight illuminated his face, showing no reaction, and she was suddenly too mad, too broken-hearted, too sliced and diced, and simply too on fire to stop, to ask him what he needed again. She was tired of always keeping space and never *taking* space, never making clear that she needed room to explode sometimes too. Noor wanted to think she was doing this for him, showing him he wasn't alone. But part of this was her serving herself up, reminding him: *You're not here with some perfect haya mage. I've been fucked over too, fucked up and broken. And if you can find a way, night after night after night, to the ocean and to me, we might both make it out of this alive.*

She spread her fingers wide enough to ache, pointed to the place where her two middle fingers trembled and wouldn't stretch as far apart.

"See how this finger can't flex all the way? Musa, the man who thought he was my master, thought I should have been able to scavenge twice the goods as I had one week—though I hadn't because I'd been too scared to go by the new British Army camp to get to the good scrap—so he took a hammer, had me put my hand on his desk, and—"

Rami froze, and a fascinated, ugly part of Noor was overjoyed. *Look, proof I'm too broken to love. If the Sword of Sidon can't bear to hear me talk about* my *hand, then nothing in me is worth anything.* The bruises around his neck looked deep, repeated. He couldn't sit in one position for long now that he'd moved away from the wall and kept shifting, face never still, an open echo of pain.

Noor continued, her voice as cold and remote as the stars above them. "I was taken by a British Army squad in Tadjoura. They held me for a month. They thought they needed some local entertainment."

Her voice could have cut iron, her words like a jambiya through an eye. "Later, after, it seemed to matter to other people that I tried to escape their camp, their compound. It was on the outskirts of town. I tried; I couldn't get out. I told people that, but eventually, I stopped saying anything at all since it seemed it made me fair game in their minds. There was no one who'd understand how grateful I was the day they left, one coming back to unlock the cage and cut the bonds, leaving me alone but free."

Her voice was too flat, too desiccated of feeling. She didn't know how to think or feel about this one, awful, horrific time in her life.

"I was in the sand where they left me, waiting for the sun, a drift of sand to die in, and I could hear someone coming. I didn't want to be raped again, to be taken to another compound, and I—I couldn't walk at that point. They'd broken something, and it had been weeks since I'd been fed right. But I heard this person coming, and I—I forced myself to crawl. It might have been magic. It might have been me. At the time, I thought it was Allah."

She shook to her deepest of bones, a thick slurry of memories like a riptide trying to tow her under. But she finished the story.

"An Afar woman found me, carried me where I asked her to, never asked me any questions, left when I said she could. I made it to the mosque, to the imam. His family took care of me, kept me from getting infections, kept me alive. Let me heal. One day, months after, in the market, I saw a little cat, one who'd been run down by a British horseman. Her back was broken. But I healed her. Gave her light and life, sipping it from every damned redcoat I could see. I healed her better than I'd ever been healed myself. My magic left her stronger in the broken places."

He met and held her eyes.

"All right." He crawled towards her, the handprints around his neck growing starker the closer he got to the fire. He sat, just out of arm's reach, then reached out to her as slowly as she'd touched him to heal the cuts on his back. His eyes remained on hers, amber-tinted in the penumbra of the fire. When she didn't shift away, he gripped her shoulder, thumb moving in an apology.

"Leave it," she said leaning away.

But he shook his head, inching a bit closer to her, twitches of pain racing across his body like a lightning storm. She scoured his face for pity, for disgust. She didn't see it in him and didn't feel anything like it rising in her chest. Just a frisson of understanding.

Rami was closer now, kneeling before her, his other arm around his stomach, and she knew how much it hurt inside when someone did something like that to you. Noor was arctic, thinking of someone holding her hands, holding him down. She hovered behind, trying to get away to safety, preparing to run, and he went utterly still, muscles tense, waiting for her to do so.

She lifted a hand to where he held her shoulder and pressed two fingers to the unbruised inside of his wrist, feeling his blood flow. On the rhythm of his heartbeat, Noor shifted back into herself, became aware again of the flow of magic around them. She diverted a stream of it from the great river and turned it to healing, touched it to his skin, restitching muscles, stopping bleeding, soothing aches. Noor diverted his blood away from the bruises on his hips, his lower back, and around his neck.

Rami continued to hold still as the fingerprints faded, and the strain within him gentled, the shape of him becoming more balanced, more symmetrical now it wasn't stiff in anticipation.

Rami's pain brought her back to that camp, and every time she remembered, her healing slowed, her grip weakening. So, she thought of other things, brighter things: The smell of Razan's hair, the sound of Usama and James's laughter, the first meal of a day, the power in her arms when she wielded her jambiya, the brightness of a new dawn. Rami's smile. Rami's unbroken skin moving over muscles built from working. Rami, whole and happy and *free*.

Noor let those memories and yearnings drift in a concurrent current along with her healing magic, slipping her light through his body, stitching together what was broken and leaving a line of bright, hard power where the cracks were.

When she rose from the flow and opened her eyes, she found his, close and searching, his hand no longer on her shoulder but cupping her cheek. She pressed into his mind: *You don't deserve any of this.*

Rami replied, *You are not broken or unlovable. You are not nothing. You are enough. Be kinder to yourself.*

He pulled his hand away, her fingers dropping from his wrist, and he breathed, "Believe me," as he faded.

*

NOOR AWOKE SOBBING into Razan's neck, her friend's arms gripping her tight, lips calling her name softly, repeatedly, like a song, like a lighthouse bringing her to shore. Noor's hands were fisted in Razan's sleeping clothes, holding her close, so tight she thought she would tear her skin or the fabric. Noor released her grip and the blood in her fingers flowed again. She felt the smooth shape of a wrist under her fingers, just for an instant.

She wanted to stifle the tears and stop herself from falling any farther or entirely apart. But then she remembered what he'd said about being kind, about being enough, and she turned and buried her face in Razan's chest, arms around her and cried until only pain remained and no guilt, cried until she felt empty. Crying brought serenity, an acknowledgement that she was smaller than some things in this world and so much bigger than others.

Her stomach and throat ached from stifling her sobs, and the front of Razan's sleeping clothes were damp through-and-through, but as Noor's breathing slowed, she felt calmer and clearer than she had in days. As with the knowledge that things pass, this was a reminder that she was affected by her emotions, and they might leave her alone if she left herself the space to feel them.

"Oh, Noor," Razan said. "Oh, Noor."

"It was bad. He was—" Noor started.

Razan held up her hand. "I don't need to know right now. I want you to have time to decide what you want to tell me. How about we get you dressed and fed, and see what the dawn brings?"

This, too, was mercy—being given comfort without the expectation of exposure in return.

Noor wrapped herself around her lover one more time, pressing the words "thank you" into her skin before carefully unpeeling herself from Razan.

As she and Razan dressed, Noor thought about what Rami had said at the end about being enough. She decided that the next time she slept, she would tell Rami he was enough too. Maybe it would feel like a lifeline to him, the way his words, his touch, and Razan's touch had been to her.

*

SHE DIDN'T SEE him for days.

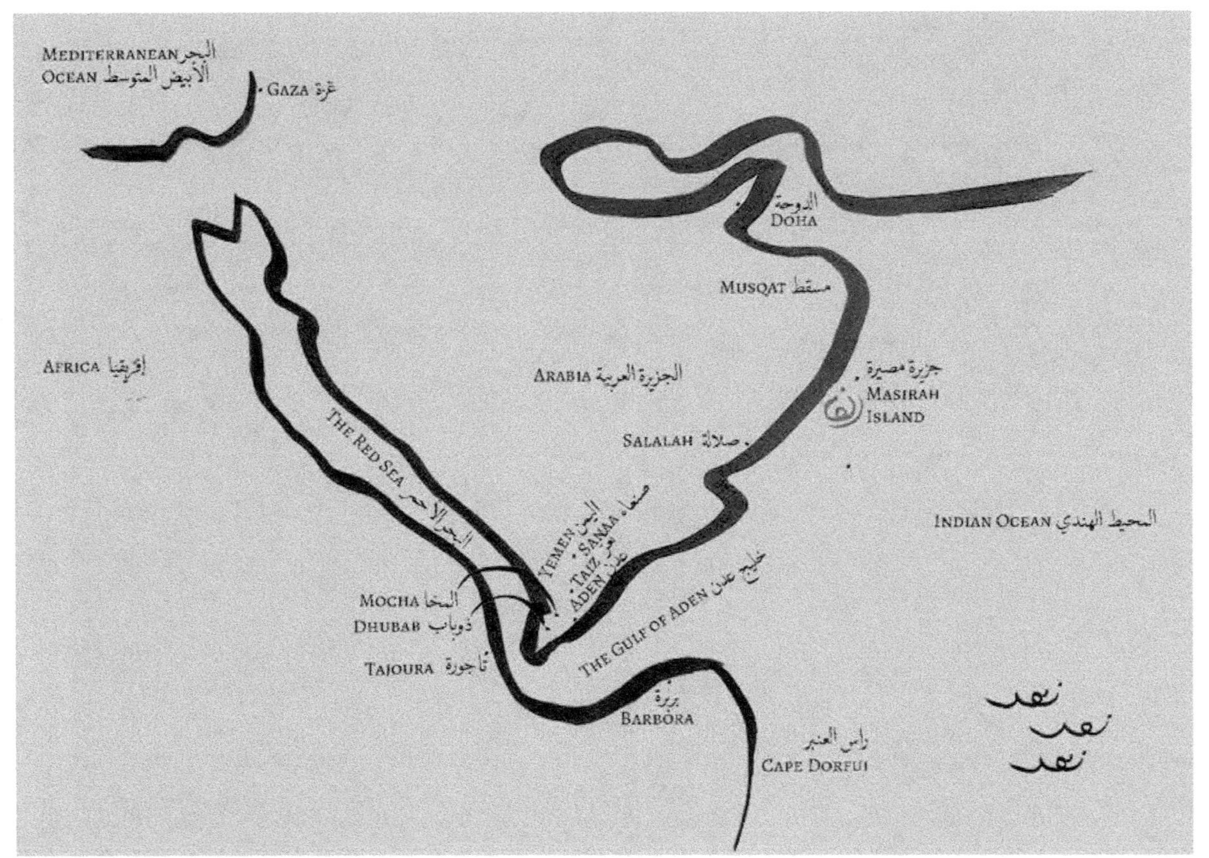
MEDITERRANEAN OCEAN
GAZA
DOHA
AFRICA
MUSQAT
ARABIA
MASIRAH ISLAND
SALALAH
INDIAN OCEAN
THE RED SEA
YEMEN
TAIZ
SAN'A
ADEN
MOCHA
DHUBAB
THE GULF OF ADEN
TAJOURA
BARBORA
CAPE DORFUI

Chapter Five

NOOR JOINED RAZAN on the deck after that last, hard dream. The slowly rising winds from a storm coming across the Indian Ocean filled the air with the smell of lighting. Noor thought it was a lightning strike when the first bomb exploded over their bow.

But lightning wasn't scarlet and didn't stink like Mysorean rockets she'd seen in the souq.

The red glare of the rockets filled the midnight sky, illuminating the coast of a great island just beyond where they were anchored. Screaming came from the coast. Another bomb, another, and another. Each flash showed more. They came from a British bark, a mid-sized ship. A fishing boat went up in flames in the harbour beside them. Families poured out of their homes. The next rocket had landed in the middle of an anchored dhow, setting the largest one ablaze.

"Where are we?" Noor hissed to Usama as he stumbled out onto the deck. The attacking ship hadn't seen them yet or at least wasn't aiming at them. Mianning worked furiously at the sails, manoeuvring them so they weren't visible.

"Masirah Island," he responded, voice flat. "There'd been a

resistance base here until a week ago when the empire found it. The British must have come back to kill the villagers who supported our cause."

"Why aren't they aiming at the houses?"

"They'd wreck themselves on the reef before they'd be close enough to try. Their rockets can't reach the houses from out where it's deep enough for their ship to stay safe, so they're destroying the villager's livelihoods instead."

Noor narrowed her eyes at the attacking bark, the Union Jack snapping in the rising wind as a storm gusted around them. "They can take their boarding boats to shore. Those are shallow enough to make it over the reef."

"And they will once they've trapped them on the island."

"We have to help them."

His smile was back. "Of course, habibati."

Noor took a deep breath, tapping into the sea floor beneath them teaming with life. Her connection to her power roared through her veins as soon as she reached for it.

"I'll hold off the rockets while you get the people out?"

"That's what I hoped you'd say, habibati," he said, reaching for his shell. "I'll let them know we're coming and we have you with us."

Noor raised her hands, calling up a dozen water spouts, tall and narrow like the bars of a cage. She arranged them in a wall, shielding the harbour from the rocket fire. After a long pause, the next bomb flew, and she whipped it out of the air, leaving it to sputter safely into the roiling sea.

Use up all your ammunition on me. Try kicking someone who can stab back.

The crew of the *Cormorant* threw themselves into saving the villagers from the British bark as Noor deflected rockets and cannonballs and musket shots around them. There were so many of them, and even with Mianning's knowledge of the reefs, sandbars, jagged rocks, and wrecked dhows, they had to work painfully slowly. All night, Mianning manoeuvered them through ink dark water as they packed every inch of the *Cormorant*. Mothers nursed their toddlers in Noor and Razan's hammocks, and chickens squawked, stuffed into the smuggling compartments.

As dawn broke, the bark sailed around the far side of the island, perhaps fearing retribution in the daylight. Noor had considered it as she watched them burn people's livelihoods, hundreds of cedar boats built by their hands and those of their ancestors.

But her magic drew from life, not death. Not pain. She feared if she used it to kill when she had any other option, it would damage her in some fundamental way.

That was her mind's reasoning. Her heart's had been every time she squinted at the deck of the bark in the next bomb's light; every sailor seemed to have James's face, boy conscripts serving at the whim of an empire who cared nothing for their lives or souls, only their bodies' ability to follow orders.

Without bombs to deflect in the daylight, Noor got to work, carrying babies and goats and rucksacks, keeping families together and all of them out of the sea. A huge crowd waited on the beach. But their ship could only hold so many, so they made the trip many times.

Sometime around noon, Razan made her sleep.

She slept without dreaming.

The next night was the same. The bark came out to hurl its bombs. Noor stopped each one. She lived in constant watchfulness, broken only by her friends forcing food and water on her whenever they thought she could spare her focus for a few seconds.

At dawn, the ship slunk away again, and Noor slept. All the while, the *Cormorant* worked its way back and forth, back and forth, from the mainland to the island.

Sometime past dinner but before dusk, Noor found herself holding a little boy for an exhausted mother with three small children, letting the little one massage her cheeks and neck and forehead. She wriggled her nose as he dragged on her hair until it was a straggled mess. When Usama saw her, he just about died laughing. The little one had some kind of green goo on his hands that he'd spread all over her face.

They'd just entered the strait when an older woman came tottering towards the wheel. She sidled through the crowd, carrying a book and some kind of wreath, made of dark leaves and tiny, bright white flowers. Noor glanced at her with a smile, making sure Mianning had the navigation covered before turning to her.

"Can I help you with something?" she asked.

"Two weeks ago, a British trade ship wrecked on our sandbar," the woman said. "We got the crew out and let them stay with us while they waited for a search party. One of those limp bastards overheard some of the young ones talking about the resistance. He told the British ship that came for the crew what he'd heard. They dropped off their survivors, then turned back around to attack us. You came right in time. You all did good work on them. In any case, the trade ship was carrying these for their Christian celebration of their prophet's birthday." The woman held up the wreath, which had a sharp, thin smell, sort of like cedar. Noor remembered something she'd heard about Christmas, but the *Cormorant* jolted in the waves, and it faded from her mind.

"When is that again?" Noor asked.

"In two days' time. Anyway, that's not what I came for. My grandson found this behind a loose panel in the hold." The woman held out the heavy book. "These are not our stories, so I suspect it is a prior passenger's."

Noor accepted it and turned over the brown, hand-tooled cover: *Tales as Old as Time.*

It smelled of weathered paper and long-set ink. The old woman hung the wreath on the wheel and wandered away, snatching a wrinkled hand in a tight grip on the robes of everyone she passed. In Tadjoura, the woman would have been a world-class pickpocket. Noor glanced at Mianning and, seeing he was still fine, flipped the book open.

The first page read, "Given to Rami ibn Arwa wa Nuri on the occasion of his birth by his loving grandmother."

Then, below it in a child's scrawl:

"R.A.N."

Her heart stuttered. A scrape of the ship's hull on sand jolted Noor, and she slapped the book shut and tucked it safely under her guntiino. She turned back to the wheel to help Mianning navigate around the sandbar blocking their path.

On the way back to the island for their last pickup, the *Cormorant* was blessedly empty except for her crew. Noor pulled the book out and let it fall open to the place where the binding was softest.

The page showed a drawing, an illustration of a broad, swirling night sky with a dark silhouette standing against it. The artist had drawn it as if looking up at the figure, but the perspective didn't hook her—the stars drew her to them. Rather than white dots, a menagerie of colour represented them, vibrant and perfect, highlighting the forested world below in gentle washes.

With such a precise view of the sky, Noor wondered if she plotted those stars into her star charts, what part of the world she would find. The facing page held a story in careful printed script, the title in Arabic. It swooped and swirled much as the stars did: *Psyche and Cupid.*

Mianning leaned over to see what she was reading. He ran his finger down the page and smiled softly. "Be careful with that. It is from Greece. Yusef said it was given to the Emira Asma, Rami's grandmother, by Athenian diplomats. They'd had some of their great stories translated into Arabic, maybe as a sign of their hopes for future trade and peace between two great seafaring peoples. You saw it is Rami's?"

Noor gentled her hands on the book. She closed it and stood, searching for a safe place to put it, knowing they would be cheek-to-jowl on this last run and not wanting to lose this precious thing now it had been found again. Mianning held out his hand, and Noor passed it to him, then watched him tuck it between his thobe and his bandolier.

As they glided to the beach and the last of the crowd waiting for them, Noor heard a bell-like noise from her lunella shell, followed by a single cold word: "Update?"

She hurried off the dispatch she should have sent days before, trying not to think of how much might have changed since then, knowing she'd be helping refugees until midnight when she could sleep again. Her dispatch to the emira said: "*He is getting worse. From the bruises and his reactions, whatever injuries they're inflicting on him now are getting deeper, more physical, more personal. We have two prisons more to search. I hope we get there in time."*

As they worked their way across the strait and towards the coast, the world felt lighter. They'd retrieved everyone who had wanted to leave, left no one behind. Now, young men and women filled the *Cormorant*, those healthy and strong enough to fight if they had had to, relief etched in every inch of their faces. They had escaped and would be with their families soon. Noor felt clean, cleared out in a way she hadn't been in weeks.

As she leaned over the side of the ship, watching the waves for evidence of the British bark returning, she caught sight something massive swimming in the dark water beside the *Cormorant*.

Grey and curving, it raced beneath the waves. She leaned farther over the gunwale to get a better vantage point, then grinned as she cried out, "Whales!"

All of the young passengers rushed over to the side, squealing as the great animals rose and breached beside the dhow, a great spout of water arcing high into the air. A moment of quiet followed as they all breathed in the warm sea air and marvelled at the massive animals sharing their journey.

*

NOOR SAID HER goodbyes to those they'd saved before returning to her hammock alone to sleep. Razan had left for the beach to help repair the tents they'd set up as temporary shelter before heading up the coast towards Muscat. The smell of worried people floated in the air, mixing with that of the wreathes that Noor had found hanging in every room, including the bilge, everywhere the grateful people could find a hook on the *Cormorant*.

The wreaths' sharp scent took Noor down into darkness.

She opened her eyes and found Rami floating deeper than she'd ever seen him before, his face ashen. She tugged on his arm; he was so heavy. Noor was weaker now, too, exhausted and keyed up and terrified. But she dragged him up, got him to the beach, and carried him across the cave floor, its rocks dark under the new moon.

Noor pressed her cheek to his chest, checking his breathing, grateful for the contact and a breath. A heartbeat. *Alhamdulillah.*

"I'm so sorry," she said, and though his eyes were bleary, his confusion was clear. She tried to explain, her voice heavy with guilt. "I wasn't here last night."

He shook his head and groaned, reaching a hand to the back of his head. She leaned over to look, her fingers light, slipping between his to a broad bump rising along the base of his skull.

"I don't think the guards from the *Victory* intended me to sleep tonight," Rami said, his voice scratching and raw, eyes steady on hers. "You didn't miss me. I haven't slept since we last saw each other. They're trying a new technique—sleep deprivation spiced up with beatings. I think to describe this as 'sleep' might be generous. 'Knocked out' might be more accurate."

Noor paused, glancing a question at him. At his nod, she pressed a bit of healing energy into the bruised skin and bone there, grateful to find no new evidence of hand-shaped bruises around his neck or across his lower back.

When she was done, Rami sighed in relief and settled back.

He tilted his head, moving now without it hurting, and raised his hand to her face, fingers light on her skin. "Why are you— Did they do something to my eyes, or are you *green*?"

Noor couldn't stop herself. She collapsed on his chest, laughing and laughing. He stilled under her, only his hands fluttering on her shoulders. The laughter came from deep in her belly, rolling up her body, and soon, he joined her, chuckling.

She felt his stomach quiver with his laughter, felt his bare skin under her hands, and when she could breathe again, she found herself staring down his body, her cheek just below his ribs. Hair, darker than the rest, trailed down, and without thinking, she followed it to the waistband of his pants, which clearly outlined something.

Noor sat straight up, pulling her hands away as if burned, caustic with herself for ogling someone going through what Rami was. His eyes shone, bright and smiling when she looked at him. She pointed to his stomach, giggling a little again at streaks of green where she'd rubbed her face.

"Sorry," she said, gesturing. "There was—" A giggle bubbled up before she swallowed it back down. "—a village on Masirah Island. The British were firing on it, punishing people for helping the resistance." She held up a hand in case he wanted to argue the point. "We were helping them evacuate. There was a little kid. His hands were kind of sticky, and it was busy. I think he smeared it all over my face."

"And did the waters of the Arabian Sea empty out as well?" he asked dryly.

She mock-glowered and tossed her hair back imperiously. "No, but some of us aren't vain princelings."

Then she softened, her voice wavering a little. "I went to sleep the instant I could. I hated the thought of missing you, of not being here when—"

"But you didn't, so it's fine," he said lightly, and she ducked her head, scrubbing her face with the edge of her guntiino.

When Noor raised her face again, he was watching her, eyes steady. When she pointed to her cheek, he sat up, slipping his thumb in his mouth, then stroked it along her jawbone.

"There you are," Rami said.

Her breathing kicked up, her heart racing. She leapt to her feet and strode to a pile of wood. She hastily arranged it into a campfire. He watched as she lit it.

"I don't know when they'll wake me up again, so I need to say this now." He turned towards her. He held his hands loose in his lap, and Noor wanted to lean forward and kiss them, rest her head in them, feel his warm palm brushing her hair away from her face. She bit the edge of her tongue to focus and nodded for him to continue.

He kept his eyes on his sword-calloused fingers. "I don't know why you decided to save me. You've been trying from the moment you pulled me out of the *Victory* cell, and I've been nothing but a pain about it. Appropriate behaviour for an alam mage, I guess. But not what you deserved. There's nothing I can do to thank you. I can tell you I will do everything I can to survive. There may be more nights when I cannot be here, but when I am, I'm sometimes one thing and sometimes another. It seems to be a part of these dreams, dipping into different pockets of my soul. But no matter how I am here, these nights are what I think of to escape the days—your stories, your brightness, your laugh. They'll come and take me away again. But until they do, tonight, I want to know you're here, no matter what happens in the waking world."

Noor shivered in spite of the fire. She wondered if he'd rehearsed that, what made him feel he needed to thank her.

"I'm going to save you," she said, keeping her voice even. "You don't deserve what they're doing to you. And, Rami—" She slid her fingertips across his hand, between the lines and calluses, a universe in his palm.

"Rami, if we can, I want to meet the free you in the waking world, when you can choose to leave or find someone else—*let me finish*—to be whoever it is you're going to be. That's what the best part of me wanted for you on the *Victory* when I left you to them. And that's what I want now, more than anything. You deserve to have a chance to do better, to get *better*."

He held her hand, staring at it, the only sound that of the fire crackling. And then he met her gaze. "Not long ago, I would have said nothing in me needed changing. But here on this beach, I know peace and a quiet in my soul I've never felt before. I don't know if it comes from the moonlight, from the water, from the darkness in this cave—or if it's just you."

She shivered and gripped him tightly as if by just holding on, they could stay here, and he would remain unharmed.

Finally, when the fire had become uncomfortably warm on her back, Noor pulled away. She glanced out the cave entrance to check their time. The new moon made the stars impossibly bright behind Rami. Then Noor smacked herself on the forehead.

"Wreath!" she shouted, and Rami startled so badly she held his arm to steady him. "Wreath," she repeated in a saner voice as he scrunched his eyebrows in utter confusion.

"There was this old woman at the wheel," Noor explained. "She had a wreath—and she had your book—*Tales as Old as Time*. And there were these stars and the British, *the British*, Rami, the British!" His eyes widened, his hands going up as if she was seawater-drinking mad.

"What about the British?" He spoke slowly, emphasising his words to break through her revelation.

She fumbled, the order of things mixed up in her mind, struggling to get it all out, then said, ticking off her fingers: "We haven't known where you are, so we can't rescue you." Another finger: "You can't tell us where you are because they won't tell you." Another: "But if you could get outside, you might be able to recognise where you are from the star charts, if I bring them next time. We'll know whether you're in Muscat or Salalah." She met his eyes and held them, willing him to understand. "Muscat's harbour faces north; Salalah's faces south."

He said, voice patient, "But they'll never let me go outside."

"The wreaths, Rami, *the wreaths*!" Her mind raced to the end of the story. "The day after tomorrow is the British Christmas. The guide we had at the last naval prison said it's their policy to let any prisoner who asks to go out to a Christian service under the stars on their Christmas. If you ask, they'll have to let you out, have to let you see the stars. It's a religious thing with them."

He got it. "Then I can tell you where I am."

"Yes," she said, filled with hope. "Then we can get you free."

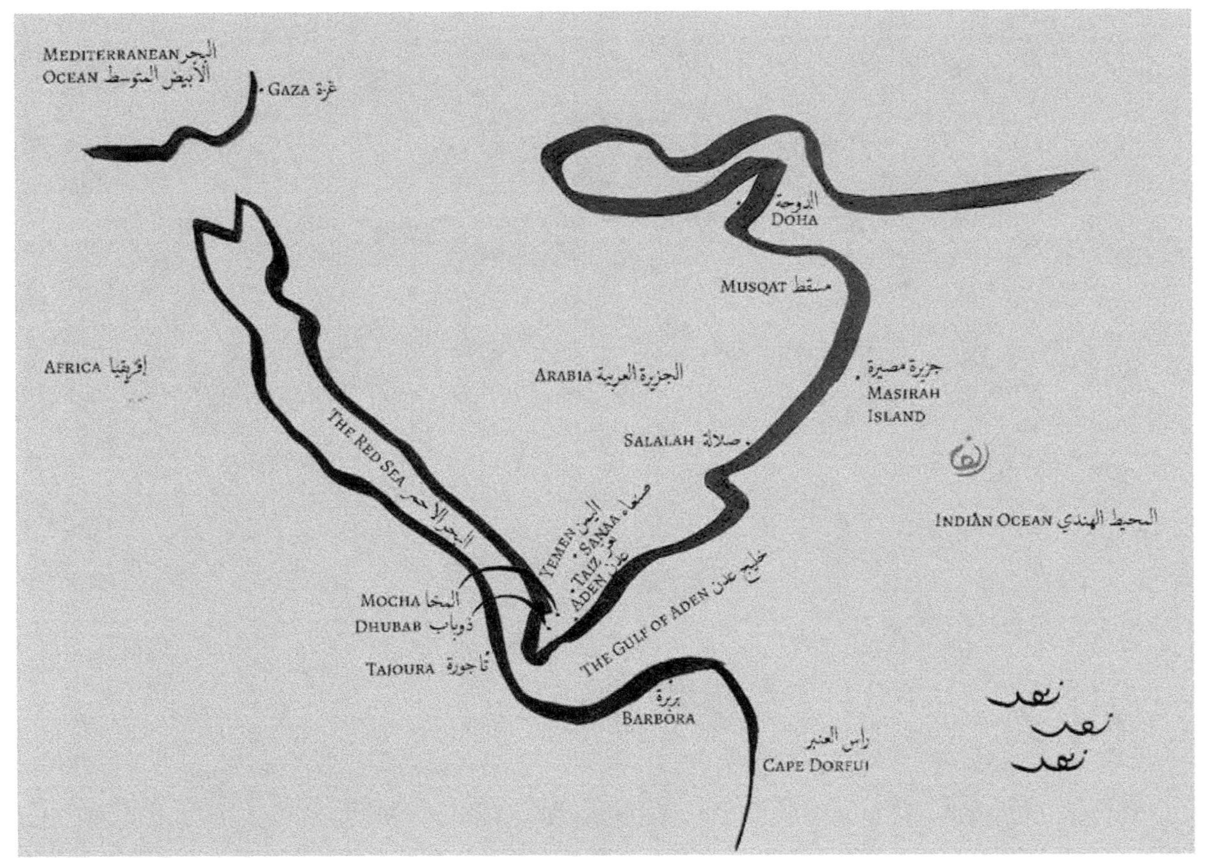
MEDITERRANEAN OCEAN
البحر الأبيض المتوسط
GAZA   غزة
AFRICA   إفريقيا
DOHA   الدوحة
MUSQAT   مسقط
ARABIA   الجزيرة العربية
جزيرة مصيرة
MASIRAH ISLAND
SALALAH   صلالة
THE RED SEA   البحر الأحمر
YEMEN   اليمن
SANAA   صنعاء
TAIZ   تعز
ADEN   عدن
خليج عدن   THE GULF OF ADEN
INDIAN OCEAN   المحيط الهندي
MOCHA   المخا
DHUBAB   ذوباب
TAJOURA   تاجورة
BARBORA   بربرة
رأس العنبر
CAPE DORFUI

Chapter Six

NOOR'S DISPATCH TO the emira took the cold, distant tone she felt her leader wanted: *"They are using sleep deprivation on him; the only rest he is getting is when they knock him out. He's experienced a lot of damage but still holds fast to hope. We have a plan that I think will work; I am hoping it will be only days before he is free. But did not tell him so in case it doesn't work; I don't want to give him false hope."*

This time, Noor received a swift reply, acknowledging receipt and ending with: *"Noor, in my experience of the world, there has never been anything false about hope."*

Noor worked with James all morning, calculating exactly which star charts she would have to memorise to allow Rami—disoriented, isolated, beaten, and sleep-deprived—to quickly tell the difference between the starscapes of Muscat and Salalah. Razan had slept even less than Noor in the past few days and was catching up in the hold.

Noor and James studied the orientation of the mouths of the ports near the two prisons, noted the time when Noor usually met Rami in dreams, and figured out every constellation that would be visible from either location. The work was long and mathematical, but James was ready, and Noor focused. Usama sailed the *Cormorant* to a point as equidistant from Muscat and Salalah as they could manage.

Noor spent the rest of the day memorizing her constellations. If Rami was in Muscat and could get outside, he would see the Lizard, the Dragon, and the Greater Bear. If he was in Salalah, he'd see the River, the Furnace, and the Sculptor's Tool.

After she could draw the star charts by hand, blindfolded, Noor had hours to go before sleeping. She grabbed James and went around the ship, going over the Arabic words for everything they saw.

"Sea is *baher*, with a hard *H*," she said, then giggled when James tried to repeat the sounds to her. She showed him how to make the hard *H*, placing her hand at the base of her throat and practicing with him until he got it.

She knelt, touching the deck. "Cedar is *arzi*—"

"And oak?"

"That would be *balout*."

He gave her a crooked smile. "And swimming?"

"*Sibaha*," she said and smiled back. "I am looking forward to learning, you know. There's something—" She glanced across the great waves around them, narrowing her eyes. It wasn't often she thought of all this wide, perfect, open space as a threat, but some part of her deep soul knew it was there, always. "I'd like to have options other than my magic if I go overboard. That hasn't always saved me in the past."

"And I look forward to teaching you," James said.

She bumped her shoulder against his. "*Sadiqi*," she said. "It means my friend, who is a man."

"And for you, I'd say…"

Noor gave him a moment to see if he could remember how to build the word himself from the parts she'd laid out.

"*Sadiqati*," he said, and she clapped.

They kept on, clambering around the ship, down into the hold, out onto the rigging, laughing and sharing words and a hope for days when the hardest task before them would be teaching James how to roll the soft part of his throat properly to say the letter '*ghrain*'.

Finally, he called a stop and flopped down on his back on the deck. She lowered herself to sit beside him.

"I want to ask you something and I don't know how to." James said, his eyes on the wildly multi-coloured sunset sky.

"You want to know how to say the letter '*ayn*' as in the word 'Arab'. It's not as hard as you think. You just meow like a cat and take the sound after the *M*—"

"No, Noor. It's about the Sword of Sidon."

She stilled, eyes drifting up to his, but then he stared over the gunwale at the white-capped waves.

"In yesterday's dispatch," he continued, "you said their abuse was getting more 'personal.' What does that mean?"

A chill, starting in her wrists, shivered at her shoulders and worked its way down her spine to twist in her gut.

"I don't know if Rami wants everyone to know the details of what he's going through," Noor started, remembering the things she'd never told anyone but Rami—just him and only in a dream.

"We need to build sympathy for him in the resistance, or at least a shared understanding that he's been punished, if not for what he did at Sidon or what he's done for years, then for his other crimes. And maybe, if enough people believe he's been punished enough, they won't fight for him to be executed when he's tried. At least there's no punishment-by-torture allowed in the resistance. But not everything that happens in that prison cell needs to be for public consumption."

James rolled his head over to her. "I'm not 'public', Noor. If we get him back, we'll be sharing water with him and sleeping quarters, since he'll probably be in the captain's cabin with us. What do I need to know?"

Noor's stomach warmed at the way he'd framed it, that it wasn't about gawking at someone else's injury.

"When he's on board, I wouldn't touch him without asking," she said, and James pulled himself up to sit and wrapped his arms around his knees until his knuckles stood out.

"All right, I can do that," he said.

They sat in awkward silence for a while, and Noor mourned it, mourned even a minute's loss of their tight friendship as he thought about what she might be saying. Then, her James was back, clapping his hand on her shoulder.

"We'll get him soon, Noor. And maybe we can finally teach you how to swim, let you be the student for once."

She felt a chill as she remembered the water going over her head, but nodded and stood. "I'd like that," she said, stretching her arms and then coughing at her smell. "I've got to clean up, and then I'm going to bed."

He tossed her a lazy salute and went to keep Usama company at the wheel.

After a scrub down with a bucket of seawater, Noor settled into her hammock, feeling her exhaustion rising. She closed her eyes, her mind quieter than it had been since Rami had flinched away from her in the cave. She'd missed spending time with her friend. The constellations she'd studied were as clear as her memory of the pattern of moles on Rami's face.

Noor rolled over and felt a lump under her pillow. She'd probably been too exhausted the night before to be aware of it. She pulled out the book, *Tales as Old as Time*, carefully bound-up in one of her thick scarves. A scrap of paper marked the story of "Psyche and Cupid" written in Mianning's broad hand.

"Yours for safe keeping until we get him back."

*

SHE SAW HIM and started swimming. Shoving with her arms and legs, she drove herself farther down because this time, he'd drifted away from the cove into the open current, his impractical coat like a sail. Noor fought against the underwater river as the temperature dropped, her lungs filled to bursting. She threw herself towards the surface, taking a massive gulp of air before pushing herself down again, using magic to sail down towards the seabed.

Rami was deathly still as Noor hugged him around the middle. She aligned herself with her magic, reaching out for the bright life above the waves, and tugged, surging up until they both came gasping to the surface. But they were far from the cave now, sweeping southwards on the current. So she struck out, towing him along in the water, until she found a low shelf of a beach, the shattered and sanded-down remains of a long-ago rockfall.

If this were the real Gaza, not the Gaza of her dreams, the fisherman would stand in the doorways of their crooked houses on the uneven sand, calling out to them with bright smiles and eyes, taking everything in, squid and sardines and other good things to eat roasting in their ovens.

But she and Rami were alone in her dreams, the only people in a moonlit world.

She barely got him ashore, her use of magic sapping her, her strength failing fast. Noor lay there, him heavy in her lap, trying to push her core warmth into his body. Finally, he coughed, spluttering as he brought up seawater from his lungs. She sat up against a rounded stone and propped him between her legs, letting him rest his back against her front, her arms around his waist as he got his breath back. Without waiting for him to speak, she passed a message into his mind:

I have the starscapes. Take them before they take you back.

He sighed and leaned his head against her shoulder. She felt his mind shift, doors open enough for her to make the connection. His hair was tangled and dripping, the long line where their bodies joined no warmer than the sea they'd dragged themselves out of, but in that moment, Noor wouldn't have traded places with anyone, not when she could feel him breathe between her legs, not when she could feel him striding along the light-drenched corridors of her mind.

She opened a door to a room without walls or shape. It was like standing inside a clear ship in the middle of the whole universe's tumble of constellations—a room of galaxies. He stepped inside, eyes sharp, his dark clothes making him like the silhouette in his book, a man against the stars. Noor stepped in behind him and closed the door. She gathered up the collections of stars he would need to memorise and tossed them to him. Rami started and caught them as he would a ball. Then he spread out his hands, expanding and shrinking the stars, twisting them this angle and that.

She stepped up to him, hands on his, gripped the edges of the world between his fingers and *yanked*, arms wide, until they stood together in the middle of a revolving star storm. Noor turned, giving him her back, and pointed out the Sculptor's Tool as it passed. He leaned down, chin hooked over her shoulder and breath warm on her cheek, to see where she was pointing.

He raised his arm alongside hers, the inside of his elbow hooking around the outside of hers, notched together like they were formed that way, while his other arm slipped around her waist to steady himself against her.

Noor's stomach tucked and tumbled as she realised how desperately close his hips were to hers, but she slowed the stars down to show him the River constellation, tracing the stars in their passage, over and over, until they lay steady in his mind. Next, the Furnace to their right. She showed him the stars of Muscat: the Lizard, the Dragon, and the Greater Bear, each in their places in her mind and now in his.

Noor started to step away, wanting to give him space to practice. But his grip on her hip tightened by a fraction, and she kept still, his body a breath from hers. Together, they lowered their arms, and she turned towards him, the heat between their bodies building as sweet things broke in her belly, fusing with hot metal only to shatter again.

She stepped forward, arms going around his chest, her face tucked into the bend of his neck. And then his arms linked behind her tight, pressing them together as though they might, for a single breath, share the same space. They held that moment, timeless, poured from gold and sealed in amber. No real time existed inside the mind, and it could have lasted eons, their bodies apart but their minds together, fused at the broken edges.

Then he huffed in her ear, and she was about to ask him what was so funny when he doubled over, hand on his stomach, sucking air as if he'd been punched in the gut. He fell to his knees like some invisible guard had struck him across the back, and she fell with him, eyes locked with his as the stars froze.

He forced the words out. "No, it's not that—they're taking me, they're—" Pain echoed in every syllable.

"Rami, we're coming—Rami, hold on—" She wanted to shout over the agony in his face, but she forced herself to whisper instead, trying to keep him there with her, away from them and whatever was happening in the waking world. His breathing had kicked up as he focused on something behind her.

He gasped out one word, "Noor—"

Then he was gone.

Noor was alone in her mind as her stars fell, clattering around her shoulders like sprays of hard metal from a smith's anvil, cooling before they reached the ground.

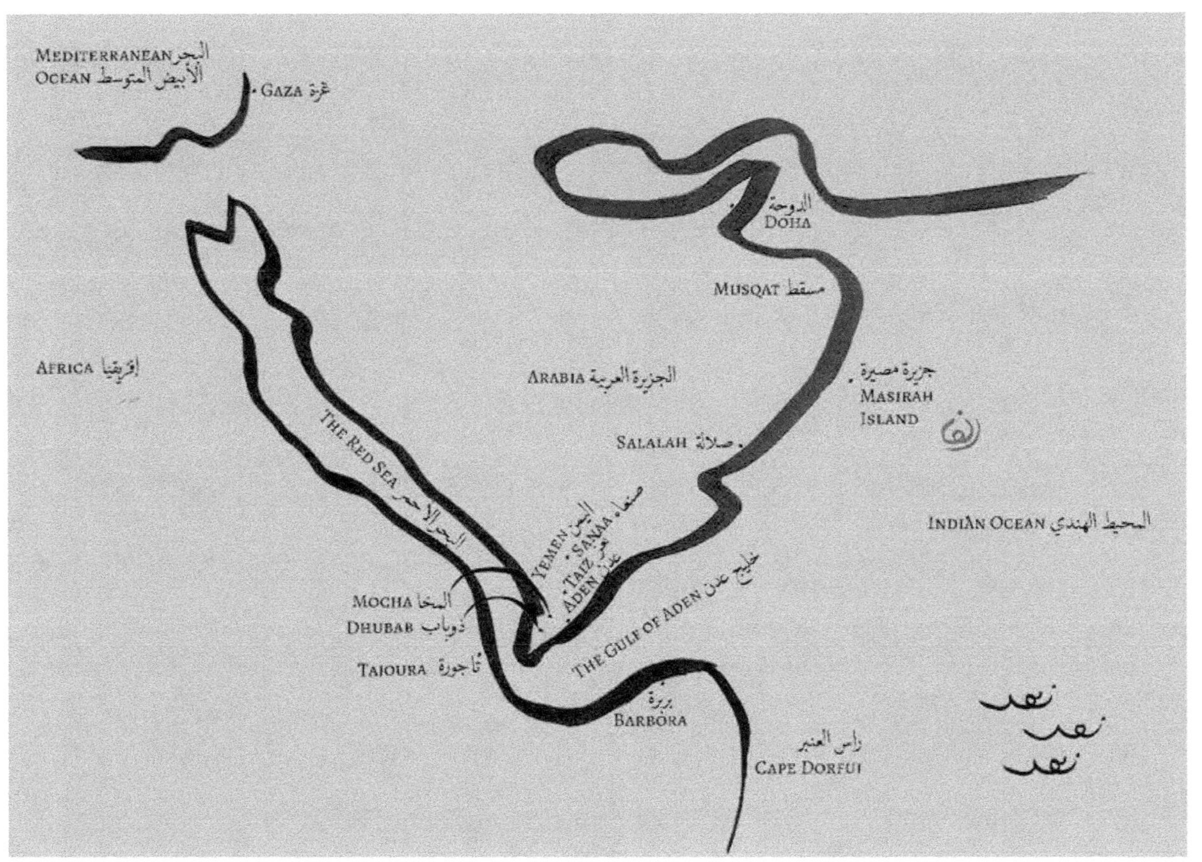
MEDITERRANEAN OCEAN البحر الأبيض المتوسط
GAZA غزة
AFRICA إفريقيا
DOHA الدوحة
MUSQAT مسقط
ARABIA الجزيرة العربية
MASIRAH ISLAND جزيرة مصيرة
SALALAH صلالة
INDIAN OCEAN المحيط الهندي
THE RED SEA البحر الأحمر
YEMEN اليمن
SANAA صنعاء
TAIZ تعز
ADEN عدن
THE GULF OF ADEN خليج عدن
MOCHA المخا
DHUBAB ذوباب
TAIOURA تاجورة
BARBORA بربرة
CAPE DORFUI رأس العنبر

Chapter Seven

NOOR AWOKE WITH a start, rolling out of her hammock and gasping, arms around her stomach. She hunched against the side of the hull, fisting her hands until her knuckles creaked, and screamed. Razan was there, arms around her waist, gripping her tight, holding her to reality. But it was so much, so much, too much—

Usama hustled down the stairs, jambiya appearing in his hands as if he was expecting the Sword of Sidon to be menacing her from under Razan's hammock.

When Usama saw her huddling against Razan, he sheathed his weapon and dropped to his knees. He patted her shoulder tentatively as she sobbed.

"James!" He yelled in a panic, and her friend came tumbling down the stairs, modesty barely maintained with a hastily wrapped sheet. Usama was also shirtless and shoe-less, his hair distinctly mussed.

For some reason she couldn't explain, the sight of them—anxious-eyed, tousle-haired, a blooming bouquet of what appeared to be fresh hickeys on Usama's throat—snapped her sobs over to laughter. She shook with them, and James knelt beside her, giving her a safe place to lean against.

"Let it out, habibati, just let it out," James said, and she did, eyes squeezed so tight she hoped nothing could come out.

Then, she eased back and wiped her tears. "Sorry," she said, and her three friends shared a worried glance.

"Come on," Razan said. "Let's get some water and food into you."

Noor brightened at the prospect of food. Razan led the way, but Noor had only walked a few steps when she raised her hand and stopped. The other three turned to her.

"They grabbed him in his sleep. I don't know what they're doing right now. I gave him the star charts. If he can survive the night and whatever comes with tomorrow, we'll know where he is."

Usama frowned. "Yes, and then we'll go and get him. But that will be hours and hours from now, and you need food, water, and rest. In that order."

"All right," Noor said and trailed behind as they all went up to the deck for a midnight snack. As she chewed, she sent her update to Emira bint Asma.

"He knows the plan and has the information. They're catching him when he's sleeping and beating him. He's getting weaker, farther away, but he'll keep fighting. He'll keep fighting until we get there."

They received the return message. *"We have redoubled our diplomatic efforts. They have received our ambassador's complaints and will be sending inspectors to the two remaining prisons. When you find him, you may have help inside."*

Noor was glad the British were reacting but didn't expect much. The crew of the *Cormorant* would have to save Rami themselves.

*

THE NEXT NIGHT, Noor went to bed early, falling hard and deep into sleep. She opened her eyes to the barest crescent of the Mediterranean moon gilding the underwater world, its light so fine it only showed the edges of things, illuminating nothing of their substance.

Focusing, she spied a black shape with its jacket tangled in the bones of a pilot whale at the bottom of the lagoon. She kicked hard and propelled herself towards the form. The moonlight caught the edges of him too: his closed eyes with tiny bubbles trapped beneath his eyelashes, shimmering in the cast-off light; the impossibly tangled jacket, darker than the grey stone of the sea floor; his dark hand, outreached and desperate for hers.

She gripped his wrist, felt his answering squeeze, and envisioned his coat cut and him loosed, and he was. He pushed up to the surface with her, arms strong, eyes open.

"I know where I am," he said with his first gasp of breath. "Salalah. I saw the night sky during their Christmas bonfire, just like we planned, and it's Salalah."

She got him to the beach, got the fire blazing. "I will be back here," she said. "But the sooner we can set course—"

He held his hands to the fire with a slight tremble but much more steadily than they'd been in weeks. "Then you come for me."

*

SHE AWOKE AND stumbled from her hammock before her eyes were fully open. Razan came to her side.

"Salalah," Noor gasped.

Razan turned and scrambled up to the deck. Noor heard her call to Usama at the wheel, and then, the ship swung wildly. The *Cormorant* pivoted nearly in place, prow pointed south, following the route James had so carefully researched.

Noor turned back to her hammock before calling over her shoulder, "Need anything from me?"

"Go back to bed, habibati," Usama shouted down the hatch. "Tell him we'll be there tomorrow night, midnight. Tell him to be ready."

*

NOOR AWOKE UNDER the surface and broke straight for the surface, feeling lighter than air, lighter than light.

She called out across the water, "*We are coming. We'll be there tomorrow at midnight,*" as she swam towards the bright fire in the cave and the dark figure in front of it.

Rami's head snapped around, and he shouted back to her, "Do you need me to come get you this time?"

"In the waking world, maybe," Noor responded, heading for shore. "But here, I can swim."

The sickle moon shone down, halfway through it course for the night and seeming so much brighter than it had before.

Rami waded in to join her in the shallows, and she grinned up at him, so happy she could crow.

We are so close.

He nudged her soaked shoulder with his dry one, his imperial uniform crisp and warm in the moonlight.

"I'm going to get your clothes all wet again," she said.

"They're not what I'm wearing."

She glanced at him quizzically, and he gestured to her guntiino.

"Is that what you wore to bed?"

"No, I'm wearing my sleeping clothes," she said, fingering the colourful fabric. "But in dreams—"

"We appear here as we think of ourselves."

He knelt beside the fire, gesturing for her to join him. She folded to her knees, leaving a space between them. He glanced at her and then into the fire, his mouth hardening.

"I remember my mother told me once," he said, "before she abandoned me to the teacher in Taiz, that for years after she grew out her hair, she would dream it was short, the way it had been when she was a girl in Aden. The book you mentioned, it was her mother's, my grandmother Asma's. She gave it to my mother for me when I was born. She's probably the only person in the resistance who will be happy to see me if this works."

"The emira isn't the only support you have in the resistance, Rami. Not then, and not now."

"I don't really think of you as being 'in the resistance'."

"You should." She pulled away, meeting his cave-light-dimmed eyes. "The resistance is my home now, my found family. Your ship attacked people I cared about in Aden. You've killed friends of people I love. But in spite of that, in spite of everything else you've done, for the past month, Razan, Mianning, Usama, and James have been hunting the world to set you free."

"They're doing it for you," Rami assured her, and Noor scoffed.

"I don't know what hold you think I, or anyone else could have on Mianning, Rami. But he has been piloting long hours, foregoing good contracts, holding off on mourning the anniversary of Yusef's death properly because he wants *you* back."

She closed her eyes, imagining the big man. "He may want you back because he wants to shout at you until he loses his voice for all of the dog-souled things you've done." She opened her eyes to Rami staring at her, his mouth slightly open. "But he didn't just let us use the *Cormorant*; he *insisted* on coming."

"Did Mianning ever tell you why he named her the *Cormorant* when he bought her years before he met my father?" he asked quietly. Noor shook her head, letting him shift the subject's course.

"In Shanghai they have cormorants," he began, "those dark, long-necked diving birds. Theirs tend to be fatter than the ones we get here—bigger, greyer, and with the patch under their eyes more golden than orange. In Shanghai, the fishermen would take them as babies and put rings of steel around their necks. Not enough to choke, but enough to stop them from swallowing the fish they caught."

"That's horrible," Noor said, remembering the feel of chains.

"I'm not saying it's right. They used them as fishing birds, like the English have hunting dogs. When they were done, the fisherman would cut up some of the fish and give it to them in small enough pieces to get past the ring. They would switch the rings our for larger ones as they got older, but they'd never get them off."

Noor thought of the ship that had brought her to freedom, and for the first time, it felt less like an oasis and more like a trap.

"I hate that."

Rami said wryly, "So did Mianning. He told me when he was a little boy, he wanted to free his father's cormorants, cut the rings from their necks, and watch them dive and swim and soar for their own pleasure. No one else's. The *Cormorant* is his freedom, his constant reminder that living things should not be in chains. That's why he helps out with the resistance; I think that's why he is helping you to come get me, even after everything I have done."

His eyes were a tideland with half-bare honesty and half-roiling dark currents. She didn't know what to say to that, but she ran her hand along the Cormorant's wheel, feeling the smooth curves of it.

"Anyway," he continued, "Usama ibn Salam can't be there for me. And is James that former British seaman, the one from Tadjoura?"

"Yes, he's the reason I got out of Tadjoura. Or really, because of Usama. But Usama—" And Noor thought about it, not wanting to sugar-coat what Rami would be walking into. She thought about Usama's anger at the Sword of Sidon, his jambiya at the ready last night, and she decided that, for tonight, she would only tell part of the truth. "Usama promised me he would tell me stories of babysitting you."

It was worth it, saving the hardest damage for later, just to hear that surprised bark of laughter from deep in Rami's chest. The weariness and pain dropped from his face, and he looked closer to her age than Usama's.

"He *wouldn't*," he said.

She grinned, full-toothed and gleeful. "I think he would."

Rami chuckled, and his hands dropped from her shoulders. He turned towards the fire.

"Have you ever met Razan?" Noor asked after a pause.

Something in her tone must have drawn his attention, because he turned to her, concerned. "I don't believe I've had the pleasure."

"Say that when you've met her, seen what she thinks of you," Noor said, words out before she could catch them.

"What did I—" He paused. "No, I can imagine any number of rea-sons why she would hate me. Is there more I should know if we're to share a vessel?"

She considered, choosing her words with more care. "I will let her tell you what she wishes to tell you. But I would tell you to tread lightly."

"I was planning on doing that anyway, but I appreciate the warning." He peered at her over the fire. "Is there anything else?"

"She and I, we care for each other. Like Usama and James do." Her heart was galloping in her chest, and she tasted copper.

"Ah," he said. "This whole time?"

"Yes. Yes, since before the second time we met on the *Victory*."

"And she is on the *Cormorant* with you?"

"We sleep together in the hold with her hammock just below mine when we're not sharing. She researched the star charts I shared with you, that told us where you are."

"So she's been in the resistance a long time?"

"Since Sidon, yes."

"Ah."

"She is brilliant and kind and fierce, and I have no idea how any of this will work." She shrugged a shoulder. "People live in multiple marriages all the time, so there have to be ways it works."

"Are we to be your harem?" he said, his voice bearing a bit more of the lightness it had before.

"Nothing like that," Noor replied, matching his tone. "I wouldn't expect you two to share a room, much less a title. I'm...I'm trying to assume nothing. Nothing about what it will be like outside of these dreams, off of that ship. We've charted a course for a quiet beach after we rescue you. I hope we'll have a few weeks before things get complicated again. For you to heal, for us all to rest. And in that time, I think we'll see what there is to be seen."

"I didn't take you for a 'wait and see' kind of woman."

She shrugged a shoulder. "I've had cares enough all my life. What I have with Razan feels better than anything else I've had, even at the worst times when she and I were at odds over you. And with you"—she raised a hand, laying it softly on his arm—"this feels important, this connection, this work. I haven't had a lot of friends before, the kind I was physical with or any other kind, but I don't know of a rule that says one's friends must all like one another. Perhaps you can both get to know me without spending time with each other."

"I hadn't even thought of an after, a quiet beach, and time to learn, to talk. That sounds far better than I had expected."

"What did you expect?"

"A long walk and a short drop, mostly. Or more of the same of what I have here but from people who share my home language and my God."

Noor shuddered. "No torture, not if I have any say over it." That was a reminder she had to get back on task. "Before we wake, I do need to ask— Is there anything you can tell us about where you're being kept?"

He shook his head, hair trailing across his face. "They kept me blindfolded my entire way out. It's not big. From the cell to the outside was fifty steps for me. No stairs, no big turns." His voice lowered. "I couldn't walk well. There hasn't been a lot of food, my connection to magic is still broken, and it's the first time they've let me out of my cell since I woke up there two months ago. Everything that happens during waking hours takes place in the cell."

He leaned away from her, weight going onto an arm braced behind his back. "It was only for a minute, but Allah, it was good to breathe fresh air, good to see the stars. Here, let me—" He reached over to grip her hand, squeezed tight, but nothing happened other than the tingles running up her arm that she tried desperately to ignore. It was as though he was trying to open his mind to her, but—

She squeezed his hand back. "It's the urodelas. They're blocking your access to magic."

"I know—I think they're prisoners too."

"Yes. I saw them in Doha. It felt like being gut punched and sat on when it first hit me." She traced her thumb over the back of his hand. "I can try to see inside your mind, see your memories of last night to get your sense of the layout, the environment."

He nodded warily.

"Other things happened that night that you might not want to experience." Noor shook her head, her resolve firm.

"The best chance we have of getting you out," she continued, "is if I know everything I can about where you're being kept. I don't have perfect control, but I will try to only see what you want to show me."

"All right."

Noor extended her magic, reaching outwards rather than inviting him in. She felt the cedar wall of a ship at her back and opened her eyes to see the image he'd made for her in his mind. She stood, and the floor tilted rhythmically. There, on the wall, was the peg where she hung her bag, but the second hook she'd added beside it for her jambiya was missing. And there, the long scar ran across the floor from some musket battle deep in the past. *It's a memory of the Cormorant. The hammock and a hanging lamp's familiar smell confirms it.*

"Oh," she said, remembering what Rami had said on the *Victory* about first creating a safe place inside his mind before opening his memories to her, a place that he shielded with his magic. Her heart ached. *Oh, Rami.*

Noor walked up to the hatch and pressed her hands against it. At first, the wood was unyielding. Then, with what felt like the permission of the mind exposed by the ship, it swung silently upwards. She climbed to the deck, but there was no one there, only her and the furled sails, alone in the empty rocking sea.

Her boots echoed on the deck as she walked towards the gunwale under the arcing moon, seeing the shape of the sea by starlight. Then Noor was doubled over, on her knees, gasping, one hand fisted on the deck, the other tight to her stomach.

When she caught her breath, she was in a British prison cell, coughing as if she was going throw up. Her hair covered her face, black, straight, and wild, and her shoulders were so broad she knew she'd have to turn sideways to get through the narrow cell door. Her body told her it was the end of a beating, not the beginning of one. This wasn't Rami as he'd been taken from her last night. It was what he'd seen in the moments before midnight of the British Christmas.

Her breathing hitched from a cracked rib stabbing into her side as the uniformed guards brought in manacles, and she catalogued her surroundings: stone floor, stone walls, iron bars; the urodelas held in cages embedded in the corridor walls, growling low in their massive purple chests, pressed to bars. Their tails switched back and forth hard enough to shake their bodies; their big purple eyes met hers with something like understanding.

It was nothing like what she'd seen in Doha. The stale air stale tasted of sweat and fear. Noor tried not to dig too far into the injuries to Rami's body, tried to respect his privacy as best she could, but his pain and hunger and fear overpowered her, drenching her in sweat.

She brought her fist up from the ground and snapped the knee of the guard in front of her. Her emotions didn't drive it; this was Rami. Even as the guard's fist connected with the back of her head, driving her face into the chipped stone and splitting the skin over her cheek, the urodelas howling, Rami's fire burned in her chest, molten and un-dimmed.

Then, a bag was over her head, her hands behind her back, wrenched up so far her shoulder blades ached under half-healed cut and slash marks. Her legs and bare feet throbbed as she stood, yet she fought her captors when they tried to drag her, forced them to let her walk.

Walking let her count the paces—fifty-three in a mostly straight line at Rami's much longer stride to perhaps seventy of hers. Then, she sensed the space opening up, the scent of fresh air and the sea, with fine sand under her feet. Noor wondered if it was her hold breaking, her con-sciousness coming back to the enclosing dream, to Gaza, to the dark la-goon, but she smelled blood from her cheek, messily smeared across her face by the bag. She also smelled smoke from a fire and cooking meat. She heard the clinking of bottles and the strumming of a stringed instru-ment: a Christmas party. A tremendous *BOOM* resounded followed by the smell of sulphur, and then she gasped when the bag was ripped from her head, her pupils contracting painfully as she stared into the bloody glare of Mysorean rockets—no, *fireworks*. That's what they called them. The last of them for the night, if the extended extravagance of the display was anything to judge by.

"You have one minute," the guard said, his hand crushing tight on Rami's biceps. Rami nodded, tilted his head up, and closed his eyes.

Noor panicked in the renewed darkness. There wouldn't be enough time for him to see the constellations. *Had he guessed at where he was? Why did he close his eyes when this could be their only chance?*

Then she felt his pupils relaxing, and she could hear the noises around him so much better now, smell the scents. A half minute went by, and then Rami snapped his eyes open, scanned the horizon— There it was, the River, the Furnace, and there, the Sculptor's Tool, on the horizon where she'd shown him it would be. *Salalah.*

His heart beat big and wild in her chest, and he searched the sky, kept dragging in every detail: the sea was a short sprint away; they were in a cove off the main harbour between two tall cliffs; the guards were getting fairly drunk.

He sucked in as much free air as he could, even as his ribs cried out. He elbowed the guard in the stomach and crouched, desperate now for details. Maybe a dozen British soldiers lounged around it, a few armed. Their housing must be near the prison.

Rami glanced back at the entrance, barely caught a hint of high, sharp cliffs diving straight into the sea, the prison dug into a cave. A massive, mostly waterproof door hung wide open beside an entrance that, from the seaweed hanging above it, would have to spend some time below the high tide line. Noor knew the tides on this coast could vary as much as the height of a man as they approached the winter monsoon season.

Noor yanked all this information into herself and stored it in a smuggler's compartment where nothing could change it as the bag went back over Rami's head.

She stayed with him as he was walked back down to the prison entrance, stayed with him as he was thrown into his cell, the guard locking the door behind himself. She stayed with him as the guard beat him, Rami protecting his head the best he could with his arms behind his back. When it was over, the guards released his hands before kicking him one last time, then rushed out and hastily locked the cell door behind them.

Rami pulled himself onto his mat on the floor and tried to arrange his battered body comfortably without much success. He faced the wall and kept his eyes open long enough to scratch a mark with his thumb on the chalky stone. She saw twelve groups of five marks: sixty days he'd been there.

Noor stayed with him until he fell asleep. She was about to pull back when she felt his body crushed beneath cold, quiet water. His lungs burned, but he was too wounded to struggle just yet as the cold compressed and soothed the aches in his muscles and numbed the sting of his cuts. Rami felt something under the need for oxygen, a bubble growing under his diaphragm: hope.

He held his breath, hearing his heartbeat slow, slow, slow, and then—a presence. He reached out, grabbing for her hand, sure of where she was, sure that she would grip him back.

Rami opened his eyes, and through them, Noor saw herself as he saw her—hair streaming back from her face, her brown eyes full of protective fire and determination, and behind her, the slight light of the moon scattered across the surface of the waves like a star field.

Noor snapped back to her own self, still disoriented by that image of herself diving down to him, by Rami's conviction when he saw her that he would be saved.

Then, Noor was back in her own skin, back in the cave. While inside his mind, she had twined her arms around him, her face buried in his shoulder, with his arms warm and steady at her back. She loosened her grip, thinking of his broken rib.

"I'm sorry," she said. "I got what I needed, but I didn't want to pry."

Rami shook his head slightly before pressing his cheek against the top of her head. "You're just in time. They'll come for me in moments, and there's something I need to do."

Noor gazed at him, questioning, searching. The split on his cheek was gone, as were the blackening and bruises she now knew mottled his face outside this dream. His skin glowed in the firelight, the constellations of his moles begging to be kissed, and his eyes—his eyes were a dark drink, with something shining in them like stars.

He traced his fingers up her back to her neck, thumbs soft across her jawline as he held her face. "Just this once," he said, brushing the pad of his thumb under her lip. "Please."

Noor closed the distance between their mouths, kissing Rami fiercely. The touch of his soft lips on hers made her stomach drop, her blood thrum in her wrists, rush in her ears, carrying the news under her skin, tingling and tapping in her gut and lower. She kissed him, digging her hands into his shoulders, pulling herself closer to him. He broke away, gasped for breath, and she pressed their foreheads together.

"Not just this once." She whispered, voice catching. "Not just this once."

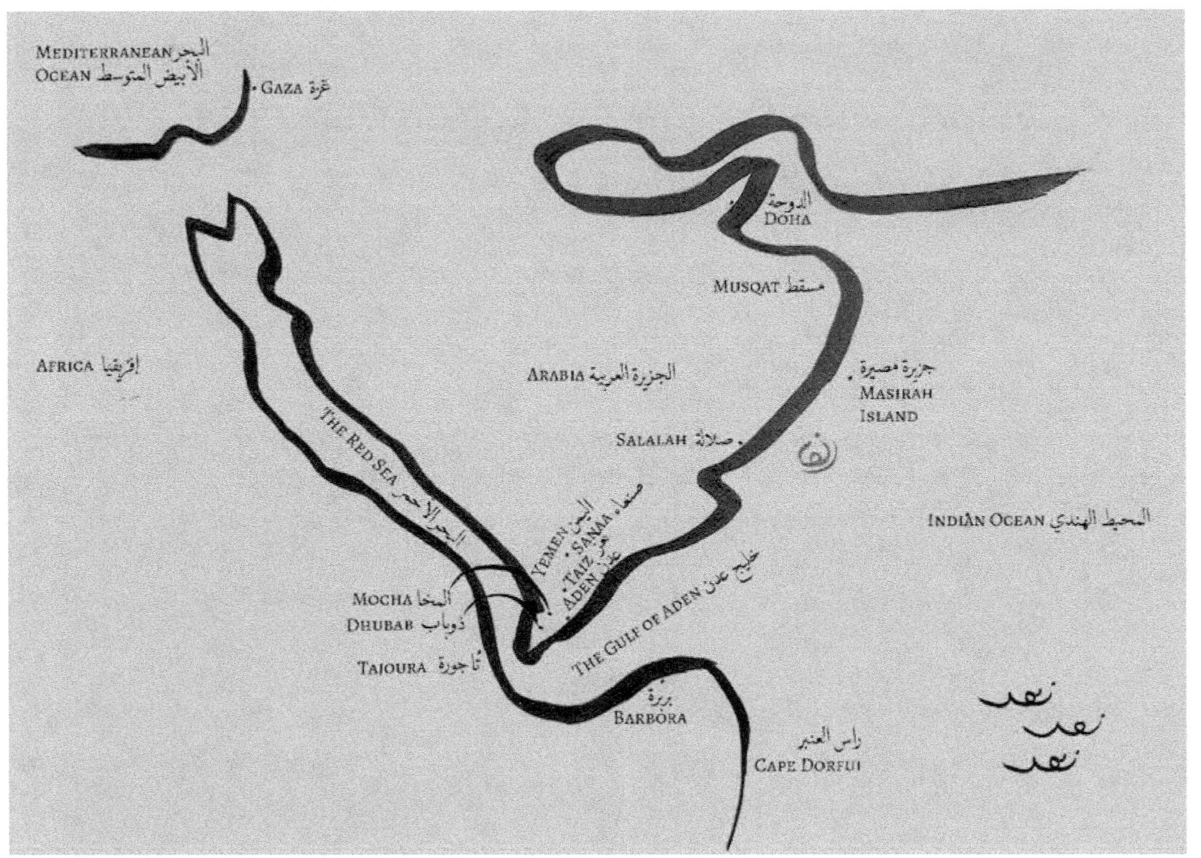
MEDITERRANEAN OCEAN البحر الأبيض المتوسط
GAZA غزة
AFRICA أفريقيا
THE RED SEA البحر الأحمر
DOHA الدوحة
MUSQAT مسقط
ARABIA الجزيرة العربية
MASIRAH ISLAND جزيرة مصيرة
SALALAH صلالة
INDIAN OCEAN المحيط الهندي
YEMEN اليمن
SANAA صنعاء
TAIZ تعز
ADEN عدن
THE GULF OF ADEN خليج عدن
MOCHA المخا
DHUBAB ذوباب
TAJOURA تاجورة
BARBORA بربرة
CAPE DORFUI رأس العنبر

Chapter Eight

ANOTHER EARLY WINTER monsoon blew in behind them. Warm rain lashed at the *Cormorant*. With Rami's memories of his surroundings and Razan's maps, Usama and Mianning made good time. The *Cormorant* would dock, an hour before midnight, on the other side of cliff face that projected deep into the sea, protecting the ship from view. The plan was simple. Noor, James, Razan, and Mianning would hike over the ridge, break in through the door by the sea, get Rami, and get out. Usama would keep the *Cormorant*'s sails ready.

"Do you have anything darker?" Noor asked as she rummaged through James's few clothes. She liked her red-and-gold guntiino, but she needed to be unseen, to avoid engaging the guards and killing anyone she didn't have to.

"There's got to be something black around here somewhere," James said, stepping over Noor's legs to poke his head out of his cabin to ask Mianning. He came back, a strange expression on his face.

"Mianning says he kept the Sword of Sidon's clothes."

Noor pulled her hair back, the last shirt she'd tried on having knocked it askew. "I didn't think you spoke Mandarin."

"Still don't," he said, "but Usama translated. Would that be weird, wearing his clothes?"

"I don't see why. Clothes are clothes. Where are they?"

It turned out, they were behind a false wall covering a *second* false wall in the hold. They found a small wooden chest, hand carved with thick iron bands holding it together and decades of scuff marks around the sides. The children's clothes started off tiny, for a baby, with carefully sewn-in initials on the back: R.A.N. The chest rocked as they unpacked it, Noor setting aside each item in a careful stack.

Lower down, they found tunics and pants—too small even for Noor. The colours got darker as she went deeper into the chest, and the fabrics rougher. Finally, she pulled out a shirt in James's size and another in hers. Or, at least, it would be close enough with a firm belting. She'd pair it with her grey pants and the sturdy boots she'd gotten in Aden. Razan's *abaya* was more than dark enough to keep her protected under cover of night.

She and James repacked the chest, and he'd nearly closed the lid when Noor shot out her hand to stop him.

"Look," she said.

There, hand-carved on the inner lid of the chest, right by the shiny iron hinges, were the words: *From Yusef Nuri to Rami ibn Arwa wa Nuri, on 1197 AH.* Noor examined it again, seeing how different the hinges were from the rest of it.

"I think this was his cradle."

James grimaced and stepped back. "So, his father, who died fighting his son's chosen empire, kept it for all of these years, tucked away where no one would find it. This family is knotted up in itself. It makes me wonder if we missed out on anything."

Noor shared an orphan's smile. "You seem to be making quite a nice family with Usama," she teased, nudging him with her elbow as they lifted the first and then the second false walls into place.

James shrugged, nose wrinkling. "Have you thought about what we're going to do after this?"

"I have. I was hoping for someplace quiet, a beach maybe, so you can teach me to swim."

James slung his arm around her waist, and she leaned her head onto his shoulder. "Then I vote we wait out the monsoon season at the beach. The British Empire will keep until the storms pass. Someplace warm, someplace sweet. I'll work with Razan and Mianning, find us one."

He shot her a look. "And if Rami needs some time to heal, getting him that will be a lot easier someplace outside of the conflict than at a resistance stronghold. I'm sure the emira would understand and give us a month or two to work our way back home. You, too, Noor. I remember when I first got free, got to Sierra Leone, I thought I had to pack all of my freedom into my first few weeks—going everywhere, doing every-thing, running up mountains, doing manhood ceremonies, eating and fighting and organizing and just—living as a free man. Never resting. The relationships you make when you're enslaved or during your first months of freedom can be *intense*. But that's not the same as strong. They can grow to be strong, but it takes time. And healing."

"You're one to talk about jumping into relationships."

He paused, then said, voice wry, "I am. Usama and I saw through each other immediately, but we've also had other relationships and know how to treat each other. I don't think you have. Which is why I'm worried for you, for this thing with the Swo—with Rami."

James took a breath. "Living after the nightmare we've been through is like trying to run on a sprained knee. You can do it; push yourself through it. But at some point, you either have to let yourself heal or accept you're going to live around it for the rest of your life. That Harmattan season in Sierra Leone, after the madness of the first few weeks, I let myself take time. I slept and ate and worked, but I spent a lot of time being quiet, thinking through what was done to me and how I wished the world was different. And it gave me what I needed. Time to survive what happened on the *Victory*. I'm telling you as a friend, as someone who has also known a life without freedom—I want you to have the kind of time I had. It's only been a few months since you killed Musa."

Noor turned to him. "I don't think I've been trying to avoid it. There just hasn't been the time. And I don't know if Mianning would let us keep the *Cormorant* out of commission for so long. There's a specific Buddhist mourning ritual that he wanted to perform at a proper temple."

"We need to make the time. We can get by without Mianning for a few months. Don't get me wrong, I love his company, but maybe that's the break we all need. He drops us off someplace, we make with the sunbathing and the *rest*. Mianning does the ritual at the nearest Buddhist temple, probably in India. We're only five days away once the storms blow through. Then he can pick us up and bring us to Aden or Sana'a for Rami to face justice from there."

At that moment, the ship jerked under them, and they scrambled for the ladder.

"Feels like we hit a reef," James said.

Through the pouring rain, they could see it was a sandbar, but one which Usama jerked them back off of at speeds and angles that left Mianning shouting with concern for his ship. Moments later, they came from behind a cliff, pointed straight on with sails tight so they wouldn't be seen against the starlight. They dropped anchor in a deserted stony cove with a small beach. The prison was just over the ridge, right on what might be the tideline. The crashing waves paired with the thrashing rain made trying to speak like shouting inside a drum filled with sand.

"Reviewing one last time," Noor half shouted through the noise as James and Mianning gathered around her. "One, we go up the cliff and rappel down the other side. Two, we break through the door and sneak through the prison—if necessary, we will fight the guards. But we'll be wildly outnumbered, so if we can keep out of their way, that's best. Three, we get Rami, get back to the *Cormorant*, and get out of here."

James descended the ladder to the shin-high waves on the beach. Noor eyed the seaweed hanging high on the cliff's edge, above the top of the *Cormorant*'s mast, and shouted down to James, "Did you check the timing of the tides?"

"What?" he yelled, cupping his ears.

She climbed down beside him, but before she could repeat herself,

Mianning and Razan landed behind them and gestured for them to stop giving away their position and get to cover.

Noor ran towards the cliff with her hand on her jambiya and Razan's map of the terrain firm in her mind. Mianning sized up the near-sheer cliff face. He grabbed Noor's rope, slung his musket around to his back, and started his free climb of the edifice. Noor heard him whistle down to them, and a rock bound-up in rope clattered down the stones to land between them, trailing a long tail back up to Mianning. Noor tugged on the cord, found it solid, and began climbing her way up.

Once Noor was at the top, she found her anchor, a massive boulder that could probably restrain a hippopotamus without an issue. She waved at James and Razan to begin climbing as Mianning worked his way down the gentler slope on the other side of the cliff. Checking on her friends every few moments, Noor turned and surveyed the prison.

Torches burned on either side of the oval door, and the moon grey sand surrounding the entrance provided no place for cover. No posted guards stood nearby. The back of her hands tingled with unease. Noor eased her haya magic through the cove, but found only fish and a faint sense of life behind the ironclad door. *Maybe they were lightly staffed for their prophet's birthday?* She pulled the magic away from her lunella shell to ensure no noise would give them away.

Finally, Razan made it up the cliff, and James followed her over the top, huffing and puffing. Mianning pulled up the rope and lowered it down the other side. Noor leaned in close to James and Razan, speaking quietly.

"I don't see any guards, but their alam mages may have enchanted spaces that allow them to hide people in plain sight; Rami said something about 'hiding magic', weeks ago. Let's make this too quick for them to muster a response."

Noor was about to start her way down the cliff side when Usama's voice came from James's pants, clear as a muezzin's athan call.

"How's it going, *habibi*?" Usama asked through the shell. "The water's getting a bit high. Thoughts on when you'll be back?"

James slapped at his pocket frantically and nearly ate the lunella shell with how close he crushed it to his mouth to reply. "We need to be quiet now. See you at midnight. I love you." He handed it to Noor to silence, head ducked.

Noor patted his shoulder. "I only remembered to silence mine because I was lounging up here, waiting for your slowpoke self." She glanced at Razan, inviting her to share the joke, but her lover's face was closed off, mouth tense.

James grumbled as he adjusted his musket on his back, "Just because I didn't grow up climbing over Yemen's mountains like Usama or use up my childhood scavenging wreckage like *some people* doesn't mean I'm not fit."

Noor grinned at him, then grabbed the rope and began to descend.

James joined them, the gentler slope easier on his arms, his face set and serious as he tied his rope to a large rock to remind them where to find it.

Once he caught his breath, he asked, "What are we waiting for?"

"You, slowpoke," said Mianning.

Noor closed her eyes and connected to her haya magic. She drew from the gritty sand around them and called up a spinner to drill through the door. Though hulking, the spinner fell to pieces when it hit the light of the torches. She tried again with water from the sea, but it shattered into raindrops within the light's circle. *The urodelas.*

"I guess we'll have to do this the hard way," James said.

They dashed from behind their cover across open sand, and Noor strained her ears for musket shots, but the pounding of their feet on wet sand was all she heard.

Then the effect of the urodelas hit her like a musket ball, making her stagger and lose her pace, breath tight in her chest, as they crossed into the circle of light.

James yelled, musket up, and eyes scanning, "Are you hit?"

Noor stumbled to her feet. "I'm cut off from my magic."

James and Razan raised their weapons, aiming at the door's hinges, firing, reloading, firing, reloading, and firing again until the rock surrounding the iron was no more than falling sand. They took up positions on either side of the door, letting it fall with a deep *thump* onto the wet sand. Noor glanced between her friends and drew her jambiya.

"Let's do this," she said and turned to face whatever was coming down the long, dark cave.

She stepped through the stone archway into a long, empty, narrow passage. She'd been wrong. It hadn't been carved by human hands, but a stream that trickled down the centre of the floor and seeped under the door. Despite the noise they must have been making, no warning bells rang, no guards' bootsteps nor shouting came to greet them.

The roar of the sea behind her faded until the only sounds were their steps on the stone floor and the *hsssshh* of old water dripping down the walls.

They arrived at an intersection, and Noor picked a direction on intuition or something better; she wasn't sure. When they reached a dead end, they backtracked, eyes adjusting to the dark and ears to the quiet.

So much for intuition.

They'd reached a gate. Thick bars stood between them and what appeared to be a row of cells. Noor studied it, considering whether she could wedge her jambiya through the padlock and snap it when Mianning nudged her to the side. From his sleeve, he pulled a full smuggler's lockpicking set and set to work. A noise came from the far end of the corridor, something rhythmic, like drums. Noor couldn't place it, but her body did, shoulders tightening until they ached. Finally, Mianning won out against the lock, the smell of old iron wafting from it.

They crept forward. The cells on either side had recently been emptied of prisoners as they still reeked of unchanged sheets and flop sweat. The block was long and curving, the cells shaped irregularly by flowing water. Noor shivered when a trickle dripped from the ceiling down the back of her borrowed tunic. The chilly, musty air in the passageway seemed heavier in her lungs with every breath.

The rhythmic strikes grew louder. It reminded Noor of something that smelled of sweat and pain.

A prison door clanged, a man screamed, and Noor took off at a dead sprint. She rounded the corner to blinding light, then reversed as pistol fire exploded against the stone where she'd been standing. She shoved James, Razan, and Mianning behind her.

"I saw him," she said, her voice a hoarse whisper and fingers cramping tight on her jambiya. A few more shots smashed into the opposite wall, then died out.

Noor continued, "It's bad. It looks like every guard in the place is around his cell, all armed."

She took a breath, trying to steady herself. "They knew we were coming for him."

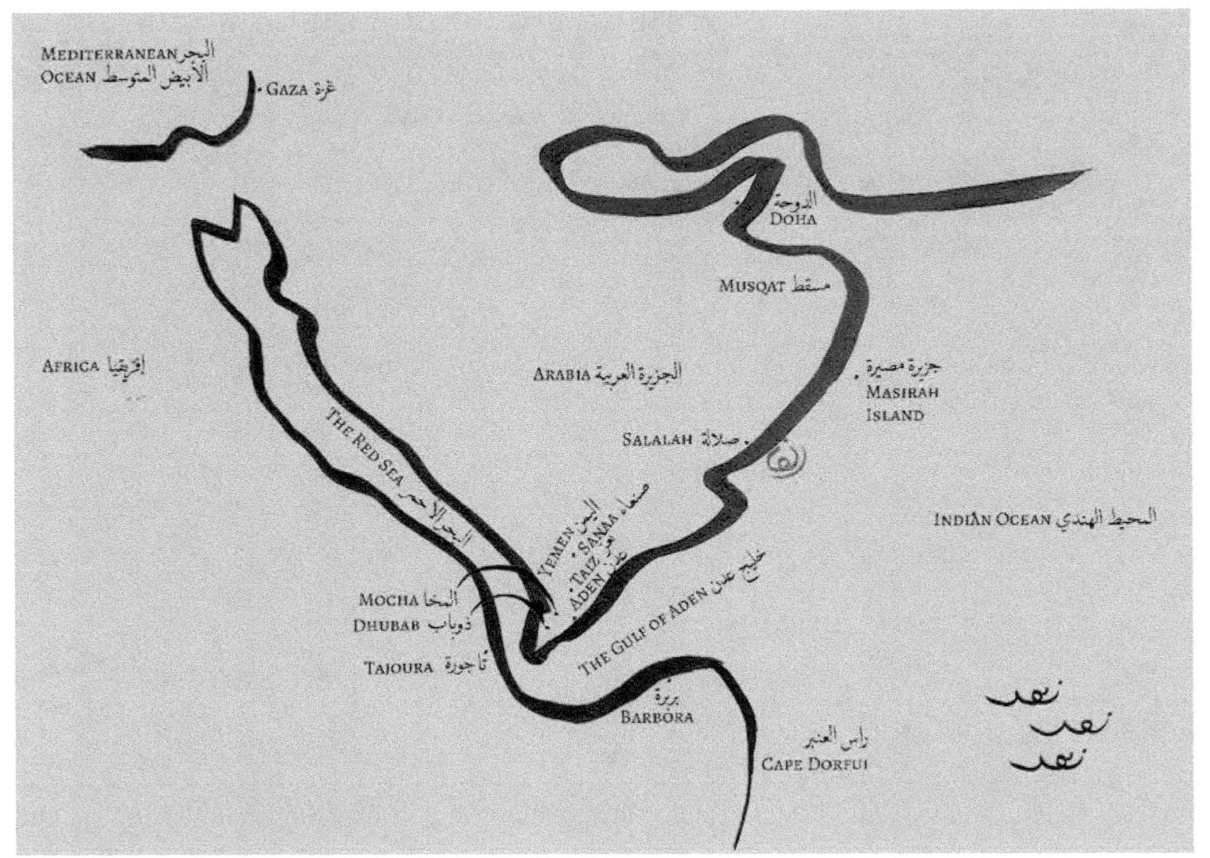
MEDITERRANEAN OCEAN   البحر الأبيض المتوسط
GAZA   غزة
AFRICA   إفريقيا
DOHA   الدوحة
MUSQAT   مسقط
ARABIA   الجزيرة العربية
MASIRAH ISLAND   جزيرة مصيرة
SALALAH   صلالة
THE RED SEA   البحر الأحمر
INDIAN OCEAN   المحيط الهندي
YEMEN   اليمن
SANAA   صنعاء
TAIZ
ADEN   عدن
THE GULF OF ADEN   خليج عدن
MOCHA   المخا
DHUBAB   ذوباب
TAJOURA   تاجورة
BARBORA   بربرة
CAPE DORFUI   رأس العنبر

Chapter Nine

"GO HOME, WITCH bitch!" shouted an unfamiliar English voice from around the corner. It came from the direction of the cell where she'd glimpsed Rami, kneeling and gaunt with one of the guards standing over him as another guard was dragged out of the cell with a bleeding nose.

Noor heard a grunt of pain from down the hallway and forced herself not to run to him, not even when it repeated. The dull sound of flesh hitting flesh echoed too loud in the curved stone prison. Behind it, under it, all around Noor, came a noise she'd never heard before, a low moaning growl. Something rammed the wall behind her, and she jumped away. It wasn't a wall but the grated door of a cage set into the stone, much too small for the scarred urodela inside.

Noor crouched to its level. Its cage had none of the plants or ample food she'd seen in the Doha prison. The lizard's violet eyes took her in before turning towards the sound of Rami being kicked. Its big head wove back and forth with worry as it flinched at each blow.

"I wish I could free you, too, big guy," Noor whispered as her friends shield away from the urodela.

"Couldn't you?" James squatted to meet the massive lizard's eyes, ignoring the growl rolling around them. "If they escaped out the door we destroyed, wouldn't you and Rami get your magic back? I bet they hate cages as much as people do."

Noor smiled, her jaw so tense it ached. She asked Mianning in Mandarin, "Can you unlock them?"

He stared at her, studied the urodelas's teeth and jambiya-length claws, then turned back to her as if she was extremely unhinged. She held his gaze until he nodded slowly.

Noor peered more closely at the cages. They might be able to free a half-dozen urodelas without entering the line of fire. She tried to think through the consequences, but the sound of Rami's beating kept interrupting her thoughts.

"Do it, please," she said, and Mianning knelt and got to work on the lock.

It seemed as though it hadn't been opened in a while, with the guards just shoving food and water between the bars, as evidenced by a dried-on mess blocking what little view they'd had.

"If you let him go, no one has to get hurt," Noor called out in English, hoping to cover the clink of Mianning's picks.

There was a harsh bark of laughter. The sounds of the beating continued.

What if they kill him, here and now, when we're so close—

Mianning dropped his tools. Cursing under his breath, he gathered them up again and switched implements.

"Here, I can help." Razan took one from him and went to the next cage.

"Thank you," Noor whispered, and then to James, "Can you help her? And stay out of sight until I have him. We don't want your former crewmates targeting you."

"I don't love sending you out there alone, Noor." James murmured.

"I'm not alone. I have you three and all of our new lizard friends. But until they're free and no longer blocking my powers, I can't protect anyone. Not me, not you, not Rami."

"Getting Noor her powers back is our top priority," Razan

whispered. "It has to be. That's what helping her means in this moment."

James frowned. "All right. But shout, and I'm there in a second, British pistols and whips be damned."

Noor gave her friend a quick, hard hug, then turned back towards the cell.

She forced herself to call out again, "Are you the men of the *Victory* whose lives I saved?"

The rhythm of the beating stumbled, pausing.

A deeper voice replied, "'Saving' us from the drowning you'd condemned us to after lighting Lord Nelson's flagship on fire with your witch magic isn't something to remind us of, little missy."

The *tap-tap-tap* of running feet followed, and an out-of-breath voice with a thick brogue barked, "What's all this then?"

"Shut *up*, Captain Hardy!" growled the same voice that had called her a 'witch bitch'.

"Sir, there's no need to take that tone. I was simply asking a question."

"You are a guest here—"

"I am," he said, his voice still breathy from running.

Not a guard then, Noor thought, glancing at James. *What is going on?*

"As I explained yesterday when I arrived," the brogue continued, "I was tasked with reviewing the treatment of Yemeni prisoners after complaints from their ambassador. As I told you then, I serve his excellency the British ambassador to the Ottoman Empire as a military attaché to the diplomatic corps."

Noor whispered into James's ear, "The emira said we might find help here, but I didn't think we would."

Mianning finished the first lock and stepped back, gesturing for Noor to do the honours as Razan paused to watch. Noor slid the door open, and the urodela poked its nose out into the open air before chancing a paw on the slick stone floor. Noor expected it to run for freedom, but instead, it waddled over to the next cell, then looked up at Razan expectantly. When Razan knelt beside it to work the lock again, the urodela then continued on to the next cell, this one containing a half-dozen pups, and flicked its tongue through the bars at them as they crowded near, staring at Mianning expectantly.

The attaché's voice echoed through the corridor again. "Captain Whitcombe, just yesterday you informed me prisoner's injuries were self-inflicted, that he had been throwing himself into walls and it was how he got all them scrapes and cuts and such."

The next lock came undone more quickly, and Mianning yanked open the door. He'd set to work on freeing the pups before the giant lizard he'd just freed had finished working its way out of its cage. It, too, didn't run, but instead, rubbed its long neck against that of the first lizard Mianning had freed. Both turned their attention to the cage with the little ones, their stares shining in the darkness.

"Just now, I heard gunfire—" the attaché said.

"Yes, you absolute ponce," Whitcombe answered. "Because the Yemenis have *broken into the prison and are trying to rescue the Sword of Sidon.*"

Then came the sound of a page turning. "The 'Sword of Sidon' is so named for his valorous work on behalf of the British Navy in the conquest of southern Lebanon?" The attaché continued, the thread of fear in his voice had been quashed, "Who played a key role in securing a dozen ports for the British Empire during his fifteen-year service on the *Victory*? Who the lord admiral specifically requested be contained here *safely* until the winter monsoon season had passed and he could render judgement as to his place in our future strategy in the region?"

A baffled silence ensued, the universal sound of men realizing they'd been operating so far outside their mandate as to be in a different nation from it entirely.

"He and the bastard sultan—" Whitcombe sputtered.

The pups were out.

Noor knelt beside them, whispering, "You can go now, you're free."

The two big adults wagged their heads at her, then turned towards the voices in the corridor. Mianning shrugged, moved to the other side of the hall, and got to work on the cage of a great monster of a urodela with a mass of white scars where one of its eyes used to be. It didn't turn to him once; it seemed to be listening intently to the conversation going on outside its cage.

The attaché continued, the same thinness to his tone. "The sultan who died in as-of-yet undetermined circumstances during the sinking of the *Victory*, who was known to use fire magic and was last seen ablaze in his own quarters, which coincidentally appeared to be the source of the inferno which engulfed the *Victory*? We have heard from our sources that the sultan routinely abused those in his charge, not for punishment under naval laws, but using his magic to manage some form of cancer?"

"It was *him* who did it—*him* who wielded the whip. I've got me the scars to prove it. You wasn't there—" Captain Whitcombe's voice shook, becoming more guttural as he stumbled over his words.

Another lock undone. None of the lizards were leaving; all stood shoulder-to-shoulder, trained on the raised voices at the end of the corridor.

"I wasn't there, that's true," the attaché replied. "Just as you weren't there when I received my orders." The sound of thick paper crinkling filled the following silence.

Razan had started on the last lock.

"'By request of the ambassador and with the permission of the lord admiral, if the prisoner Rami ibn Arwa wa Nuri is found to have been mistreated the following actions are to be taken forthwith. In recognition for his fifteen years of service to the Crown, he will be remanded to the custody of his ancestral people if a suitable representative makes themselves available. Anyone taking custody of him must agree to make him available to the Crown if he desires to continue his service.'"

"What the *fuck*," said Whitcombe.

Grumbling from the other guards rose up, and the last urodela climbed heavily from its cage. It waddled towards the voices, but when it reached Noor, it gestured with its long snout towards the voices.

"Why would the lord admiral allow that?" another guard demanded, his voice flat with disbelief.

"The strategy of the admiralty is not your business," the attaché responded, "but suffice it to say, there has been a concern about the effect the sultan's treatment had on the moral of the sailors, resulting in multiple high-profile desertions and, as I do not have to remind *you*, the loss of the former lord admiral's flagship. The current lord admiral is interested in a different approach and is ready to close the chapter on this unfortunate business."

The big animal nudged Noor's knee with its snout and turned towards the voices. She shifted her jambiya to the small of her back and knelt before it. "They may shoot us," she whispered to the urodela.

It huffed with something like lizard derision.

"I feel the same way," Noor replied.

She stood and started towards the voices.

"Noor—" Razan gasped.

But then, she was in the flickering lamplight of the corridor.

She saw Rami first, kneeling, confused and furious and desperate, and then took in his swollen face, split cheek still untended, and his mouth, gagged with a dirty grey rag. They had him on his knees, manacles stretching his arms tight behind his back.

He wore tatters that barely covered the thickets of cuts among vast ranges of bruises and welts on his skin. She wanted to count them and flay them into the skin of every guard in this place, slice for slice, wound for wound. Rami was so much thinner than he'd been in their shared dreams, his ribcage showing stark against his dark skin.

The guard in his cell—Whitcombe—had his gloved hand fisted in Rami's hair, forcing him to kneel at an unbalanced angle that made him easier to kick. Whitcombe had a silver-shined pistol in his other hand, pressed into Rami's ear.

Noor took a breath, thinking what she wanted to say in English, holding Rami's gaze with a promise like a wildfire. Then she raised her voice and lied.

"I don't want to hurt any of you." She spoke deliberately, like stones dropped into deep water, building a spiral staircase to the light. The other guards turned to stare at her, all of them in naval blues, except for the one holding a notebook, who wore a black brocade waistcoat, shiny and unmarred. His dark grey hair, streaked with white, fell across his sun-browned face. He stood frozen, stunned at her sudden appearance.

Noor stepped forward, her hands casually at her sides, the urodelas flanking her. She heard Razan and James and Mianning working the keys, increasing their numbers. *If the urodelas can't leave and return my magic to me, they will make fine body guards.* The urodelas in the cells on either side of her began a low, throbbing growl, and the other guards' weapons came up, pointing solidly at her chest.

"I am here representing the Yemeni resistance," she said in an even voice, her focus never leaving Rami. "I am sorry about your door. We had no idea our ambassador's requests had been heeded or that you were here, Captain Hardy. I am here for Rami ibn Arwa wa Nuri."

Whitcombe shook his head, a sneer twisting his face, and he spoke before the attaché could. "We knew you were coming; we've known since Doha. You think any British citizen would betray us, for what—a slot on the empire's execution list? Ian Tone informed on you before you left the harbour." He spat, and thick saliva hit the wall above Rami's sleeping mat and slid down his scratch-mark calendar.

Noor forced her attention back to Rami's.

"Your own government tells you to give him to me," she said, her voice low and pleading. "Take your hands off of him. Please."

The guards in front of the cell wavered before her slow approach, her quiet voice. The urodelas in the cell watched her and their freed brethren. Their growls followed her as they paced alongside her in their cages, fixed on Rami.

"This is the mage you claim sank the *Victory*?" Captain Hardy said. "She's just a girl—"

"She's the bitch who whipped our guns right out of our hands with waterpipes she made from nothing but magic and the sea in Tadjoura Bay. And ordered the winds to rip our sails to shreds in Mocha like a fucking monsoon queen! She's the bitch who—"

"Now, Captain Whitcombe, there is no need to use such language—"

"Shut *up* Hardy! Shoot the witch!" Whitcombe screamed, his hand still in Rami's hair.

The guards outside the cell squinted nervously between them, pistols wavering. The urodelas's growls softened, lowered to purrs. Whitcombe's grip on Rami's hair remained firm, his finger held inside the trigger guard.

A urodela screamed as one of the younger guards raised his pistol, but the attaché, Captain Hardy, pushed the young man's arm down as he peered over his shoulder at Whitcombe, a worried line forming on his forehead.

"How did you say he got those scrapes again?"

"He did them to himself," Whitcombe hissed. "He's a traitorous bastard, a blaspheming witch who got what he deserved."

The urodelas's growling rose to a buzz, the soft, dry scraping of their bellies insistent on the stone floor alongside Noor's quiet steps. Captain Hardy leaned closer, peering through the bars, now seeing the words on Rami's back. His face greyed.

"He wrote 'Arab Lord' on his own back, sir?" Hardy demanded with a rumble of revulsion, his tone cold and precise. In *English*? I've seen some bar tricks in my time, but that would take the cake."

The other guards shuffled their feet, eyes darting between Captain Hardy and their captain. Noor walked towards them again. Ten paces to go. Now five. She was within touching distance of the nearest guard, and they barely noticed, all of them staring at Whitcombe.

Captain Hardy spoke. "Guards, please unlock the door, per the lord admiral's command."

Whitcombe screamed, "How *dare* you, you Scottish poof. Men, arrest him!"

When the others made no move to obey, Whitcombe went scarlet with rage, and Noor was so close. If she knelt and reached her hand through the bars, she could almost touch Rami's shoulder.

Captain Hardy glanced down at her, at Whitcombe, and then at her again. He sucked air through his teeth and unhooked an enormous ring of keys from the belt of a nearby guard with a courtly nod.

"*I* heard Captain Whitcombe say he wanted the prisoner released. Did everyone else hear that?"

There was a general affirmative nodding, and he unlocked the cell.

"Hold on," Noor whispered to Rami, her attention riveted to him.

Captain Hardy crept carefully towards Whitcombe, slipped his hand around the pistol's barrel, and pointed it away from Rami's head.

Then he tugged it out of Whitcombe's hand.

Captain Hardy knelt beside Rami and, hands gentle at the nape of his neck, searched for the knot of the gag. Whitcombe held tight to Rami's hair, baring his throat. Captain Hardy got the gag free and used it to wipe some of the saliva from around Rami's mouth, and Rami broke eye contact with Noor to meet the other man's steady gaze.

Still kneeling beside Rami, Captain Hardy glared up at Whitcombe until the man released his hold on Rami's hair. Rami sagged briefly, rolling his neck before sitting up on his heels.

Noor held her breath.

Captain Hardy stared Rami in the eye. "Son," he said, "we haven't properly met. I just got in yesterday on a bark that got a bit distracted on the way here, and then I wasn't allowed in the cells on my first day. I need you to tell me, truly, did you do this to yourself?"

Rami shook his head, tried to speak, then had to clear his throat. He answered in English, "No," his voice a cracked whisper, more hoarse than anything Noor had heard in the dreams. A twist of pain and hope shot through her at hearing his real voice for the first time in months.

Captain Hardy seemed to expect that answer. "Who did it?"

Rami glanced at Whitcombe before turning back to Captain Hardy. "They didn't make a point of introducing themselves, but nearly every guard on this block must have heard what was happening. The only objections I ever heard were from the urodelas."

Captain Hardy froze as the displeasure of the great lizards rose again in a war-drum rumble that seemed to travel through the stone floor and into Noor's very bones. Hardy turned to the assembled men, none of whom would meet his eyes.

"Is that so?" he asked them.

There were no affirmative nods this time. Just hidden faces.

Captain Hardy stood, pistol casually pointing at Whitcombe's stomach as the man took a step back.

Then Captain Hardy turned to Noor. "Madam mage, what should I call you?"

She walked forward, and the guards shuffled out of her way as she entered the cell, *so close now*. "My name is Noor."

"'Light'? Is that right?"

"Yes." Rami answered in English. "Her name is Light."

Captain Hardy continued, "Madam Light, will you take custody of the prisoner per the conditions I believe you heard me read?"

"I will."

Captain Hardy nodded. But when he leaned over to unlock Rami's manacles, Whitcombe screamed and dove for the captain's pistol as every urodela howled with rage.

Noor threw herself onto Whitcombe, fighting for control of the pistol as a shot ricocheted off the ceiling. She shoved her knee up between his thighs, and he doubled over. Noor knocked him to the floor, hands on his wrist, landing on his chest with her knee slamming up again for good measure. At the same time, Hardy shoved Rami into the corridor, using his body to protect Rami from the fight.

Noor reared back, yanking the pistol free of his grip and going for her jambiya at the small of her back when a urodela darted in past her. Its massive jaws opened wide, then clamped on Whitcombe's face, crunching down. Noor felt him go limp under her, and she shoved herself off of him as the other urodelas crowded in quickly, their teeth clacking as they tore him to pieces. Within moments, Whitcombe's body had disappeared beneath a writhing mass of massive lizards.

Noor backed up, turning to where she'd last seen Rami. He crouched behind Captain Hardy, still surrounded by guards with pistols pointed at the urodelas, at Noor, at Rami, and at the floor.

Captain Hardy cleared his throat. "All are ordered to return to their quarters," he said in a strong voice, directing his words to the guards. "We will determine what is to be done with you in the morning."

For a long moment, no one moved, then one after the other, they all lowered their pistols. At once, most of the urodelas left Whitcombe's body, each of them towards a separate guard. Some of the men backed away and found themselves chased. The pups snapped at the men's ankles, but the adult animals opened their bloody mouths and showed their rows of teeth.

"I believe the urodelas will keep guard through the night," Noor said. "And given the swarming behaviour we just saw, I would encourage the guards not to try to harm even the smallest of them."

Captain Hardy watched as the guards exited through a side passage, escorted by gape-mouthed urodelas.

When they were alone, Captain Hardy sighed deeply in relief and leaned over again to unlock Rami's manacles. Before they hit the floor, Noor was in Rami's arms, face buried in his chest, his hair tickling her cheeks. *Alive and here, alive and here* was the sound of his heart against her ear and all the words her mind could give her. He was warm and smelled like she'd expected, but when he breathed in, and she felt his chest move, it was as if every hope she'd held lit up like butterflies in her belly, circling and winding and *free*.

"I've got you," she whispered.

"I know," he replied, too low for anyone except perhaps Captain Hardy to hear.

The sound of Captain Hardy shuffling awkwardly brought them back, and Noor stepped away from Rami but held her arm around his waist as he sagged gratefully against her.

"Razan, Mianning, James, can you come and free the urodelas in this hallway?"

Her friends emerged from around the corner and got to work on the cages.

Noor adjusted her grip on Rami, and he gasped as the rough material of his shirt brushed the scrapes on his back. Noor nodded to the captain and turned to the door, away from the still feasting lizards.

"All done?" She asked Mianning as he stood.

"Yes," he said to Noor but focused on Rami. James scanned Rami's brutalised face, his ribs stark against bruise-mottled skin, and the cataclysm of cuts across his shoulders and back. Razan's face was unreadable, and when Noor made her way slowly down the corridor, Razan took up the rear.

Rami's bare feet trod softly on the cold stone, steps faltering and breathing ragged. A part of Noor was aware of the moaning-purr of the urodelas as they watched them leave. But most of her attention remained on Rami and the impossibility that he was *here* and *alive*. She caught him when he stumbled and swayed against her, his face twisting as he struggled to breathe around his broken rib. But he forced his head back up, and with every step he took away from the cell, the stronger he seemed.

They made it around the corner.

*

WITH MORE ROOM in the corridor, Mianning reached out a well-calloused hand to grip Rami's forearm, then released it. Noor tightened her arm around Rami, and he leaned into her, fingers plucking at the fabric of her black shirt as they walked away from his cage and towards the distant crash of waves. Mianning started to leave, but Noor stopped him.

"There were baby urodelas in the other prison. I need to do a sweep, make sure we didn't leave any behind."

She turned to Rami and saw agreement there, so she handed him over to James who took his weight with no issue. Razan kept an eye on the exits while Mianning followed Noor back into the light, where she approached Captain Hardy, still observing the urodelas feasting on Whitcombe's corpse with fascinated horror. Mianning began searching through the rotting food and torn blankets in the cages with sturdy precision.

"They didn't have these at Sandhurst," Hardy murmured to himself before noticing her.

"Madam Light," he said to her, "how may I help you?"

Noor observed the cage where Rami had been kept. The large urodela with the missing eye pulled away from Whitcombe's body and waddled over to her. She knelt, holding out a hand for it to smell like a big market cat. It did so, its pupil pulsing with an inner light. Noor wiped a smear of blood off the side of its face.

Then she saw it, as clear as day: A vision, feelings, not words. The guards in chains. British sailors escorting their comrades onto a Yemeni dhow, not the *Cormorant* but another of Razan's designs. Noor leaned closer, tried to see more clearly. The bright purple of the lizard's iris glowed in the dimness of the prison, and the vision faded.

Noor finally turned to Captain Hardy. "I believe tomorrow morning, the urodelas will offer you a choice." She heard herself speaking as if at a distance, as if her words weren't her own. "Either they will eat the guards who separated them from their babies, starved and wounded them—as well as torturing the other prisoners—or, like Rami ibn Arwa wa Nuri, they will be turned over to Yemeni justice."

"I don't know if my superiors will accept that." Captain Hardy's voice wavered in the face of the scarred urodela's stare.

Noor smiled as Mianning finished the third lock and turned to the final one. "I don't think the urodelas will give you a third choice. And I can't say I disagree with them."

She stood, wiping her hands on her pants. "I wanted Rami ibn Arwa wa Nuri free, so I didn't demand justice from Captain Whitcombe. We would have left without allowing him to come to harm if he'd have done the same."

Captain Hardy began to speak, but Noor raised her hand.

"I want to make sure you know what happened here," she said in a harsh whisper. "Rami ibn Arwa wa Nuri has been your captive for sixty days." She pointed to the marks on the cell wall, now spattered with blood before continuing.

"In that time, he has been tortured, beaten, burned, starved, raped, sleep-deprived, beaten again, humiliated, and nearly killed. Yemeni justice is justice. There will be a trial, an evaluation of the evidence. No one will be tortured or starved. Your diplomats may visit the guards at will in Aden. Once we are free of this place, I will have a ship sent to collect them. You have no other support here besides the guards, so I suggest you not try to interfere. Do you understand?"

Captain Hardy's face went cold. "I will be requesting a ship to transport them to Doha for a naval trial. I will send it on the next mail ship."

Noor smiled again, viciously now. "We'll see who gets here first then—ships of cedar or ships of oak." She spoke over the magmic rumble of blood in her ears. "In case a far simpler solution occurs to you or to your superiors, I want you to understand I have ways of finding out. If I hear that a single scale on these urodelas's heads was harmed, I will hunt you down. And you will see a side of me you will not like."

He nodded, quick and jerky. She checked over her shoulder, and Mianning now stood, waiting. The last of the captive urodelas had been freed.

Noor and Mianning made their way back to the others, accompanied by soft slip of scales against stone as the urodelas waddled, once again, towards the body in Rami's cage.

James and Rami were braced against the wall where she'd left them. Rami's breathing hitched when he saw her, but he didn't ask any questions. He heaved his arm over her shoulder as James released his hold and then tucked himself close against her, his dark hair mixing with hers. They shuffled on, nearly to the final corridor when he bent his head, lips brushing her ear.

"Are you wearing my shirt?"

She stifled a giggle at the small smile in his voice. *Alive and here. Alive and here.*

They'd made it to the last corridor when something smelled wrong.

Mianning picked up his feet. "What the—"

A waist-high wave crashed through the shattered door, slapping them against the rough walls.

"The tides!" Razan and Noor said together, as James said, "What?" Then, Mianning was shoving them all out and into the storm, through the thigh deep waves and towards the *Cormorant*.

An early winter monsoon season storm surge? Maybe the urodelas's magic helped hold off the sea before? Noor stepped past the now-extinguished torches, and the oppressive barrier between her and her magic dissolved.

Rami sucked in a huge breath, straightening with it, holding more of his own weight. Noor didn't have a moment to savour how the world shot into colour, how the life of the universe roared back to life around her as she staggered out of the ocean onto the rain-whipped rocks, where they'd tied off their rope. James awakened his lunella shell and heard Usama yelling.

"It's nearly midnight. Do you hear me habibi? What's happening down there?"

Rami stared at James, confused to hear Usama's voice coming from the shell.

Noor held it to her mouth, a victorious grin heating her face as she said, "We've got him, Usama. Tell the emira we've got him."

"Allah, it's good to hear you, Noor. But we're going to have to wait on that. The storm pulled up the waves like a monster just after you left. I had to head into deeper water to avoid getting smashed against the cliffs. You should be able to swim out from the cove."

Noor's stomach dropped at his words, but James agreed with Usama. He found the rope and began working his way up the cliff, Mianning free climbing beside him in the streaming rain and Razan following close behind. Rami and Noor stood alone together, waiting for their turns. Rami stood stronger but still shivering cold, and Noor held on to him tighter. Her mind sang with him safe beside her, *alive and here.*

"The beach where we left the *Cormorant* was lower than this one," she said.

Rami shrugged. "Like Usama said, he's set anchor farther out, and we'll swim to him."

Noor turned to him, hoping the darkness of the storm clouds hid her heating cheeks. "I can't swim."

He stared at her, his face a mask of incredulity under the cuts and bruises. "But every night—"

"I do a lot of things in dreams I can't do in the waking world," she said sharply.

Rami tightened his arm around her waist. "It seems I might need to save *you* this time."

"Let's hope not. I don't like the height of these seas."

Rami stretched his arms out to the side, then flexed them behind his head, his shoulders popping. He tipped his head back, the rain dripping down his front rinsing off some of the dried blood and leaving his skin a stark dark canvas. Dark slashes crossed it, as well as a scattering of moles she wanted to trace with her fingertips. Noor clenched her hands into fists.

"I can reach my magic for the first time in two months," Rami said smugly. "If I didn't think I would pass out before we landed, I would just fly us there. Leap up and over the cliffs and fly us wherever we wanted to go."

"Don't get cocky," she said. "I've got a lot of healing to do before you can do anything more than sleep, eat, drink, and sleep some more." He nodded, growing serious.

"I'm grateful for the help," he said, voice low and rough again.

"None of that. Razan's at the top. It's your turn."

He gestured for her to go ahead of him. "Ladies first."

"You heard how I threatened Captain Hardy, so you know I'm no lady. Get going, Rami."

He climbed up the slope with sure, steady movements, perhaps using his magic to do so. Noor wondered as she watched if he *would* be able to fly when he was all the way healed.

She wondered if she could fly with him.

The water, higher now, yanked at her ankles, the rope's lowest knot deep beneath the waves. She began her climb. A crack of thunder slapped across the water, and she stumbled, slicing her knee open on a rock. She staggered at the stabbing pain but forced herself to keep going.

She met James on the ridge. Mianning had climbed all the way down and now swam out to where the *Cormorant* was anchored. The ship's ladder clipped the top of each long wave that rolled in a little higher than the last. She tossed the rope over the edge into the water, where the depth must be far above her head. And a dozen arm lengths yet remained to where the *Cormorant* huddled on the white-topped waves like a seabird in a hard storm wind.

Noor gulped in a breath.

James leaned into her. "Rami reminded us— I'd forgotten you can't swim, Noor."

Razan met her eyes. "What do you want to do?"

"Not drown."

"Agreed," Rami said, overlapping with Razan's, "Of course."

They both gazed at each other, and then Razan nodded sharply.

"Rami, you're injured. I'll help Noor to the ship."

"I can help—"

Razan held up a hand. "We don't need to prove anything right now, and we're running out of time before this storm gets worse. We'll both swim with her, on either side."

"Fair enough."

"I'll go down first," James said, "and stay at the base of the ladder, help guide you three in. Are you sure you want to go to the beach after this, Noor? Haven't had enough of the sea yet? I picked one out for us, with a little collection of former French coloniser's beach houses at Sayn. You'll love it. But maybe you'd prefer someplace with a bit less sand."

"Ha ha ha," Noor said flatly. "I was raised near sand. And no changing my plans on me. You owe me those swimming lessons."

"That I do," James said, clapping her on the arm.

She gripped his hand tightly once and jerked her head to the waiting ship. "We'll be right behind." Noor said.

James seemed worried but he began climbing down the cliff face.

"He cares for you greatly," Rami said, something indiscernible in his voice.

"He was my first friend," she said simply before giving Razan a quick smile. "And he and Usama make an adorable couple."

James had entered the water and now swam strongly to the ladder.

"Usama ibn Salam always needed someone to keep him on the good side of trouble," Rami said above the crashing waves.

Razan's eyes narrowed. "That used to be your father."

"It did." Rami said, an empty space where his brief cheer had been.

Razan stared at him but seemed to deflate when he didn't fight back.

"It's time," she said finally. "I'll head down next. Reach for me in the water, all right, Noor?"

Noor gave her a tight hug. "Yes."

Noor and Rami stood alone, lashed by cool rain, gazing out at the wind-tossed waves and roiling, black, rich storm as it raged towards them.

"I wish I could offer you more than storms," Noor said. "But monsoons are all I see in our future."

"We've got a ship with sails and a safe harbour to aim for. What are a few storms against that?"

Noor shook her head. "Optimist."

"Not usually. Not unless it's with you."

Noor swallowed; Razan had reached the water.

"Your turn," she said to Rami.

When Rami reached the bottom, he treaded water, keeping a hand on the end of the cord, and gestured for her to come down. On her descent, she glanced down at him the rain streaming around her like stars in the night, framing his dark, upturned face and steady, dark eyes. When her feet touched the water, her stomach spasmed. But then Razan's hand was around her calf, guiding her down. Noor tried to tread water as she had in so many dreams, but dipped right under, the trick of it eluding her.

"Stop wiggling," Razan said, hauling her up, and Noor stilled in her arms, letting her strong stroke carry them towards the *Cormorant*, Rami right behind.

They were feet away when a wave overtopped them, the undertow rolling Noor away from Razan like a feather in a dust devil. She struggled, arms flailing, trying to find her centre, get to magic, get to anything that would get her back to the air. Then her shoulders hit something hard, forcing the air from her lungs.

She'd hit the seafloor, pressed flat to the packed sand she'd walked on an hour before, maybe twice her height below the surface. The hull of the *Cormorant* wavered before her with each wave.

And there, coming for her like an oncoming storm, was Rami ibn

Arwa wa Nuri with Razan right behind.

For a flash, Noor remembered how she'd appeared through his eyes: determined, protective. She wondered if she had the same fire as she saw in him now, the same power he used as he reached for her.

She grabbed his hand as he pulled her arm over his shoulders and began kicking up.

Her lungs burned and something told her to open her mouth, to try to breathe. Instead, she tucked her face against his shoulder and forced herself to hold on.

When they broke the surface, Noor sucked in a breath. Rami, his arm tight around her, lifted her in the water until her cheek was on Razan's shoulder. She gasped into Razan's neck, heard her chant.

"Just breathe, love, just breathe. We've got you. Just breathe."

And she did, the waves heaving around them, her lips never dipping beneath the waves. In moments, they were at the *Cormorant*'s rope ladder.

Mianning, dangling from the end of the ladder, reached down into the water and scooped her up like it was nothing. At the gunwale, James grabbed her arm, and Usama, taking her other arm, pulled her to the soaked deck. James patted her face to make sure she was all right, but she leaned over the edge, searching for Razan and Rami in the dark waves. Razan was already on the ladder, climbing quickly.

Then, Mianning reached down into the water for Rami, clasped his forewarn, and lifted him out of the waves, holding him tight.

Noor heard Mianning say something about *thanks* and *you're safe* and something about *welcome home, kid.*

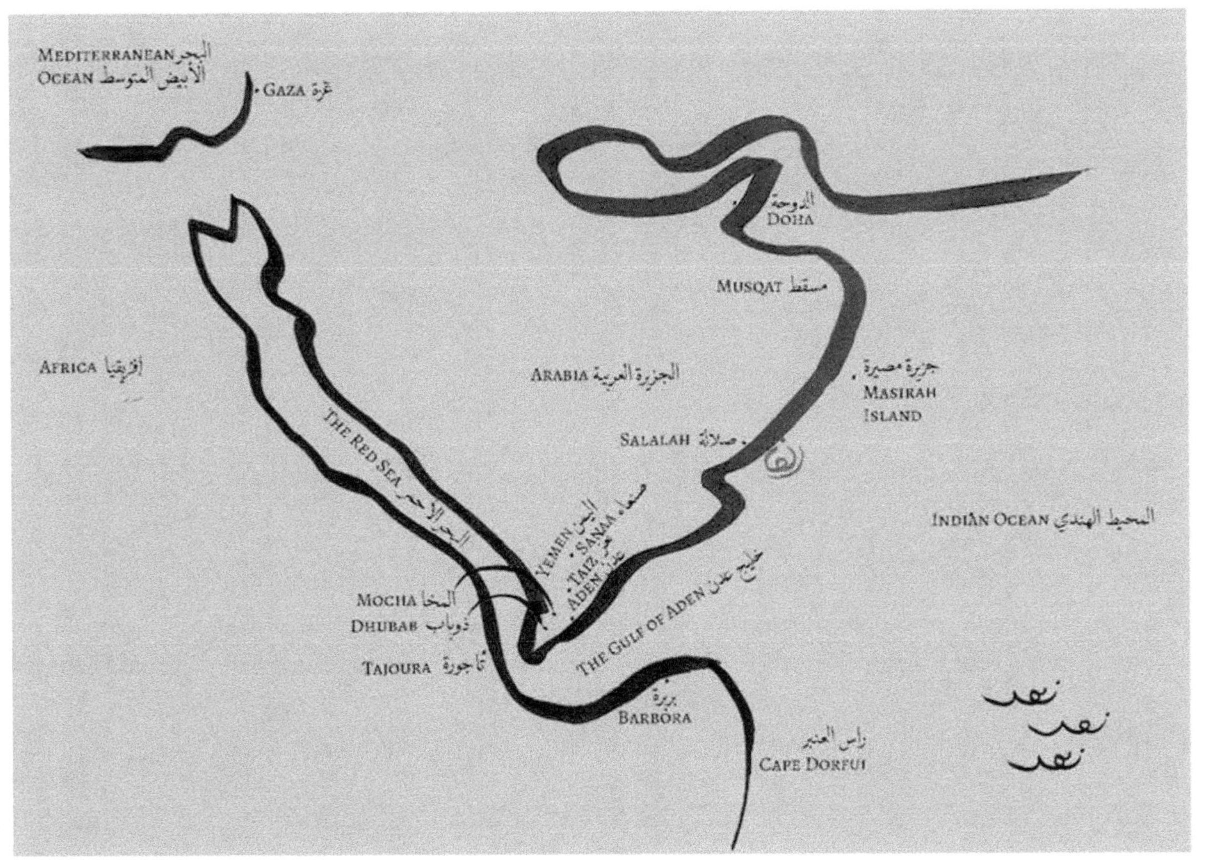

MEDITERRANEAN OCEAN البحر الأبيض المتوسط
GAZA غزة
AFRICA أفريقيا
DOHA الدوحة
MUSQAT مسقط
ARABIA الجزيرة العربية
MASIRAH ISLAND جزيرة مصيرة
SALALAH صلالة
INDIAN OCEAN المحيط الهندي
THE RED SEA البحر الأحمر
YEMEN اليمن
SANA'A صنعاء
TAIZ
ADEN عدن
MOCHA المخا
DHUBAB ذوباب
TAJOURA تاجورة
THE GULF OF ADEN خليج عدن
BARBORA جزيرة
CAPE DORFUI رأس العنبر

Chapter Ten

USAMA HOLLERED AT Mianning to get his butt back on the *Cormorant* so they could get out of *all of this weather* as Noor and Rami stumbled out of the driving rain and into the hold. Above deck, Usama, James, and Mianning worked together to steer them away from the rocky coast, getting them on course to a safe harbour.

Noor shivered and gestured for Rami to sit on Razan's hammock. He'd found his sea legs nearly immediately, even in the storm-tossed waters, a small gift from spending a decade and a half at sea with the British Empire she expected. He dripped seawater everywhere. Some of his cuts still bled, and it was hard to find a patch of skin not mottled with bruising. Noor turned to the bundle on the wall and pulled out every spare blanket and towel.

"I'd tell you to wash up first, but until we get those cuts handled, you're just going to bleed everywhere. Will you be all right if I heal you first?"

"Please," he said. She passed him a towel to dry himself, and she did the same.

"I don't have anything to change into anyway," Rami said as he patted his hair dry, his voice muffled by the towel. "It's not like Usama ibn Salam and I can share shirts."

"We found a chest of your old things in a smuggler's compartment. I think your father kept them. Or Mianning. They would have been too small for you, before, but—" She noted the thinner lines of his chest, his starvation-carved clavicle, and his hollowed cheeks. Her voice was quieter when she finished. "I think they'll fit you just fine."

Rami set the towel down. His black hair haloed out around his face as he leaned on one hand, giving her a look that would have made Usama smirk. He plucked at the sleeve of her black shirt.

"Is that where you got my shirt?"

"I don't own anything black, and we needed to be stealthy," she muttered, flushing.

His shoulders shifted in his ragged shirt as he tugged at her collar, his fingernails scraping against the rich black-on-black embroidery.

"I think I wore this to Nuha bint Nasser's wedding," he said.

Noor shook her head. *These people owning multiple sets of clothes.*

Then she sobered and stepped closer to him. "Where are you most injured?" she asked, keeping her voice steady.

He closed his eyes, thinking. "There's something deep, south of my stomach that could become a problem," he said, his voice hoarse but tone even. "Probably an injury from that last-ditch beating this morning. The malnutrition is something that will take more than magic to manage. None of the cuts were tended, or the blades used treated, so I would appreciate anything to stop the fever."

He paused, throat working before saying, "And there's quite a bit of damage up here." He tapped on the side of his head with a self-mocking smile. "Probably not the kind magic can heal, at least unless there've been major advances since I was last in school. For example—" He glanced at the open hatch. "—I find myself checking every few breaths to make sure that hatch hasn't shut and blocked my exit."

Noor marched over to the open slatted hatch and pulled the bolts out of the hinges. She wrestled it down and onto the hold floor, with the rain following after, and then tied the whole thing against the wall with straps called over by her magic.

"All right?" Noor asked.

Rami nodded, seeming a little stunned, and she wondered how long it had been since someone took his needs seriously.

She couldn't bring herself to ask.

Noor moved about an arm's length away from where Rami swayed on Razan's hammock and held out her hand. Rami took it without hesitation.

"Are you ready?" she asked.

"I am."

"This is going to hurt," she cautioned.

Rami gripped her hand, pulling her closer to him until she stood between his spread knees. He ran his other hand from her shoulder down her arm to her hand and slipped his fingers between hers. Then, he took a deep breath and inclined his head.

Noor echoed his breath and connected instantly with her haya magic. It was as though it had been waiting for her. She was close enough to pull from the lives of the British men in the prison and felt a dark joy in doing so.

The damage was extensive. If she thought about the story it told, she wouldn't be able to focus, to finish healing him, so she closed her eyes and divided him into parts. Top-down, outside-in. She had enough time to heal the stinging surface pain first before getting to the worst of it. She could take her time, be thorough, and know her work would last past waking.

With a plan in mind, Noor raised their interlocked fingers and touched the backs of her hands gently to the side of his face, stitching the split skin over his cheekbone and easing the swelling. She dragged her knuckles lightly over the bone bruises until the bones were pale and milky white again. She tapped his cheek, startling a smile out of him. Next, Noor checked the scar she'd left across his face with her jambiya when they'd fought on the *HMS Victory*. It had healed well, a thin line down his cheek. He'd been focused on his knees, but now he peered up at her intently.

The air they shared between them grew hot, tight with combined energy. Noor realised it wasn't just her connection with magic flowing through her, but *theirs*, his thin connection to the haya magic trickling in to join the river of her power.

She pressed their hands together against his cheek, diving deeper, finding the bruised parts of his brain from the head blows he'd survived, and then healing them through and through. Scar tissue ran along his spine, something thick and knotted, rough in her mind's eye, but it was old, and he gestured her away from it. Noor went, willingly, setting that aside for another time.

She eased her fingers free of his to reach behind his neck, and he let her, keeping contact by tracing his hand up the back of her arm, calloused fingers tickling the thin skin there. Noor traced the bones in his neck with her fingertips, softening the stiff muscles and healing the underlying damage caused by whiplash and being knocked around when he couldn't brace his falls. She swept her hand down his back and asked him a question in his mind— *Skin or bones?*

He shrugged, and she widened her connection to her magic, rippling and trickling across the mass of cuts across his back as she'd once done in their cave. She reached around him to hover her hand over them, seeing in her mind's eye that they were ragged, feeling the heat of fever coming from them. Noor unlaced the sickness from his skin, slipping it out of his blood. He grunted, surprised at the intrusion, then sighed and allowed his head to fall onto her shoulder, thick hair soft around her ear, body softening against her.

She dove farther down to the muscles that protected his spine, strained and nicked though they were. People always underestimated backs, how much pain a little slip or a tiny strain could cause. But people used their backs for everything, and without healing, the injury would be an ever-present and corrosive force in his life. Noor buttoned the muscles back into place, asking them to relax.

Rami shifted experimentally and then gasped. Noor ran her fingers down the edge of his spine, checking for more serious damage, and found it there again, tight around his nerves—bundles and bunches of scar tissue a decade or more old. She shook her head, moved away without him needing to tell her to, and slid her palm to the cool skin of his belly, bared through his tattered shirt.

The scars there, old ones from combat and training, weren't the cause—there were bruises enough for that. Now she could see them, going into his skin, boot print after boot print across his stomach. Noor couldn't keep her distance, couldn't stop herself from telling the story of his pinging ribs, a half-dozen bruised internal organs, and the faded handprints on his hips where fingers had *dug in*. She gasped, tears pulling free from her, quiet sobs surprising her as much as him.

Rami's hand shifted from her shoulder to the back of her neck, pulling her closer to him. He ran fingers through her hair, soothing her as she poured healing light into him, spreading it out, reshaping everything to what it had been before he'd been dragged down to Salalah. Noor settled once the last bruise was healed and sighed, rolling her head against his shoulder.

"I'm sorry."

He clucked in disapproval. "It's likely to be my turn soon enough."

Settling his hands softly on her bowed neck, Rami breathed steadily beneath her cheek.

"What happened to me," he said, his voice rumbling smoothly and comfortably from his chest, "I dealt with as it happened, or mostly did. But you're getting all of it, all at once, one big mess, no chance for a break."

Noor traced his Adam's apple, pressing in her haya magic, his vocal folds repairing as he spoke. His voice was nearly entirely healed now, no longer cracking and hoarse.

"Even worse for people like us," Rami continued, "you're getting the blow-by-blow without the ability to fight back." He pulled away from her, hands sliding down her arms to interlace with her fingers. He showed her a deep nick on the back of his hand, and she started to direct her healing towards it, but he shifted back.

"No, don't. I want to keep that one."

He grinned at her questioning expression. It wasn't kind, but it fit on his newly healed lips,

"I took out one of the guard's teeth; must have been three days ago," he explained. "That's the imprint it left." He gestured to a rubbed-red area on his knee like a ghastly rug burn. "The guard who did this to me will not be having children, not naturally at least."

Noor drew in a breath to object, to ask him not to be flip, but he stopped her.

"I'm not saying it's all right," he said. "I want to kill them all." And Noor remembered what she'd made Captain Hardy promise. "But I know what happened. I was there. It's not new for me. It'll be new for you, probably always will be since you were never there;"

He paused, reconsidering. "You were there in the ways that mattered the most. You're the reason I slept well enough to stand up and fight back, every time, no matter how many of them came in. You're the reason I knew I had to hang on, just had to get through it."

He raised a warm palm to her face, cupping it and wiping a smudge of tears away, "You were my light."

Noor buried her head in his shoulder and muttered, "*You* are a *sap*."

He chuckled, low and deep in her ear, and something unexpected twisted inside her belly. She crushed it down, praying he was too focused on his own body to sense anything about hers through their connection.

She caught her breath and said, "Ready to get back to it?" At his nod, she considered, "We're nearly done, then you should be able to wash with the sea water in peace; take your time. The food will be ready when you get out."

Rami frowned down at himself, at the rags he still wore, and adjusted his seat on the table.

He took a deep breath. "When they—" He couldn't finish the thought, his inner defences locking down with a clang.

Noor waited, but he seemed to not be able to get past that thought, his face warping through emotions, too fast for her to catch, too varied for her to characterise, not a single one of them pleasant. His hands spasmed in hers, arms shaking until she squeezed his fingers, bringing his gaze back to hers.

She interrupted whatever was happening in his head, her voice low and gentle. "I'll take care of all of the internal damage. I have some idea of what to look for."

He raised his face, stark with his aching. "All right."

Noor stepped back a little and said, "Do you want a minute, need some space? We can do this any way you need to."

Rami shook his head, reaching for her, pulling her close to him until her arms were pressed between her chest and his, his warm ones around her. He laid his head on her shoulder, and she wrapped around him as he stuck his cold nose against her neck. She only stopped herself from squeaking when he spoke again, his voice so, so small.

"I just want it over with."

Noor got to work, forehead against his, breaths intermingling. She started with the bones in his legs, some bruised, some cracked. Some had long-healed breaks, maybe a turned ankle when he was small. But the strong bones hadn't missed many meals growing up, and what he'd eaten had been good for him.

She tried to think of him like that—a tousle-haired boy, dark eyes filled with the same fire of curiosity she saw in the man today, climbing and jumping and learning about the world with two parents next to him. She healed the strains in the muscles of his feet, caused by being forced to go barefoot after a lifetime in boots. She found lacerations, some in long lines, as if the soles of his feet had been struck by something thin and sharp like a branch or— Noor refocused on the image of the bright boy. She wondered if he'd worn big boots or thin-soled slippers when he played growing up as she stitched the muscles and skin of his feet back together.

A part of her wanted to put her hands around his foot, to feel if it was strong, flex it back to check if she'd given him black his flexibility, kept the suppleness on the arch. She didn't need to, and she was trying to keep her hands to herself.

Noor healed his shins next, fixing a nick here, a pulled muscle there. She left the notch on his knee as he'd asked.

She paused for a moment, letting her breathing guide his, slow, and deep, and even. She moved to the thick quads bracing his thigh bone. These were injuries she recognised. Biting her tongue, she tried to think of him in pieces, tried to think of that bright boy in her imagination. But the evidence was too strong, and it told a story she'd hoped never to see again. Strains, pulls, muscles torn from being spread by force, being pulled together in desperation. She had no idea how he'd walked out of that prison, but she knew sometimes you just had to crawl to get away.

Noor squeezed her eyes shut, bracing her forehead against his shoulder and tried again to give herself some distance before finishing. Some piece of magic must have taken mercy on her because the last healing went quickly, smoothly, with torn soft tissue repaired, brutalised muscles mended, pain gentled. She was grateful again for the magic that made it possible and for being saved from reliving her own pain.

Noor took a sharp breath in when she was done. "Is there anywhere else you hurt?"

His chest touched hers with every inhalation, evenly, steadily. As he shifted his hips, Noor sensed a small song of surprise thrill through him when it didn't hurt. Rami rolled the shoulder under her forehead, and she took that as a cue to lean away. His arms were loose around her, giving her space, but something like shame or disappointment flickered across his face that made her remove her hand from his side.

His eyes darted everywhere but at hers, and Noor took a deep breath and passed a thought into his mind.

I see someone strong in front of me, someone who survived something unsurvivable. I know some of that strength because I carry it in my own bones, my own sewn-back-together guts. I know something of how hard you had to fight.

Out loud Noor said, "Go rinse off, then get some food, and have some real, uninterrupted rest. We'll be at our destination in a few hours."

"Where are we heading?" He spoke quickly, his voice as deep and warm as it had been in their magic connections. But it was different hearing it in person, the way the sound flowed between them, tickling her ears and making her light up.

"Sayn, south of Berbera on the Horn of Africa. Usama's sources let slip that ten years ago, it was a former French nobleman's favourite secret spot. He had three Provence-style cottages built there at great expense and trouble. Then, he was called up to fight for Napoleon, promptly killed, and the cottages were just—forgotten. He had French kitchens, European furniture, the whole thing. It'll be odd and probably uncomfortable but serviceable enough. Some families from Beereda took them over, used them as a hide away for visitors and meetings they couldn't take in town. The emira has used them several times recently for meetings, when things were calmer. I believe Usama's summary was 'low imperial patrol traffic, nice beaches.' He showed me a memory of it—winding hills, a river for water, lots of places to hide. Defensible."

"And then?"

If she'd never met him before Noor would have thought the question light, casual, such as when asked about the weather or some political issue that would never affect him. But she'd stepped through his mind and knew what he meant.

"The emira agreed to give us a few months to heal," she said, trying to ground herself in what she knew to be true. "And to continue her sympathy campaign."

He nodded, seeming to remember the updates Noor had been sending for wide distribution in the resistance for weeks.

"Then, there will be a trial," she said.

Nothing changed in his body; he breathed calmly, remained warm. But without reaching out with anything other than her intuition, Noor knew his mind raced, howling down windless corridors of possibilities. She tried to keep her tone neutral, to say everything she needed to with words alone, even when the space between them felt like oceans.

"I made no promises about you," she continued, and at this, he glanced down at her quizzically, so she clarified, "I never told the emira you would give up secrets, sell information for safety." She hurried to add, "And she never asked. She said she just wanted you back. How did she say it? 'Whole and repentant.'"

Noor didn't look at him to see what he thought of this, had no idea if he believed he had anything to repent for. Suddenly bone tired, she raised a hand to push away the headache building in her forehead.

"I don't know if going back to the resistance is going to be the right path. I don't know what you think, but if it's not the right path, I will do what's necessary to see real justice done."

Noor left that there, hanging in the air as he sucked a huge breath in, something happening inside his head she couldn't guess at. When she glanced up at him, his face was a whirl of emotions, flurries and torrents, and she had to close her eyes lest she get swept away by them. Then she felt fingers around her elbow, pulling her back to this moment.

"We have two months until the winter monsoons pass, right?" Rami asked and, at her nod, continued. "I don't know about you," he said, "but I am just about dead on my feet,"

Rami slipped out of the hammock and stood before her. Noor shifted back to give him room. Now, he moved without pain; he was so *fast*. He could stand comfortably, and he was so *big*. A part of her shied away, wanted safety from this body so much larger than her own. But a bigger part knew the sound of the blood in his veins like an old tune she could hum while working on a dhow. The rhythm of his heart, the same hard beat, ticked under her cheek as it had in the cave.

He held his hands out to the side as if inviting an embrace. She gently lay a single finger on the back of his hand, and he opened up his mind, just enough to show her an image of a brief hug, nothing more. A small piece of comfort in the storm for two exhausted bodies. Noor considered overthinking it but let her body want what it wanted and leaned in to him on the next ocean swell. His arms raised slowly, settling around her in increments as if giving her every opportunity to change her mind. She ducked her head under his chin, letting her eyes drift shut as he held on *tight*. Her arms, first loose at her sides, hugged him around his waist, tangling together in the sway of his lower back. She squeezed back with enough strength to make him change his breathing, and then she heard a chuckle.

"How'd you get so strong?" he asked, his voice low over her ear.

She shrugged. "You know in the plays at the souqs, where the guy and the girl are fleeing disaster, and he falls over a cliff," she said, light and easy, "and she can't pull him back, and he dies?"

"I didn't get to watch a lot of plays growing up," he said with an edge of teasing. "Too much time spent studying magic and doing princeling stuff."

"Or like in the plays, where the girl and the guy are running, and the guy gets shot, and she can't carry him back?" Noor drove on, questioning his newly healed shoulder where she'd buried her face. "Or the one where the girl dies because she can't climb a cliff or a compound wall to safety to save her own life?" She huffed, and he shivered at her lips moving against his skin through one of the many holes in his shirt.

"Well," she continued, "I decided at about the age of five when I first saw one of those stupid plays that I was never, *never* going to be one of those girls, the kind men make up when they write plays, who are nothing like the women I know. So, I always made sure I was strong enough to lift myself and anyone who needed help to safety."

She squatted, tightened her grip, and deadlifted Rami a solid three handbreadths off the floor. He wiggled a little in her grip before going perfectly still. When she set him down gingerly, he wrapped his arms around her, laughing softly in her ear.

"That is—that's not the kind of strength I meant," he said. "But that was excellent. And I dare you to try that on Mianning. I will give you ten pounds if you do that to Mianning."

Rami thought for a moment. "Actually, I have no money. I'll do your laundry for a week, how 'bout?" And Noor was chuckling, pulling back to smile up at him. His eyes were soft and easy now, with none of the tension he'd held when he'd pulled her to him a moment ago. His moods were like the desert wind, constantly shifting.

As if the quiet moment gave it voice to make itself heard, the small cut on her knee from the climb down decided to sing out, and she grimaced.

"Noor? What's wrong?" Rami asked.

"I caught my knee on a rock. It's all right. I'll take care of it while you're cleaning up—"

"Time was," Rami said slowly, "I could heal something like that with a thought." He took a breath. "So much lost time."

Noor held her quiet, giving him space to think it through.

"Perhaps—"He ducked his head. "Perhaps I can learn to connect to my haya magic again."

"No time like the present." Noor reached for his hand. She sat, tugging him down with her. He followed, radiating befuddled acquiesce.

"All right," she said and laid his hand over the cut on her knee, her hand on his. "Follow me."

She sought her magic once again, letting him follow her at his own pace, his trickle to her river, flowing lightly but still flowing after all this time.

Noor healed herself, letting his magic intertwine, mould, and then dissolve into and mix with hers until her skin was as whole and dark and warm as it ever had been.

"There," she said and lifted their hands off her knee. Her soaked pants were torn and dirty, and she plucked at them. "I'm afraid these are done for."

"Speaking of laundry," Rami said, picking at the awful remains of what he was wearing. "How about we burn this?"

"Head for the washing barrel," Noor said. "We just hauled them up. I'll get the clothes from the deck and be back right away. And I'll change back into my own things, but I'll be fast."

"If you think I'm going to take such little time for my first wash in *two months*, being a haya mage has left you entirely cracked," he said.

She batted at his arm, and he grinned, stepping away from her and heading for the washing area.

*

NOOR WAS NEARLY asleep when Rami returned to the hold, searching for the clothes she'd set aside for him.

He paused before whispering, "Noor, are you awake?"

She groaned, barely opening her eyes. "I need sleep. If you need entertainment, help yourself to some books and take them with you to the men's cabin."

Rami followed her rough gesture to the sealed waxed leather bag. He carefully opened it and took the book O'Reilly had given her out.

Rami leaned against the hull near her hammock, opening a page with its vertical script and reading aloud from it. "'The metal must be boiling hot but not hotter than the surface of the pot, or it, in its profusion, will crack it.'" He smiled, a bit of smirk at the edges. "Trust the Japanese to use three words where one would do."

Noor returned his smile, letting her eyes open a little. "I didn't know Japan had its own script," she said and sat up. She reached over to trace a fingertip across the page and its indecipherable words.

"Yes. Some parts of it are like Mandarin, but not all. They've kept their language through empires and invasions, and typhoons and volcanos, and the Dutch East India Company." He gave her a wry smile. "We had traders come through Aden all the time, and during the stormy season, they'd get bored and teach random children who approached them with questions, if we were lucky. You should ask Usama to speak Urdu with you sometime. My mother ensured all the kids tumbling around her were very well educated, and she wanted me to learn as much as I could before sending me to Taiz."

Noor stilled the book in his hands, flipping back to the description of the scar-flaunting, metal-healed bowl.

"I got this book from one of the harbour prisons we visited," she said, tone soft. "It's one of the other three British harbour prisons that hold mages." His hands hardened in hers, and someplace else, too, so empty of the touch and meaning they'd shared just a moment before.

"The old mage had made friends with them—the urodelas," she rambled. "He was the only one in that block. He had all of these books. I said I would write him; I should, once we're on the beach."

"Who?" Rami asked.

"Sean O'Reilly. He's the one who gave me that book."

If possible, Rami went even more still. "You met Sean O'Reilly?" he asked in a mix of disbelief and excitement. "How did—how did you manage that?"

"I just said. He was the only mage in the British prison we visited and"—she was confused by his response— "he seemed nice." She'd really enjoyed those illustrations, the stories they told, and hoped O'Reilly hadn't done something terrible.

Rami traced the title. "In the imperial navy, he was a ghost, a legend, one of the few Irish haya mages to serve. He was rumoured to have used alam magic as well, which we were all taught was impossible."

Noor had been taught that too. But the past few months had her doubting that was the whole truth.

"Maybe you can write him when we get to Sayn," she said, fighting through a yawn.

Rami finally seemed to remember his manners and stood, wished her a good night, and went to the ladder.

Noor fell asleep to the assured sway of the seas, the echo of her friends' boots on the deck above her, and the subtle and entangled spice of salt and cedar.

*

NOOR WOKE IN the middle of the night to Razan climbing down into the hold. She stopped to stare at the hatch door, lashed to the far wall.

Noor pulled herself out of her hammock. "Is everyone up?"

"Everyone except Rami. He went into the men's quarters with your book and shut the door. He didn't say anything."

"I'd like to debrief with the crew." Noor turned to Razan. "Come with me?"

"All right," she said.

Everyone was huddled around the table, the remains of a quick meal spread between them. They'd outrun the storm and had anchored off the shore of an island, water still dripping from their sails and spattering the slick deck.

"Where are we?" Noor murmured.

"Socotra," Razan said, a bit of humour in her voice. "Again."

"It was the nearest port we could reach," James explained, offering Noor a chunk of bread. She took it gratefully.

"So," Usama started, narrowing his eyes. "How is he?"

"Not dead," Noor said through her full mouth. "Not insane. Very tired. He knows the plan." She gave him an exhausted smile. "Thanks again for finding us a safe harbour."

"It's what I do," Usama said with a smile. "It sounds like things were both worse and better than you expected in Salalah. Anything we need to know about?"

Noor swallowed, taking the skin of water Mianning offered her. "The emira's diplomacy worked. We had friends inside." She met Usama's eyes. "Ian Tone is a turncoat. We need to cut him out of any information chains."

"Probably not the only thing we'll cut out of him, but thanks for the update."

She grimaced, but continued. "The urodelas are safe. We rescued them too. They were grateful. They seem...invested."

"Is it odd I found them kind of beautiful? Once you got to know them," James asked.

Razan shuddered. "Too many teeth for my liking, but what they did to that bastard guard, that I could get behind."

Noor nudged her shoulder. "I thought you might."

Usama glanced at Razan. "And you're fine with him bunking down on the same ship as you?"

"I can stand it for one night. We'll be at Sayn by midday. I intend to stay in a different cottage than him."

"There are three of them, so that won't be a problem," Usama said.

"Noor," she said after a pause. "You're welcome to either my cottage or the one we'll be installing Rami in. I can't promise to visit that one if you're there, but you'll always have a place with me."

Noor stretched a tentative arm out and was relieved when Razan folded up against her side. "Thank you, habibati."

Razan gave a stiff nod but then handed Noor a piece of mango and watched as she ate it.

James stifled a yawn. "I'm done for. Usama and Mianning have first watch. I'll take second with you Razan, if that's all right?"

She echoed his yawn but stood. Noor wondered if she should offer to take her place, and Razan smoothed a finger over Noor's scowl lines until she relaxed.

"You need sleep too," Razan said. "You've got your work cut out for you with us."

"It's not work when it's for you," Noor said, gazing at her friends. "For all of you. I can't…I can't say how much I feel for all of you, how much you're woven into my heart now."

"You're our friend, Noor," said Usama. "That means something to us."

"All of us," Mianning added.

"Oh!" said James. "There was one more key detail that came up."

Usama cocked his head. "Yes?"

James met Noor's eyes. "The British jailers have a new nom de guerre they've come up with."

"For Rami?" asked Razan, and Rami turned to her, startled.

"No. For Noor."

"Don't hold out on us," Usama said.

"One called her 'Monsoon Queen.'" James grinned.

"'Monsoon Queen," Usama said. "I like it." He caught her eye. "Noor? What do you think?"

"I'd rather be 'nap queen' right now, or possibly even one day, 'fully rested queen'," Noor said plaintively. "Can we talk legends and legacies after I've had at least one in-depth strategy session with the insides of my eyelids?"

Usama laughed and shooed her and Razan towards the hold.

There, they got ready for bed in contented quiet, the easy rocking of the waves gentle enough to catch their tired staggers more often than causing them.

"I could use some comfort tonight," Razan said, eyes not quite meeting Noor's, as she sat on her mostly dried out hammock.

"Me too," Noor said.

Razan lay back, and Noor crawled in after her, wrapping them both in their thick blanket before sleep wrapped them in dreams.

Glossary

أ

ALAM / ALAM MAGE—a type of magic / a type of mage, drawing from the Arabic word "ألم" which means "pain"

ALHAMDULILLAH—all praise is due to Allah

ALLAH YARHAMHU—"may Allah have mercy on him," a common Arabic phrase used in response to hearing of someone's death, similar to "may his memory be a blessing" or "rest in peace"

ARZI—cedar

ATHAN—the call to prayer, vocalized by a muezzin, often from the minaret

EMIRA—a title used for a secular female leader, often of a large area; the male form is "emir." European aristocratic titles are roughly analogous. Often pronounced "amira." Historical examples of emiras include Arwa al-Sulayhi (c. 1048 – c. 1138), a sole ruler of Yemen and Asma bint Shihab, her mother-in-law, whose reign preceded hers.

إ

IMAM—a religious leader for some Muslims

ب

BAHER—sea

BAKSHEESH—a money bribe

BALOUT—oak

ث

THOBE—an ankle-length shirt, often white, with long sleeves and buttons down the front worn by some Arab men

ج

GUNTIINO—a long women's wrap worn like an Indian sari (Note: this is a Somali word, so the Arabic language transliteration is approximate.)

JAMBIYA—a dagger with a curved double-edged blade, worn in the belt; called by many names in many Middle Eastern, South Asian, and Central Asian societies; the term "jambiya" is specific to the Yemeni iteration

ح

HABIBI, HABIBATI—an endearment meaning "my dear, darling, love." The lack of an "a" before the "ti" denotes the loved one is a man. It draws from the Arabic root word " حب ", that is, "love." Notes: most Arabic words draw from 2 – 3 letter roots. and an "ee" sound at the end of a noun in Arabic means "my [noun]."

HARAM—not permitted by Islamic law, forbidden

HAYA / HAYA MAGE—a type of magic / a type of mage, drawing from the Arabic word "حياة" which means "life"

خ

KHAMEEZ—a long robe, often available in different colors, worn by men and women

د

DHOW—a small boat with sails and made of cedar often harvested from the mountains of Lebanon

س

SADAQA—literally means "righteousness," referring to the voluntary giving of alms or charity

SADIQUI / SADIQATI—a male friend / a female friend

SALAH / SALAT—a ritual prayer made five times daily, standing, and with alternating inclinations and prostrations, facing Mecca

SAMBANDHAM—derived from the Sanskrit for "equal alliance", a mode of traditional marriage

SHARIA—Islamic religious law

SIBAHA—Arabic for "swimming"literally means "righteousness," refer-ring to the voluntary giving of alms or charity

SOUQ—a market

ش

SHEIKHA / SHEIKH—an Arab leader with a strong grounding in reli-gious law; the lack of an "a" at the end denotes a male leader

ظ

DHUHR—the second daily prayer offered by many Muslims in the early afternoon

ع

ABAYA—a loose-fitting, full-length robe worn by some women in and around the Arabian Peninsula, often mostly or entirely black

ASR—the third daily prayer offered by many Muslims in the late after-noon

AYN—a letter in Arabic and one of its most distinctive sounds. Non-Ar-abic speakers are sometimes taught to say it by asking them to imitate the sound of a cat miaowing. The first letter in the words "Arab," "Oman," and "Iraq."

ISHA—the fifth daily prayer offered by many Muslims in the late even-ing

ف

FAJR—the first daily prayer offered by many Muslims in early morning, before dawn

غ

GHRAIN—an Arabic letter; refers to the letter ghayn (غ)

ق

QAT—a shrub found in the Middle East and Africa whose leaves and buds are the source of a habit-forming stimulant. Qat is chewed or used as a tea

ك

KIDEM—a delicious Yemeni bread

م

MAGHRIB—the fourth daily prayer offered by many Muslims just after sunset. The word shares a root with the word "المغرب" which refers to North Africa (other than Egypt); the Arabic dialect spoken in North Africa; and is the Arabic name of the country of Morocco.

MAJILIS—the area where a sheikh or sheikha gathers community leaders to sit together, usually at the same height, in a circle, looking each other in the eye to discuss shared problems and solutions (Modern note: the legislature in Qatar, Iran, and other countries in the region is called a majilis.)

MUEZZIN—a highly skilled figure in a mosque who vocalizes the call to prayer

و

WAHHABI—a religious revivalist movement within Sunni Islam named after eighteenth-century Hanbal scholar, Muhammad ibn Abd al-Wahhab.

Acknowledgements

Thank you to my cultural experts who read this in its early stages and guided it to safe harbor: Alina, Ayan, Fadia, and Wafa, you were incredible. Thank you to Nadiah who came in at the end to make sure I got the details right.

Thank you to Misha, the Zen Buddhist librarian at my elementary school who taught me the word "qat" to win points in afternoon games of anagrams and got me started caring about Yemen. Thank you to Cath, Jay, Kat, Nox, Megan, and Hal for your wonderful support. And to Grace for sharing all the different ways families can be built and grown.

Thank you to my wonderful editor, Elizabetta, whose humour, kindness, and fierce pen are lifesavers.

Thank you to my wonderful family, who are my world.

About the Author

Jo Carthage is a bi, cis woman from Silicon Valley. In her career, Jo has worked with survivors of labor and sex trafficking in DC, helped get incredible women and queer folks elected to state and national office, and thinks politics and science fiction go together beautifully. Jo has visited, taught, worked, or studied in a third of the countries in the Middle East (from Doha to Beirut, from Cairo to Gaza), speaks conversational Arabic, and has enjoyed time in West Africa. She is currently completing graduate work in history focusing on these regions.

Jo was honored to have an early version of the War Between Cedar and Oak Quartet favorably reviewed by several Yemeni friends living in Sana'a as well as a Somali American friend from earlier in her career when they were both working to support survivors of trafficking. As a writer, Jo loves slow burn, hurt/comfort, queer history, enemies-to-lovers, and happy endings.

Email
jocarthage@proton.me

Facebook
www.facebook.com/jocarthage

Twitter
@jocarthage

Website
www.jocarthage.com

Instagram
www.Instagram.com/jocarthage

Tumblr
www.Jocarthage.tumblr.com

Other NineStar books by this author

Nuclear Sunrise

Connect with NineStar Press

Website: www.ninestarpress.com

Facebook: www.facebook.com/ninestarpress

X: www.twitter.com/ninestarpress

Instagram: www.instagram.com/ninestarpress

BlueSky: bsky.app/profile/ninestarpress.bsky.social

Threads: www.threads.net/@ninestarpress